A MORE
PERFECT
UNION

B.G. Thomas

J. Scott Coatsworth

Jamie Fessenden

Michael Murphy

Published by
DREAMSPINNER PRESS

5032 Capital Circle SW, Suite 2, PMB# 279, Tallahassee, FL 32305-7886 USA
www.dreamspinnerpress.com

A More Perfect Union
© 2016 Dreamspinner Press.
Edited by Nicole Dowd

Flames © 2016 J. Scott Coatsworth.
Jeordi and Tom © 2016 Michael Murphy.
Destined © 2016 Jamie Fessenden.
Someday © 2016 B.G. Thomas.

Cover Art
© 2016 Reese Dante.
http://www.reesedante.com
Cover content is for illustrative purposes only and any person depicted on the cover is a model.
Hands photo by J. Scott Coatsworth.
Authors photo by Michael Murphy.

ISBN: 978-1-63477-331-7
Digital ISBN: 978-1-63477-332-4
Library of Congress Control Number: 2016902323
Published June 2016
v. 1.0

Printed in the United States of America

This paper meets the requirements of
ANSI/NISO Z39.48-1992 (Permanence of Paper).

CONTENTS

This morning, the Supreme Court recognized that the Constitution guarantees marriage equality. In doing so, they've reaffirmed that all Americans are entitled to the equal protection of the law. That all people should be treated equally, regardless of who they are or who they love. … This ruling will strengthen all of our communities by offering to all loving same-sex couples the dignity of marriage across this great land. … It's a victory for gay and lesbian couples who have fought so long for their basic civil rights…. This decision affirms what millions of Americans already believe in their hearts: When all Americans are treated as equal we are all more free…. There's so much more work to be done to extend the full promise of America to every American. But today, we can say in no uncertain terms that we've made our union a little more perfect.

~ President Barak Obama on the Supreme Court decision for marriage equality

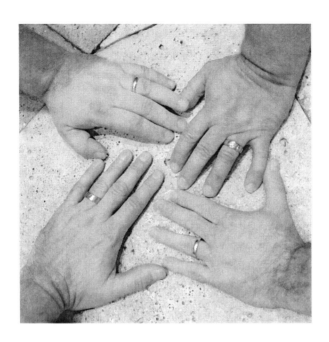

More Than Just a Piece of Paper

On June 30, 2014, my husband and I became legally married. We had to go to Baltimore to do it, but ironically, even though we couldn't get married in Missouri, we lived in a state that chose to recognize same-sex marriages from other states.

A few weeks later, same-sex marriage was legalized in Kansas. People asked me, "Don't you wish you had just waited?"

All I could do was stare at them and say, "*Are you kidding?*"

Take a half-hour drive, get married, be home an hour or so later…

…or take an amazing romantic trip to Baltimore, a gorgeous historical city, and get married in a wonderful, beautiful way? A marriage that was mostly paid for by my fans and fellow writers. A wedding that I would always remember.

Two years later later, I look down at my hand, and I see my wedding band, and I still can't believe it. Still can't fathom it. I am married! I am *legally* married! It's not a Holy Union or a so-called Civil Union. It is a legal marriage.

Ten years ago the love of my life and I had our own ceremony. Two hundred some people came, and it was beautiful, and we jumped both the sword and the broom and were married in our hearts—the way it was done for thousands of years. That was when we were *really* married. After all, wasn't the legal thing just a piece of paper?

And yet….

And yet I have found it wasn't "just" a piece of paper.

When we got legally married on that June day, when two friends came down from Washington, DC, to be our witnesses, when that representative of the court stood before us under that tacky arch and gave us our vows, when we repeated them, when he declared us married…

…and when we were handed that "piece of paper"?

In that moment I discovered something.

That piece of paper was far more than *just* a piece of paper!

For now, in my fifties, I finally had been given the same basic human right as every heterosexual person I knew. I was flying! I felt high! I couldn't believe how *different* I felt.

Story ideas began to take wing.

I got home, and straight married people said to me, "So after all these years of you two being together, being married doesn't feel any different, does it?"

But it did!

And gay people? Gay people said, "So don't you feel *different*? We feel so different. So amazingly different!"

They agreed with me.

We began to talk about it. And we came to a conclusion.

When someone is straight, they grow up knowing several things. They know they will go to high school and go to the prom and go to college and get married. They know it. It is taken for granted. Their whole culture tells them that. They expect it.

But gay people? We grow up reinterpreting everything. Adapting. We fantasize that maybe we will be brave enough to try and take a same-sex partner to the prom. Most don't. We certainly didn't when I went to high school. Or that we'll find a neighborhood where the neighbors won't mind that a same-sex couple has moved in next door. Or somehow find a job where our spouse is welcome at the company Christmas party.

We grew up knowing we would never get married. That the best we could hope for is some ceremony we made up, or a Holy Union, and maybe—just maybe—a Civil Union.

Never in my life did I ever expect that I would be legally married to another man!

And I am.

I think that is why I feel different.

I think that is why now, as I type this two years later, when I look down at my hand and see that ring, I am still flying. Because now when I say "husband," it is more than husband of my heart—he is my *legal* husband! And oh, the joy!

And that joy has come out of me as pure inspiration. Inspiration in the form of stories. The stories still want to pour out of me.

So I began to plan them and plot them.

And then it hit me.

What about other gay men? Other gay authors who grew up in my world, thinking we could never get married? Other gay authors who are now legally married?

Were they being hit with these wondrous feelings? This amazing power? Did they feel grateful like me? Were they high? Were they flying? Were they being inspired to write stories from this energy as well?

Might they want to join me in writing some stories about men getting legally married? Might they want to take this soaring feeling and write from that energy?

I checked.

They did.

I asked J. Scott Coatsworth, a young author who I like to think I discovered. I bought his first story for my anthology *A Taste of Honey*.

I asked Jamie Fessenden, a writer whose work I am crazy about and from whom I have yet to find a story that I don't love.

I asked Michael Murphy, whose novel *Little Squirrels Can Climb Tall Trees* is one of my favorites. He is also, by the way, one of the two witnesses for my marriage, and he took amazing photographs to forever commemorate our wedding day.

They all said yes.

So here it is. An anthology of novellas, written by gay male authors who are legally married and who all thought it would never happen in our lifetime. Four authors who took that stupefied, grateful, excited energy and wrote stories from that magical place in their hearts.

I think you will love them.

I know I did.

"I do."

Namasté,

B.G. Thomas

FLAMES

BY J. SCOTT COATSWORTH

To Mark.

The one I knew I'd spend the rest of my life with, even if we couldn't get married.

The one who fought next to me for all those years to help make it happen.

And the one who stood by my side on that rainy afternoon in November in San Francisco, looked into my eyes, and said "I do" without reservation.

I couldn't do this without you. And I wouldn't want to.

Prologue

THERE WAS only this moment. This place. Alex holding Gio's hand, gently because of the burns on the back of Gio's arm. The sounds of the breathing machine came in regular soft sighs.

The little green box held in Alex's other hand—and all it symbolized between them.

All their life together had shrunk down to this moment, this place, this plea. "Please wake up, Gio. *Amore mio, svegliati.*"

Chapter One

Saturday, September 12. Two weeks earlier

ALEX WAS late getting home, and he was in a foul mood from the long, difficult day at work. One of the properties he'd made a bid on had fallen through, and another client had all but called him a bald-faced liar.

He was looking forward to getting home, taking a long hot shower, then crawling into bed.

Alex was startled to find a huge meal, complete with wine and candles, laid out on their dining room table. Gio must have spent the whole day cooking.

Alex was late. He'd been delayed with his angry client, and to make matters worse, his phone had up and died halfway through the afternoon and he'd been without his car charger.

He was already annoyed when he walked in the door.

"Welcome home, *amore*," Gio called from the kitchen.

"I had a hell of a day…." He caught a whiff of whatever Gio was cooking.

"Come sit down. I've got everything ready."

The dining room looked like a Martha Stewart production of a telenovela Thanksgiving. "I'm sorry. I'm not really hungry. Things were the shits at work today."

"Sorry to hear that. Have a seat." Gio grabbed his elbow and urged him toward his chair. "Food makes everything better."

Alex was starting to get annoyed. "Look, I'm sorry, but I'm not hungry. I just want to wash up—"

"That's just the job talking." Gio took his arm again.

"Knock it off! I'm not in the mood tonight."

Gio looked hurt, but Alex plowed on, too incensed to stop.

"This isn't some kind of June and Ward Cleaver thing."

"I just—"

"You have to let go of your stupid, unrealistic expectations of me and this relationship."

Gio frowned. "That's bullshit, and you know it. Just because you had a bad day at work, there's no reason to take it out on me."

He was right. But Alex couldn't admit it. "Just leave me the fuck alone," he said, grabbing his phone charger and storming out. He'd find somewhere else to sleep tonight.

ALEX WOKE, still groggy from the immense amount of alcohol he'd consumed the night before.

Where am I? Memory slowly returned through his aching brain. The Super 8 Motel. It had been close and cheap, and he hadn't wanted to go back home after the binge he'd gone on.

He sat up and pulled back the motel sheets and bedspread from his naked form. If Gio had been mad at him before, he'd be livid now. And he had the right to be.

The cow skull in the watercolor painting on the wall glared down at him as if in judgment.

God, his head was pounding. He stumbled into the bathroom and ran the water until it was hot. Then somehow he managed to get himself into the shower. He breathed in the steam deeply, and the pressure in his head abated a little, enough that he could start to think.

There was no choice other than to go home and face the music. This whole thing was his mess—he'd made it, and he'd have to live with it. But he could delay his hour of reckoning, at least for a little while longer. He stayed under the warm spray, letting himself forget what waited for him at home.

Eventually the water ran cold and he had to leave the shower.

Alex dried off and checked himself in the mirror. He didn't look too bad, considering. The eyes were a little red, but they'd have to do. He rubbed his temples with his thumbs, willing the pain to go away.

Alex didn't have a fresh change of clothing with him, so he pulled his old ones back on. He could change when he got home.

Then he noticed his phone where he'd plugged it in to charge upon reaching his room. At least he'd remembered to grab his charger on his way out of the house.

He had it on Do Not Disturb because he hadn't wanted to talk with Gio last night, not in the condition Alex had been in. He unplugged the phone from the wall charger. It was fully juiced up now, so he activated it, and a flood of texts and messages arrived.

Jesus, had the Paxton deal gone south? He'd hate to lose that commission.

The thought fled his mind as he scanned the texts. Most were from their friend Oscar.

Alex, they're calling me. Something happened to Gio. Where are you?

On my way to the U of A Medical Center. Hope to see you there.

At the hospital with Gio. It's bad…. Alex, where are you?

By the time Alex read the last one, he was at the car, fumbling to find his keys in his briefcase. He fished them out and hopped inside, not bothering with checkout. He threw the case in the passenger seat and peeled out of the motel parking lot.

"Hold on, Gio, hold on," he whispered to himself. "I'm coming."

He reached the University of Arizona Medical Center in record time, thanking the traffic gods when he didn't have an accident and wasn't stopped for a ticket. He parked his car in the first visible spot in the garage and jumped out, not even bothering to lock it, and ran toward the hospital lobby. A couple walking past shot him a sympathetic glance, but he ignored them.

There was only Gio.

He reached the front desk, panting, hands outstretched on the cool surface as he fought to catch his breath. "I'm looking… for… Giovanni."

The woman at the desk put her hand on his. "Calm down, sir. Catch your breath."

He closed his eyes for a second, willing himself to be calm. "Better?" His eyes threatened violence if she didn't say yes.

She seemed to sense his urgency. "Giovanni, you said?"

Alex swallowed hard and nodded. He took a couple of deep breaths and tried again. "I need to find Giovanni Montanari."

"Let me look," she said, her voice full of sympathy. "When was he brought in?"

He checked the messages on his phone. "I don't know. Late last night, maybe?"

She nodded. "Okay, I found him."

"How is he?"

"I'm sorry, sir. I can't tell you that. You'll have to talk to the doctor."

"He's still alive?"

She nodded again. "Yes, sir. He's in the burn ward. Take the elevator down that hall"—she pointed—"up to the third floor. Then follow the signs."

He ran down the hall toward the elevator. *Burn ward?*

THE DOORS opened, and Alex sprinted out of the elevator, pausing only a second to see which way the burn ward was. He almost knocked down a nurse carrying a tray of urine samples.

"Sorry," he called back.

He ran headfirst into a bear of a man.

"Hey there, slow down," the man said, catching him before he could fall.

It was Oscar. His friend helped him back up and guided him to a bank of chairs along one wall.

"Where is he?" Alex was on the verge of panic.

"He's okay for the moment." Oscar rubbed his eyes. "They brought him in last night after the fire."

"Fire? Oh God, what fire?"

Oscar shook his head, narrowing his eyes. "Where the hell were you, man? The fire that burned your house down."

If Alex hadn't already been sitting, he would have collapsed then and there. "We had a fight last night," he said softly, looking down at the tile floor. Then he couldn't sit any longer. "I need to see him. Where is he?"

"I'll take you to him, but Alex"—Oscar put his big paw on his friend's shoulder—"he looks pretty bad." He led Alex down the hall to Gio's room and opened the door quietly.

Alex pushed past him and stopped dead.

There he was, the love of Alex's life. Gio lay in the hospital bed, looking small and forlorn, with a breathing mask attached to his face. The machine made soft sounds as air flowed in and out of Gio's lungs. The outsides of his arms were covered with burns and some kind of salve, and an IV dripped fluids into his veins. His face was battered and bruised.

Alex stood at the end of Gio's hospital bed, afraid to touch him for fear of hurting him. "How bad are they?"

"Mostly first degree—it looks worse than it is. They think he'll heal just fine."

Alex breathed a sigh of relief. "Has he been awake at all?"

Oscar shook his head. "From what they tell me, which isn't much, he's in a coma. His brain shut down from the trauma." He put an arm around Alex's shoulders. "They pulled him out of the house after it had partially collapsed."

Alex pulled up a plastic chair next to the bed, searching for a part of Gio's body that wasn't damaged. He finally took his right hand and said gently, "Gio, can you feel this? It's me, Alex. I'm so sorry we fought. That I didn't come home last night. Maybe if I had…."

"The hospital tried to reach you," Oscar said. "Then they called me—I guess they found our numbers in his wallet."

"My phone battery died, and later I was too drunk to check it." Alex was beating himself up inside. This was *his* fault. His and no one else's. "I'm so glad you were here for him. I saw your texts this morning."

"Gio and I go way back, to when we first volunteered together at Wingspan a decade ago. There's one more thing…," Oscar said.

"It can't get any worse. Can it?" Alex looked at Gio, so small and fragile and broken on the hospital bed.

"I'm not so sure about that." Oscar stroked his thick beard. "They called his mother."

CINZIA MONTANARI and Alex had a *complicated* relationship.

Well, maybe not so complicated, Alex mused. *She hates me with a passion.*

In her mind, Alex had committed three unforgivable sins.

First and foremost, he was gay. Gio's mother had an almost unrivaled commitment to the Catholic Church and all that it embodied. Although she'd known Alex for going on ten years, her opinion on the whole gay thing had remained unchanged… yet somehow Gio seemed to get a pass on that one.

Second, Alex had taken away her beautiful little boy. Gio would always be her *bel bambino*—and no one came between an Italian mother and her son. It was a cliché, but for a reason.

And third, Alex had kept Gio in America. Gio had been due to return to Italy after a two-year program as a visiting professor with the University of Arizona, but once they had met, Gio extended his stay indefinitely. Although it had at least as much to do with the university offering Gio a permanent position as it did with their relationship, at least initially, Cinzia Montanari would not be swayed. She still hated him.

Her last name meant "from the mountain," and she was as immovable as one.

As Alex sat holding his partner's hand, he thought about the trips back to the *bel paese*—the beautiful country. They had visited Gio's family three times over the last ten years to try to calm the waters. With little success. Two of those trips had ended in shouted curses and one in thrown pieces of pottery.

And now, for the first time, *la signora* Montanari was on her way here to the United States.

It was too much for him to think about right now.

He held Gio's hand and caressed the back of it gently, where the skin was not burned, with his other hand. The doctor had been by to discuss Gio's condition an hour or two earlier. It was hard to keep track of the passage of time in here. The big clock on one wall said it was already four, but Alex didn't believe it. He'd gotten here close to nine, and surely seven hours couldn't have passed already.

There was no visible response from Gio. The doctor said his body had gone into a coma to allow itself time to recover and heal. Gio's worst burns were on his forearms and shins. The firefighters had found him huddled in a corner of the kitchen, with his back to the wall and his arms wrapped over his head for protection.

Alex's heart was breaking, over and over again, to see his beautiful Gio like this. To know he hadn't been there to protect him. He wished with all his might to turn back the clock and do the last night over. But time, always eager to rush forward, refused to turn back.

The doctor had said he had no idea how long the coma might last. Gio's MRI had come back clean, so the doctor didn't think there was any permanent brain damage. He hoped it would only be a week or two until Gio wakened, but in some cases comas could continue for years.

Alex didn't know how he would bear *years*.

The door opened, and Oscar popped his head into the room. "Hey, Alex," he whispered. "I just got back from my afternoon youth session at the center. I can sit with him for a few minutes."

Alex shook his head. "I don't want to leave him."

Oscar sat next to him, pulling up a chair. "The doctor said he's stable. Your job right now is to take care of yourself so you will be here for him when he wakes up. Go eat something. I'll be here, and I'll text you if anything happens."

Alex looked at Oscar and then over at Gio, uncertain. Surprisingly, he *was* hungry. "I don't know...."

"Do you trust me?"

Alex nodded.

"Go. I'll take care of Gio."

"Okay." Alex stood, unsteady on his feet because his left leg had gone to sleep. "Where's the cafeteria?"

"Down the hall that way, make a left. You'll see the sign."

Alex bent over to kiss Gio lightly on the forehead. "Oscar's gonna take care of you now for a couple minutes," he whispered. "I love you, Gio."

He would make it quick.

GIO SAT on the floor. At least he assumed it was the floor. It was white. Everything was white. The ceiling, the walls, the floor. His breath.

"Hello?"

The atmosphere muffled the word like a thick mist, although it wasn't cold or damp. He stood, putting his hand out in front of him. It disappeared about a foot away, enveloped by the strange thick air.

He was naked.

His right hand was warm, as if someone was holding it, but when he brought it up to eye level, there was nothing else there.

"Is anyone out there?" he called again. As before, his words were muffled.

The room seemed to press down on him like layers of soft cloth, pushing in on all sides. His heart beat faster, and he struggled to breathe. He started to panic. He was trapped, boxed in on all sides. He could die here.

And then he realized he couldn't even remember his own name.

He jumped up and pushed forward into the bright murk, trying to run. But the bonds of the white air seemed to tighten around his arms and legs. It was like running underwater.

He was going to drown here.

He redoubled his efforts, but the air pushed back harder.

Then he felt something else. Warmth suffused his forehead, and a disembodied voice spoke clearly to him.

Oscar's gonna take care of you now for a couple minutes. I love you, Gio.

Of course! He remembered. He did have a name.

It was Gio.

ALEX FOUND a quiet table in the corner of the sterile cafeteria. The room was painted a pale green, broken only by the wide picture window that looked out at the campus to the west and the distant Tucson Mountains. The sun was edging toward the horizon.

He picked out a premade egg salad sandwich, an apple, and a bottle of orange juice. He wolfed down the sandwich, though it tasted like cardboard and paste, and chased it down with the juice. His hunger started to subside.

The place was practically empty. Only two other tables were occupied, which suited Alex because he wasn't in the mood to talk. He polished off the apple and stepped out into the hall.

First he called work, explained the situation, and told his boss he'd need some time off. Liz was aghast at what had happened and promised to find someone to cover Alex's clients.

Then he made a call to their insurance agent. "Hi, Janis," he said, finding a bench to sit on. "It's Alex Gutierrez."

"Hey, Alex! Good to hear from you. How are you guys?"

Alex took a deep breath. "Gio is…." His voice broke. He couldn't finish the sentence. "Gio is—"

"Alex, where are you?"

"At the hospital."

"What happened? Is Gio… is he okay?"

Alex shook his head, even though he was aware that she couldn't see him. "He's not. He's in a coma."

"Oh my God." There was a long pause. "What happened?" she asked finally.

Alex closed his eyes. "The house burned down. He was there. I… wasn't." He waited for her judgment.

Instead, she snapped into business mode. "Okay, here's what we're going to do. I'll get someone over there to survey the damage. You don't worry about that. We can talk about it later."

"Okay."

"Do you have someone there to help you? Someone who can run errands or make calls or whatever?"

"Our friend Oscar is here."

"That's good. Ask him to call some of your other friends. You're going to need support to get through this. How about family—anyone close by?"

"No, just my mother, but she's at Saguaro Hills."

"Okay. If you need me to arrange a hotel room, just let me know."

"I think I'll stay here, at least until I know more."

"Sure. Listen to me, Alex. You guys are going to get through this." Her voice took on a more personal tone. "You are strong together, but right now, Gio needs you to be strong for him."

Alex nodded. "I know. I'm just not sure I can. I'm going crazy here. I don't know what to do for him."

"That's okay. Tell you what. Can you get some paper and a pen?"

He frowned. "Right now?"

"No, after we talk."

"Yes, I think so." What did she want him to do, write a letter?

"Okay. I want you to start making a list of all the things you guys owned in that house. It'll help keep you busy, and we'll need it when you file the claim."

He thought it over. "I can do that."

"Okay. I'll call you once I hear back from the adjuster about the house. And Alex?"

"What?"

"Hang in there."

ALEX SAT in Gio's room, staring at him. The sheet over Gio's chest rose and fell with a steady rhythm. Oscar had gone home a couple of hours earlier, promising to "rally the troops" for the next day.

The clock said it was almost 9:00 p.m. Alex looked down at the yellow legal pad he'd procured at the hospital gift store. He'd started jotting down the things that were in the living room, but his heart wasn't in it. So far, he had:

> *couch*
> *rug*
> *love seat*
> *TV*

His mind drew a blank beyond that.

He *knew* this. He *should* know this. But every time he tried to concentrate on the list, his eyes kept straying from the page to Gio, lying in the metal bed in the room painted in soft desert tones—"to promote healing," the brochures said; Alex had practically memorized them to kill time—while the heart monitor beeped in a steady rhythm.

One of the nurses came in through the open door. She looked to be in her midforties, with close-cropped salt-and-pepper hair. Her scrubs were covered with monster trucks.

She saw him and smiled. "I'm here to check on Mr. Montanari. My name's Rosalind."

He stood and reached out to shake her hand. "I'm Alex, Gio's… partner."

"Gloves, sorry," she said, refusing his handshake, showing her purple hands. "Yeah, I figured. Your friend Oscar mentioned you."

She checked Gio's pulse and heart rate and entered the information on the terminal in the corner of the room.

"He did?"

She nodded. "Want to help me lift him? We need to shift him a bit so he doesn't get bedsores."

"Sure."

Together they lifted Gio gently and moved him over a little, settling him in a new position.

"How long have you two been together?"

"About ten years."

"Nice. My wife and I have been together for twelve. You guys get married?" She tucked the sheets back in as they talked, then gently lifted Gio's head and fluffed his pillow.

"Not yet." There'd been many discussions about that. Alex didn't believe in marriage—imitating the straights and all that. "We talked about it," he said noncommittally. "Before… before…." He couldn't get the rest out. Instead he began to sob like he had when he was ten years old and his father had died in the military. "What if… I… lose him?"

The nurse put her arms around him, hugging his waist and forgetting all about her gloves. "He's gonna be okay, baby," she said softly. "Come over here and sit down for a minute."

He allowed himself to be led over to one of the chairs.

Rosalind looked at her watch. "I've got a few minutes before my next rounds," she said, sitting down next to him. "Why don't you tell me what happened?"

GIO WOKE again. His eyes slipped open. This time he was in a bed. Some kind of substance was all around him—a sense of walls and ceilings and floors, but they had an ethereal feel to them, as if they were made of mist and pixie dust.

He lay there for a long time, trying to feel his body. There was a vague sensation of weight and a dull, aching pain, but his limbs would not respond to his will. He felt like less of a person and more of a fat, helpless slug.

Then he felt that sense of warmth again, as if hands touched him along the sides of his body.

What had happened to him? He remembered making a romantic dinner for someone. Then there had been light and heat, a terrible heat. He turned away from the memory of the pain, and other details eluded him.

He lay there for a while more, then dropped back down into oblivion. The "room" dissolved into dust around him.

ROSALIND FOUND Alex a chair that folded out into a makeshift bed so he had a place to sleep in Gio's room. It was cramped and not particularly comfortable, but Alex was exhausted, and after about an hour, he dropped off into a dreamless sleep.

Chapter Two

Sunday, September 13

ALEX WOKE several times in the middle of the night and got up to check on Gio before relieving himself in the hospital room's small bathroom. Nothing had changed.

One of the nurses popped in at about 3:00 a.m. to check on her patient. Alex rolled over, glared up at her, then fell back asleep.

At just after five in the morning, he decided he couldn't sleep anymore and folded up the chair. He sat in front of the window, looking out over the quiet city, the predawn glow throwing the Catalina Mountains in the distance into shadow.

He checked on Gio, who was still unconscious but breathing easily under the respirator. Sighing, Alex grabbed his notepad and set out for the cafeteria.

They weren't serving yet, but he found a table in the back of the room, near the big picture window, and sat down to work on the list.

Something had shifted during the night, because now the words just flowed out of him. He started in the kitchen, seeing it in his head, and plates, bowls, silverware, and the beautiful De Grazia painting they'd found for next to nothing at a yard sale on the east side of town all flew onto the page. The gorgeous blue and gold Italian platter with the lemons that Gio's sister Caterina had given them for their pottery anniversary two years before. The butcher block they'd bought together at IKEA. The prickly pear tablecloth from Penney's. Gio always did have a thing for kitsch.

Even their telescope, the one they'd bought together that first year.

In his head he continued on, walking through each room in their small house, remembering all the things that collectively described the life they had built together, the physical evidence of their relationship.

Now all those things were gone.

Where does that leave us?

When he finally finished, it was six thirty and the kitchen was starting to serve breakfast.

Alex stared at the list for a long time, at the things the fire had taken. It was a lot like being orphaned.

He put the list away and grabbed a plate of eggs and bacon, sitting down again at the table to eat. He managed to down about half of it, then sent a text to Caterina.

She responded almost immediately. There was an eight-hour difference between Arizona and Italy, so it was midafternoon over there.

How does he do?

He smiled. Cat's English was only slightly better than his own mangled Italian.

Sleeping still. Looks peaceful. When I know more, I will tell you. TVB.

I love you guys too.

Throughout the rocky times with Gio's mother, his sister had always been supportive. Different generation, he supposed. Even in Italy it worked that way. His phone buzzed again.

Mamma will be there at 3.

"Fuck," Alex said, eliciting a few glares. He smiled back sheepishly. "Sorry!"

Of course she should be there. She was Gio's mother.

Cinzia Montanari had made no bones about her feelings for Alex and their relationship, so her arrival could only spell trouble. He'd only been half joking when he'd referred to his partner's mother as "Mussolini with better legs."

He scooped up the list of things they'd lost to the fire, along with his coffee, and headed back to Gio's room.

OSCAR WAS waiting for him, along with Dax and Mario, two of their friends from the Tucson gay couples group.

Alex embraced all three of them. "Oh my God, I am so glad to see you here. Thank you, guys, for coming." He felt a renewed sense of hope, seeing their friends here to support them. He might be able to make it through another day of this hellish wait for Gio to awaken.

"How is he?" Dax asked. Dax was the whitest man Alex had ever known, short of actual albinism, with a spray of freckles across his cheeks and bright red hair cropped short. He also had an infectious smile. "Any news?"

Alex shook his head. "Nothing yet. He's been in a coma after the fire, and it could take weeks or months for his body to heal and for him to wake up again." Alex felt tears resurfacing and wiped his eyes angrily with the back of his hand. He would not cry again. Not now, not here in front of their friends. He looked at Oscar. "Cinzia is coming this afternoon."

"Not surprised," Oscar said. "Hey, I've got to get to the center, but Dax and Mario said they can stay here for a bit while you take care of yourself—get freshened up a little."

"I'm not sure I can leave...."

"I already asked the doctor. Gio is stable, and you can use my place. You don't want to be a mess when *mamma* arrives. You can get a quick shower, shave, whatever."

"I don't have any clothes." The realization underscored his sudden homelessness, and emotion threatened to overwhelm him again.

Oscar put his hands on Alex's shoulders. "Hey, don't worry. I got you covered." He picked up a bag off one of the green plastic chairs and handed it to Alex. "Here's a change of clothes." He must have seen the look on Alex's face. "Don't worry. They're not mine. I know you'd be swimming in mine, and the pants would only reach your ankles. These were Peter's."

Alex nodded. Peter had been Oscar's partner, who'd died the year before in an accident. "Thank you. That means a lot to me."

Oscar smiled. His own eyes were just a little moist at the corners. "I also picked up some toiletries. Not sure what you use, so I had to guess. I hope you like Axe."

"It's perfect." He felt overwhelmed. "Thank you, guys. I'm not sure how I can repay you."

"You can start by getting your stinky hide clean," Mario said, smirking.

Alex laughed involuntarily. "Asshole." He'd needed that.

"And here are the house keys. Just lock up when you're done. Come on. I'll walk you out."

Alex hugged his friends once more, kissed Gio on the cheek, then followed Oscar out to the parking lot.

GIO WALKED through the empty white space. Unlike before, he no longer had the sense that he was in a confined area, nor was the mist closing in on him.

Instead he felt as though he were in the midst of an infinite space, a wide-open, featureless white plain that extended all around him.

He'd started off in one direction, if it could be called that. There were no markers here to tell him what was left or right, north or south. Only up and down had any existence for him. He'd been walking for hours, or so it seemed, with no way beyond the beating of his own heart to judge the passage of time.

As he walked, little bits of memory—fragments, really—filtered into his head. He remembered a person named Alex. Someone important to him, though he couldn't say exactly why.

There was a house. A place he had lived, maybe? A little gray bungalow with a slightly peaked roof and a white picket fence.

And there were flames.

When he thought about the flames, he felt a searing pain all over his body and quickly pushed the memory out of his head.

Something bad had happened to him.

He kept on walking.

ALEX RETURNED to the hospital an hour and a half later, feeling a little more human. Fortunately, Oscar's house wasn't too far away.

Peter's clothes fit him well enough. They were not what he would have chosen for himself—a plaid long-sleeved shirt and a well-worn pair of jeans with holes in the knees. But they were clean and they had been given to him with love.

Dax and Mario were waiting for him in Gio's room. Mario was texting, and Dax was sitting next to Gio's bed.

"It's weird, right?" Dax asked, looking down at Gio's sleeping form.

Alex nodded. "I keep expecting him to open his eyes and say... I don't know... 'Where's breakfast?' Thanks again for staying with him."

"Of course," Dax said. "No changes. Just a nurse a little while ago." He glanced over at Mario. "We have to get to work, but Oscar's got one of his friends checking in around lunchtime, and I'll stop by this evening. Can I bring you anything?"

"Something to eat would be great. The food here... well, it's hospital food."

Dax nodded. "Enough said. Okay, we're off. Come on, love." He pulled Mario up by his sleeve. "Take care, Alex." Dax kissed him on the cheek.

"You too."

Then they were gone, and Alex was alone again with Gio.

He stayed there for the rest of the morning, sending texts and making calls to rearrange his schedule for the next few weeks. He checked their bank balance—they could manage for a bit. Thank God for Gio's health insurance through the university.

A little while later, some of Gio's friends from the astronomy program stopped in to see him. They didn't stay long, but they did leave Alex a basket of halfway decent snacks.

After they left, he settled in to wait for the arrival of *la mamma*.

IT WAS just after four when he felt the air change. It was like the ionic charge that preceded a monsoon—a sense of tension in the air, accompanied by a strange calm that came before the thunder and lightning and heavy rain.

Alex looked outside and saw that a monsoon was gathering. Towering, gravid purple storm clouds marched across the sky, presaging rain.

That wasn't the only thing that had caught his attention, raising him out of his semislumber.

"Dov'è mio figlio?" a feminine voice demanded, sharp and forceful.

"I'm sorry, ma'am," one of the nurses said. "I don't understand you. Let me find someone who speaks Italian."

"Where does you have my son?" Her English was heavily accented.

Alex swallowed hard, then stepped out of the relative safety of the room to greet her. "Mamma Montanari," he said, holding out his arms to her. "Benvenuti agli Stati Uniti." His Italian was elementary-grade level, but he could at least manage that much.

She turned and saw him, all five foot three of her, her blonde hair twisted into curls on top of her head, her face still beautiful despite the addition of years and a few more pounds on her hips. She glared at him, then pushed past him into Gio's room. He followed her inside reluctantly.

She took in Gio's condition with a single glance, then pulled him up in her arms.

"He's tender," Alex protested. "*Stai attenta!*"

She laid Gio back down and kissed him on the cheek gently. Then she turned on Alex. "*Dove eri*? Where you go? Why you let this happen?"

"I am so sorry. I was away from home…. *Ero fuori.*"

I didn't know this would happen.

A young woman poked her head in. "They called for an Italian translator? I'm Stefani."

"Parla italiano?" Gio's mother asked.

She nodded. "Sì, più o meno. Mi chiamo Stefani."

"Piacere. Sono Cinzia," Gio's mother replied, then let out a torrent of words, gesturing first to Alex and then at her son. He caught a few of them here and there: angry, my son, rights. The rest eluded him.

Finally she finished and Stefani turned to him. From the look on her face, he could see it wasn't going to be good. "She says she's this man's mother."

He nodded.

"And she says you will claim to be related, but that you are not, in fact, a family member."

"She what? Listen, Gio and I are a couple. We've been together for ten years."

Stefani looked sympathetic, but she asked, "Are you guys married?"

He shook his head.

She frowned. "Do you have his power of attorney?"

Again he shook his head. "We talked about it, but we never quite got around to it."

"Then I'm sorry…?"

"Alex."

"Alex. I have to ask you to leave. As his mother, Ms. Montanari here has asked that only family members be allowed to remain."

Alex shook with anger. She couldn't do this to him. He turned to her. "Mamma Montanari, wait. Don't do this. I need to be here with him!"

Stefani shrugged. "I'm so sorry, Alex. I wish I could change it, but I don't make the rules. Maybe she'll change her mind." She called someone on the intercom. Then she turned away to speak to Gio's mother again.

One of the orderlies, a bear of a man, appeared at the door to escort him out. "You can't do this to us," Alex said, starting to get frantic. "I love him! Gio!"

The man pulled him out of the room. "This is not the time or place," the orderly said. "Get a lawyer. Fight this thing out in court if you have to. But right now, you have to leave."

A crowd had gathered outside the room to witness the spectacle. Alex looked back and forth, but he saw no way to turn this around. Not here, not now.

"Okay." He shook off the man's hand. "I'll go." He slipped through the crowd and started to run down the hall toward the elevators.

"Alex, wait," someone called.

It was the nurse from the day before. Rosie? Rosalind? Alex turned around reluctantly.

"I just heard what happened," she said, giving him a quick hug. "Here, take this." She handed him a scrap of paper. "It's my number. Call me later tonight, and I'll try to help you." Then she turned away and disappeared down the hall.

He stuffed the paper into his pocket and fled the hospital.

GIO LOOKED up from where he was sitting. He'd finally given up walking after untold seconds or minutes or hours—who could say in this strange place? Every now and then, out of the corner of his eye, he thought he glimpsed something other than the formless white plain, but whatever it was melted away into dust and nothingness as soon as he looked at it.

Maybe it was better to stay still for a while. He sat down on the flat surface that was strangely neither opaque nor transparent, neither shiny nor matte white. Nothing seemed to make sense.

He noticed that the soft white glow around him was changing. Dimming. Like when he was in a restaurant and they turned down the lights for ambiance. The conscious mind wasn't quite aware of it, but it impinged on the senses anyway.

Restaurant. He rolled the idea around in his head. He used to go to restaurants with someone before this new thing had happened. With…

with Alex. He smiled a little. That was something, wasn't it? Some little piece of what was missing?

But his happiness soon turned to concern, then worry, and then fear, as it continued to get darker and darker all around him. His heart beat faster as the light slipped away. He jumped to his feet, looking left and right, but there was nothing but the gathering gloom. He'd thought the empty white was awful, but this darkness was worse.

And then the howls began.

ALEX PEELED out of the parking lot, unsure of where to go. Oscar might be able to help, or at least be willing to listen, but right now Alex was too angry, too distraught to speak with anyone.

He'd known Cinzia disliked him, but to throw him out of Gio's room like that? He and Gio were... they were partners, for sure. Lovers, yes, but Alex had always resisted the idea of *marriage*. Marriage was for other people. Surely he and Gio didn't need it to prove their love for each other?

Only now his own reluctance had been used against him. And in the end, what was he afraid of? Was it really a principled stand against society's expectations, or was he just scared shitless of the commitment?

Either way, Cinzia was with Gio and Alex was out there alone.

He found himself driving up the old road to the top of A Mountain, the lonely volcanic peak, more of an oversized hill really, that looked out over downtown and the Tucson valley. It was named for the whitewashed letter *A*, a tribute to the university that had been a city tradition for almost a hundred years. The clouds above looked threatening, ready to unleash their monsoon rains.

He knew why he was there. This was the place where the two of them had met, ten years before. He pulled the car into the parking lot and climbed out. The wind buffeted him as the storm grew toward a fever pitch. He shouldn't be up there right now—he was exposed to the wind and rain, and lightning often struck this peak when storms passed through.

He didn't care. He *needed* to be there.

Alex climbed the short trail to the peak, stepping up to the edge to look down at the valley below. Tucson stretched out in front of him, from the majestic Catalina Mountains to the north to the Santa Rita Mountains to the south. In the distance, he could also make out the Rincon Mountains to the east.

The clouds crammed the horizon.

The creosote smell was strong in the air tonight, the scent that had, for as long as he had been alive here in the Sonoran Desert, signaled the coming of a monsoon rain.

On the slope below him was the *A* the mountain was famous for. He closed his eyes as the rain began to fall in heavy sheets from the skies and remembered the day when he had first met Gio.

The evening had been warm and clear as Alex made his way up the road to the top of A Mountain—the perfect night for stargazing. He had taken up the hobby with his ex, Jason, who had often used his own small telescope to spy on some of their neighbors.

Alex had always had more than a passing interest in space and astronomy, and he'd turned the telescope to a higher purpose. Literally.

Now he had a better model, one where you could enter the coordinates of what you wanted into the onboard computer and the telescope would find your target for you. He'd scraped together a couple of paychecks to buy it.

He was excited to use it for the first time. It was the night of the full moon over the Tucson valley, and he'd been waiting for this night for weeks. It was a Saturday, so he could stay out late without totally screwing up his workday on Monday.

As he neared the parking lot, he realized he wasn't the only one who'd had the idea. It was jam-packed with cars.

Alex finally found a place to cram in his VW Bug off the edge of the road and pulled out his telescope in its protective case. He slung it over his shoulder, grabbing his backpack with his other hand, and climbed up to the peak of the mountain.

There were about thirty people already there, many with scopes, some cheaper than his and a few much nicer. He chose a spot to set his up his own telescope and pulled it out of its bag. He glanced at his watch. It was just about five forty-five, so he still had a three-quarter-hour margin.

The sun would set over the Tucson Mountains behind him just minutes before moonrise, so it promised to be a spectacular show.

"Nice scope," the man next to him said with a smile, glancing over at his equipment. He was a good-looking guy in his midtwenties, about Alex's age, with a slight accent.

Alex laughed. "Yours is bigger."

"Have to wait and see about that one." This time the guy's grin was wider and infectious.

Alex laughed. "I'm Alex Gutierrez," he said, holding out his hand.

"Gio Montanari."

"Ah. Italian?"

"What gave it away?" Gio asked.

"Um, the name, the accent, the classic Italian good looks...."

"*Capito*. And I'm guessing you're Mexican heritage?"

Alex nodded. "What gave it away for *me*?"

"Name, accent, classic good Mexican looks...."

"Hey, I ain't got no stinking accent," Alex said, acting wounded.

They were getting some looks from other people nearby, but Alex didn't give a shit. He *liked* this guy. "So, what brings you up here tonight?"

"Graduate student at the U of A," Gio said. "Thought I'd score a little extra credit with the professors in the astronomy program. You?"

Alex laughed ruefully. "Ex got me hooked on telescopes. This is my first full moon with the new one." He patted it, and the tube shifted. "Oh crap."

It was already after six. Alex pulled his manual out to get the thing readjusted so he'd be ready when the moon rose.

"Here, let me help you with that."

Gio put his hand on Alex's, and a thrill went up his arm. His new friend took the manual and quickly entered the correct coordinates into the scope. It swiveled around to face the eastern horizon.

"Won't be long now," Alex said.

Together they waited to see the rise of the full moon. The sun set behind them, painting the Catalinas a vivid pink. Then the moon rose, glorious against the velvet blue sky.

They stayed there together for hours, until almost everyone else had gone home. Until monsoon clouds blocked the view and the rain started pouring out of the heavens.

Laughing, they gathered up their equipment and ran back to the parking lot.

Once they stashed their gear in the trunks of their cars, Alex followed Gio back to his apartment, and they shared a passionate night together that surprised both of them with its intensity.

Two weeks later, they moved in together.

The rain was coming down in torrents, soaking Alex to the bone, but it was still warm out, and he didn't really care. The water washed away his fear and anger and worry, rinsing him clean again even as thunder boomed in the valley below.

In that moment Alex's life was reduced to its essence: the feel of the raindrops pelting his skin, his heartbeat, his breath, his love for Gio.

Alex opened his eyes.

The swirl of the storm around him lessened, and the valley below slowly came into view, gleaming under the clouds, the lights of Speedway and Broadway paralleling each other into the distance. Faraway lightning flared up along the Catalina Mountains, and a stiff breeze pushed the storm along to the east.

At last Alex turned and made his way down the trail from the peak, walking among the desert broom, rabbitbrush, creosote bushes, and mesquite trees to the parking lot, and set out to find Oscar.

"YOU NEED a lawyer." Oscar pulled the fitted sheet up over the mattress on his guest bed. "You have to fight this."

Alex shook his head. "There's got to be another way. I'm not suing Gio's mother. He'd never forgive me. You know how Italian guys are."

"Mammoni!"

"Yup, mother's boys." Alex laughed. It was a longstanding joke between the three of them. "Thanks for letting me stay here."

Oscar nodded. "Hey, it's the least I can do."

Alex pulled his keys and wallet out of his pockets and found a folded-up piece of paper. Curious, he opened it up. It had Rosalind's name and a phone number. "Damn, I forgot about this." Fortunately it was still legible, even after the soaking he'd gotten.

"What is it?"

Alex set it down to help Oscar with the sheet and comforter. "It's the number for a lesbian nurse I met at the hospital."

"Damn. I never get anyone handing me their number anymore."
Alex stuck out his tongue.

"You should call her."

Alex hesitated. "I don't know. I'm not sure what she could do for me."

"Never know until you give it a try." He shook out the comforter,
brightly colored Day of the Dead print, and let it settle down over the
mattress.

"You're probably right." He sat down on the edge of the bed and
called the number on his cell.

After about five rings, she picked up. "Hello?"

"Hi, Rosalind? This is Alex. Alex Gutierrez."

"Alex?"

"From the hospital. Gio's partner."

"Oh, Alex! Where are you? Are you okay?"

"Yes, I'm at a friend's house. How's Gio?"

"He's the same. Your mother-in-law is going to her hotel."

He was quiet for a moment.

"You still there?" she asked.

"Yeah. I just wish I could get back in there to see him."

"About that. I have an idea. Can you come over now?"

"Sure. I can be there in ten minutes. Thanks so much for this,
Rosalind. You have no idea how much this means to me." He hung up
and kissed a surprised Oscar on the cheek. "The coast is clear. My new
favorite nurse is going to get me in to see Gio while *la mamma* is at her
hotel." He grabbed his notes, his keys, and his wallet.

"You still have my key?" Oscar asked as Alex sped out the door.

"Yup. Thanks again! Sorry to eat and run!"

"Just don't wake me up when you come home."

The front door closed behind Alex, and he hopped in his car and
sped out of the driveway. It was after 10:00 p.m., so he tried to keep it
quiet, but his tires might have squealed. Just a little.

He made great time down Speedway and hung a hard left at
Campbell, and in less time than he'd planned, he was at the hospital.

The parking garage was quiet at this hour, and he found a spot on
the ground level. He got out of the car. An ambulance sped by outside,
shattering the silence for a moment. Streetlights pooled their brightness,
leaving patches of darkness that the waxing moon tried to fill.

Soon he was in the hospital lobby, lit by harsh fluorescents. He texted Rosalind.

Five minutes, she texted back.

He waited off to the side of the lobby, counting off the time impatiently. Despite her assurances, he needed to see for himself that Gio was okay.

Eventually Rosalind appeared and dragged Alex off down a hallway. "His mother gave orders that you're not to see him, but I have friends on the night shift, and I saw how you two were together. If it were my wife…."

He nodded. "Thank you."

She took him up a back stairwell, and they reached Gio's room virtually unseen. Slipping inside with him, she made sure the blinds were closed.

"You have until 5:00 a.m.," she said. "The shift changes between five thirty and six, and you need to be out by then. It's about eleven now."

"I understand."

"If they find you here and trace it back to me, I could get fired. So set your alarm, or whatever you need to do. And talk to him. He may not show it, but he can hear you."

Alex swallowed hard. "Okay, gotcha. Rosalind?"

"What?"

He hugged her.

"Well, okay, then," she said, a little nonplussed. "I'm going home, but Chelsea will be the shift nurse tonight. She knows the score. She will be in later to check the dressings on his shins. I'll be off tomorrow night, but you can come in the same way I showed you, after ten. Now go be with him."

She slipped back out of the room, and Alex turned to see Gio lying there peacefully. He sat down next to his partner, taking Gio's hand in his, grateful that they could be together again.

If only for a little while.

GIO LAY still in the darkness. He was terrified, curled up in a fetal position, praying the howling things would go away and leave him alone. Their claws scratched the ground as they circled around him, and he could feel the swish of their passage and smell their hot breath and fetid odor as they breathed on his neck.

They were *demons*.

Soon enough one of them would end this little game and devour him whole.

Then he realized that he hadn't actually heard any of them howl for a while. In fact, now that he put his head up a little, he couldn't hear them or smell them anymore.

It was silent. A shocking silence after all the howls and grunts and growls.

He sat up. It was growing warmer, brighter. He had survived the darkness.

His hand felt warm again.

Alex. Alex was with him.

He wasn't sure how he knew it. He just did, and it made all the difference.

"TALK TO him." That was what the nurse had said.

Alex cast about for something to say to Gio. Something that might help him find his way back from wherever he was. His eyes fell on the notepad he'd brought, the list he'd scribbled down of things they had lost in the fire. He picked it up off the other chair with his free hand and flipped through it, looking for something.

"I don't know if you can hear me in there, Gio, but the nurse said you would. She told me to talk to you, so I'm talking."

Kitchen. Bathroom. Bedroom. "I'm making a list for the insurance company of the things that we lost." His voice caught a little. "The things the fire destroyed. Oscar told me that we lost everything, Gio… so many things are gone." Then he saw it. "Do you remember Devin, the little stuffed Wildcat we used to keep on the bed with us ever since I won him for you at the county fair? He was so cute…."

THE UNIFORM whiteness that surrounded Gio began to shift, taking form. He stood up as the floor beneath him became dark gray, hardening into pavement broken by myriad cracks and craters. The white sky above darkened too, becoming a vault of stars. Around him a row of forms arose slowly out of the ether, becoming carnival booths and stalls. There were smells too—greasy hot dogs, cloyingly sweet cotton candy, and the delicious aroma of Indian fry bread. Suddenly there were people, so many people, walking past, laughing and shouting.

"Come on," Alex said, pulling his hand.

Gio looked down. He was no longer naked but was wearing tight jeans and a black T-shirt. He followed Alex through the crowd, his heart thrilling at the sight of him and of so many things!

They stopped in front of one of those milk-bottle booths, the kind where you have to toss a ring over the bottle to get a prize.

"I'm going to win you that one." Alex pointed at a giant teddy bear almost as big as he was.

"You're crazy. Where am I gonna put that?"

They'd been dating for seven months, and they were now both living in Gio's crappy little apartment.

Alex grinned. "Where's your sense of romance? Five, please."

He handed a five-dollar bill over to the carnival huckster, who pocketed it in his apron and handed Alex fifteen rings.

"Good luck. You're gonna need to land ten of those for that big guy."

"Wish me luck," Alex said, planting a kiss on Gio's cheek.

"Hey, not in public." Gio glanced around to see if anyone had noticed.

"Chicken." Alex tossed his first ring, and it landed right on one of the bottles. "Score!"

Gio grinned in spite of himself.

Two and three went wide of the mark, but four was another score. So were five and six. But seven missed, falling short by a foot.

By the fourteenth ring, he was nine and five, with just one to go.

Gio leaned forward, eager to see his lover make the final shot. Even if it did mean he was taking home a five-foot-tall teddy bear.

Alex leaned forward as far as he was allowed, moved to throw once, twice, and on the third move he let go of the bright red ring. It flew through the air, perfectly parallel to the ground, and settled down on one of the milk bottles… around, around, around the neck… before slipping off and falling to the ground with a clatter.

"Porco cane!" Gio shouted.

Alex turned to him, a puppy-dog look of sadness on his face. "Well, I came close. You said he was too big anyhow."

"Here you go." The man behind the booth handed Alex a much smaller prize.

Alex's smile returned, and he handed the stuffed animal to Gio. "Let's name him Devin. For our grandfathers, Desi and Alvin." Devin was a little Arizona Wildcat—the U of A's mascot.

"He's perfect," Gio said, "and he'll fit in the apartment."

Alex kissed him again.

The memory and Alex melted away, but Gio held on to the little stuffed animal. Somehow his clothing stayed with him too.

It was a small memory. He sensed that he had lost so many more, and in the ocean of his mind, this one was a single grain of sand.

But it was something.

ALEX WASN'T sure, but when he finished telling Gio about the night at the county fair, he thought that Gio's lips twitched upward just a little.

Alex sat with him for the rest of the night. He followed Rosalind's advice, setting an alarm on his phone for 5:00 a.m., and after Chelsea, the night-shift nurse, came in one last time at 3:00 a.m., he crawled onto the bed and very carefully snuggled against Gio to catch a couple of hours of sleep.

At five in the morning, Alex packed up his things, kissed Gio on the cheek, and left the room before the morning shift or Gio's mother could discover him there.

Chapter Three

ALEX WOKE in a strange bed, looking around wildly for a moment before remembering where he was.

The room was decorated with Día de los Muertos memorabilia—Oscar was a big Day of the Dead fan. There were little statuettes of skeletons getting married, riding bikes, surfing, and eating at little cafés.

On the walls were framed posters of sugar skulls, and dolled-up skulls of women at the park stared down at him. Even the comforter sported a Day of the Dead theme. It was a little creepy.

His thoughts turned almost immediately to Gio. He looked at the clock next to the bed. It was almost three, so he had another seven hours before he could see his partner again.

He showered, shaved, and dressed, and put in a call to his insurance rep to ask if she could recommend a lawyer. He might need one eventually if he couldn't work this mess out with Gio's mother.

Then he sat down on the bed with a sigh, as the full weight of what had happened finally hit him. Everything he knew, all that he had become in the last ten years was suddenly thrown into question. Their home was gone, a pile of ash and wreckage, along with pretty much everything he and Gio had owned. Alex's work, the other thing that defined him, was on hold indefinitely. He was banned from being with his soul mate, except in the wee hours of the night.

If they were married, he would have had the right to be with Gio, no matter what Cinzia said. A couple of years before, he'd effectively slammed the door on the idea of getting married.

It was his fault.

Alex pulled his Jetta into the driveway. He'd just had a big sale fall through when the sellers got cold feet. It had been a shitstorm of a day because his assistant had quit the day before, his car had stalled out on the freeway, and just about everything else he could think of had gone wrong too.

He entered the house and threw his jacket up on the coatrack.

"Is that you, *bello*?" Gio called from the kitchen.

"Yup, I'm home. Gonna go take a shower before dinner."

Gio appeared in the doorway, his red-checkered apron covered in flour and pasta sauce. "I made my mother's specialty. *Nidi di rondine*."

"That sounds delicious." Gio knew that it was one of Alex's favorite Italian dishes. Alex frowned. "Gio, what did you do?"

"Niente, amore," Gio said, laughing. "Go shower. Dinner will be ready in about fifteen minutes."

Alex took a quick shower, but the warm water ran out halfway through. Then he banged his toe on the foot of the antique bathtub. It had been one of those days. "Fuck!" He hopped around for a minute while the pain gradually subsided, then managed to get dressed and limp out to the dining room.

The room was lit with candles, the flickering light lending the yellow walls a romantic Tuscan feel. Gio was just coming out of the kitchen with dinner—skinny strips of pasta curled around in circles like little bird nests, smothered in a red *pomodoro* sauce.

They sat down together, and Gio served him a little *nido*, or nest. He poured them each a glass of red wine.

Alex took a bite of his pasta. He spat it out. "Crap, that's hot. I think I burned my tongue." He took a long gulp of the wine to try to cool his mouth. "What's this all about? You never make this for me unless you're trying to apologize for something."

Gio looked hurt. "It's not *about* anything." He wouldn't look Alex in the eyes.

Alex put down his fork. "Hey, I'm sorry. Look, I had a lousy day. Everything went wrong. Damien quit. I lost a big sale. Come on. Tell me. What is it?"

Gio looked up at him cautiously. "It's just…."

Alex waited for him to finish. When he didn't, Alex asked, "Just what?"

"I thought we could talk about getting married. We've been together for almost eight years. Lots of other couples are doing it."

Alex frowned. "We're not other couples. You know how I feel about it."

Gio stood, pushing back his chair noisily and throwing down his napkin. "I knew you'd say that. *Cazzo*, you're such a hypocrite, pretending you're opposed to marriage because it's some sort of heterosexual institution that gays shouldn't subscribe to."

"It is."

Gio's eyes flashed. "Not anymore. Look around you, Alex. Everyone we know is getting married. Dax and Mario, Shira and Cheryl. They're not scared of it."

"Lesbians aren't scared of anything," Alex pointed out, trying desperately to lighten the mood.

Crap, I've stepped in it now.

"They're not scared of commitment." With that, Gio left the house, slamming the door behind him.

He was gone for a couple of hours, while Alex waited and tried to figure out what he'd done wrong.

When Gio came back later that evening, they dropped the matter.

Alex had had his chance to marry Gio, and he'd blown it. Because, God help him, he *had* been scared. Scared to lose even more of himself. Scared to say, finally and irrevocably, "This is the best I can do."

Now he saw it clearly in retrospect. Gio *was* the best he could do. Why had he ever thought otherwise? Gio was *the best*, and Alex had been a fool not to take that next step when Gio offered.

Alex needed to go back to where it had happened. He needed to see it for himself, even if the house was nothing more than ash.

It was time to go home.

ALEX LOCKED the door to Oscar's place and glanced up at the sky. The thunderclouds were moving visibly overhead. It looked like it might rain a little later, but he judged he had a couple of hours. The day itself was warm, with the sun peeking through the clouds at intervals.

He climbed into the car and eased out onto the road. His heart was suddenly heavy in his chest—an actual sensation of weight beneath his rib cage. He wasn't sure he was ready for this.

They'd bought the house together five years before, after Gio had finished his graduate studies. They'd been desperate for more space. It wasn't huge, but compared to Gio's apartment, it was a palace.

The neighborhood wasn't great—it had been a barrio when they moved in. But more importantly, they'd been able to afford it, and it was close to Tucson's small downtown, where Alex had just gotten a job as a real estate agent, and it was not far from the university.

Over time the neighbors had come to accept them and even rely on them. They had keys to half the houses on the block, to water plants or feed pets or generally take care of things when folks were away.

They had been in the vanguard. New young couples, straight and gay, were moving into the neighborhood every couple of months then. Starbucks was reportedly eyeing a spot just down the street and around the corner, a sure sign the place had achieved hipster status.

They had built a life together there. And now it was gone.

Alex felt like an orphan.

He drove through downtown, wondering if and when Tucson would ever truly grow up. He loved the city, but its downtown had remained basically unchanged for decades. The new light rail system was a good start, but it was still a pilot project that didn't really go anywhere.

He turned off Simpson onto Elias Avenue, and his heart broke.

The little one-story bungalow they had called home together, halfway down the block, was nothing but charred stucco walls. The structure still stood, but its roof was gone, and even after the heavy rain, the smell of ash hung heavily in the air.

He pulled the car up in front of the house and got out, staring at the sight without truly understanding what he was seeing. The palo verde tree in the front yard was singed but looked like it would probably live, and the saguaro had been spared too.

"Alex!" someone called from across the street.

He turned to see Marta, one of his oldest neighbors, approaching. In a big floral dress, she hobbled across the street to give him a *grande* hug. "*Mijo*, how are you? How's Gio?"

He hugged her back. The tightness gripping his chest eased, just a little. "He's okay. I mean, he's alive—he's in a coma, but the doctor thinks he'll come out of it soon."

She nodded. "*Ay, dios mio.* I'm sure he will." She glanced over at the ruins, frowning. "I am so sorry about the house. It was such a beautiful home."

"Thanks, Marta. It's my first time back since the fire…." His voice caught a little as he glanced at the ruins.

"I saw it all, *mijo.* It started inside and spread like… well, like a wildfire. If there's anything we can do…."

"Gracias, senõra."

She gave him one last hug, then squeezed his hand, stretching up to kiss his cheek. Then she left him with the burnt-out shell of his home.

Alex opened the gate to the white picket fence they'd built. The yard still looked mostly the same, although the rock landscaping was a bit in disarray from the firemen and all the water. The black plastic sheets that kept the weeds from sprouting showed through from underneath the rocks and soil here and there. But the front door was gone, broken to blackened kindling, probably by the axes of the firemen. Alex imagined them rushing in to search the house and finding Gio there on the kitchen floor, curled up to try to fend off the flames.

He closed his eyes, warding off the pain, his hand on the charcoal that used to be the doorframe. When he opened them finally, his hand came away black.

If only he had been there.

He left the mark on his hand, certain that he deserved it.

Cautiously he stepped inside. The roof had burned and collapsed, so their home was mostly open to the sky. The rain had poured in the night before, and although it had dried under the hot Arizona sun, it left a mess of hardened ashes and bits and pieces of their life together that Alex crunched underfoot.

Near the fireplace, he found a silver picture frame, partially melted by the heat of the fire. It was impossible to make out what it had held, but he knew. It had been a photo taken on a sunny day in Tuscany, standing in the shadow of the Leaning Tower of Pisa—the obligatory shot of Gio "holding" the tower up with his hands.

Alex had that one on his phone. Some things could be restored. The silver frame, however, which they'd bought on the same trip, was a lost cause.

He looked into the kitchen. The appliances were still there, scarred and broken. The old Saltillo tile floors might be salvageable, but the tile countertops had collapsed as the wooden cabinets under them burned, and many of the tiles were broken.

Finally he ventured into the bedroom. The metal bed frame still stood, but the beautiful headboard, hand carved and painted in Mexico with fanciful colors showing a jungle scene, had been completely destroyed—just a bunch of broken pieces of charcoal.

Next to it, Alex found the remnants of one of the matching nightstands, the one on Gio's side of the bed.

They'd chosen which side they wanted when they first met. Alex liked being close to the window, but Gio felt more secure away from it and closer to the bathroom for late-night trips. And it had stuck.

Alex knelt down to pick up one of the charred drawers from the nightstand. It fell apart in his hands. Something fell out, landing with a small *thunk* on the hardened ashes. Curious, he knelt down and picked it up.

It was a small green box, a bit melted. Alex really had to pull at it hard to get it to pop open, but he managed it at last.

Inside were two matching silver rings, inlaid with turquoise.

Gio had planned it all: the romantic dinner, the candlelight, the rings.

And Alex had ruined it.

He closed his hand around the box, forcing it shut, and began to cry.

GIO SAT in the nothingness, holding Devin the Wildcat tight. The howling demons hadn't come back. It was still dark in this strange place, but it was no longer pitch black. Every now and then, he thought he heard some carnival music or voices passing close by.

He wondered when he would see Alex again. Everything was better when Alex was there.

ALEX WAITED in the parking garage for ten o'clock to roll around, responding to some of his backed-up e-mails on his phone to kill the time. One of his escrows had gone off track, and his new assistant, whom he'd never even met, needed some advice.

Then there were e-mails from his mother—he'd have to go see her tomorrow. He hadn't told her what had happened yet.

A text flashed on his screen.

My spies tell me that the prima donna has left the building.

He grinned. It was Rosalind's not-so-subtle code to let him know he could come in.

He grabbed his things, locked the car, and was up in Gio's room in less than five minutes. He set down his briefcase, sat next to the bed, and pulled out his list, looking over all the things they'd had together for something to talk to Gio about. His eyes lit on something he'd seen that day at the house. Unconsciously he grasped the ring box in his pants pocket.

"Gio, remember how I told you about Devin last night and how we got him?" He held Gio's hand. "Tonight I thought I'd remind you about the bed we chose together, just after we bought the house."

He squeezed Gio's hand gently, hoping for some sign of recognition—a flicker of the eyes, a squeeze back, anything to show that Gio heard him.

Nothing.

Nevertheless, Alex continued. "We were on that trip to Puerto Vallarta…."

THE AIR around Gio was changing again. He looked up at the sky, which was becoming so blue it almost hurt to look at it. The ground turned to cobblestones, warm underfoot, and the colonial Mexican architecture that filled Old Town Puerto Vallarta surrounded him.

Alex was holding his hand. "The guy at the hotel told me about this great little shop," he said, his eyes dancing. "They'll ship things home for us cheap, if we find something we like." He peered at a map, glancing around at the street signs. "Come on. I think it's this way."

He pulled Gio after him down the street, past a gaggle of bemused tourists on a walking tour, a garishly colored piñata hanging above them on a pole.

Must be their tour guide, Gio thought, before being pulled around a corner.

"Here it is," Alex announced proudly.

The shop was in an old stone building a little off the street, with shiny new windows showing off a display of brightly colored Mexican trinkets clearly designed to bring in the tourists.

Gio followed Alex inside, and there it was, the most wildly decorated bed frame he had ever seen. It must have been seven feet tall, carved out of a light-colored wood and hand painted with a fantastic tropical scene, with palm trees forming the corners and a menagerie of creatures prowling the jungle floor amid ferns and sago palms.

They looked at each other and said at the same time, "It's perfect."

They were furnishing their new home together and still sleeping in Gio's old student bed, but Alex's new job as a Realtor afforded him a bit of extra cash.

"How much is it?" Gio asked.

His job didn't earn him *that much* extra cash.

Alex turned over the price tag. "Holy crap!" He showed it to Gio.

"Seriously? $399?" Gio read, his eyes widening.

Alex nodded. "And it comes with two nightstands for the price."

"Sold!"

Gio knew they were supposed to haggle, but it was already such a great deal, it just didn't feel right. "Alex," he said, taking his partner's arm, "I want to pay my share."

"Are you sure? I can swing it. The new job—"

"It's *our* bed." Gio took Alex by the shoulders and looked into his eyes. "Please let me do this. Although it might take me a couple paychecks to come up with my share."

Alex studied him for a moment. "All right. Look at this thing—it's gonna be magnificent when we get it into the house."

He found the owner and arranged the payment and shipping. Gio watched him.

That's the man I'm going to marry. Hell, it's even legal in some states!

Once again the scene melted away, returning Gio to his strange, empty white world.

But this time, both Devin and the bed remained.

ALEX FINISHED telling his story and leaned forward, looking intently at Gio.

There!

The tiniest of smiles stretched its way across Gio's face.

He was sure of it now. Gio could hear him.

"Gio, I'm here," he said, taking his hand again. "It's Alex. I'm here. I just want you to wake up so I can tell you—" He couldn't get the words to come out. "—so I can tell you…. God, this is hard."

Gio didn't wake up. Didn't open his eyes. Didn't even smile again.

"That I'm so sorry," Alex whispered.

He sat there, holding Gio's hand, for another hour before curling up beside him to get some sleep.

Chapter Four

MORNING CAME far too soon. Alex's phone alarm blared, bringing him out of a light sleep. He shut it off and climbed down from the hospital bed carefully, stretching and glancing over at Gio. He was as still as ever, as if the life had already gone out of him, but Alex *knew* he was still in there.

He packed up his few things and gave Gio a kiss, whispering "I love you" in his ear. Then he set off, taking the stairs back down to the ground floor.

He stepped out of the stairwell, and there was Cinzia Montanari in the lobby. Fortunately her back was to him. She was speaking to someone on her phone. He ducked back into the doorway.

Things couldn't go on like this—he had to call the lawyer again today. Alex peeked around the doorframe again. She was still there. He retreated to his safe place and checked his messages—there were three from work that he would have to answer sooner or later.

After another five minutes, he looked out again, and fortunately by then she was gone.

Alex made a beeline for the door to the garage and made it out of the building without being seen, exhaling a sigh of relief.

He hopped into his car, threw his briefcase on the passenger seat, and drove back to Oscar's house for a quick shower. The water helped counteract the exhaustion that was settling in on him, at least for a little while.

"Hey, handsome," Oscar called from the kitchen when he stepped out of the bathroom. "Want something to eat?"

Alex popped his head into the kitchen. Oscar, in his underwear, was making some eggs at the stove. He wore an apron that gifted him with the painted-on physique of a go-go boy.

Alex smiled. "Something quick, please. I'm going to go see my mom, let her know what's going on."

"Sure. Give me five minutes, and I'll have some scrambled eggs and toast up for you."

Alex pulled out a bench and sat down at Oscar's kitchen counter. "Hope I didn't wake you when I came in."

Oscar shook his head. "I was already up. Heard you in the shower and thought it would be nice to touch base over breakfast." He pulled out a glass and filled it with fresh-squeezed orange juice. "Here you go— keep you healthy. You're gonna need the strength."

"Thanks." Alex gulped down a few swallows. "Oh my God, this is good."

"You're welcome. So how is Gio? Any change?" Oscar cooked the eggs like a chef.

"He smiled last night."

Oscar turned around. "Seriously? Alex, that's great! Are you sure?"

Alex nodded. "I saw him do it. When I was talking to him about the list."

"The list?"

"The one I made for the insurance agent, about the belongings we lost to the fire. I was recounting some of the stories to Gio. You know, when we bought this, what happened when we bought that. I think he heard me in there."

Oscar served up the eggs on a bright yellow Fiestaware plate and buttered a piece of toast to go with it. Alex attacked it, suddenly starving.

Oscar sat down to eat his own breakfast. "And Gio's mother?"

"Close call today," Alex said between bites. "She almost saw me when I was sneaking out."

"You have to talk to her. Or get a lawyer, or something. What if she decides to take him back to Italy?"

That brought Alex up short. He hadn't considered that possibility. "What if she did?" He finished his eggs, but he wasn't really hungry anymore.

"Why don't you ask your mom what to do? She used to work for the State Department, right?"

Alex nodded. "She's not a lawyer, though."

"Still, she might have an idea."

"I'll ask." He took the dishes to the sink and rinsed them off.

"Just leave 'em there," Oscar said. "I'll put them away. I'm very particular about my dishwasher."

"You're very particular about everything."

Alex gave Oscar a peck on the cheek. Oscar started, apparently caught by surprise by the affection.

"I'm off. Thanks again for everything you've done—that you're doing for me."

"Don't mention it. Let me know what your mother says."

GIO AWOKE alone in his bed. Their bed. Alex wasn't there.

He knew Alex meant more to him than anyone else in the world, but he couldn't remember how they had met, or much of anything beyond the time at the fair and the trip to Mexico.

It was becoming clear to him that he was damaged.

He sat up, leaned his back against the headboard, and stared out at the emptiness that surrounded him. It was no longer white or black, but instead a kind of muddled gray, like fog rolling across a damp, hidden marsh.

Something had happened to him to rob him of his memories. And with them, his sense of self.

Some of them were coming back. Alex was making that happen; Gio was sure of it.

But what if the rest never did? What if he was stuck here forever, in this limbo? What kind of life would that be?

Where was he, really? Was he lying on the floor at home, unconscious? Was he in a hospital bed somewhere? Or was he dead already, a ghost between worlds?

Gio pulled Devin to his chest and hugged the little stuffed animal, beginning to despair. He couldn't live like this. No one could.

He hoped Alex would come back to him again. Soon.

ALEX TOOK Speedway through town, heading out toward the eastern end of the city. Speedway and Broadway, the main east-west drags through the center of Tucson, were collections of eclectic construction periods dating from the fifties to the present.

As he drove past auto shops and car dealerships and fast-food joints, he wondered how his mom would take the news. She loved Gio like a second son, and he'd been afraid to tell her what had happened. She was not as strong as she used to be, and he didn't want to scare her.

He stopped at the eegee's, an only-in-Tucson fast-food experience, to get her favorite frozen drink—the piña colada. His mother had practically raised him on the only-in-Tucson slushies.

Ten minutes later, he pulled into Saguaro Hills. The broad metal gates, cut out of ionized copper to resemble the desert hills and the cacti that populated them, swung open wide to let him in.

He drove through the neat, curved streets of the planned development, past the desert landscaping that was typical of homes built in the last thirty years.

The assisted-living complex offered independent living for seniors like his mom, with a communal kitchen and on-site activities. She'd moved in there last year, and Alex felt much better having her in a place where help was just the push of a button away.

He missed her old house, though. It was the place he'd grown up in, with a big yard that backed onto open desert, where he'd roamed at length in his early to mid teens.

He pulled into his mother's driveway and sat there for a moment, gathering his courage. Then he went up to the front door and rang the bell.

His mother answered the door. At five four, she was a head shorter than he was, and her hair was as white as snow. It matched her embroidered blouse. Alex remembered when she had been raven-haired, the beautiful Southern belle who had won his father's heart when he was a day laborer, struggling to find work every day. Theirs had been a true romance, one his mother was still fond of talking about, whenever she could bend Alex's ear.

"Alex!" She took the eegee and smiled. "What a pleasant surprise." Appearances were deceptive. Although she looked frail, her thin arms held a defiant strength as she hugged him close. "Come in, come in!" She gestured him inside. "Come have a seat. I was just making some coffee. Can I get you a cup?"

"Yes, please." He sat down on her cowhide sofa. For a Southern belle from Atlanta, she'd taken to desert decor wholeheartedly. A cow skull hung above the round adobe fireplace, the walls were adorned by hand-woven Native American tapestries, and all the available surfaces were covered with every type and size of kachina.

His mom breezed back into the room. Alex noticed she was wearing one of the silver and turquoise necklaces he'd brought back from Santa Fe. She handed him a steaming cup of coffee in a mug that read "Tucson—the Old Pueblo."

"It's black, just like you like it."

Alex took the cup and held it. The warmth of the ceramic felt good in his cupped hands.

She sat down opposite him. "So out with it," she said without preamble.

"Out with what?"

"I raised an independent son, and I'm proud of the fact." She chuckled. "You never come here without a reason. So tell me."

He sighed. She was right. He really ought to visit her more. "It's Gio, Mom. He's in the hospital, at the U of A. I don't know when he'll—" He choked up a little.

She came to sit by his side, taking his hand in hers. Her hand was marked with age, but it was beautiful. "Tell me what happened." She rubbed his shoulder gently with her other hand.

"There was a fire…." He recounted the events of the last several days, getting through it bit by bit. The messages, the mad dash to the hospital, the waiting, the arrival of Gio's mom.

The whole time, she held his hand and listened.

When he was finished, she was silent for a moment. Then she surprised him by saying, "I'm sure it's been hard on Gio's mom, even after all these years. It was hard enough for me when you came out, and you were right here to talk to me about it." She laughed ruefully. "I had to get my head stuck on right to realize you were better off this way. That you would be happy, with Gio."

He pulled away. "I can't believe you're taking her side," he said, feeling a little hurt and betrayed. "You're my mother, for Christ's sake. You're supposed to support me."

She cupped his face gently in her hands and looked him right in the eyes. "And I do. One hundred percent. But Alex, she's his mother, and she's just been told that her son, whom she loves more than anything else in the world, is in the hospital and might die. What would you do to protect him?"

Reluctantly he said, "Anything I had to."

She nodded. "You're not her enemy. You have to find a way to make her see that. That you're better for him at his side than out of the room."

He nodded. "You're right. I know you are. I just don't know how to get through to her. She hates me."

"How could anyone hate you, sugar?" She pulled him into a hug, and her silver bracelets jangled. "And if she won't listen, I'll sic someone from the State Department on her."

He laughed and gave her a big hug. "Thanks, Mom. He hears me. I know he does."

"I have no doubt."

He stayed another couple of hours for lunch, then kissed her good-bye and went back to Oscar's place to get a little sleep.

GIO SQUEEZED his eyes shut, trying to remember what had happened to him and how he had come to be in this desolate place. He searched what was left of his memory, but there was nothing there but heat and light.

He opened his eyes and looked down at Devin. The little Wildcat's glass eyes stared back up at him. He smiled and held the stuffed animal to his chest, taking some comfort from it.

In the last few hours, wisps of other memories had started to come back to him. Memories from his childhood in Italy. He remembered his mother, a beautiful, strong woman from Sicily who had settled down with his father.

His father.

The man had never accepted the fact that Gio was gay. When he'd come out, his father had refused to speak to him again, a wedge between the two men that had lasted until Gio's father's death.

He remembered the trips to Lago di Como as a child, and the weekend visits to Venezia together. As he sat there on the bed he and Alex had bought in Mexico, he felt his connection with his past growing, just a little.

But he still didn't know where he was or how he had gotten here.

ALEX SET his things down in Gio's room, happy to be back by his side for the night.

As he sat next to his partner's bed, Nurse Rosalind slipped in.

"Thought I saw you," she said.

"Any changes?"

She bit her lip. "Maybe," she said at last. "His mother sat here with him all day, speaking to him in Italian. I think she was talking to him about things that happened in his childhood. She told Stefani, the translator, that he didn't move an inch."

"He smiled for me," Alex said. "When I was talking with him about some of the things we bought together."

"That's a good sign," she said.

"I hope so. Listen, I am so grateful for what you've done for me."

"If I were in your situation, I would hope someone would do it for me too. How come you guys aren't married?"

He flinched. "Because I'm a stubborn ass."

She shook her head. "I don't think that. And I'll bet he doesn't either."

"Thanks. But it really is my fault. I wasn't ready for the commitment."

"And now?"

"I'd say yes. In a heartbeat."

"You'll get your chance." She gave his arm a quick squeeze. "I have to go on rounds, but I'll check in on you guys later."

"Thanks." He watched her slip back out and turned his attention back to Gio. "It's just you and me, love." He pulled out the list again. "Remember that mask we bought together in Venice?"

Once again Gio's world transformed. The drab, swirling gray around him took on shape and color and texture as palazzi rose out of the mist—two- and three-story buildings in the Venetian style, painted in rust and gold, with peaked windows.

The ground beneath him coarsened and became a cobblestone street, and Alex was beside him once again. Gio looked behind them, but the bed and Devin were already gone.

They strolled hand in hand through Campo Santo Stefano in Venice, the sky above cloudy and threatening showers. It had rained for three days so far, and the tiny rental unit they had found just off the square had leaked like a sieve. There were little pots and pans scattered throughout the unit—whatever they could find—and they'd put their suitcases on the tall bed to avoid any flooding should the leaks get worse. But hey, the place was cheap.

Alex had jumped at the chance to practice his Italian this trip. They'd been together four years, and he still didn't speak it all that well, but he was trying. Even the disastrous three days they'd spent with Gio's mother hadn't turned him off.

"Mi scusa, dove essere quell'indirizzo?" he asked a passerby.

Gio grinned to himself. Only three errors in that one. And hey, at least his boyfriend was *willing* to ask for directions.

The man pointed down the street.

"It's right down here!" Alex smiled.

Gio glared at him. "In italiano?"

"Um, I mean, *eccolo!*" Alex led him to a shop just a block down with a window filled with Venetian masks.

Gio was from Bologna, which was practically next door, so this whole Venice thing was a bit pedestrian for him, but this was Alex's first time, and he was like a kid in a candy store.

They entered the shop, crossing the high threshold that helped to keep out the annual floods that usually came with the fall. Venice was a sinking city, after all.

"Che belle maschere," Alex said, picking up one, then another. The shopkeeper looked on, concerned. "Beautiful masks."

Gio mouthed, "È americano," and she laughed.

"What are you saying?" Alex asked, looking at the two of them suspiciously.

"Nothing, handsome," Gio told him reassuringly. Then he saw it.

The mask was made out of leather, stained a beautiful mahogany brown. And it was the spitting image of Alex's face. Gio pulled it down from its peg reverently. "This is the one."

Alex looked at it. "Why?"

"Because it's you."

Alex looked at it again and then up at Gio. He took it gently from Gio's hands and laid it over his own face. It fit like a glove.

It was a sign—they were meant to be here together.

"Vieni a vivere con me," Gio said.

"What?"

"Let's get our own place together."

Alex looked shocked for a moment, and then a smile spread across his face. "Even though your mother wouldn't approve?"

Gio nodded. "Even so. I'm not a *mammone*."

"You *are* a mamma's boy," Alex said, still grinning. "But the answer is yes." Then he wrapped his arms around Gio. "And this will be our first piece of art to decorate our new place together."

"It's perfect," Gio repeated. "But *you're* the *mammone*," he whispered in Alex's ear.

"Mammone."

Gio said it so softly that Alex thought he was mistaken, that he hadn't really heard it. Then it registered. "Oh my God, Gio… you heard me. You remember." He teared up as he searched Gio's face for a sign that he was in there, that maybe he was waking up.

But there was nothing more.

He waited a few more minutes to be sure, then crawled up onto the bed and gently lay next to Gio, careful not to hurt him where he was burned. "I'm here, Gio," he whispered.

He missed Gio's snoring. It surprised him a little, because Alex had always hated it at home when Gio sawed logs. But he'd always known Gio was there, still alive, still his. The silence at night was unnerving, as if it contradicted the other evidence that said Gio was still in there somewhere.

But Gio had spoken. Alex was certain of that.

He lay there for a long time, listening to the steady rise and fall of Gio's breathing.

At some time in the middle of the night, he fell asleep.

GIO SNUGGLED with Alex in their bed. Devin was tucked between them, and for the first time in an untold amount of time, Gio forgot he was trapped in a strange place.

Alex was here. That was all that mattered.

Chapter Five

Wednesday, September 16

A HAND on his shoulder woke Alex up. He glanced up blearily at the clock on the wall. It was 7:00 a.m., and he'd forgotten to set his alarm.

"Oh crap," he said, disentangling himself from Gio.

He sat up and turned to face his awakener. It was Cinzia, Gio's mom. She took three staccato steps, her heels clicking on the tile floor, and faced him across the bed.

They stared at one another, like two gunfighters about to draw, and the moment stretched out.

At last she said, "Vattene," and pointed to the door with a perfectly manicured nail.

Alex shook his head. The moment had come to confront this. He would not leave without a fight this time. "Parliamo," he said. "I want to talk to you."

His right hand tightened around Gio's.

She shook her head and pointed to the door again. "*Va' via*. Go."

She turned as if to call someone, and Alex took her hand. She looked back at him, her tight curls snapping back into place.

"He spoke to me, Cinzia." He pointed at Gio. "Mi ha parlato."

That stopped her. "Quando? Cosa è successo? Si è svegliato? Dimmi!" Her grip squeezed his hand almost painfully.

"Un momento." She was going too fast for him. "*Mi scusi*… um, excuse me," he called out the door to a passing nurse. "We need the translator."

The nurse held up a finger to indicate they should wait.

Cinzia nodded. "Figlio mio." She laid her hand on his forehead. "Parlami!"

Gio was silent. Eventually his mother sat down next to the bed. Alex let go of Gio's hand, and stepped back toward the door, not wanting to risk breaking this fragile treaty between them until Stefani arrived to translate.

Alex was powerfully hungry—he'd skipped dinner the previous night—but he had to get through this first.

At last Stefani came in, looking like she'd been roused from sleep. She gave him an appraising look, as if to say she didn't know he'd had it in him. Then Alex started to describe what he'd been doing: the nighttime visits to see his partner, reading the list of the things they'd lost in the fire and talking about the memories they brought up for him.

How Gio had responded.

"Ha fatto in sorriso," the translator said, miming the smile for Gio's mom.

"Veramente?" Cinzia asked, looking at one, then the other.

Alex nodded. He guessed from her question that Gio had been unresponsive to her. "Last night I talked with him about our trip to Venice. I reminded him that I'd called him a mamma's boy."

He waited for the translator to repeat that in Italian and saw Cinzia's mouth quirk up in a slight smile at the word *mammone*. "And then he said that word. *Mammone*."

She looked over at Gio and back at him, considering.

"He doesn't snore anymore," Alex said, not quite sure why that was important.

Stefani dutifully repeated what he said.

Then Alex took Cinzia's hands, and the translator stepped back to give them some space. As Cinzia looked up into his eyes, he said, "Lo amo, mamma," pleading with her with his eyes. "*Cerca di capire*. Let me stay with him."

She searched his eyes. "Anche a me manca il russare del mio amore. Da nove anni ormai."

Alex looked at the translator questioningly.

"She says she also misses her husband's snoring."

Alessandro Montanari had been dead for nine years. Alex nodded and put his arms around her, and something melted between them. She squeezed him tightly, and when she let him go at last, he knew she would let him stay.

The two of them sat together next to Gio's bed, silent. Cinzia seemed lost in thought.

Alex kept quiet, afraid to disturb this new balance he'd so precariously achieved between them. He and Cinzia had a difficult history that had started when she first discovered Gio was not only gay but had brought his American boyfriend home for the holidays.

It had only gotten worse since.

Alex looked over at her and found her staring back at him with a curious look on her face.

"Mi ricordo bene quando ci siamo conosciuti," she said.

"She says, 'I remember well the day we met.'"

He nodded. "I remember too."

"Yes. I like you then."

Before she had known he was gay. "*Mi eri piaciuto*—I liked you too. It was raining."

The rain was coming down *a dirotto*—in buckets. Gio and Alex sat in the rented car in Bologna, outside Gio's mother's house, and looked out the window dubiously.

"I have to tell you something," Gio said at last.

Alex looked at him curiously. "That it always rains like this in Italy?"

Gio laughed and shook his head. "My mamma doesn't know."

"Doesn't know what? That I'm coming?"

"That I'm gay."

Alex stared at him. He'd lost the ability to speak.

"I told her you're a friend from college who wanted to come with me to see Italy."

Alex looked out the car window at the little house, with its porch light aglow, awaiting them. "You're just telling me this now?"

Gio shrugged. "I didn't know how. My English not so good."

"Bullshit," Alex said, but he cracked a little smile. "So, what? You're going to tell her while we're here, right?"

"I don't know."

"We're not doing the whole 'sleep in separate beds' thing, are we?"

Gio looked away.

"Shit, we are." Alex's smile was gone when Gio looked at him again. "I'm sorry. I'm not going back in the closet. Not for you, not for anyone. It was bad enough the first time."

"Just give me a day or two. Then I'll tell her."

Alex looked out the window at the house again. "Tell her by the day after tomorrow. Or I will."

"I promise," Gio said. "Come on. I want you to meet her."

They got out of the car, and Gio led Alex up to the front porch. He knocked on the door, and soon his mother opened it. When she saw who it was, she flashed him a big smile and beckoned them inside. "Entrate, entrate, belli," she said. "Maria, il fratello è a casa!"

Gio breathed in deeply. "Mamma is telling my sister Maria that I'm here."

The house smelled like home, full of *pomodoro* sauce and *salsiccia* and fresh-cut flowers. His mother ushered them into the kitchen, where she was making *la pasta fatta a mano*.

Gio settled in with Alex at the kitchen table to watch.

He could come out to her tomorrow. Right then he just wanted to enjoy being home.

AT LUNCHTIME, Alex and Cinzia sat down together in the cafeteria to have some lunch. The place was busier than usual, but they found a table in the corner where they could have a little privacy.

Alex was tired of hospital food, but he was hungry and needed to eat something. And he really wanted to work things out with Gio's mother.

They opened their plastic-wrapped sandwiches.

"Che brutto," Cinzia said, wrinkling her nose at the prepackaged meal. "Questo sarebbe un panino?"

"Sandwich? In name only. *Solo in nome*."

She snorted, the first time he'd ever heard the usually dignified Italian woman make such a coarse sound. She took a bite and spat it out. "Fa schifo!"

He took a bite of his own sandwich—the label claimed it was egg salad. He gagged. It was pretty bad. "Lo so," he agreed. The apple and chips were much better.

They were silent for a few moments, eating what they could stomach of their lunch. Finally, he cleared his throat.

She looked up at him, her eyes narrowed.

"Grazie, signora Montanari," he said, addressing her formally. "Gio è molto importante per me."

She sighed. "Lo so, Alex." The way she said it sounded like *Aleex*. "But is hard for me to accett… accept."

"The Church?"

She nodded. "They say it is… *come si dice? Peccato?*"

"A sin," he guessed.

"Sì."

"We've been together for ten years. *Dieci anni*! I love him."

She took his hand. "I see it. Perhaps… *forse La Chiesa su questo si sbaglia.*"

His heart beat a little faster. "Maybe they *are* wrong. About this."

She squeezed his hand. "*Devo pensarci.* Time. Some time." She stood and leaned over to give him a quick kiss. "*Grazie di averlo aiutato.* Thanks for help… him."

Then she walked away, leaving Alex a little bemused. Maybe things were shifting between them.

He needed to talk with someone else, so he called Oscar.

"Hello?"

"Hey, Oscar, you have a sec?"

"Alex? Sure. Did something happen? How's Gio?"

"Everything's fine. He spoke to me."

"Holy shit. He's awake?"

"Not yet. But he said a word to me. And even better, his mother said I can stay."

"That's great news. What did you do?"

"I told her he was responding to me. And that I loved him." Alex looked down at the remnants of the disgusting hospital sandwich on his plate. "Hey, can I ask one more favor?"

"Of course. Whatever you need."

"Can you stop by Rigo's and pick up something for us to eat for dinner after work? The food here sucks."

Chapter Six

THE NEXT few days passed in a blur. Alex and Cinzia set up a schedule—Gio's mother was with him during the daytime, and Alex was there at night. It made sense, as they had already gotten used to it. But there was a difference—each day they passed an hour together for breakfast and an hour at dinner, talking and comparing notes.

Cinzia Montanari was a fascinating individual, as Alex was discovering now that they'd gotten past the whole antigay thing. *At least for the moment.*

She'd been an *avvocato*—a lawyer—in Italy before Gio was born and now worked in a nonprofit for out-of-work Italians—the *disoccupati*.

Alex found himself picking up more Italian during their conversations. Stefani often sat in to facilitate the conversation and to get a little practice with someone from Italy.

Alex himself had studied the language for a couple of years when he and Gio first met, and those old lessons came back into his head bit by bit. He was nowhere near fluent, but he could understand a fair amount and could make himself generally understood.

The three of them talked about Italian and American politics—both apparently sucked. They discussed friends and family and the way each had grown up.

Most of all they talked about Gio.

Alex learned that his partner had been a shy child, prone to spending time alone in his room with his older sister's science textbooks. Alex told them Gio still had a few of them at home… or used to. Cinzia learned that Gio had developed a surprising passion for spicy Mexican dishes during his time in Arizona and that he still missed her every day.

Their friends organized a food delivery service and brought in homemade dishes interspersed with restaurant fare. All of it was better than what the hospital served.

Every night Alex sat with Gio for hours, going over some of the things on his list, hoping to prod Gio's memories. He'd sent the insurance agent a copy, and the claim was being processed, but he hadn't had the heart to return to the house again.

Gio sometimes smiled when Alex told his stories, but he didn't say another word.

In the morning, after breakfast, Alex would return to Oscar's house to catch up on his sleep and keep track of the day-to-day things he still needed to do.

But he was starting to worry. After the initial signs, Gio wasn't getting any better.

When did you go from a coma to a permanent vegetative state?

GIO SLOWLY began to adjust to his new normal. He would sleep in his bed for hours at a time, with the covers pulled up over his head so that he didn't have to stare at the strange gray fog that constantly roiled all around him. He snuggled Devin in his arms, a reminder of the time before this one, of the life he used to live.

He still couldn't describe that old life with any clarity, not even to himself. Not that there was anyone else to talk to here, although Devin was a good listener.

He was slowly accumulating memories of specific past events. He assumed they were his, but how could he really know? They felt more like movies, very realistic, interactive movies of someone else's life. They were missing continuity and connection, the glue that should have held them all together in his head.

On a regular basis, during what he'd come to call *day* in this limbo, Alex would appear, and together they would relive another memory.

Over time, Gio had noticed a pattern. Each of the memories was tied to a specific object—the bed, Devin, the mask, a pair of chopsticks they'd bought in Hawaii. Why that should be so, Gio had no idea.

The items were collecting around the bed in small piles, some stacked on the pieces of furniture that he had relived. The whole place was starting to resemble a bizarre yard sale in heaven.

Every now and then he pushed against the invisible door in his head that he felt might hold some answers. And every time he was blown back by heat and flames.

He looked forward to his visits from Alex. He understood by then that they were a couple and had been together for a long time. Five years? Maybe ten?

Gio found these visits increasingly frustrating. They weren't so much visits as reenactments, and he longed to pull Alex aside in one of them and have an earnest conversation. To ask him where Gio was, and why.

At the same time, he became aware of another sensation. It was hard to describe, but then again, what wasn't in this place? It was a sort of yearning, or maybe gravity. The sense that if he just let go, something would pull him out.

He felt it especially strongly after Alex left him. If he closed his eyes, he could almost picture it. Like one of those laser shows in the old Flandrau Planetarium on campus, bathing him in its light.

Like the invisible door, he didn't know what was behind it. And he wasn't sure he was ready to find out.

So he continued in this strange existence, waiting for Alex to return.

ALEX SAT at Oscar's dinner table one afternoon, holding the little green box with the rings and flipping it open, then closed, then open, then closed. They were truly beautiful and had somehow escaped the wrath of the fire— two white gold bands, inlaid with matching parallel lines of turquoise.

He pulled them out of the box and held them in his palm. His brain was telling him that this whole situation was his fault. He should have been there for Gio when it happened. His own bad mood had caused all of this. He certainly didn't *need* to be married. After all, it was an outdated heterosexual tradition that dated back to biblical times when women were sold off like chattel. What did it have to do with being gay?

Maybe he didn't *deserve* to be married.

And yet his heart looked at the rings, and he felt an almost overwhelming feeling of love for Gio. In the face of Cinzia's disapproval, of conservative Arizona society's opinions, even of his own uncertainty and ambivalence, Gio had taken this step into the unknown and had planned to ask Alex to take it with him.

It had been two weeks since the incident—the fire. Alex looked over at the well-worn notepad where he'd listed everything they'd lost.

Well, not everything.

They'd lost each other too. And the cost of that one made the rest pale in comparison.

The doctor had tried to sound encouraging when they'd spoken with him that morning, but Alex was a Realtor—he knew how to read between the lines, a skill he'd honed over years of negotiations. *Cozy* meant *tiny. Fixer-upper* meant *total wreck.*

And *we're still hopeful* meant *anything but.*

If Gio didn't wake soon, it was likely he never would. And then what?

A car pulled up outside. He hoped it was Oscar. He needed someone to talk to about all this, and he certainly couldn't discuss same-sex marriage with Cinzia.

The sound of a key in the lock confirmed it, and a minute later, Oscar walked into the kitchen. "Hey there," he said, looking at his phone. "Aren't you due at the hospital shortly?" Then he saw what lay in Alex's hand. "Oh shit." He sat down abruptly at the table, across from Alex.

"Yeah, *shit* is about right." Alex set the rings down on the table between them. "Gio bought them. Before the fire."

"May I?"

Alex nodded, and Oscar picked one of them up between his thick fingers.

"Nice. Where did you find them?"

"At the house a week and a half ago. I think he was going to propose."

Oscar nodded. "Sure looks that way." He set the ring down and leaned back in his chair. "So, Gio was going to propose to the King of No Commitments?"

Alex hung his head. "I've been killing myself over these. When I came home that night, he had this romantic dinner ready for me. But I was in a mood. I had just had a shit day, and I didn't want to talk."

Oscar put a hand over his. "You couldn't have known."

Alex looked up at his friend. His voice broke as he asked, "What if he doesn't come back to me?" He blinked back tears.

"Don't be crazy. He's coming back. Gio's a fighter."

Alex couldn't tell if Oscar was really sure or was just trying to convince himself. But he nodded. "He is."

"Alex…."

Alex looked at his friend expectantly.

"You have to tell him."

"Tell him what?"

"What you just told me. And you need to give him an answer."

Alex swallowed hard. *An answer.* He nodded. "You're right." The rings lay between them like an accusation.

Or was it a promise?

ALEX MADE the short drive back to the hospital, half an hour later than usual. The monsoon storms from earlier in the week had moved on, and the last of the clouds were making the beginnings of a brilliant sunset over the desert, their pink hues stretching across half the sky and deepening into orange and red and almost to black.

The early night sky held that particular deep, velvety blue color it took on sometimes when the conditions were right, just before the stars began to wink into view. Alex rolled down his window, breathing in the fresh desert air.

For a few minutes, he let his concerns and fears and guilt melt away in the wind, his car almost driving itself down this, by now, well-worn path.

Then he arrived at the hospital. He parked, gathered his things, and entered the lobby, feeling a little sick to his stomach. His heart pumped a little faster than normal.

The elevator seemed to take forever to climb the two floors to where Gio waited for him. Oscar had been right. He needed to tell Gio some things while there was still time to say them, just in case—

He couldn't finish the thought. It was better that he say them *now*.

Cinzia was waiting for him, a concerned look in her eyes. "Sei un po' in ritardo. Tutto a posto?" she asked.

He nodded. "I know I'm late—*mi dispiace.* Just had some thinking to do. *Dovevo pensare.*"

He entered Gio's room. Rosalind was there, tending to Geo's burns. Already his skin looked better and healthier on his forearms. His shins were still an angry red.

She finished and nodded to him, starting to leave.

"Can you stay a moment?" he asked. He could use all the support he could get for this.

"Sure," she said, sounding surprised. "Whatever you need."

Alex realized that Cinzia had also followed him into the room. Nothing he could do about that; she would have found out soon enough.

He sat down next to Gio, took his hand, kissed it, then took a deep breath and started to speak. "Gio, I know you can hear me. Somewhere deep inside there, you hear what I'm saying." It was more a plea than a statement. "I have some things to say to you. Important things. And I'm afraid if I don't do it now, I may never have the chance."

He took another breath. He was having a hard time getting the words out, but he couldn't delay any longer. It was time. "Gio, I am so sorry I wasn't there for you that night. If I could change just one thing in my life, I would stay. I should have stayed to protect you. I should have…." Alex was, for a moment, physically unable to speak. He squeezed Gio's hand as hard as he dared, then forced himself to go on. "It's my fault you are here. If I hadn't been such an ass, if I hadn't run away…. If I lose you, I'll never forgive myself."

He felt Rosalind come sit next to him, putting her arm around his shoulder. He glanced at her, grateful for the small kindness, then looked back at Gio, hoping for some sign that he'd been heard. Gio's chest rose and fell at the same even pace, and his face was as peaceful and unmoving as a painted angel's.

He pushed ahead. "All those times you wanted something more from me, when I said I wasn't ready, there was something wrong with me, not you.

"When I said we didn't need to be like straight couples, that just living together was enough of a *fuck you* to the world. I was wrong. I need you to come back to me. Nothing would be the same without you." Alex sobbed but pulled himself back together.

He felt another hand on his shoulder. He looked up and was surprised to see Cinzia. She bent down and took his face in her hands and kissed him on the forehead.

"Continua pure."

He nodded.

Stefani had come in at some point and was whispering to Cinzia. There were others from the hospital too, standing in the room, bearing witness to Alex's confession, and before he could go on to the final part, Oscar, Dax, and Mario came in together. Each one came up behind him and gave him a quick hug.

"Got your back," Oscar whispered, shooting a sidelong glance at Cinzia.

Alex smiled just a little. "Here goes," he whispered to himself. He put his hand in his pocket and pulled out the fire-warped ring box, opened it up, and took out the two rings. There was an audible gasp, but he could only see Gio. The room narrowed down to just the two of them.

"I found these at home among the ashes. The one thing the fire didn't destroy." He held the rings up, and they sparkled in the florescent light. "Gio, I love you with all my heart. I was a fool when I said I didn't want to get married before. I see that now. I'm yours, if you will have me."

There was only this moment. This place. Alex's hand holding Gio's, gently because of the burns on the back of Gio's arm. The sound of the heart rate machine came in regular soft beeps.

The little green box in Alex's other hand and all it symbolized between them.

All their life together had shrunk down to this moment, this place, this plea. "Please wake up, Gio. *Amore mio, svegliati.*"

The whole world seemed to spin to a stop while he watched Gio for a response. A word, a smile, his eyes opening. Even a change in his breathing.

Alex waited.

Nothing happened.

After a moment, Alex's shoulders slumped, and he began to sob uncontrollably. Gio was really, truly lost to him.

He had waited too long.

GIO WOKE up in his bed, expecting one of Alex's memories to come for him, but this time there was nothing. No change in the air. No new scene for him to behold. No shiny object for him to bring back to his little rabbit hole.

Alex isn't coming back.

Gio knew it in his bones. The strange alchemy that had allowed them to reach one another in this limbo was gone.

He sat up, pushing the sheets back. Devin was lying there next to him, his glass eyes staring vacantly up at the sky.

Once again Gio felt that strange pull, and this time he stood and looked around, trying to tell where it came from.

He was tired of this half-life in the shadows. He was tired of disjointed memories that faded away into the mist when they had run their course.

He was drained, and Alex was gone.

Over there.

Gio felt the strange attraction, like the air rushing out of a bubble. There was a current in the mist, and he decided to follow it. It pulled him along, ever so slowly, away from Devin and the bed and the mask and the chopsticks and all the other things he'd collected from memory lane, and out into the ether.

He walked slowly through the mists along with it, and as he did, he felt a pleasing numbness start to settle along his shoulders. It worked its way inward, like Novocain at the dentist's office, and soon he was feeling no more pain. Another few moments and he would walk into blissful oblivion.

"*Gio!*"

He spun around at the sound of his name. *Alex.* He could still see the bed and the memories Alex's visits had brought to him in the distance, lit up as if by a spotlight.

They seemed so far away. It would be so much easier to keep walking away from them all.

If I lose you, I will never forgive myself.

It *would* be easier to walk away. But sometimes you had to fight for what you wanted.

He started back toward the bed, forcing one foot in front of the other, but it was like walking through water—or syrup. Behind him, oblivion whispered his name too. Once again he almost stopped.

"*Gio, I love you with all my heart.*"

Alex was speaking to him. Not the memory of Alex. Alex himself was here with him, somehow. Gio redoubled his efforts, struggling against the mists that held him back.

Then he felt the heat behind the invisible door, the thing that had happened to him, that had damaged him and left him in this place.

The one thing the fire didn't destroy.
The fire. The thing that had happened was a fire.
All at once he was in hell.

Gio cried after Alex stormed out. He grabbed the plates off the table and threw them into the sink along with the food, hurt and angry at Alex's reaction. He had planned everything so carefully, been so *sure*.

Alex hadn't even listened.

Gio grabbed one candlestick and knocked over the other in his haste to erase the evidence of his horrible mistake. He watched as it fell onto the colorful tablecloth they'd bought together in Mexico and looked on in horror as the cloth caught fire, flaring up as if it were covered in gasoline.

He ran into the kitchen, grabbed a pot of water, and ran back to fling it over the flames, but the grease in the pot only fueled the fire, which was already spreading up to the rafters above.

He had to get out of the house.

He ran into the bedroom and grabbed Devin, but the fire had already cut off his escape route through the dining room to the front door, and the curtains and wall in the bedroom were on fire. He backed away into the kitchen as the smoke quickly filled the house.

There was fire everywhere he looked. How had it spread so quickly? There was no place for him to run. He dropped down to the floor to try to escape the heavy black smoke, which burned his nostrils and throat with a strong chemical smell.

It was a temporary reprieve. The smoke filled the house in billowing waves, the heat of it making him sweat, until there was no clean air left even along the floor. He huddled against the wall as the air turned hot and foul around him, his heart pounding and his eyes watering from the burning air. Gio held Devin to his chest, trying to back away from the flames and heat and smoke, but they were everywhere. He couldn't breathe.

He gasped for air.

He was going to die there.

Everything blurred, then went black, and the heat finally went away.

Gio opened his eyes to find himself once again on the white plain.

Alex was standing before him in the gray mist, holding the rings in his hand. The rings Gio had bought for them. He watched in awe as something he'd never expected to see in his life happened: Alex knelt before him and said, "I'm yours, if you will have me."

The mist was suddenly gone. Everything began to change around him. All the stories Alex had told him, the memories he'd viewed, began to stitch together in time, each connected to the others by a series of other events. They filled him up like a sponge absorbing water. Each one was connected to him, a part of who he used to be and who he was now—who he would become.

He opened his eyes.

Chapter Seven

Monday, September 28

"ALEX," SOMEONE said, shaking him awake. Alex was too far gone in his misery to recognize who it was.

"Alex!"

He opened his eyes, his chest heaving. He squinted at the clock on the wall. It was 11:00 a.m. He must have fallen asleep in the waiting room outside of Gio's room. "What happened?" he said blearily.

"It's Gio," Oscar said. "Come on!"

Alex followed Oscar, afraid to hope, afraid to even think. He entered Gio's room and stopped, stunned. *Gio's eyes are open.*

He was at Gio's side in a flash. "Oh my God, Gio. Can you hear me?"

Gio's lips moved, but no sound came out.

"Get me some water," Rosalind called, and one of the other people rushed out of the room. "Alex, help me prop him up."

She lifted the head of the bed, and they managed to get Gio into a sitting position.

The water arrived, and Rosalind gave Gio a few sips.

Finally Gio opened his mouth to speak again. This time his voice was firm though still soft. "Yes."

"Yes, what? You can hear me?"

Gio laughed softly. "Yes, I'll marry you, you idiot."

Alex hugged him as tightly as he dared. It was a long time before he let go. When he did, he found Cinzia staring at him. "Look, I know you don't approve—"

She cut him off with a hug. "Mi hai riportato il mio bambino," she said. Then she turned to hug Gio herself.

"She says you brought back her little boy," Stefani said.

"I got it." He turned to Oscar. "I need a wedding officiant. Someone who can come down here as soon as possible."

"You're gonna get married *today*?"

Alex grinned. "No time like the present." He wasn't going to let the opportunity pass him by again.

Oscar rubbed his hairy chin. "Janine Rogers is an officiant, and she's a friend of mine. I'll call her." He put a hand on Alex's shoulder. "Are you sure about this?"

"Yes. Never been surer of anything in my life."

"Okay. You're gonna need a license. Usually both of you have to go down to the courthouse together, but they make an exception for inmates and hospital patients."

Alex laughed. "Well, Gio fits one of those."

"Hopefully not the convict one," Oscar rumbled with a big belly laugh. "Janine can bring a marriage application and notarize it for Gio here. But then you'll have to take it into the Superior Court office to get the license."

"Got it." Alex would fit that in somehow.

Oscar nodded. "I'm so thrilled for you guys." He gave Alex a bear hug, then left the room to make the call.

Everyone else was chattering excitedly.

"Not here," Gio said clearly, cutting through the noise and activity.

Alex turned back to his fiancé. "What?"

"I don't want to get married in a hospital room."

Alex sat down on the bed, deflated. "Well, I guess we can wait—"

"No," Gio said firmly, "I'm not letting you get away. I want to marry you now, today. Just not here."

Alex looked up at Rosalind.

"You guys could get married on the roof tonight. Under the stars. I heard it's going to be beautiful out this evening."

Alex looked back at Gio with one eyebrow raised.

"That will work."

The activity started up again. "Rosalind, can you get things ready up there?" Alex asked. "It should be romantic. Well, as romantic as a hospital roof can be."

"Got it. What will you be doing?"

Alex leaned in and kissed Gio. "I have to go get my mom, and then we need to get the license."

"Go," Gio said. "I'll be here waiting for you."

ALEX HAD never made the trip across the valley so quickly. The lights on Speedway were all green for once, and not a cop in sight. He was there in twenty minutes. As he pulled into his mother's driveway, he was almost on the verge of tears.

He pounded on the door. "Mom, it's Alex!"

"Hold your horses. I'll be there in a minute," she called out from inside.

The door swung open, and she stood there before him in her robe and slippers, her hair rolled up in curlers. His tears dissolved into laughter.

"Alex, what's happened?" She pulled him inside, and they sat down on the Santa Fe print couch together. "Is everything okay?"

"He woke up. Mamma, Gio's awake!"

She threw her arms around him, and this time he did cry, or rather, they cried together.

"Oh my, that's wonderful news, sweetheart."

She smelled of roses and hand lotion, and for a minute he was five years old again.

They separated, and he wiped away his tears with the back of his hand, offering a Kleenex for hers. "There's more, Mamma. I'm going to get married."

The sound she made could have shattered glass as she jumped up into the air and did a little dance. "Oh, sweetheart, I have waited so long for you to say those words to me. Y'all have no ideah." Her Southern accent slipped out, just a little. "When? I'll make sure I'm free…. Hell, I *will* be free."

"Um"—he looked down at his feet—"tonight?"

"Are you kidding me?" She looked herself up and down. "I can't go like this."

"You look beautiful to me," he tried, but she was having none of it.

"Give me five minutes to whip myself into shape. I will not go to my only son's wedding dressed in a robe, bunny slippers, and curlers."

An hour later they were on their way.

The officiant met them in the garage with Gio's notarized application, and after a short delay at the clerk's office to verify all the paperwork was in order, he had his marriage license.

THIS TIME Oscar and Dax met them in the lobby. "Ms. Gutierrez, Dax will escort you to the wedding venue," Oscar said.

Dax was dressed in a shirt and tie. Where he'd gotten them in such a short time, Alex had no idea.

Oscar took him by the arm. "Alex, you're coming with me. Can't see the bride before the wedding."

He led Alex down a hallway to an abandoned office, closed the door behind them, and presented his surprise.

It was a beautiful crisp black tuxedo. With a white shirt.

Alex was on the verge of tears again. It was gonna be one of those nights. "How did you—?"

"It was Peter's. Should fit you well enough. He would be thrilled that someone was getting such a good use out of it."

He shook his head. "Oscar, I can't."

"You can and you will, and you're gonna be *fucking grateful*. Now get out of those clothes."

"On my wedding night? Really?" He shot Oscar a sly grin.

Oscar laughed. "Come on. Your groom awaits."

Alex did as he was told. The shirt and jacket fit well enough, finished off with a classic black bow tie. But the pants were too loose, and there was no belt.

"Hang on just a sec," Oscar said, rooting around in the desk. "Ah, here we go." He displayed his prize, an oversized binder clip. He spun Alex around, doubled the waist of the pants in the back, and slipped the binder clip over them to hold them tight.

"Oooh, that's cold."

"Nope, cold would be turning down a gift from your best friend on your wedding day." Oscar pulled down the jacket's tails to cover up the clip and spun Alex around again. "Almost perfect." He took a bottle of hair gel out of his backpack and smoothed it through Alex's hair, styling it to his satisfaction.

Alex laughed, unused to being primped like that. "How do I look?"

Oscar stood back and gave him a critical once-over. "One last thing."

There was a red rose lying on the desk. He picked it up, snipped off the stem, and used a paper clip to fashion a boutonnière attached to Alex's lapel. "Courtesy of Mrs. Nivens in 201C."

"Oh my God. You've gone and gotten half the hospital involved in this little affair."

Oscar shook his head. "It wasn't me. It was the nurses. They've taken a shine to you two. Now come on. You've got a date to keep." He hustled Alex out the door.

Before I can change my mind, Alex thought with a grin.

GIO GOT the star treatment—a private sponge bath from a hunky male nurse who also washed his hair, a mouth washing with Scope, and a firm tooth brushing administered by his mother.

Guess that's the bachelor party.

Someone had found him a tux coat and shirt and cut the sleeves away so they wouldn't rub painfully on his burned arms. He managed to get some sweatpants on with his mother's help over the dressings on his legs. He'd finally gotten the chance to look at his burns. His forearms and shins ached, but it was nothing he couldn't handle.

The whole time, his mother sat next to him, even when he tried to shoo her out during his bath.

"Ho visto il tuo corpo per prima," she said.

Yes, you've seen my naked body. But not since I was six.

When Gio was ready, Cinzia whisked the others out of the room and closed the door. She sat on the bed again, taking his chin in her hands. "Are you sure?" she asked in Italian. "Do you love him, truly?"

"Of course I love him," Gio said. *We've been together for ten years, after all.* But he didn't say that part.

She sighed, then seemed to come to a decision. She took off the necklace around her neck, and Gio saw what hung there. It was Papa's ring, a beautiful, simple, heavy gold band.

"Then I want you to have this. For Alex."

Gio was speechless. Clearly things had shifted between Alex and his mother while he'd been gone. He accepted the ring, then hugged her gently but fiercely. "Thank you, Mamma." *For more than just the ring.*

There was a polite knock on the door. Dax popped his head in. "Cassandra's here."

Gio nodded. "Send her in."

Alex's mom entered, looking like she'd just stepped off the cover of a fashion magazine.

How she'd been able to accomplish that in the little time she had had, Gio had no idea. "Cassandra, this is my mother, Cinzia. *Mamma, ti presento Cassandra Gutierrez, la madre di Alex.*"

They embraced. "I am so pleased to meet you," Cassandra said. "I have so many things to talk with you about."

Gio translated.

His mother nodded.

"Welcome back to the land of the living," Cassandra said to Gio, giving him a careful hug.

"Thanks."

Here we go....

Dax popped in again. "Time to go."

Several of the nurses came in to take Gio up to the ceremony. One of them brought a wheelchair and transferred him into it along with his IV. There were garlands and flowers wrapped around the armrests and wheels.

Where the hell did they find all these things?

THE ELEVATOR doors opened. Alex stepped out ahead of Oscar and stopped, dumbfounded.

A crowd packed the rooftop. Two sets of chairs lined a central aisle that was scattered with rose petals. Two hundred people turned to look at him, every last one of them smiling.

Along the edges of the rooftop on either side, little Bunsen burners cast their flames, giving the scene an amber glow.

There were flowers everywhere. His friends and the hospital staff must have raided the flower shop and most of the rooms in the place to come up with so many bouquets.

Above, the moon hung in a sky full of stars, beautiful and full.

Like the night we first met.

Gio waited for him up in front, looking as handsome as he'd ever been, even if he was in a wheelchair. Someone had set up an arbor for the two of them, wound with garlands and flowers. He laughed when he realized it was made out of bed frames.

"How did you do all of this?" he asked Oscar, who was standing beside him.

"You have a lot of people who love you." Oscar grinned. "Plus a lot of the hospital staff turned out." He directed Alex's attention up to the front. "I think your moment is here."

On that cue, the wedding march began, played on someone's phone. Alex's mother appeared at his side and took his arm in hers, looking up at him, fiercely proud. They walked up the aisle together, one measured step at a time.

After all his misgivings, fear, and shame, this finally felt right.

GIO WATCHED Alex approach. It was surreal. He'd spent so much time these past few weeks in bed, watching life happen in disjointed scenes around him, that he had to pinch himself to be certain it was real.

Then he looked up and saw the full moon hanging above them on this warm September night and knew they had come full circle.

His mother stood next to his wheelchair. Gio glanced at her. She was crying. He hadn't seen his mother cry since his father died, all those years ago. He squeezed her hand, and she smiled down at him.

Alex arrived, and Gio's mother let go of his hand, whispering, "Tocca a te, caro," as she joined Alex's mother in the front row.

My turn, indeed.

One of the nurses started to turn the wheelchair around to face the officiant, but Gio shook his head.

"No, thank you. I'll stand with my fiancé."

Rosalind lowered the footrests. With Alex's help, Gio stood but almost immediately fell back into the chair. He smiled sheepishly.

"Maybe I better stay in the chair."

Alex smiled and whispered so only he could hear. "We'll just say it's your throne."

"Dearly beloved," Janine, the officiant, said, "we are gathered here to witness this couple as they enter into holy matrimony in this most unusual of circumstances."

She winked at them, and Gio squeezed Alex's hand.

She spoke to them about life and love and commitment, but all Gio noticed was the rise and fall of Alex's chest. Alex was here, in the flesh, in front of him, and Gio didn't intend to ever let him go.

Suddenly he realized that everything had gone silent. "What?" Gio looked around in confusion.

"He just came out of a coma, so we'll cut him a little slack," Alex said to the assembled crowd, kissing him on the cheek. "Your vows?"

Gio shook his head. "You go first. I'm still working on them."

The assembled crowd laughed.

Alex took a deep breath. "Okay, here it goes. Giovanni Montanari, I've loved you since the day we met, on a mountaintop under a full moon." They both looked up at the sky above them. "I was too scared to take the next step. I didn't think I was worthy.

"But life is short. I'm ready, if you are, to spend the rest of my life with you, husband and husband. I'll never let you fall again."

Gio's heart swelled. It was his turn. "Alex Gutierrez, these last couple weeks, I was literally lost without you. I almost gave up. You have no idea how close I came to walking into the light. Then I heard your voice, really heard it for the first time in weeks, and I knew I had to come back. I don't ever want to leave you again." He felt a tear on his cheek.

"Alex, do you promise to take care of Gio for the rest of your life, when he is sick and when he is well, whether you are rich or poor, in sunshine and under the light of the moon?"

"I do."

"Gio, do you promise to take care of Alex for the rest of your life, when he is sick and when he is well, whether you are rich or poor, in sunshine and under the light of the moon?"

Gio looked into Alex's eyes and saw home. "I do."

"You may now exchange rings."

Alex took Gio's hand and slipped on his white gold band. "With this ring, I thee wed."

Gio held up Alex's matching ring and then set it aside. Alex looked at him quizzically.

Gio reached into his pocket and pulled out another ring. It was a wide solid gold band. "This was my father's," he whispered.

The two of them looked over at Cinzia, seated in the front row. She nodded and smiled.

"With this ring, I thee wed." The ring slipped over Alex's ring finger perfectly. Gio's chest tightened with emotion—he could feel his father's presence.

The officiant put her hands on their shoulders. "Then by the power vested in me by the State of Arizona, I declare you husband and husband."

The audience cheered, and someone called, "Go ahead. Kiss the groom!"

Gio did, and Alex's lips had never tasted sweeter.

THAT NIGHT, they celebrated until Gio needed to go take a nap. "I've had enough sleep to last a lifetime," he murmured to Alex, but he fell asleep almost instantly when they laid him down in bed.

Tucked in Alex's arms, he woke up in time to watch the sun rising over the Tucson Mountains through his hospital room window.

Epilogue

A WEEK later, the doctor officially discharged Gio, giving him the okay to go home with Alex. Not that they had a home to go to really, but the insurance agent had set them up with an extended-stay hotel while their claim was processed.

It was a start.

Gio was sitting in the wheelchair, and Alex was about to push him out to the parking lot when Rosalind came in with a plastic bag.

"Don't want to forget your personal belongings," she said, handing it to Gio.

"His clothes from the fire?"

She nodded. "And his wallet and keys, and a stuffed animal."

"A what?" Alex didn't dare to hope.

But Gio was already searching through the bag. He pulled something out and held it up triumphantly.

It was Devin.

The Wildcat was a little dirty, covered with smudges of soot, but otherwise he was none the worse for wear.

Alex knelt next to Gio, and they looked at the little guy in wonder. "I had him clutched in my arms in the kitchen," Gio said. "I thought he was gone."

Alex shook his head. "He's too tough for that. He is a Wildcat, after all."

More than one thing had survived the flames.

J. SCOTT COATSWORTH has been writing since elementary school, when he won a University of Arizona writing contest in fourth grade for his first sci-fi story (with illustrations!). He finished his first novel in his midtwenties, but after seeing it rejected by ten publishers, he gave up on writing for a while.

Over the ensuing years, he came back to it periodically, but it never stuck. Then one day, he was complaining to Mark, his husband, about how he had been derailed yet again by the death of a family member, and Mark said to him, "the only one stopping you from writing is you."

Since then, Scott has gone back to writing in a big way, finishing more than a dozen short stories—some new, some that he had started years before–and seeing his first sale. He's embarking on a new trilogy, and also runs a support group for writers of gay sci-fi, fantasy, and supernatural fiction.

He lives in Sacramento, California, with his handsome, supportive husband Mark. Together for twenty-three years, they were married twice, the first time in 2004 in San Francisco. The California Supreme Court invalidated those weddings, but then legalized same-sex marriage in 2008, and Mark and Scott were married in San Francisco for the second time in November. That time it stuck.

Facebook: www.facebook.com/jscottcoatsworth
Author page: www.jscottcoatsworth.com

By J. Scott Coatsworth

Between the Lines
A Taste of Honey (Dreamspinner Press Anthology)
A More Perfect Union (Multiple Author Anthology)

Published by Dreamspinner Press
www.dreamspinnerpress.com

Jeordi and Tom

By Michael Murphy

To Danny, for a wonderful thirty-two years together.
Here's to thirty-two more!

Chapter One

WHEN THE front door of the trailer slammed shut with a loud bang, followed immediately by an animalistic howl of rage and frustration, Tom knew Jeordi was home. He snickered and shook his head.

"Hey, babe," Tom called out. "I forgot this was the day you were going to visit your parents. It went that well, huh?"

One glance at his boyfriend told Tom all he needed to know. Despite the scowl and look of anger and frustration on Jeordi's face, it only took one glance at the man to ignite the most sensitive parts of his nervous system (and everything connected to it).

He couldn't help but smile at the sight of Jeordi. He wasn't handsome in the New York runway model sense, but was handsome in the real man sense. Jeordi turned heads every time he walked down the street, although he consistently missed the many glances people cast his way.

All Jeordi saw when he looked at himself was that he wasn't tall, and he felt his ears were too big. Tom daily told Jeordi that he was the most studly man he'd ever known—and he quietly gave thanks that the man was all his.

Tom felt two strong hands wrap around his waist as he stood at the sink in their kitchen. Carefully setting down the dish he'd been washing, he leaned his head back against his boyfriend's solid shoulder, brushing his smooth cheek against Jeordi's fuzzy cheek—fuzzy not from a beard but from a strong five o'clock shadow the man dependably had every day by late afternoon. Jeordi hated it, but Tom loved it and loved rubbing one part or another of his body over the stubble.

"Love you, babe," Tom whispered. "I'm glad you're home."

"Why?" Jeordi whispered into Tom's ear. "Why? Why? Why do I keep subjecting myself to the same crap?"

"So, they didn't throw their arms open and tell you they've joined PFLAG and ask for your advice on what to wear in the next Pride Day parade?"

Jeordi snorted. "Um, that would be a great big no."

"What did they do this time?" Tom asked.

"Prayed—and then some. They tried to have some kind of healing service to rid me of the evil that had 'grabbed ahold' of me, to quote my mother. They said they needed to cast the devil out of my body."

"Oh, isn't that special," Tom joked.

"Not so much," Jeordi disagreed.

"Was it just your parents?"

"Oh, no. That's what made this one more frustrating. They had their minister there. He brought a backup minister—poor kid looked freaked out just being in the same room with a known homosexual. Don't know what he thought was going to happen."

"They upped the ante, I see," Tom said.

"Oh, there's more," Jeordi said.

"More?"

"Hell, yes. They had some of my more uptight brothers there with them this time."

"They succeeded in getting any of your brothers to be in the same room at the same time? How the hell did they swing that one?"

"Don't know. Must have been one hell of a bribe. They, of course, brought their wives, I guess to show me how a good strong Christian heterosexual marriage works. They pissed me off so much I slipped and asked Beau how he could take part in something like that when he'd been off screwing half the women in the county. He didn't appreciate it. I guess his wife didn't know he was a hound dog she needed to keep on a tighter leash."

Tom stopped what he was doing and dropped his head back, deep in thought. "Hmm, your brother Beau would look damned good in a collar—and naked," he said. "Now, if you maybe added a blindfold, put him on his knees with his hands cuffed behind his back—now that's just freaking hot. Maybe I should call his wife and give her a few suggestions. How do you think she'd take that? I'd be doing it strictly to help her out since I doubt she'd ever come up with an idea like that on her own. And of course I'd need to be there to help her, you know, to consult."

"Don't go there," Jeordi warned with a chuckle. Beau was beautiful, but unfortunately he knew it and wasn't at all opposed to spreading his beauty around to any and all women who'd have him. "At least that got the two of them out of the whole ritualistic crap my mother had planned for the weekly visit."

"Two down, ten to go," Tom said.

Tom turned around and wrapped his arms around Jeordi, kissing his neck. "I love you, babe," he whispered into Jeordi's ear as he held tightly to his man.

"I'm so glad you do. My family certainly doesn't."

"Oh, they love you. They just don't understand it because the playing field has changed since you came out," Tom said.

Jeordi had come out to his family a few months earlier when he and Tom decided to move in together. He hadn't planned to do so, but he'd been so frustrated with his parents making snide comments about why he was moving in with a man and why he hadn't found a woman yet to date and marry and knock up. In a moment of weakness, Jeordi had let slip that there was no woman and there would never be a woman—that he was in love with Tom, and he'd appreciate it if they'd all behave a little more politely with him.

Tom could still remember watching the look of pure horror pass over the face of Jeordi's mom. One minute she'd been standing in the living room of their newly shared trailer, talking about what they needed to make the place habitable, and the next minute, she was looking madder than a cat someone had just doused with a bucket of ice cold water.

And her words: "No one in our family has ever been something as evil as a homosexual, and you are not one of those people. No, you're not."

Jeordi and Tom still laughed, because his mother's brother was serving a prison sentence for murdering a woman during a bank robbery. To someone in her world, murder and armed robbery were less bad than being gay.

"So after you got the first two out of the way, what happened next?" Tom asked.

"Oh, it keeps getting better. Then the minister's backup decided to get into the act and try to play big man. The guy was clearly quaking in his boots when he stood up. I don't know if he was freaked about Beau being a cheating skank or if he was scared of me for being gay."

They released one another but stood close enough to touch.

"Was he at least cute?" Tom asked.

"Unfortunately, yes. I wasn't paying all that much attention to what he was saying, so I had lots of time to study his face and check out his body."

"How did you get rid of him?" Tom asked.

"He was the easiest one. All I had to do was to stand up and take a couple of steps toward him. He freaked and took off. I never laid a finger on him. All I did was step toward him."

"Did you have that intent expression on your face?" Tom asked.

"How the hell should I know?" Jeordi asked.

"You get that look every time you get super focused on something. You get it when we're having sex and you get close."

They snickered together for a moment.

"So you had one more down."

"I did. A couple of the sisters-in-law were starting to back away by that time. One dragged her husband with her. I guess she was afraid I'd reveal something about her dearly beloved that she didn't want to hear. Anyway, before long it was just me, my mom and dad, and that scum-sucking pig of a pastor of theirs."

"I do dislike that man," Tom said with a grimace at the thought of the pastor.

"Me too."

Before they could continue their conversation, though, there was a sharp knock at the door.

"What fresh hell awaits us now?" Jeordi muttered. Opening the door, he found another one of his brothers, one who had not been present earlier at the afternoon inquisition—the joys of coming from a very large family.

"What the hell are you doing this for?" the man asked as he pushed his way into the living room.

"Do come in, Jessie," Jeordi said.

"Answer the question," Jessie ordered.

"Excuse me?" Jeordi said.

"Cut the crap and answer the goddamned question, Jeordi. Why are you so determined to embarrass Mom and Dad in front of the whole community?"

Jeordi glanced to Tom, who shrugged, not understanding the question any more than Jeordi.

"Didn't know that I was, so I'm afraid you've got to be more specific than that," Jeordi said.

"Why is everything a fight with you?" Jessie demanded.

"It isn't, as far as I know," Jeordi said. "Now what the hell are you talking about?"

"This whole *gay* business," he said, clearly unhappy at even having to say the *G* word aloud.

Jeordi stood as tall as he could. "I don't see where you're going with any of this, Jessie, so I'm afraid you've got to explain yourself a bit better."

"Cut the crap. You know how embarrassing it is for Mom and Dad for you to be prancing around like some girl with another guy for the entire world to see. So just what is it that they did to piss you off so much? Huh?"

Jeordi shook his head. "Do you really not get it? Do you really think me being gay is some way to get back at them for something?"

"Well, of course it is. You're not gay. I've known you your whole life, and you never gave any hints of being… one of those people."

"I was just really good at keeping who I actually was hidden from all of you because I knew how poorly you'd all deal with the truth."

"Bull. You couldn't hide something like that. You don't prance around like some ballerina."

"Excuse me?" Jeordi said, his voice rising a little in strength.

"You look and act like a *guy*."

"Thank you," Jeordi said. "I think."

"So what's really going on?" he pushed.

"What's really going on is I love Tom and he loves me. We are happy. He's the first person I've ever been able to be myself with. He's the first person who has ever loved me for me, not for some superficial cardboard representation of the person everyone wants me to be."

"Huh?" his brother said, obviously confused.

"Oh hell," Tom said, grabbing Jeordi and planting a big, lingering kiss on his boyfriend's lips. "Now I ask you," Tom said, "does that look like something your average straight guy does?" Tom dropped one of his hands to Jeordi's crotch, grabbing hold of the man's clear sign of interest. "See? Does your dick get hard if a man kisses you?"

Jeordi's brother looked absolutely horrified. "I don't know what you've done to my brother, but somehow we'll get this sorted out and fix him," Jessie angrily announced before he turned and fled, the door to their trailer slamming for the second time in as many hours. And even though they knew it was coming, both Tom and Jeordi jumped at the sound.

"It's official," Jeordi said. "I want to be an orphan."

Tom stepped behind Jeordi and wrapped his arms around his boyfriend. "I'm sorry, babe. I don't know why they all can't just trust us to live our own lives."

Jeordi hung his head and focused on the arms wrapped around him, drawing comfort from the man he loved and trusted more than anyone else in the world. "Love you, babe," Jeordi said. "I'm happy coming home to you at the end of each day more than you could possibly know."

"I know because I feel the same way," Tom said. He gave Jeordi a quick squeeze before he released him. "Dinner should be ready by now. You hungry?"

"You'd think after all the crap I've been getting today that I wouldn't be, but for some reason I am."

"Well, then, come on and let's eat. Got to keep my man happy and healthy and as studly as ever."

"I really think you need glasses. Every time you call me that, I think you must be nuts. I just don't see it."

"You don't have to. I got ya covered, babe. Trust me. In my eyes you are the hottest of the hot. When you walk into a room, heads turn to try to take in your beauty. Both men and women," he added.

"I still don't get it," Jeordi said.

"Don't worry about it. On this one, my opinion is all that counts," Tom joked.

Tom pulled the oven door open, taking care to hold on to it for fear it would fall off. Their new rental home had a few issues that needed to be addressed, but their landlord had yet to respond to any of their concerns. As he pulled a covered dish from the oven, the kitchen was filled with a delicious aroma of pumpkin, chicken, apples, and something else Jeordi couldn't identify. Cinnamon? Yes, he decided. Cinnamon. He closed his eyes and savored the scents.

As they sat at the table and ate, talk was deliberately on anything other than Jeordi's family. Talk of their days allowed both of them to release some of the burdens the outside world tried to heap upon them.

Chapter Two

ON TUESDAYS Tom typically got home an hour before Jeordi. He'd barely been in the house long enough to change his clothes when he heard someone knocking on the door. He almost hoped it was some Bible-thumper so he could take out some of his built-up aggression on the person. Instead it was worse.

"Sandra," he said, surprised, when he found Jeordi's mother standing outside the door to their trailer. "Jeordi isn't home yet," Tom said as he greeted her.

"I know that," she said as she pushed past him into the living room.

"Okay," Tom said hesitantly. "Do come on in. This is a first. What brings you over here today if not to see your son?"

"You and me—we need to talk."

"We do?" Tom asked, playing it calm. "What is it we need to talk about?"

"Whatever you've done to my son, you need to back off and let him go. You've had your fun. I don't understand any of it, but he needs to get back to the life he's supposed to be living."

Tom arched an eyebrow at the last statement, even though nothing she'd said so far had surprised him. He crossed his arms over his chest and stood staring at her, deliberately putting the pressure on her.

Most people hated silence, so it only took a moment of silent staring at her to get her talking again.

"My boy is a good boy," she said.

"He's a good man," Tom agreed with clarification. "He hasn't been a boy in many years."

"And he needs to get back to life as he is supposed to live it."

"Oh, I thought he was. I know he thinks he is. And I happen to agree with him."

"Well, he's not," she said decisively.

"Have you thought about asking him about this? It is his life, after all."

"Of course I've tried talking to him. He's too damned stubborn to listen."

"He is related to you, after all," Tom said, but the comment went entirely over her head.

"I don't care how you go about doing it, but we cannot have him prancing around in front of the whole community acting like some damned fruit. It's embarrassing to me and everyone in his family."

"He's not acting," Tom said.

"Of course he is," she said.

"This is something you and he need to talk about," Tom repeated.

"You aren't listening to me," she said, a strong hint of exasperation quickly creeping into her voice. "He won't listen to reason, so I'm forced to come to you. I don't know what you've done to him. He was always a good boy who never gave us this kind of trouble. It was only when you came onto the scene that everything started to go all to hell with him. So stop it."

Tom stared at her for a moment, trying to decide how much of his anger should be allowed out.

"Since I disagree with your entire premise, I can't help you."

"I don't care what you think—"

"Sorry, but I do."

"I don't care. Fix this mess."

"I cannot and will not simply because I don't see what you refer to as a 'mess.' What I see is a man I love and a man who loves me."

"Men aren't supposed to do things like that," she said angrily.

"Men and women have been doing this for thousands of years. You've just been oblivious to it. Your son has been gay all of his life— you just didn't see it."

"No son of mine is one of those people. I raised my kids right."

"Being gay has nothing to do with the way one is raised. Someone is gay because of something in his or her DNA and not from what someone did or did not do. He no more chose to be gay than you chose to be straight."

"No one wants to see such distasteful, sinful stuff shoved in their faces."

"Likewise," Tom agreed, which only confused her more.

"Enough," she yelled. "I've told you what you are going to do, and I'm not going to stand here and tell you again."

"And what would that be, Mother?"

Neither his mother nor Tom had heard Jeordi arrive home, so his question caught both of them by surprise.

"Since you will not listen to reason, I had no choice but to come talk to"—she waved her hand vaguely at Tom—"this one to tell him to fix the mess he's created."

"Why in the world would you ever do something like that, Mother? There is nothing wrong, other than you not getting the message that I don't need or want you meddling in my life."

"I'm your mother. It's my job to keep you on the straight and narrow and to help get you back on course when you get into trouble."

"Good to know. If I ever get into trouble, I'll be ready."

"Will you stop being so goddamned stubborn?" she yelled at him. "Everybody sees you behaving like this, and they're all going to think I didn't do a good enough job raising you right."

"I think you'd better go now, Mother."

"I'm not leaving until you see reason."

"No, you're leaving now," Jeordi said, taking her by the arm and walking her to the door.

"You're throwing your own mother out?" she demanded of him.

"If you had any manners and didn't come into my home to abuse and misuse the man I love, then you would be welcome to stay. But clearly you are not capable of that, so I guess I am throwing you out. Good-bye," he said as he closed the door with her on the other side.

Chapter Three

AFTER A quiet weekend, Monday morning dawned cold and wet and dreary, a constant drizzle falling from the leaden sky. Monday mornings were always the toughest days to get up and get going, and that morning, being nasty, was only more so. But they had no choice. Work awaited both of them, so they reluctantly got out of bed and started moving through their morning routines.

Tom's job was closer, but he started work earlier than Jeordi, so Tom left first. Since finances were so tight for them, they did not own a car. To get to work, Tom walked, but Jeordi's job was a couple of miles away, so he rode his bike. A bike ride on a wet morning was far less appealing than it was on other days of the week.

The drizzle had turned into a steadier rain by about the halfway point of Jeordi's bike ride to work. He was just passing an especially congested part of his ride when a car, going too fast, apparently did not see him and turned right, hitting him from the side, knocking him to the road, and sending him body surfing across the hard blacktop of the pavement.

When his body first connected with the pavement, his head bounced on the hard blacktop with enough force to leave him feeling quite disoriented. It was this disorientation that probably prevented him from feeling the pain that would normally have accompanied the horrible slide he took on the road.

If he had not been getting a face full of rain, he likely wouldn't have tried to move as soon as he did. The only problem was that he wasn't very successful in making his body do what he wanted it to do.

"Don't move," someone said. Jeordi didn't recognize the voice.

"Here, I'll use my umbrella to keep the water off your face," he heard a woman say from close by. He was having a hard time sorting out who was talking and what they were saying. Since the cold water was no longer hitting his face, though, Jeordi had less urgency about getting up. He lay back down and lost consciousness. At least that was his best guess, because the next thing he knew, someone was moving him from the ground up onto something softer than blacktop. He roused enough to see what was happening, but unfortunately the first thing he happened to spot was the mangled form of his bike. He groaned at the sight. It wasn't new, but it was how he got around. He didn't know what he was going to do without that bike, and he certainly couldn't afford one.

"Hey there, buddy," an unknown man said to him in the back of an ambulance. "How you feeling?"

"Don't know," Jeordi answered truthfully.

"Hell of a way to start the week," the unknown man said as he skillfully inserted an IV into Jeordi's arm.

"What's that?" Jeordi asked.

"Fluids. You've been bleeding. Standard course in an accident like you had."

"What happened to me?" Jeordi asked.

"I don't know. I didn't see it. Looked like a car hit you and sent you flying."

"Right," he said. "I remember—I think."

Jeordi was a bit confused about the order in which things happened, but at some point the ambulance reached a hospital and he was wheeled into the emergency room, where someone checked him out almost immediately, ordering a series of tests and scans, the names of which meant nothing to Jeordi.

One test completed, Jeordi lay on his bed in the ER waiting for the next test when he heard the familiar voice of his mother.

"Oh my God, baby, are you all right?"

"Mom?" he said, not expecting her.

"I'm here, baby. Oh, my heavens, look at you. You're so scraped up. What happened to you?"

"I think a car hit me," he said. "Is Tom here?"

"I haven't seen him," she said.

"Call him, please, and make sure he knows what happened."

An orderly appeared to push his bed off for his next test. An hour later when they returned him to the ER, other members of his family were there, but there was no sign of Tom.

"Where's Tom?" was his first question.

"I don't know," his mother said before quickly going on about something else entirely.

When someone came to draw blood, everyone stepped out while the technician did his work. A nurse was in the room at the same time, so Jeordi asked, "Has anyone called my partner?"

"What's her name, sweetie?" the nurse asked.

"His name is Tom," Jeordi said.

"You got a number?" she asked.

"It's in my phone. Where's my phone?"

"Sorry, baby, but you didn't have one when you were brought in. Maybe it fell out when the car hit you?"

"Crap," Jeordi said, his frustration piling up. First his bike and now his phone. Digging into his memory, he gave her the number for Tom's workplace.

"I'll go call for you."

Jeordi lay back, slightly comforted by the thought of Tom getting there to share in the hellish way in which his Monday had started. Jeordi hurt, and if he were honest, he was also scared. But it was only Tom with whom he would share the existence of that fear. He was certainly not about to show his fear to his parents or anyone else in his family.

"Mr. Boone, I need to start cleaning up some of the injuries you sustained," another nurse told him upon entering his space. "I'll do my best to be gentle, but there may be some pain with some of the deeper parts, especially where I've got to try to remove foreign bodies."

"Foreign bodies?" Jeordi asked.

"Most likely gravel and dirt, things you picked up when you slid along the road and the shoulder of the road."

"Sounds like fun," Jeordi said.

His mother chose that moment to pop her head back into the room. "You okay, baby?" she said.

"Doing great," he said dismissively. "Is Tom here yet?"

He wasn't looking at her, but Jeordi could hear the hitch in her voice. "I haven't seen him. I'll be out here if you need me, baby."

With her gone, Jeordi sighed and mentally shook his head in frustration.

The debridement, to use the technical term—a term he learned when the nurse's assistant tried to distract him from the nurse digging into an especially deep and sensitive spot—was not pleasant.

"This is going to require some stitches," she said before stepping out to summon a doctor.

As Jeordi waited, he had nothing to do other than feel a throbbing in a huge section of his chest, not to mention his face, and he wasn't even ready to think about his leg. He couldn't move much since he was covered with sterile cloths, and the nurse had warned him about not disturbing them.

Trapped as he was, Jeordi noticed the distinctive smell of the hospital. If asked, he couldn't have identified what the chemicals were that created the scent, but there was no question it was there and it was very real.

The wall to the right of his location looked a bit battered. Clearly it had seen a lot of people brush up against it. Gurneys had been bumped into it, along with an untold number of the rolling trays of instruments that dotted the room at the moment. He'd also seen some big but portable devices being wheeled around into other spaces, and he guessed that some of those had added to the damage. If that wall could talk and tell the story of each ding, dent, chip, and scuff, what a story that would be.

The light in the room was dramatically different than that in most of the rest of the world. Since he was flat on his back, his face was getting the brightness full blast. And the nurse who had been working on his injuries had an even more intense beam, this one with a huge magnifying glass attached to it with yet another light source. If there was something that those two didn't reveal, it must be tiny.

His gaze drifted upward, not to the lights but to the square panels that made up the remainder of the ceiling. Clearly those were not new but had been there for some time. A number of them were chipped or had pieces missing, most likely from being pushed up or removed multiple times over the years. There were any number of smudges, probably from hands dirtied by whatever was on the upper side of those panels. Some of the stains were clearly handprints, but others were not so easily identifiable.

This combination of dinged, dirty, and damaged surroundings made Jeordi wonder if perhaps the sterile cloths the nurse had used were enough, given the environment in which she was working. He made a mental note to mention that. But he also made a note to ask her for something for his headache, which was getting worse.

A moment later he heard the nurse return and begin to pull on a fresh pair of surgical gloves. She was accompanied by a man, presumably a doctor, who did the same thing. He looked a bit harried, like he needed to be somewhere else more urgently at the moment, anywhere but in that room.

"Okay, let's see what we're dealing with here," he announced as he spread the deepest scrape on Jeordi's chest.

"Ow!" Jeordi cried out.

"Did that hurt?" he asked.

"What the fuck do you think?"

"Not unexpected. It looks like you've damaged yourself quite a bit. How did this happen?" he asked as he continued to poke around.

"A car hit my bike and sent me flying."

"Motorcycle?" the doctor asked.

"No. Bicycle bike." Jeordi's opinion of the man was dropping precipitously, especially when he felt another sharp pain in another spot. "Ow!" he yelled, a little louder this time.

"You shouldn't be feeling that," the doctor announced, as if that would clear up the problem.

"Well, I did feel that."

"The anesthetic should have numbed the area."

"I haven't given the patient anything yet, Doctor."

"What?" he demanded of the nurse.

"You know I'm not allowed to do that."

The doctor sounded pissed, which made Jeordi even less happy with the man poking around on his body.

"All right. This is going to take longer than I realized. I need to go finish up with another patient first," he said as he left the room.

"Nurse," Jeordi said. "Is there anyone else other than him? I don't like him. He seems mad at the world. I don't think I want him working on me in that state."

"I'll see. He's really a good doctor, but he is stretched a little thin right now. You lie here for a few minutes and we'll be back."

As suddenly as it had started, Jeordi was once again alone with nothing to do and no one to talk with. The usually placid, mostly quiet emergency room was apparently getting busy, at least based on the noise Jeordi was hearing from somewhere away from his location. Voices were raised, joined moments later by the sound of running feet and more commotion. He couldn't make out the words nor tell who was speaking.

Whatever was happening, it took a few minutes to resolve and involved one loud metallic crash before it was finished.

Ten minutes later when a nurse poked her head in to check on him, Jeordi asked, "Has my boyfriend, Tom, got here yet? Someone called him quite a while ago. I need to see him as soon as he gets here."

Jeordi glanced her way when she didn't immediately respond and saw an expression of... something unidentifiable on her face. "What?" he demanded.

"Um, there was... well, there was just a dispute of some kind between the front desk personnel and someone who was trying to get in to see a patient. Those people who have been checking on you got involved somehow, but I didn't hear what they said or what really happened."

"Oh, hell no," Jeordi said, knowing instantly what had happened.

Pushing himself upward, Jeordi felt a moment of dizziness and disorientation that only got worse as he swung his legs around to sit up on the table.

"What are you doing? You can't move!" the nurse yelled at him. "I had you all sterile. Now we'll have to do that all again."

Jeordi stood, even though he still had the IV in his arm and wasn't wearing anything other than his white cotton briefs.

"Get this out of me," Jeordi ordered, pointing to the IV.

"No, I can't. You need fluids."

"I'm leaving to go see if my parents have done what I think they've done. I need this thing out while I do that."

"I can't let you leave. You haven't had your stitches yet, and we haven't finished debridement. We have a lot of work to do on you yet."

"I'm coming back, but I've got to go check this out first."

"This is a really, really bad idea," she said.

"You can do it, or I will do it," Jeordi said. "It will probably be safer if you do it."

She gave a huge sigh and pulled something free from the needle the ambulance crew had placed in his arm.

"I've disconnected the line, but the port is still there."

"Good. Thank you," Jeordi said.

Unsteadily, Jeordi made it to the door of the room, halting only when he heard the nurse tell him, "You're not dressed."

"I'll be right back," Jeordi said.

Every step he took hurt, sending reverberations of pain through his entire body, from his twisted ankle straight up to his aching head. His dizziness made him stop a couple of times, waiting for the world to right itself. But each time, he did not let his physical condition hold him back.

"Baby," he heard his mother shout when he reached the waiting room.

"What just happened?" he said loudly, which unfortunately made his head hurt just that much more.

His brother, Jerry—where had he come from—stood and tried to support Jeordi.

"Shit, man. You're a mess," Jerry said. "I hope they're not done with you yet."

"What happened out here?" Jeordi repeated. "Where's Tom?"

His previously animated family was suddenly silent.

"I said, where's Tom?" Jeordi asked again.

"He's not here," his mother said, but Jeordi could read her well enough to know why he wasn't there.

"Where?" he asked, turning.

"Where you going, bro?" his brother asked.

"To find my boyfriend," Jeordi answered, starting to step away from his family.

"Jeordi, behave yourself," his mother said sharply.

"Get out of my way, Mother," Jeordi said without turning back or stopping. With one hand on the wall to support himself, Jeordi limped to the doors, which automatically opened as he stepped near them. Proceeding outdoors was tougher because there was no wall for him to hold on to. Consequently, he had to move from one pillar to another. But at least he had a destination now. His destination was crystal clear. He was headed directly to the man who sat crumpled on the curb outside the hospital ER. Jeordi could hear the man weeping and knew now why Tom hadn't appeared.

"Jeordi," his brother said, trailing along after him.

"Not now," he said. Then, "Babe?"

Instantly Tom's head rose and whipped around toward him.

"Jeordi? Oh, thank God," Tom said, jumping to his feet. "Are you okay?"

"No. I'm a mess, actually," he said, grabbing on to a pillar. "But I heard something happening, and the nurse told me my family had been involved in the commotion. It didn't take a rocket scientist to figure it out. I've been asking them about you ever since I got here, telling everyone to call you. I couldn't figure out why you weren't here."

"I've been here. I couldn't.... They wouldn't—" Tom started to say, cutting himself off in midsentence. "I'm here now, babe. I want to hug you, but I don't know if I should. You're a mess. What are you doing out here? You need to be in there so they can fix you up."

"Help me?" Jeordi said.

"Of course. How?" Tom asked.

Once they had it arranged, they carefully took each step until they were back inside. Tom tried to move him along, but Jeordi insisted they stop at the front desk. The woman behind the counter looked up as they approached.

"Do you see this man?" he asked her sharply.

"Yes, sir," she answered.

"Good. He's my family. He's my only family. He's the one I want with me. He's the one that gets to make decisions about me if I can't make them myself."

"Does he hold your durable power of attorney?" she asked.

"What's that?" Jeordi said, never having heard the term before.

"You'll need to see a lawyer to get that paperwork prepared. We cannot have nonrelated individuals making any decisions without the appropriate authorized paperwork in hand."

"Fine. When I save the money, I'll see a lawyer and get the paperwork. If he was a woman, would you be telling me the same things?" he asked sharply.

"What do you mean?" she asked.

"I mean, if we were a male-female couple."

"Of course not. Those are real couples."

"We are a real couple," Jeordi started to lecture, but they were interrupted by a man that neither of them recognized.

"Excuse me," he said, addressing the woman behind the counter, "but you are incorrect. The president issued an order back in 2010 to ensure that same-sex couples had full visitation rights in hospital settings."

"He says lots of stuff. We're a small country hospital. We have our own way of doing business."

"Thank you," Tom said to the stranger, "but I need to get some help for Jeordi." Turning to Jeordi, he said, "Let's get you back to your room and fixed up so we can get out of here."

They turned to leave, but the woman behind the counter felt compelled to have the last word.

"I'll pray for you and your sinful souls."

Jeordi stopped in midstep, but Tom urged him on.

"Never mind the bigots, babe. Let's get you fixed up and then get out of here and go home."

"You'll do no such thing," Jeordi's father announced. "He's going home with us, where he belongs, where we can take care of him. We're his family. We've had enough of this horseshit."

Both Tom and Jeordi were startled, not realizing anyone else was that close to them.

"No," Jeordi announced to anyone who cared to listen. "I have a home. I have a boyfriend. I'm going home to that place with this man when this horrible nightmare is over."

Despite a lot of sputtering and muttering and complaining all around them, Tom urged him onward once again, gently but forcefully.

"You gonna make it?" Tom whispered to him.

"Now that you're here, I will," he said softly, giving Tom a quick smile.

Tom grabbed a nurse and instructed her, "Help me get him back to his room. Can you tell me what's happening and what needs to happen next?"

Together they got Jeordi settled on his back before summoning the doctor. By the time he arrived, she had a fresh set of sterile cloths draped over him and had a fresh tray of instruments prepared.

When the doctor did something that caused Jeordi to wince, Tom immediately spoke sharply at him. "Hey! Be careful. How would you feel if that was your husband or wife lying there?" He wasn't sure if there was some homophobia at play, but regardless he wanted to nip it in the bud immediately either way.

"Sorry," the doctor told him. "Okay, Mr. Boone, you'll feel a sharp pinch for a second. I'm injecting a local anesthetic so that you don't feel me working. Let me know if it feels uncomfortable for more than a moment or two, okay?"

"Okay."

Tom watched Jeordi's face and detected no signs of sudden pain.

"Okay, the anesthetic is all on board. I'll wait just a moment for it to fully take effect."

"While we're waiting for that, do you have anything for a headache?"

"Yes. Let me take a look at the last scans to see if they show anything unusual."

Tom watched him pull up a series of images on a nearby computer monitor and study them intently for a moment.

"They are unremarkable, so I think we can give you something." Turning to the nurse, he ordered, "Let's give him fifty milligrams of tramadol and see if that takes care of it."

"Right away, Doctor," she said, then retrieved and administered the medication.

"Wow," Jeordi commented. "That stuff works fast."

"Your headache easing a bit?" the doctor asked.

"Yes, it is. Wow, that feels so much better. Thank you. The headache was the worst part." Jeordi audibly exhaled in relief.

For the next forty minutes, the doctor worked on the many scrapes and cuts that covered the front of Jeordi's body. Jeordi was quiet, and at one point Tom even thought he had fallen asleep. When the doctor finished and the nurse cleared away the sterile cloth, he handed Jeordi two prescriptions and a sheet of printed instructions.

"Let's get you up, big guy," Tom told Jeordi, helping him to his feet. "Where are his clothes?" Tom asked the nurse.

"They were all torn up by the accident. Let me get some scrubs for him to wear home."

A moment later she was back with the promised clothes, and Tom helped Jeordi get dressed. The usual activity gave him lots of trouble that day, despite the fact that he'd done the same thing thousands of times before. The stitches and dressings made movement difficult, at least as far as bending and stretching to pull on clothes.

Leaning heavily on Tom, Jeordi walked out of the room and toward the desk.

"Hi, we're leaving," Tom said decisively to the previously difficult person. "Do you need anything else from us?"

"How would you like to settle your bill?" she asked, retrieving a copy of Jeordi's statement from the printer beside her desk.

Both men leaned over to look, their eyes going wide with shock at the number that greeted them.

"Holy crap," Tom said first.

"Do you have insurance?" the woman asked.

"No," Jeordi answered.

"I need to get him home and off his feet. Can I deal with this another time?"

"Give me your address so we can bill you," she said with no emotion over the clear anxiety this bill was causing them.

"I'll take care of the bill," Jeordi's father said.

"No," Jeordi said sharply. "I don't want your money. I'll deal with it myself."

"Just how the hell are you going to do that?" his father demanded.

"I don't know, but I will not owe you folks a penny. I don't want your help because I know how many strings come attached to any offer of help."

"Stop being so goddamned stubborn," his father ordered, tossing his credit card down on the counter.

Jeordi reached out to grab the card back, but the woman behind the counter was faster, swiping the card through a reader and producing a sales slip for signature. Jeordi used the opportunity while his father was distracted to start walking away, with Tom holding tightly to his side.

It was only when they got outside that they confronted the next issue. How the hell were they going to get home? They didn't own a car, and they didn't have the money to take a cab. Jeordi's family was not giving up, though.

"Baby, we'll drive you home," his mother said, appearing by his side.

"No, thank you," he said without looking. "I told you before, I'm not going to your home. I'm going to our home."

"Stop being so damned stubborn," she ordered. "We will drive you."

"No, thank you. I know how you work. You'll get us in the car and then do what you want and to hell with what I already told you."

His mother sighed in exasperation, although it was unclear whether she was frustrated with arguing with her son or that he was that much onto her style and techniques.

Jeordi's brother stepped up next. "Come on. I'll give you a ride," Jerry told them.

"Where?" Jeordi asked.

"To your place. That's where you live. Don't worry. I don't play Mom's games."

"Good. No one is as good at them as she is," Jeordi said.

"Stay here. I'll go get my truck and come pick you up."

"We'll be waiting here," Tom answered for him.

Unfortunately, though, not fifteen seconds after Jeordi's brother went off to get his truck, Jeordi's mother descended upon them again.

"What in the name of all that is holy are you doing?" she demanded angrily.

"What?" Jeordi asked, not understanding what she meant.

"Get your hand out of that other man's hand. Men do not hold hands, especially not out in public where anyone could see you."

"Get over it," her son told her, holding fast to his boyfriend's hand.

Not satisfied with their lack of activity, though, she put a hand on her son's arm and Tom's arm and tried to separate them.

"Get your hands off me," Tom ordered loudly, the first time anyone of Jeordi's family had ever heard him raise his voice and speak sharply to anyone.

"Sandra." Her husband tried to distract her.

"What?" she demanded.

"Leave the boy alone," he said simply.

"Not until he stops acting like such a blooming idiot and takes into consideration someone else's feelings than his own," she angrily told him. "I didn't raise my son to be so ignorant of other people's feelings."

Jeordi ignored her, which became easier about thirty seconds later when his brother drove up and Tom helped Jeordi into the truck, then slid in after him.

"You take him home," his mother yelled, but Jeordi's brother waved a hand dismissively at her as Tom pulled the passenger side door closed.

Chapter Four

TWENTY MINUTES after leaving the hospital parking lot, Tom helped Jeordi up the three steps into their living room. At Jeordi's encouragement, his brother didn't come in but went on to his own home.

Jeordi moaned as Tom helped him to sit back on the sofa.

"Lock the door," Jeordi ordered while Tom took off his coat.

"Why?" he asked.

"Just do it, please," Jeordi said.

"All right," he said, doing as Jeordi asked. "All done."

"Good. Thank you."

"You hungry?" Tom asked.

"Yes, I am, but I don't know why. All I've done is lie around all day."

"Don't forget the body surfing on the asphalt part."

"Trust me," Jeordi said. "I'm not going to be able to forget that anytime soon."

When the food was ready, Tom brought it to Jeordi where he sat on the sofa, then sat down beside him. They rested their heads against one another. Tom sighed.

"I'm so glad you're okay," Tom said.

"I'm not sure I would use the word 'okay' to describe my condition right now," Jeordi said with a chuckle between bites of the pasta. When they had finished eating, Jeordi continued. "Um, babe, I'm worried."

"What about?" Tom asked.

"Money. I'm pretty messed up, and I don't think I'm gonna be able to get myself to work tomorrow. And I obviously didn't make it today. If my boss didn't fire my ass for not showing up, he's gonna be mighty pissed at having me out for two days in a row. And then of course there's the problem that I don't get paid when I don't work. But the bills keep coming in. The rent's got to be paid. There's an electric bill sittin' there on the table."

Tom sighed in understanding. "I know." He sat quietly for a moment. "I'll ask tomorrow if I can take some extra shifts at work."

"You know they won't do that," Jeordi said. "It's the same with me. If we work too many hours, we have to have benefits or overtime, or something else they don't want to pay."

"Until you're back on your feet, maybe I can find a second job."

"Babe, no," Jeordi pleaded. "You'd wear yourself out, and that's no good. I'll get back to work as quick as I can."

"You haven't seen how you look yet, J. Trust me. You need more than a day. I've seen how torn up you got. You've got a whole lot of stitches, and those all need some time to heal. If you try going back to work too quick, you'll rip everything open and only make it all worse. You need time to heal. Let me think a bit and see what I can come up with."

"We're not taking money from my parents," Jeordi said.

"Hell no," Tom said in complete agreement.

Jeordi nodded but stayed silent.

For twenty minutes they were both quiet, Jeordi watching something mindless on TV. Tom sat beside him, but his mind was clearly not on the television.

Jeordi clicked off the television and turned to Tom. "What are you thinking?"

"What do you mean?" Tom asked, caught off guard.

"Come on, babe. Talk to me. I know you. I can see you've got something on your mind. Talk to me."

Tom hesitated for a moment.

"That good, huh?" Jeordi said.

Tom sighed and leaned back, his gaze on the wall across the room. "I've been thinking," he said.

When he didn't go on, Jeordi said, "'Bout what?"

"Ways to make some money."

"And you've got something that's gonna upset either you or me?"

"Damn, babe, you're good."

"So spit it out. What's your idea?"

"I…. This is not ideal… but… I could… maybe… you've said I have a good body… maybe I could make some money using it."

"How?" Jeordi said tightly.

"You remember last month when… that guy… asked me to… pose for him so he could take some pictures of me?"

"Nude pictures," Jeordi shot back.

"Yes," Tom said simply. "Remember he offered to pay me a hundred dollars to pose. We need the money. It would make some money for us."

"No," Jeordi said.

"You got any other ideas?" Tom said.

Jeordi was quiet before he said, "No. But I can't stomach the thought of you... degrading yourself in that way. I hate that. I can't handle that."

"Jeordi, we're two guys in rural Kentucky. We've got our high school diplomas, but we don't have that many doors open to us. You know as well as I do that what I'm talking about is something I can do without some advanced degree."

"The idea of some other guy or guys looking at you naked, is... it's not something I can stomach." He was quiet for a moment. "Would you mind if I lie down for a little while?"

"Of course," Tom said quickly. "Let me help you up. In bed, I assume?"

"Yeah, I want to lie down there."

Together they made their way into their bedroom and the bed they'd shared for several months now, the same bed that had his parents so much in an uproar. Very gently, Tom got Jeordi down onto the bed and covered him with a blanket.

"Lie with me, babe?" he asked. "Just for a few minutes?" He carefully rolled onto his side so Tom could get behind him.

"Of course. I never turn down the opportunity to hold you and touch your body."

"You may not think that way after what I did to myself today."

"Hey," Tom said. "You didn't do anything. The fault is with that car that hit you. You are not to blame unless you did something I wasn't aware of."

"What happened to the car that hit me? Did the person stick around?"

"I don't know. I wasn't at the scene of the accident, and by the time I got to the hospital, the police, if they had been there, were long gone. Maybe someone in your family got the information. We can find out."

"I hate this," Jeordi said. "Can we just not talk about this for a while?"

"Absolutely," Tom said.

"Oh, fuck," Jeordi said suddenly. "My bike. Crap. That's more money. Fuck."

Tom stroked his arm and said, "Shhh. We'll worry about that tomorrow, babe. Focus on the here and now. Just you and me. Together. No one else. The world is out there. In here, it's just you and me."

As much as his injuries allowed, Jeordi pushed back against Tom in an effort to draw him closer. All was quiet, and then Jeordi slept.

Chapter Five

THE SOUND of raindrops hitting the roof of their trailer was the first thing Jeordi heard when he woke up. While he'd slept the rain had changed once again from drizzle to a flat-out downpour. The sound of drops hitting the windows in their bedroom told him the wind had picked up along with the rain.

The warmth of the blanket Tom had draped over him and the dimness of the room were both comforting and made Jeordi want to burrow deeper and never move. But his bladder had a completely different point of view, which forced him to get up. He moved slowly and carefully, feeling frustrated that it was such an effort to get up off the bed.

After he finished in the bathroom, he started down the hallway at the same pace toward the living room but stopped suddenly when he heard voices. He'd feared his family sticking their noses into his business once again. Now he just had to find out who was first up. That, plus thank Tom for running interference and letting him sleep. He hated leaving his boyfriend so much at the mercy of his family because he knew how difficult and pigheaded they could be.

Carefully Jeordi moved down the hall and toward the living room, listening carefully with each step, trying to figure out whose voice he was hearing. He figured it out just as he caught sight of the person. The reason it had taken him so long to recognize the voice was because it belonged to the last person he expected to find sitting in his living room.

"There he is," Jeordi's boss, Marvin, said in his typically boisterous manner.

"Hey," Jeordi said cautiously as he moved the last few steps into the room. He hated the fact that he was walking like a ninety-year-old man. Being less than vibrant ran completely contrary to everything Jeordi had always known.

Tom was by his side, lending an arm and helping get Jeordi settled into a chair.

"I heard you had a rough start to your day," Marvin said to him.

"Yeah, not exactly my usual. Sorry I didn't make it to work this morning. I was on my way when this happened."

"I know. I heard. Your buddy Tom was filling me in on what all happened to you."

"Good."

"I heard you got pretty banged up."

"I did. Scraped off a bunch of skin. I think I had to have some stitches somewhere too."

"Ninety-eight of them, Tom was just telling me," Marvin said.

"Ninety-eight?" Jeordi asked Tom, not trusting what he'd heard Marvin say.

"That's right," Tom said. "And that's why you have to take it easy for a few days while everything heals."

"Marvin, I'm probably not going to make it in tomorrow. I'm really, really sorry about that, man. I know this leaves you shorthanded, and I hate to put you in this bind."

"Hey!" Marvin spoke sharply. "None of that. You hush up and sit still and get better. You got a lot of healing ahead of you, and trust me, I know, you can't rush that stuff."

"Okay," Jeordi said curiously, not believing what he was hearing from his boss. "How did you hear about what happened?" Jeordi asked.

"Your buddy Tom called me to let me know you'd be off work for a few days. I won't lie to you—when he told me you were going to be out for a few days, I was pissed. I'm afraid I said a few not so nice words until he told me to shut up so he could explain why you were going to be missing work. You got a good friend with Tom," Marvin said, continuing to surprise Jeordi, who had only known him as a tough, hard-as-nails boss who put up with no guff from anyone. He was seeing an entirely new side to him, one he'd never even known existed. He kind of liked this Marvin and hoped he wasn't just dreaming.

"Well, I'm gonna get out of your hair," Marvin said, rising from his seat. "And you don't move," he ordered Jeordi. "You take it easy, and I don't want to see you back until you're not about to hurt yourself by being there. Okay?"

"Okay," Jeordi said, since he quite honestly didn't have a clue when he would be fully recovered or able to start back to work.

Marvin left Jeordi looking confused, and Tom smiling.

"Who was that?" Jeordi said.

"I hope you don't mind, but I called him this afternoon while you were sleeping to fill him in on how badly hurt you'd been this morning. His wife fixed some kind of chicken casserole for us for our dinner tonight. It looks like she made enough to feed an army."

"Wow. I... I can't believe he did that."

"They did. He told me he values you because you're his best man, working circles around everyone else."

"He said that?" Jeordi asked, not believing what he was hearing.

"He did. We talked quite a bit. He apologized that he isn't able to pay you while you're not working and said he would if he could. He did tell me that your job would be waiting for you when you are able to get back to work."

"Wow," Jeordi said again. "That's not at all what I expected to hear when I spoke with him. I thought he'd be pissed and fire me on the spot."

"I think he was going to at first until I got him to shut up so I could tell him what happened to you."

"Thanks, babe. I owe you one. A big one."

"No, you don't," Tom said. "You're my guy. Of course I'm gonna do what I can to take care of you."

Jeordi nodded.

"Um," Jeordi started hesitantly. "About what we talked about earlier?"

"Yes?"

"Don't."

"That's... good. I've thought about it too, and I would do it, but I don't want to do it. That's something only we get to share with one another. Mind you, if you needed something and it was the only choice open to me to be able to take care of you, I'd do it in a heartbeat."

"We'll find a way to make it all work. I don't know what it is, but we'll find it. Things are gonna be rough for us for a few months with me out of work for a while. With my bike ruined—I'll need to replace that or start walking like you do."

"All true, but tell you what," Tom said. "Think about all of that tomorrow. For tonight just pretend you're a good Southern belle, pretend you're Scarlett O'Hara, and leave all of that for tomorrow."

"Deal."

Chapter Six

THE FOLLOWING morning, as much as it pained him, Tom hauled himself out of bed and got himself ready for work. Like Jeordi, he too had missed most of work the day before. When he'd received the call to come to the hospital, he'd dropped everything and run. He knew this morning he had to redeem himself.

Showered, dressed, and fed, Tom took a last quick gaze at the sleeping form of his boyfriend, the man he so desperately loved and wanted to protect and safeguard. Even though Jeordi was simply lying in bed, his chest regularly rising and falling in silent rhythmic breathing, Tom could have watched him forever. It pained him so much that Jeordi was such a mess from the accident the previous day.

It was only with supreme effort that Tom tore his eyes away from his boyfriend's sleeping form and quietly exited their home to head to work. He'd prepared things for Jeordi to eat when he woke up and left him written instructions on medications and food.

The rain of the previous day had ended sometime during the night, leaving the air thick with humidity. Cicadas were calling to one another from what seemed like every single tree he passed on his walk to work. Their calls were both comforting and annoying. They were such a part of the season, but the noise they made could become so grating after a while.

Twelve hours later, Tom dragged himself home, finding Jeordi asleep on the sofa in their living room, the television on in the background. Stepping lightly to avoid waking his partner, Tom showered and changed clothes before returning to the living room. He was afraid that if he turned off the television Jeordi would wake, but the man slept on. Grabbing a beat-up paperback he was in the middle of, Tom settled into a chair to read and watch his boyfriend.

Jeordi was the most incredible man he'd ever seen or known. Sure there were others who were more classically handsome, men who were taller, men who had this or that feature, but they all lacked one thing—they didn't have the passion and heart Jeordi possessed. Jeordi was so much more than just a pretty face. He was an awesome man who was loyal beyond words, fierce, unafraid to confront threats or to go into conflicts if need be to stand up for himself and Tom. Jeordi's heart was his biggest attribute, and it belonged unquestionably to Tom.

The room was quiet for another hour. The only sounds disturbing the silence were the occasional car driving past outside, the pages of Tom's paperback flipping, and their ancient air conditioner cycling on and off periodically as it struggled to cool the hot and humid air that crept into their sanctuary.

When Jeordi finally stirred, he clearly was confused at first as he tried to wipe the sleep from his eyes. It was not at all typical for him to nap in the living room, so he was unaccustomed to waking up there. His gaze traveled around the room until it settled on Tom.

"Hey," he said hoarsely.

Immediately dropping the book he'd been reading, Tom was out of his chair and kneeling on the floor beside the sofa where Jeordi lay.

"Hey, babe. How're you feeling?"

"Okay. I guess I slept for a while. What time is it?"

"About nine o'clock."

"In the morning?"

"No. At night."

"Huh?" Jeordi asked, clearly confused.

Tom helped him to sit up.

"Those pain pills really knock me out," Jeordi said.

"You had a lot of pain today?" Tom asked with concern.

"Yeah. I held off taking one as long as I could, but I finally had to give in and do it. They work, but they make me sleep too."

"I suppose that's good. Keeps you from moving around too much and doing something to injure yourself again."

"I want to take a shower," Jeordi announced.

"Sorry, babe. Can't get your stitches wet for forty-eight hours."

"So no shower?"

"No shower. But I can give you a sponge bath if you like," Tom said with a smile.

"That… that could be fun."

"Damned right it could."

After Tom got Jeordi into their bedroom and helped him out of his clothes, for the first time Jeordi could see the extent of his injuries.

"Jesus, look at me. I'm a total fucking mess. I'm gonna have such awful scars after this."

"Some," Tom agreed, "but the doctor said it won't be too bad."

Jeordi sighed. "I only hope he's right."

Worry or concern about scars quickly evaporated, though, as Tom took off his own clothes and set to work with a washcloth and a basin of warm water. Carefully, tenderly, sensually, he worked his way over his lover's body, gently washing him with bodywash before wiping it away with clean water.

Despite the awkwardness created by his stitches and bandages, Jeordi became incredibly aroused, especially as Tom cleaned around his penis. Before he'd even touched the organ, Jeordi was rock hard. Tom dispensed with the washcloth for a few moments, replacing it with his tongue as he first toyed with Jeordi's erection, then sucked him deep into his throat. Jeordi grabbed Tom's head, his fingers threading their way through Tom's thick dirty blond hair as if to keep him there—not that he had anything to worry about. Jeordi was almost embarrassed with how quickly he reached orgasm.

"Gosh, you'd think I was a teenager. I couldn't even last a minute."

"Hey," Tom said with a happy smile, "I'm good."

"No argument there," Jeordi agreed as Tom snuggled up next to him, Jeordi's once thick, hard erection now lying swollen and sated on his thigh, a mere shadow of its former grandeur.

"I want to do you, but I don't know how since I can't move much," Jeordi complained.

"Not gonna happen, babe," Tom said. "We are not risking it. In a few days, you'll be much more able to move around, and you can have your turn then."

"But I want it now," Jeordi whined like a five-year-old.

"Tough. Get better first, and then you can transport me to sexual paradise."

Sighing, Jeordi agreed. "Fine. Thank you for that. It felt fucking awesome. Sex with you is always great, no matter what we're doing, because it's with you. It doesn't matter if I'm in you or you're in me, just so long as it's the two of us connected. I love you so much, Tom."

"And I love you too, Jeordi Boone."

Chapter Seven

DAPPLED SUNLIGHT made its way into Tom and Jeordi's bedroom the following morning. With only an ancient window air conditioner to handle their bedroom, the room was warm and sticky. Jeordi lay naked on his back, the covers kicked off sometime during the night. Tom lay on his side facing away from Jeordi, equally naked.

The grinding of a garbage truck somewhere in their trailer park woke Jeordi. Instinctively he tried to roll over to cuddle up behind his boyfriend, but his injuries prevented that move. With some difficulty but a bit more finesse, Jeordi made it up off the bed and shuffled toward the bathroom.

Startled a moment later by Tom, he accidentally peed on the floor when he lost his aim. Tom wrapped his arms around Jeordi and chuckled as Jeordi cursed.

"Don't worry, babe. I'll clean it up," Tom assured him.

"Just don't scare a guy like that, okay? I could have peed on your feet or something like that. No guy wants that."

"True."

Finished, Jeordi leaned back into Tom's warm embrace.

"Is that a gun in your pocket, or are you just happy to see me?" Jeordi joked.

"No pocket. I'm naked," Tom said teasingly.

"But I feel something solid, and I could swear it's loaded."

"Could be. We'll deal with that later."

"But I want it now," Jeordi whined again.

"Don't whine, dear. It's unbecoming."

"Fuck you," Jeordi joked.

"Not till you're better, and I get you first. Then you can have me."

"I can live with that," Jeordi agreed readily.

They made their way to the kitchen. While Jeordi sat, Tom made coffee and toast for the two of them. With breakfast, such as it was, finished, Jeordi grabbed Tom's hand when he started to get up to put the dishes in the sink.

"Hold up a minute, babe, if you can."

"Sure. What's up?"

"Aside from my dick because I'm seeing you naked, you mean?"

"Yes."

Still holding Tom's hand, Jeordi said, "I've been doing a lot of thinking."

"Should I be worried?"

"Probably, because it all involves you."

"Go on."

"You are the best thing that has ever happened to me in my entire life," Jeordi said. Tom immediately sensed that whatever Jeordi had to say wasn't going to be a simple thing.

"From the moment I first saw you sitting in that church just a few feet from me, I was blown away by you. Your beauty, your mind, your zest for life. Each day I learn something more about you and become just that much more impressed and in love with you. You've hung in there with me through all the crap my family has thrown at us.

"I guess what I'm trying to say…. No, I know what I want to say. I've given this a lot of thought. I've spent hours and hours mulling this over.

"The whole hospital thing pissed me off, and it scared the life out of me. Just when I wanted you and needed you the most, my family stood between us. I don't want that to happen again." Jeordi sighed but kept a firm hold on Tom's hand.

"What I'm trying, and failing, to say is, Tom Goodwin, you are the love of my life. I love you more than I can believe. I cannot even imagine a life without you in it. I want you with me, by my side every day, for the rest of my life." Locking his gaze on Tom's, Jeordi finally got to his key point. "Tom Goodwin, will you do me the honor of marrying me?"

Tom stared at Jeordi blankly for a moment.

"What?" he finally said in a whispered voice.

"Will you marry me, Tom? I want to be with you and only you for the rest of all time. I want the world to know that you are mine and I'm yours. I want it clear to everyone that we are husbands, mated for life. So I'm asking you to marry me. Please. You will make me a very happy man."

Tom continued to stare at Jeordi, his face still not revealing anything going on inside his mind.

"Tom?" he finally asked.

"Huh?"

"Here's where you say yes and tell me you accept my proposal of marriage."

"Um… I need to think a little. Is that okay?" Tom asked, pulling his hand free from Jeordi's for a moment. Carrying the dishes to the sink, Tom stood facing away from Jeordi, whose mind was a whirlwind of thousands of arguments, celebrations, fears, and so much more.

A moment later Tom whirled around and asked, "Is this because of what happened at the hospital?"

"Some of it," Jeordi admitted. "But I've been thinking of this since before that happened."

"You have? You were?" Tom said.

"Yes, I have. I truly do love you with all my heart. I'm yours, babe, if you'll have me. You see my flaws, you know I'm damaged goods, you know the baggage I've got. I know it's a lot to ask any one man to take all of that, but I can't imagine waking up in a bed without you or at least your scent there. I want to go to bed with you each night, wake up with you each morning, and have an untold number of days to show you how much I love and adore you. You've made me a better me. You're the only man who has ever freed me to be who I really am. I absolutely adore you, Tom. Please marry me."

Tom stood, leaning back against the sink, his arms crossed over his chest, his gaze on nothing somewhere in the vicinity of the floor. He finally nodded slightly. "Just give me a few minutes to get this all sorted out in my mind, okay?"

Jeordi, not getting the words he wanted and had expected to hear, slumped in his chair.

Tom disappeared, returning a moment later dressed in jeans and a T-shirt.

"I'm gonna just take a walk around the block and try to sort this all out in my head. Okay?"

"Is it because of how much of a mess I am now, physically?" Jeordi blurted out.

"What? Good Lord, no. Just… just give me a few minutes, okay?"

"Okay," Jeordi said.

And Tom slipped out the door, leaving Jeordi freaking out inside. Any erection Jeordi had had from looking at Tom's naked body was long since vanished, much as Jeordi's excitement. He wondered what he'd done wrong. This was the most important moment of his life, the biggest decision he would ever make, and somehow he'd blown it. But he didn't know how.

When Tom returned about fifteen minutes later, Jeordi was dressed in shorts and a loose shirt and sitting on the sofa, close to tears.

Quietly Tom closed the door and stepped over to sit next to Jeordi. Taking his hand, Tom said simply, "Yes."

"Yes?" Jeordi asked, his heart ablaze with excitement once again.

"Yes," Tom said, nodding and smiling his way.

"Kiss me," Jeordi ordered, so Tom leaned over and they locked lips in a searing kiss.

"Thank goodness," Jeordi said. "I was sitting here freaking out, wondering what I'd done wrong. I couldn't blow this. This was the biggest moment of my life."

"You didn't blow it," Tom said. "You just caught me off guard. My first thought was that this was just a way to get us some legal protections because of the hospital thing. But then, as I walked, I calmed down a bit and thought why not take those protections that are there already for people who are married. I said yes because I love you and because I know you love me. The legal stuff is secondary."

"I love you, babe," Jeordi said. "Help me get dressed so we can go to the courthouse and get our license."

"Right now?" Tom asked, startled.

"I want to get it in our hands. That's not to say we'll use it immediately, but when we've got everything worked out in a few days, we'll have it ready."

It took some serious work to get Jeordi dressed and then to find someone in the park who could drive them to the courthouse. When Tom had found a woman driving that way to work, he asked for and got a ride from her.

Neither man had ever needed to visit the courthouse before that day, but with the help of a couple of security guards as well as a map on the wall of the building, they finally managed to find the county clerk's office.

It being a weekday and the middle of the day, there was no line, so the clerk appeared almost immediately when they walked in.

"How can I help you, gentlemen?" she asked.

"We'd like to get a marriage license, please," Jeordi said.

"All right, and who is it for?" she asked.

"Us," Tom said.

"The two of you?" she asked. "I'm sorry, but we do not issue marriage licenses to anyone except traditional male-female couples in this office."

"Excuse me?" Tom said, his anger rapidly rising. "Haven't you heard that the Supreme Court recently overturned all state laws prohibiting same-sex marriage? We're now legal, so we'd like to get a license, please."

"And I'm telling you that I will not be party to such an abomination in the eyes of the Lord."

Jeordi noticed a woman who had entered the office behind them pull out a smartphone and use it to record what was happening. Tom recapped for the recording.

"So you're telling us that you will not obey the law and issue us a marriage license?"

"I cannot in good conscience do that. It is against my faith, and I will not be party to the commission of such an abhorrent sin in the eyes of the Lord."

"I thought this was a courthouse," Tom said. "Surely you must have people around here who will tell you that you have to follow the law. The Supreme Court ruled we can get married anywhere in this country."

"Then you'll have to go somewhere else, because I cannot issue you a license. It is in opposition to my faith, and my faith is the most important thing in my life."

"So let me get this straight. You will not do your job, the job for which the taxpayers pay you, because it goes against your faith?"

"This part of the job is contrary to my beliefs, and I will not be party to sin."

"Then, ma'am, you need to quit and get a different job, because you don't have a choice. You do what the law requires, or you get out so someone who will abide by the law can take over."

"I have to ask you to leave," she said officiously. "I will not stand here and be verbally assaulted by two homosexuals. Repent, and there might be hope for your eternal souls."

"Really?" Tom said. "This has all been a fascinating, eye-opening experience." When he asked for her name, however, she refused.

Somehow while they'd been talking, a security guard had arrived on the scene and asked them to leave the building. Without a word, they did.

Chapter Eight

ONCE THEY were out of the courthouse, Jeordi let loose with all of the anger he'd held inside.

"I don't fucking believe it," he practically shouted. "She can't do that. It's her job."

"I agree, but she did," Tom said. "And she had us removed from the building."

"I'm… I'm… I don't know what, but I'm gonna fight her. This isn't right," Jeordi said.

"Gentlemen?"

"Yes?" Jeordi said, turning to find who was speaking to them.

"Hi, I was in there."

"I remember you," Tom said. "You were recording that woman, weren't you?"

"You're damned right I was. You're not the first same-sex couple she's done that to, but if I have anything to do about it, I want you to be the last couple she denies service to. She's way out of line, and she needs to put her faith aside and do her damned job."

"I couldn't agree more," Jeordi said, smiling. "But how are we ever going to change something like this?"

"With your permission—and you better agree—I'm sending that video to Channel Six news, and I'm gonna demand that they broadcast the story of that employee paid by the taxpayers denying constitutionally guaranteed services to those same taxpayers."

"Wow," Jeordi said. "Thank you!"

"Now, I need some information from you, like your names."

They exchanged information, and she was off to get the video to the news reporters in the hopes of getting it on the air that evening.

"Okay," Tom said. "I need to get you home so I can get to work. I'm gonna be late as it is."

"Go," Jeordi said. "I'm feeling a lot better and could use a little exercise. I'll walk and take it really slow. If I can't for some reason, I'll just wait until someone I know comes along and hitch a ride with them."

Tom looked quickly at his watch. "I don't like that, but… I need to get to work. Are you absolutely sure?" he asked.

"Of course. I don't lie to you. You know exactly how I'll do this. So go. I'll be fine. I'm not going to run, but I'll make it home at my own pace."

"I hate this. I wish we had a car so you—"

"Go," Jeordi ordered, pointing Tom in the direction of his workplace.

WHEN TOM got home late that night, he was absolutely exhausted. He had been convinced that he would find Jeordi in bed and asleep, so he was surprised to find his best friend, his partner, his lover sitting in the living room wide awake and still dressed.

"What are you doing up?" he asked. "I thought you'd be asleep by now."

"I was waiting for you. You're late."

"I was able to pick up an extra shift because someone called in sick. We need the money. Sorry if I worried you."

"I suspected, but I always worry about you. You're my guy," Jeordi said with a smile. "You're off work tomorrow, aren't you?"

"Yes, tomorrow is my day off. I volunteered for a shift, but they wouldn't give it to me because it would put me over some magic number of hours or something. Who knows."

"Good. I've made plans for us for tomorrow."

"Oh? What do you have planned?" Tom asked.

"We're going on a little adventure."

"An adventure?" Tom asked, curious.

"Yes. It starts early, so I suggest you get showered then meet me in bed so we can both get some sleep."

"You're gonna try not to tell me?" Tom asked, his arms crossed over his chest.

"I will tell you—just not right now. In the morning you'll know everything. You. Shower. Now," Jeordi ordered.

Ten minutes later they were in bed together with the lights out. No matter how many times or how many different ways he asked, Jeordi would not reveal his plans for them.

Jeordi's alarm clock went off at five thirty in the morning. He gingerly got out of bed and dressed before shaking Tom awake and forcing him out of bed.

"No," Tom whined, pulling the pillow over his head to try to make the distraction go away, but Jeordi was insistent that he get up.

Thirty minutes after he'd gotten out of bed, Jeordi pushed Tom out the door to his brother's waiting truck.

"It's still dark out. This is uncivilized. Nobody should be up at this hour," Tom complained.

"No argument there," Jeordi's brother Jerry said.

"Where are we going?" Tom asked at the twenty-minute mark.

"You didn't tell him?" Jerry said.

"Hush," Jeordi said.

"Fine. I don't see why you can't tell him," Jerry said.

"Drive the truck," Jeordi said.

"I hate you both," Tom said as he closed his eyes and tried to get some more sleep. He actually did manage to fall asleep so that Jeordi had to wake him when they got to their destination.

"Come on, babe," Jeordi said, shaking him gently.

"Huh?" he said, only half-awake.

"Come on. It's time. We're ready for part one."

"Part who?" Tom said, trying to scrub the sleep from his eyes.

"Come on," Jeordi said, pulling Tom toward him and the open door of the truck. Turning to his brother, he said, "Thanks, Jerry. I appreciate the ride."

"Where are we?" Tom said.

"We're at the airport," Jeordi said.

"Why?"

"Because that's where they keep the airplanes," Jeordi said.

"You're not making any sense at all. Why are we here?"

"Come on. You'll see."

Inside the small airport terminal, Jeordi looked around and led them to a Southwest Airlines ticket counter. Tom listened, but the conversation he heard made very little sense. The story didn't get any more clear when Jeordi led him through a security check that was more intense than anything he'd ever gone through in his life.

"All right, I need to know what's going on," Tom demanded, now wide awake as he put his shoes back on and put his belt back through the loops.

"We're going to do what we tried to do yesterday," Jeordi answered.

"Why does that involve us going through security at an airport?"

"Because we have to get on an airplane to do it."

Tom's eyes went wide with shock.

"I've... I've... I've never been on an airplane. I'm... I'm not qualified. I don't know what to do."

"You don't have to do anything but sit down. The airplane does all the work. Or at least so I've been told."

Tom pulled Jeordi close. "I'm scared, Jeordi."

"Me too. That's why we've got each other."

Their small airport didn't have a lot of space. In fact there were only two gates. Jeordi directed them to Gate Two, which somehow felt exotic, definitely better than lowly Gate One.

For two hours they sat or paced the short distance available for people to walk, both becoming more anxious with every passing moment. But their nerves took a backseat to something strange. A very loud noise sounded just as a large jet came into view and rolled quickly toward their location. The engines on the machine were very loud as it parked.

As soon as the engines had shut down, a truck with stairs mounted on the back end drove up and parked so they touched the edge of the plane. The driver jumped out, raced up the steps, knocked on the door, and opened it. Almost immediately a steady stream of people began to exit through that door. Tom watched the people come in through the door they were supposed to leave from.

While people were still exiting the plane, someone announced, "Ladies and gentlemen. Boarding for our flight will begin momentarily. If I could have everyone in group one please line up for me, as soon as we get the all-clear we can begin. Ground time is minimal, so I appreciate your cooperation in getting everyone on board and seated as quickly as possible so our flight can have an on-time departure."

"I didn't understand half of what that meant," Tom said.

"Me neither," Jeordi whispered back. "All I got was boarding group one. We're in second, so I guess we need to be ready to go next."

"Jeordi, why are we doing this?" Tom asked.

"Love, darlin', for love," Jeordi said, giving Tom one of his million-watt smiles and a quick kiss.

They stood and watched the last people from the plane come through the doors, followed almost immediately by the people in group one moving out to take their places. When boarding group two was called, they were the first in line and therefore the first to nervously lead the second wave toward the plane.

Stepping outdoors, Tom and Jeordi both detected the odor of some kind of fuel. A person gestured them toward the stairs. Jeordi went first, holding tightly to Tom's hand. His injuries made him move a little slower on the steps than usual, but neither one of them were upset by the pace.

"Welcome aboard," a perky female flight attendant greeted them as soon as they were on board the plane.

"Thanks," Jeordi said. "Um, where do we sit?"

"Take any open seat," she said with a smile.

Jeordi, still holding Tom's hand, led them back to a spot where there was an empty seat by the window and another beside that. He took the window and got Tom seated in the middle seat. Instructions were given in the midst of people boarding, stowing their luggage, and finding seats, so both men fastened their seat belts and made sure they were secure.

"Ladies and gentlemen, the cabin door is now closed. Please ensure that all seat backs and tray tables are in their upright and locked position for taxi and takeoff. We will be underway momentarily. Flight attendants, arm doors for departure. All-call and cross-check."

Faster than seemed possible to the two novice flyers, the engines of the mighty machine sprang to life and powered up sufficiently to start them moving forward and turning away from the terminal. They rolled along the taxiway leading to the one runway at their rural community airport.

"Ladies and gentlemen, we are number one for takeoff. Flight attendants, please be seated."

Without slowing down, the engines got louder still, and they were pushed back into their seats as the airplane raced down the runway faster and faster until the thump-thump of the tires on the pavement stopped.

"Oh my God," Tom said. "Are we in the air? Holy shit. Do you see how high we are already? How is that possible? I can't believe it. Everything looks so small on the ground already. Wow. I had no idea planes were so powerful. Holy fuck."

"Amazing" was all Jeordi said from his seat by the window. No one had taken the empty seat on the aisle, so they did not hesitate to keep their hands locked together.

A few minutes later, the pilot came on the loudspeaker system and said, "Ladies and gentlemen, we have reached our cruising altitude of 37,000 feet. Our projected flight time today is one hour and fourteen minutes from takeoff to touchdown, which will put us at the gate a few minutes ahead of schedule. We do not anticipate any major turbulence today, so I've turned off the fasten seat belt sign, but we advise you to keep your seat belts fastened while seated, just like we do up here in the cockpit. In the meantime, sit back, relax, and enjoy our short flight this morning. We'll be back with more updates as we get closer."

"I can't believe we're doing this," Tom said, leaning over toward Jeordi, quickly planting a kiss on his temple. "Thank you."

"You're okay with this?" he asked Tom.

"Getting married and having an adventure with you? Hell yes, I'm okay with it. My only concern is how are we paying for this? Flights aren't cheap."

"This one wasn't too bad, at least according to people I talked to yesterday."

"But how are we going to pay for it and pay our bills? What are we going to live on?"

"Love, babe. We're gonna live on love."

They remained cuddled together for the duration of the flight, watching with great interest when their plane started to descend into Washington, DC. When the wheels touched down on the runway and the mighty engines reversed to brake their forward motion, they heard a flight attendant calmly say, "I'd like to be the first to welcome you to our nation's capital, where the local time is 10:02 a.m. Please remain in your seats with your seat belts fastened until we have parked at the gate and the signal has been given that it is safe to get up."

While everyone around them wrestled heavy bags, they didn't have anything with them, so when it was their turn to move down the aisle, all they had was each other. It was only once they were in the terminal, this one substantially bigger than the one they had flown out of a little over an hour earlier, that they both seemed to realize they didn't have as much of an idea of what they were doing as everyone else seemed to. People zipped around them, while they had to stop and read signs and check with one another about each decision.

Following instructions from someone at the information desk, they exited the airport and entered the subway system, purchasing fare cards and boarding the proper train toward their destination. Even though Jeordi knew their destination, he anxiously checked at every stop to be sure they hadn't somehow missed the proper station.

Getting into the courthouse was a little easier than getting into the airport had been, but only slightly. With just one wrong turn, they found the room they needed. The room at least was quiet, so they didn't have to wait to see a clerk. There were two other men in the room, both substantially older than them. They seemed totally engrossed in reviewing photos on the back of a digital camera and paid no attention to Tom and Jeordi as they came in and checked out the place.

"Hello. Can I help you?" an obviously bored clerk asked.

"We'd like to get married."

She slid a clipboard toward them and said, "Fill this out and come back when you have it completed. Bring a photo ID with you to verify your identities and ages."

The form was relatively easy to complete except for a box that asked them who would be performing the ceremony.

"Ma'am," Jeordi said, handing the form back to her. "We don't know what to put down in that box there."

"Where are you getting married?" she asked.

"We were hoping to do that here," Jeordi said.

"All right," she said, tapping keys on her computer. "The next available opening is two weeks from Tuesday at ten fifteen in the morning."

Both men fell into the chairs before her desk. "Two weeks?" Jeordi said, suddenly feeling completely deflated. "We don't have two weeks. We have to get this done today. We're flying out tonight."

"You can use any minister or judge of any court to officiate."

"How do we go about finding someone?" Tom asked.

"You just start calling around, I guess," she said.

"There's really no one here who can do it for two weeks?"

"Sorry," she said with a smile that almost made them believe her.

"And you can't issue the license if we don't have the name of someone who will marry us?"

"That's the way it works," she explained, "at least as long as I've been here."

Tom and Jeordi stood from her desk and walked a few steps away. "Shit," Jeordi said. "Fuck, fuck, fuck. I can't believe I fucked up so bad. I should have found this all out before we ever left home."

"It's not your fault, babe. Who knew they'd need so much advance notice?"

"I should never have tried to do something this crazy."

Tom could see tears in his boyfriend's eyes, and he leaned over to quickly wipe them away.

"You did a beautiful thing today, Jeordi. Don't you dare to talk that down. You planned this super spectacular surprise that I will never forget. You got us onto an airplane. We had our first flight. We're just two country boys from nowhere, Kentucky, and you got us to Washington, DC—by airplane. I call that pretty fucking spectacular," Tom argued.

"You can try to sugarcoat it," Jeordi said, "but I blew every penny we had, and we're still not gonna be able to get married. This is two strikes against us now."

Tom wrapped his arms around Jeordi and held him, stroking his hand over his boyfriend's head, trying to comfort him and tell him it wasn't the end of the world.

"Excuse me," they heard a male voice say from nearby.

Looking up, they spotted one of the two older men they had noticed in the room when first entering. He was no longer sitting with the other man but was now standing close to them.

"I couldn't help but overhear your conversation. I'm sorry for eavesdropping. Please, come over and sit with me and my husband and talk for a minute? Would you do that?"

Tom and Jeordi glanced at each other, wordlessly confirming that they didn't see a problem with the request. Once seated and facing the two men, the one who had spoken said, "You're here to get married?"

"Yes," Jeordi said.

"We flew in to do this, but we're only here for the day," Tom explained. "We wanted to get married here, but they just told us there's a two-week wait, so I guess we flew here for nothing."

"Will you return?" one of the two men asked them.

Jeordi's gaze dropped to the floor. "No. I don't see how that's possible. We spent every penny we had to get here."

"Why did you want to get married here? Marriage is now legal nationwide."

"Yeah, well, someone needs to tell that to the clerk in our county at home. She refused to issue us a marriage license and had us removed from the courthouse yesterday."

"Oh my," the stranger said, an unhappy expression on his face. "I'd heard rumors about people like that trying to pull those stunts. It's terrible to see the lives those people are hurting with their bigotry." He shook his head. Suddenly, though, his look of sadness vanished and was replaced with a huge smile. "Okay, I may have an idea. Would you mind if I made a phone call and tried to find someone who could marry you today? I can't guarantee anything, but if you'd agree, I'd like to make a couple of calls. Would that be all right?"

"You... why would you do that? We're complete strangers," Jeordi said.

"No we're not. We're brothers. We're part of the brotherhood of gay men. We take care of one another. That's just what we do. We're family. Sometimes our other families don't understand us, the real us, but your gay brothers understand exactly. We take care of one another when and where we can. And by the way, I'm Hank and this is my husband, Bill."

"I'm Tom, this is Jeordi. Nice to meet you."

Hank got up, pulled out his cell phone, and made a quick phone call. That call was followed by another and then a third. Finally, after ten minutes of conversations, he turned back to them with a smile on his face.

"Okay. Good news, boys. Want to get married in about a half hour?"

"Yes," Tom and Jeordi both practically shouted at nearly the same second.

"Then let's get that license for you."

He accompanied them back to the counter, and when the clerk asked for the name of the officiant, he wrote something on a pad of paper and handed the paper to her. She then dutifully transferred it to her computer.

Their fees paid, ten minutes later they held in their hands a license to get married. Once again there were some tears, but this time for a very good reason.

"Let me get a picture," Hank said, posing them as he wanted them, side by side, each holding on to the license. Another set of photos was required outside in front of the courthouse, each time carefully posed, right down to who was looking where in each one.

"Come on," he ordered, leading them to a car his husband had pulled up in front of the courthouse. "Do you know our fair city?" he asked.

"No. We've never been here before today," Tom said.

"We've never been anywhere before today," Jeordi said.

"It's a big day for us," Tom said. "First time out of Kentucky, first time on an airplane, first time in Washington, DC."

As they sped over busy city streets, Bill expertly handled the traffic while Hank gave a running commentary on what was what. Wherever they were going, they had apparently arrived, because they parked and Hank led them to a huge, ornate building that looked old. Whatever it was, it must be important. It sat directly across the street from an even bigger building.

"What's that?" Jeordi asked their host.

Bill answered, "That's the Capitol building, where Congress sits… and does largely nothing." Pointing, he explained, "That side is the House of Representatives, and that side," he said, pointing to the other side, "is the United States Senate."

Jeordi and Tom's mouths hung open in surprise.

"Holy… fuck," Tom whispered to Jeordi.

"Amen."

"Come along," Hank directed.

Everything was happening so fast.

Entry into this building involved security, just as so many other things had that day. Jeordi couldn't remember ever having to be frisked as many times as he had been that day. Once they were all approved, Hank led them to another guard, who stood beside a closed door.

"Hey, Hank," the guard said with a smile. "What are you doing here? I thought you retired, man."

"I did. Got an appointment with the chief, though."

"Good deal, man."

The guard turned around and keyed a code into the door. The clicking sound it made upon being unlocked was loud enough to be heard by all of them.

Holding the door open, the guard said, "Good to see you again, Hank. Retired. You lucky dog."

"Yeah, and loving it too," Hank said.

Hank was moving forward down a hallway that he had clearly been in many, many times before, because he walked like he owned the place. For a short guy, he carried himself like a man supremely confident about everything. Jeordi envied him that ability.

Since he couldn't walk as fast, Jeordi was in the back of their little pack, walking beside the other half of the couple that was rapidly becoming their new best friends.

"It sounds like Hank used to work here?"

"He did indeed. He worked here for thirty-five years. He just retired last month, and between you and me, he's been bored to tears in retirement. He's needed something to do, someone to help, so I've got to tell you that your arrival today, you needing help, the timing was absolutely perfect. You cannot imagine how much good this is already doing him."

"Really?" Jeordi asked. "How—"

"How can I tell? Easy. He's smiling, laughing, animated, active, everything he used to be. He'd been getting depressed, kind of listless, not getting any enjoyment out of anything. When he retired he kind of lost his reason for being, although he's too damned stubborn to admit that. But look at him up there with your man. He's absolutely alive and happy as can be, so thank you and your partner for being there today. He really needed this."

"Okay," Jeordi said, not entirely believing Bill.

They walked in silence for a few seconds before Bill asked, "Are you okay? You seem to be favoring one side a bit."

"Yes, sorry. I had a little accident a couple of days ago. A car hit my bike as I was riding to work. I sort of body surfed across the pavement. I couldn't prove it to you, but I guess they put ninety-eight stitches into me."

"Holy hell, man. Should you be walking at all?"

"I need to. I want to marry Tom so desperately. He's the one, Bill. He's my guy, and I want to protect him and show him off to the entire world and say, 'He's mine and I'm his.'"

Jeordi stopped and looked at Bill. He didn't know the man at all, but something made him talk to this stranger more than he would have to a friend back home.

"Bill, when Tom got the call that I'd been injured in an accident, he came to the hospital—and they wouldn't let him in. Between my family and the good Christian woman working the front desk in the ER, they kept him from even knowing if I was dead or alive. I needed him with me, and at the same time, he was being thrown out of the ER by hospital security. I swore that I would do everything in my power to make sure he never had to go through that again. He's my man. I needed him then, I need him now, and I don't want to ever give anyone the ability to keep us apart when we need one another."

"Good man, Jeordi," Bill said with a smile and a hand on Jeordi's arm.

Even though Tom and Hank had disappeared by that point, Bill knew where they were going, guiding Jeordi to an office just in time to see Hank sweet-talking an older woman sitting behind a desk in a very attractive waiting area. Hank seemed good at what he was doing, because the woman behind the desk was chuckling and blushing as Hank talked with her.

Bill and Jeordi stood beside Tom, and Bill observed, "That's my man. Thirty-eight years together and he still loves toying with straight women—and they love it and completely understand what he's doing."

"You doing okay, babe?" Tom asked Jeordi. "You need to sit down for a minute?"

"No, I'm good. Just needed to walk slower. Bill walked with me and told me a bit about them. Thirty-eight years. That's longer than I've been alive. Hell, that's about how long the two of us put together have been alive."

"Enough of that," Bill said. "You're making me feel old, and I do not want to be yet. I'm not ready for that. If somebody could just tell my body that and make it work like it did when I was twenty, then I'd be all set."

Hank rejoined them, beaming with delight.

"You trying to get a date, babe?" Bill asked. "You switching teams on me?"

Hank snorted. "Oh, please. You know as well as I do that I couldn't do it with a woman to save my life. You're stuck with me."

"Good," Bill said with a smile.

A door beyond them opened, and a tall, slender, distinguished-looking African-American woman stood there, immediately smiling when she spotted Hank.

"Hank! How good to see you," she said, giving him a hug.

"Chief! I've missed you."

"And we miss you too," she said. "Are these your two friends in need of some assistance?" she asked, turning to Tom and Jeordi.

"Yes, they are, and thank you so much for taking my call and being willing to help out an old friend. I know how busy you are, so thank you for seeing us on such short notice."

"Just working on my annual report to Congress. You know how much I hate doing that, so I am absolutely delighted to be able to help. Where would you like this to happen, Hank? My chambers? The courtroom?"

"How about the courtroom? Do you think that would work?"

"I don't see why not. Give me just a minute to get myself together." She stepped back into her office and returned perhaps thirty seconds later wearing a beautiful black judicial robe with a white collar. "Follow me, please," she instructed, leading them a short distance to a courtroom unlike any Jeordi or Tom had ever seen before.

"Where does the jury sit?" Jeordi whispered to Tom.

Hank happened to overhear and immediately answered, "There is no jury in the Supreme Court. The nine justices that sit at the bar are the jury."

"Okay," Jeordi said. "Did you say Supreme Court?"

"Yes," Hank answered.

"Gentlemen," the justice said to get their attention. "If you would stand here." She indicated a spot in front of the big bench in the front of the room. "Hank, I assume you will be taking photos?" she asked.

"Of course," Hank said, beaming with joy.

With everyone in place, the justice started. "Tom and Jeordi, you are about to enter into a union that is the most important one you will ever join because it will bind you together for life. You are entering into a relationship unlike any other, a relationship so close and intimate that it will profoundly influence you and your entire future.

"Marriage is not something to be taken lightly or to be entered into casually. Its hopes and disappointments, its successes and its failures, its pleasures and its pains will be confronted and handled together from this day forward.

"So I ask you, Jeordi, knowing these things, do you take Tom to be your lawful husband, to love, honor, and keep in sickness and in health, in good times and bad, and forsaking all others, keep yourself only for him? If so, please say, 'I do.'"

"I do," Jeordi said.

"And Tom—" She started to repeat the question.

"I do. I absolutely do."

Everyone chuckled at his earnestness.

"Are you exchanging rings?" the justice asked.

"Yes, ma'am," Jeordi said, pulling another surprise out of his pocket.

Tom gaped. "How—"

"Jeordi, place the ring on Tom's finger and repeat after me. With this ring I thee wed and pledge my faith."

"With this ring I thee wed and pledge my faith."

Tom did the same, still stunned that somehow Jeordi had managed to get them rings and that the one he'd placed on his own hand actually fit.

"For as much as Thomas Goodwin and Jeordi Boone have consented to live together in wedlock, and having declared their intentions before these witnesses, I am pleased and honored to be able, by the power vested in me by the United States of America, to declare to all present that they are now legally married and are husband and husband. Jeordi and Tom, you may kiss your husband."

Bill applauded briefly while Hank was busy snapping pictures with his camera, which he'd been quietly doing throughout the ceremony. Even though Tom and Jeordi didn't necessarily want anyone to see it, they both shed tears of joy at the unexpected turn of events and the two strangers who had swooped in and saved their day.

They got some pictures with the justice standing between them and a few with her to the side and them holding hands. They even got someone to come in and take some photos of Tom and Jeordi, Hank and Bill, and the justice all together.

"Let's return to my chambers and sign the paperwork," the justice instructed. Hank helped her remove the robe and hung it up, somehow knowing where she kept her judicial robe.

Seated behind the most ornate and largest desk Jeordi had ever seen, the justice signed the document and asked Bill and Hank to sign as well as witnesses.

"Return this to the courthouse and they will issue your official marriage certificate."

"That's where we're headed right now," Hank told her, giving her a quick hug. "Thank you so much, Chief. This means so much to all of us."

"My pleasure, Hank. You know that if I'm here and can do so, I'll always have time for you."

"Madam Chief Justice, you are awesome," Hank said.

Each in turn shook hands and thanked the justice, Tom and Jeordi both at a loss for the proper words, managing only a simple "Thank you."

Back in the car, Bill drove them across town to the original courthouse where they had started. By comparison, this building looked more like an industrial warehouse than anything else, especially compared to the building they had just left.

Hank again took the lead, quickly navigating them back to the office where they'd started. The hallways were much less busy than they had been earlier, so there were fewer crowds through which they had to weave.

When they handed the license to the clerk, a different one from earlier, her eyes went wide with surprise. "Is this real? You got married by the chief justice of the United States Supreme Court?"

Tom and Jeordi looked at Hank, who nodded and smiled.

"Holy fuck," Tom whispered to Jeordi.

"Is that all right?" Jeordi asked. "Is there a problem? Is it… legal?"

"You can't get much more legal than that, honey," she said with a smile.

Ten minutes later they held in their hand three official copies of their marriage certificate. Hank insisted on more pictures, clicking away.

As they were exiting the building, Jeordi leaned over to Bill and said, "He likes to take pictures, doesn't he?"

"He does. And he's damned good at it. He's been doing it for a long, long time."

"What time is your flight back?" Hank asked when they were in the car but still parked.

"Um, nine o'clock," Jeordi said.

"Perfect. Home, Bill. I need to take care of a couple of things, and Bill is going to see about getting us all something wonderful to eat."

"Um, you don't have to—"

"Nonsense," Hank said before Jeordi could even get the words out. We're family, and we take care of one another. That's one of the first rules of being gay. Remember it, live it, and you'll have a great life."

"Okay," Tom said, smiling. "Thank you, for… everything. I can't believe it all. I'm going to be thinking of this for years, each time realizing something I missed the first time."

Hank and Bill's house was in the Georgetown neighborhood of the city, an older part of the area with absolutely incredible older homes. The one Hank and Bill shared was the grandest home either Tom or Jeordi had ever seen.

Bill gave them a brief tour, Hank disappearing immediately to go do something else. Ending up back in the kitchen, which was perhaps larger than their entire trailer, Jeordi and Tom seated themselves at the counter and talked with Bill while he cooked, preparing things they couldn't identify but that smelled fantastic.

An hour later the four of them sat at the dining room table to a meal unlike any in which Tom and Jeordi had ever participated. There were cloth napkins at each place, the silverware was intricately carved, the dishes on which the food was served were all similar but slightly different, appearing to be hand painted.

"My God, this is wonderful," Tom said after a couple of bites.

"Oh wow," Jeordi said, echoing Tom's observation.

"Isn't he a good cook?" Hank asked with a smile.

"I'll say," Jeordi said.

"Can I ask—?"

"Anything, little one," Hank said.

"These plates. They're beautiful. Is there a story behind them?"

"I love this set. We bought them on our last trip to Turkey. There was an artisan whose work we both adored, and we decided we simply had to have some of his work, so we bought this set."

"Turkey?" Jeordi said. "Turkey, as in the Middle East?"

"Not quite the Middle East, but Middle East adjacent at least," Hank said with a smile. "A truly magnificent place to visit, one of my favorites of our world travels."

Jeordi nodded, stashing that bit of information away for future reference.

The remainder of their afternoon passed faster than seemed possible, Hank disappearing again before dessert was served along with coffee and tea in a room they called the "drawing room," for some reason. An excited Hank dashed in at six o'clock and handed a large book to Jeordi and Tom. Sitting together, they flipped the cover back and saw a photo from their wedding. Flipping the pages, they found another, and another, then another. The entire volume was filled with photos from their day, primarily the wedding ceremony and afterward but including a couple of them at the courthouse with license in hand from that morning. And they were good—really good.

"Oh... wow."

"Sorry it's not better put together, but I was working under some serious time constraints. We need to leave to get you two to the airport so you can catch your flight. Traffic at this time of day will be... um, intense. You'll find a digital copy of all of the photos on a CD tucked into the back of the book."

"How can we ever thank you for everything you've done?" Jeordi said.

"By simply passing it on down the line when you find another gay brother or sister in need someday."

"Okay."

"And while I hate to cut this short, to get you onto your flight, we need to leave and head for the airport."

When he had said traffic would be intense, Hank had not been exaggerating. Traffic was indeed a mess. Tom and Jeordi were not accustomed to seeing so many people, cars, pedestrians, or so much traffic and congestion, but Bill, once again behind the wheel of their car, handled it as if it were nothing. Before it seemed possible, they were giving one another hurried hugs at the airport while a cop insisted they move along.

Chapter Nine

AFTER THE whirlwind of a day they'd had, Tom and Jeordi actually fell asleep on the plane ride back home to Kentucky. Tired but clutching the book of their photos along with their certificates of marriage, they exited their tiny airport to find Tom's sister waiting for them. This time there was no cop telling them to move along quickly, but they were exhausted, so they didn't need anyone telling them to do so.

"So, how was it?" she asked.

"You know where we were today?" Tom asked.

"Yes. Jeordi and I talked. And I wouldn't agree to pick you up until he spilled the beans about what he was planning."

"I see that I have to work on finding new ways to get information out of him," Tom said with a smile that bordered on frisky and evil.

"Hey, injured man here," Jeordi pleaded.

At home, despite wanting to climb all over one another physically, they lay down and were both asleep in almost no time. It had been a very long day.

The following morning, before Tom left for work, Jeordi surprised him yet again.

"Tonight when you get home from work, I'd like you to go with me to see my parents."

"You would? Why? What did I do wrong? I thought you reserved that punishment for capital offenses."

Jeordi chuckled, recalling how he'd actually said pretty much those words. "I want us to go together and show them what we did yesterday."

"Really?" Tom asked.

"Really."

"Okay."

And that was how, at six o'clock that evening, Tom and Jeordi stood hand in hand at the front door to the house where Jeordi's parents lived, the same one where he'd grown up.

It only took one poke of the doorbell before Jeordi's mother was pulling the inside door open. She broke into a big smile at the sight of her son but lost it when she saw Tom was there with him. When she spotted them holding hands, her face became a frosty scowl.

"Get in here. What the hell are you doing? Don't you know people can see you?"

"Let 'em look all they want," Jeordi said. "I've got nothing to be ashamed of."

"You're not the only person affected by your outrageous behavior," she said. "Did you ever think about that? We live in this town too, you know," she scolded.

"Son," Jeordi's father said, walking slowly into the room. "I'm surprised to see you here. Tom," he said, acknowledging Tom's presence with a nod.

"We have something to show you," Jeordi said. He nodded to Tom, who stepped up, holding the book and opening it to the first page.

"Your incredible son did the most amazing thing. Without telling me what he was up to, yesterday he flew us to Washington, DC, where we got married." He flipped the book to a photo showing them facing one another, holding hands, with the chief justice standing between them.

"Is that...?" Jeordi's father started to say before the words died away.

"Yes, Dad, that's the chief justice of the United States Supreme Court."

"What did you do?" his mother demanded. "How did you get in trouble bad enough that you had to go there?" Her tone was accusing.

"We didn't do anything wrong, Mother. We were there to get married. The chief justice married us yesterday."

His mother asked, "How—"

"Family," Tom said. "Family up in DC helped us out when we needed them."

"We don't have any family in DC," his mother complained. "And Tom, your people certainly don't have anyone up there."

"Our gay family, Mother," Jeordi said, flipping to the photo of the four of them standing with the chief justice. "Our big, extended, incredible, glorious gay family. When we hit a snag yesterday, they were there when we needed someone, and they just immediately pitched in and fixed our problem in a way we never saw coming. It was incredible—the flight, seeing the nation's capital, getting married, meeting two incredible guys who took care of us every step of the way."

"What did you have to do for them for all of this?" she asked with a curl to her upper lip.

"All we had to do was agree to pass it on to someone else when we were able. So when we spot a gay person or couple in need, all we have to do is what we would do anyway—reach out a helping hand, give them a shoulder to lean on, and do something for them that we can do but they can't do for themselves. That's all.

"You know," Jeordi said with a particular twinkle in his eye. "This reminds me of a hymn that Grandma used to sing when she worked in the kitchen—something about casting your bread upon the waters and it will come back to you. Do you remember that, Mother? I'm sure you heard your mother sing the same hymn. It was one of her favorites."

Jeordi's father nodded, looking thoughtful.

"I need to get Tom home. He's worked all day and probably is still tired from all the running around we did yesterday. But I wanted to be sure to come show you the wedding photos. You couldn't be there, but we wanted you to see them."

His father nodded. His mother said nothing.

At the door, Tom said, "Good night."

Jeordi's father, however, surprised them all by pulling his son into a quick hug before saying, "Good night, guys."

Jeordi could not remember his father ever doing anything like that with any of his sons, including himself.

Their trailer was only a couple of blocks away, so it was an easy walk to get home.

Jeordi pulled the screen door open to unlock the main door, surprised when an envelope fell out.

"FedEx," he said. "You expecting something?"

"No," Tom said. Since the package was addressed to both of them, while Jeordi was busy unlocking the door, Tom pulled it open to see who had sent something to them. Inside was a much smaller envelope, greeting card sized, with their names handwritten across the front.

After opening that second one, Tom pulled out a card featuring two gorgeous shirtless men in a tight embrace. The words wished them all the best on the start of their life together as a married couple. Flipping the card open, Tom saw that it was signed by Hank and Bill.

But that was not all that was inside.

"Holy fuck," Tom said, his voice low and gravelly.

"What's wrong, babe?" Jeordi asked.

"Holy fuck."

"Tom? What's wrong?" Jeordi asked, worried.

"Um, nothing wrong," Tom said. "Quite… the opposite actually. It's a card from Hank and Bill congratulating us on our marriage."

"That's great, but I wonder why they sent it by FedEx," Jeordi said.

"Because of what was inside the card," Tom said, holding something out to him.

"What's this?" Jeordi asked, taking the paper that Tom held.

"Holy fuck."

"Yeah, think I said that," Tom said.

"Holy fuck," Jeordi repeated.

"Okay, so we're on the same page now," Tom said. "There's a note in the card. 'Jeordi and Tom—Thank you for letting us be part of your special day yesterday. It was wonderful beyond measure to meet the two of you and be able to do something to help someone else. It sounded like you were facing a few unanticipated expenses because of Jeordi's accident, so we wanted to send you the enclosed check to help you get over the hump and get back on a firm footing. As hard as it might be to believe, we were once your age and remember how hard it could be when money was tight. We are most fortunate now that money is not a consideration for us, and we are delighted to give you the enclosed wedding gift to get yourselves back on your feet and maybe even take a honeymoon trip somewhere, if and when the time is right. All our best, Hank and Bill. PS—Don't even think about sending the check back. PPS—I had a talk with the chief about your county clerk, and we watched the video that was broadcast on your local channel. The chief was not amused and immediately got on the telephone. I don't know all the details, but knowing her, heads were going to roll before the day was over.'"

"I… I'm speechless," Jeordi said.

"I can't believe they did that for us," Tom said.

"Of all the people we could have run into, how did we get so lucky as to meet them? What are the odds?"

"They may be better than you think," Tom said. "Remember, we are everywhere."

Jeordi snickered. "I love it." Thinking for a moment, he went on, "I can't believe I remember this, but one of the Bible verses I had to learn as a youngster has stuck with me. I think it was from the Old Testament, the book of Hebrews, and it was simply 'Forget not to show love unto strangers: for thereby some have entertained angels unawares.'"

"Spot on, babe," Tom said. "Spot on."

"You tired?" Jeordi asked.

"More than you could possibly know," Tom said. "You?"

"Not as much. Too bad you're so tired."

"Why?" Tom asked suspiciously.

"I don't know. Why don't you check the locks, turn off the lights, and then come into the bedroom and see your... husband about the matter. I have it on good authority that he might have an idea or two."

Tom rushed around to do as directed, suddenly more awake and excited.

MICHAEL MURPHY met his husband Dan thirty-four years ago during a Sunday service at MCC in Washington, DC, when a hot, smart man sat down beside him. Due to a large crowd and a shortage of hymnals, they had to share. The touch of one hand on the other in that moment was electric. Sparks flew that day. Though neither had planned it, they spent the rest of day together followed by the night. From that day, for more than three decades, they've rarely been separated, each finding in the other their soul mate.

In the District of Columbia, where they live, marriage became possible in early March 2010. The minute it happened, they were in line to get a marriage license, only to be stumped because the license required the name of the person who was going to marry them. There was such a sudden rush of same-sex couples wanting to get married that the office already had a two-month backlog before an appointment could be secured. Since they weren't at all convinced that the Congress wasn't going to step in and do something stupid to take away this right, they started calling everywhere to find someone who would marry them. It might be legal, but finding someone to marry them was proving to be a challenge.

When an article appeared in the newspaper telling of a small local United Methodist Church that had decided to go against general church policy because marriage equality mattered deeply to them, a conversation started. After a series of e-mails and phone calls, suddenly they were seated with two retired UMC ministers who were willing to risk it all to do the right thing. A few days later, license in hand, surrounded by a handful of friends and their best dog, Shadow, they were finally legally married.

Please stop by www.gayromancewriter.com to learn more about him.

By MICHAEL MURPHY

Book Fair
Breaking News
Evac
It Should Have Been You
Little Squirrels Can Climb Tall Trees • Mano's Story
A More Perfect Union (Multiple Author Anthology)
A Night at the Ariston Baths
The President's Husband
Swan Song for an Ugly Duckling
Walls That Divide
When Dachshunds Ruled the Serengeti
You Can't Go Home Again

Published by DREAMSPINNER PRESS
www.dreamspinnerpress.com

DESTINED

BY JAMIE FESSENDEN

For my amazing husband, Erich.

Destined is the more or less true story of how Erich and I met and spent years figuring out we wanted to be together. It isn't 100 percent accurate, but memories rarely are. And this is our fairytale, so I reserve the right to make us handsome, charming, and maybe even a bit heroic.

Prelude

JAY AND Wallace were convinced they met for the first time in 1999, but they were wrong. They'd met five years earlier than that, in 1994. But neither of them remembered.

Jay had just graduated from college with a computer science degree and found himself a job two hours west of the university doing tech support for a mail-order company called PC Connection. A coworker found out he was looking for an apartment in the area and told him his wife managed an apartment building. So that was how Jayson Corey ended up in Keene, New Hampshire, in the midnineties with a job, an apartment, and no friends to speak of.

He was social enough. He made some acquaintances at work. The support department went out for drinks every Wednesday night after work, so he got to know his coworkers a bit better. But apart from work, he didn't have much in common with them. And none of them were gay.

There was a gay men's group in town, so Jay went to one of their meetings. The men were nice—and some were pretty cute—but he didn't immediately connect with anyone. In retrospect, perhaps his friends in college had been a little on the fringe. They'd introduced Jay to role-playing games, medieval banquets, fire dancing, skinny-dipping....

He could imagine some of these guys skinny-dipping—and that was pleasant to think about—but they clearly wouldn't have fit in with his friends back at UNH. He supposed it might be time to move on. After all, he wasn't in college anymore. But that thought didn't cheer him up at all.

Then he saw the flyers on the table. They were largely flyers for other gay groups in New England, some too far away to appeal to him at present. But one intrigued him. It was a flyer for Gaynemede's Crossing, a group for "gay, straight, lesbian, bisexual, and trans pagans" in Cambridge, Massachusetts. Jay wasn't a very religious man, but he'd attended some Wiccan gatherings in college. The circles had been peaceful and beautiful experiences. He found the thought of dipping a toe back into that scene intriguing, especially as a contrast to the stressful, high-tech business environment he now worked in. And Cambridge was just north of Boston, about an hour's drive away.

HIS FIRST attempt at going to the group was a dismal failure. He'd never driven in the Boston area, and he wasn't prepared for the chaos in and around the city. He drove an hour to get there, then spent another hour driving around hopelessly lost, until he finally found himself on a highway heading north, passing an abandoned car in the breakdown lane that was literally on fire. He said, "Fuck it!" and kept going until he hit the New Hampshire border. Then he went home, vowing never to try anything so foolish again.

But one month later, he was back on the road. Jay wasn't sure why he was so determined to go to this one group, but this time he was armed with better directions and a phone number.

He got lost again. As the beginning time for the meeting came and went, he found himself at the ass end of Boston, surrounded by crumbling, mostly empty buildings and road construction. He had no idea where he was, though it resembled a portal to the underworld. Eventually Jay came across a Dunkin' Donuts that had a pay phone. He dialed the number for the group, and a man answered.

"Hello?" Wallace said, having no idea he was about to hear the voice of the man he was destined to marry.

Frustrated, his nerves stretched to the breaking point, Jay skipped over romance and went straight for, "Where the hell are you? I've been driving around looking for you guys for forty-five minutes!"

"Um… do you know who you're calling?"

Jay hesitated. Maybe he'd dialed the wrong number. "Sorry. Is this Gaynemede's Crossing?"

"Oh. Yes."

"I wanted to come tonight."

"The meeting's almost over."

When Jay spoke again, he was embarrassed to hear a catch in his voice, as if he were on the edge of tears. "I drove all the way from New Hampshire…."

"Well, where are you now?"

Jay wasn't sure. But he described the Dunkin' Donuts and the bridge outside, and his suspicion that it led to one of the nether hells. To his surprise, the man recognized it.

"Gods! How on earth did you end up all the way down there?"

"I have no idea."

The man on the phone was silent for a long moment, and Jay waited for him to say "Sorry. Better luck next time." Then Jay would have to find his way back home, having failed again. He braced himself for it.

But instead the man said, "You'll need to turn around and head back the way you came, until you cross the bridge into Cambridge." Then he proceeded to give Jay directions and describe the neighborhood and what the storefront looked like.

Jay had no idea what the man's name was or what he looked like. But he knew he loved him.

WALLACE HAD to help Adrastia clean up after the ritual. Not that the ritual itself had been particularly messy, but they had to make sure all the chairs were put back against the walls, all the snacks had been carted away, and all dirty paper plates and plastic cups were tossed in the trash. A quick sweep didn't hurt either. Gaynemede's Crossing was allowed to use the basement room of the store on the condition they not inconvenience the owner.

The shop itself was a vaguely New Age occult shop selling herbs and paraphernalia for religions ranging from Wicca to Hinduism to Santeria. Wallace often bought candles and herbs there for his personal use, and they had a decent stock of occult books. Unfortunately it was well past closing, so no one was there to sell him the scrying mirror he'd had his eye on. He'd have to remember to grab it before the ritual next month, if it was still there.

As Adrastia shooed everyone outside, Wallace took one last look around and then locked up with the key the owners had entrusted to him. It was past eight, but it was late June, so the sun was still in the sky and the air was deliciously warm. A few people from the group were still straggling by the front steps, knowing a quest for Vietnamese or Thai food was likely to be next on the agenda.

A man approached them along the sidewalk, eyeing them with trepidation. Frankly, that wasn't unusual. Outsiders often found the group a bit… eccentric. Adrastia towered over everyone, and her broad shoulders made it obvious she was trans to all but the most clueless. Others were dressed head to toe in black or purple, with pentacles and crescent moons and other pagan symbols adorning them—necklaces, earrings, tattoos, the whole nine yards. Wallace himself dressed blandly in jeans and a T-shirt. He didn't wear jewelry and had no tattoos—not even in interesting places. His most unique feature was the pair of Coke-bottle glasses he despised.

Everyone gazed at the stranger with mild interest, waiting for him to say something, but he seemed a little intimidated. At last Adrastia asked, "Can we help you?"

"I called here about fifteen minutes ago," he answered uncomfortably. "I was the one looking for the group…."

"I'm afraid you've missed the evening ritual."

"I know—"

"Hey!" Wallace interrupted, hurrying down the three slate steps to the sidewalk. "That was me on the phone. I'm Wallace."

The man looked relieved. "Hi. I'm Jay."

THAT WAS how they met. They even had dinner together at a nice Vietnamese restaurant, but there was no chance to talk privately—not with eight people at the table. Wallace thought Jay was kind of cute. A little skinny perhaps, but handsome, with dirty-blond hair and soft emerald eyes. And Jay thought Wallace was nice in an understated way. The glasses made it difficult to see his eyes, but he had a boyish face and sensual lips that Jay would have been tempted to kiss, if they ever found a moment alone together.

But they didn't.

When dinner ended Jay said good night and drove back to New Hampshire. He thought about going to the group the next month, but by then he'd begun to make some friends in Keene. As he grew less lonely in his new hometown, the desire to reconnect with the Cambridge group faded. Considering how many people lived in the Boston area, it was unlikely Jay and Wallace would ever bump into each other again.

But they did.

Part One

Chapter One

1999

DOUG HAD seemed terrific when Jay first met him. He was funny, attentive, good in bed, and Jay's family thought he was great. At family gatherings, that is—not in bed. They were living together in short order.

But after two years, things weren't going so well. They'd moved to Dover, which allowed Jay to get back in touch with some of his college friends, but their relationship seemed to grow rockier by the day. They fought constantly, though Jay was never really sure what they were fighting about. They just didn't… fit anymore.

But still he tried. Jay was nothing if not stubborn.

His ties to the pagan/Wiccan world had long ago faded away, since Doug thought that stuff was weird and creepy. In fact, his ties to anything outside the tech industry had pretty much withered to nothing. He worked long hours, during which he thought about nothing but computers and switches and routers. It paid well, and raises were frequent, so he was caught up in the game his coworkers played—pushing for promotions or transfers every six months to a year in order to get salary increases. Like his coworkers, he had an E*TRADE account and spent time between support calls attempting to build a stock portfolio. He had the sense not to gamble the small amount of savings he had, but it was a fun game to play.

But he was unsatisfied. He couldn't quite put a finger on why until one Saturday, when he was sitting at Café on the Corner and his friend, Steve, happened by. Steve had been part of the medieval reenactment group Jay hung out with in college, and apparently he was still involved with them.

"Michaelmas is coming up," Steve pointed out, referring to one of the large feasts the group put on every year. "It's going to be at the Unitarian Church. You should come."

Jay couldn't see that happening. He no longer had any of his medieval "garb," and Doug was likely to turn his nose up at the idea of hanging out with a bunch of reenactors all day.

Jay said diplomatically, "I'll think about it."

"Well, at least stop by the monthly Wiccan group. Julie's usually there, and Mark. A whole bunch of the old crowd. That's tomorrow. Same place."

It would be nice to see some of them. And Doug was working on Sunday. "That might be fun."

"Are you still writing?"

He wasn't. Jay had written a lot of science fiction stories in college, and he'd talked about getting published one day. But that, like everything else he'd enjoyed in those days, seemed like nothing more than a dream he'd once had, barely remembered.

This conversation was getting depressing.

"So," he asked, trying to change the subject, "do you still sing?"

Steve grinned with excitement. "Yeah, man! My band is putting together our second CD. It's gonna be awesome!"

The more he talked about his life, the more it became clear Steve was barely scraping by financially. But he was doing what he loved, and he seemed just as happy with his life as he'd been in college. Jay, on the other hand, had plenty of money. He had a career now, a boyfriend, a new car, and a nice apartment. He'd thought he was doing okay, but now he realized exactly why he'd been feeling so uneasy. His life had veered off course. In just five years, he'd lost touch with everything that had been fun and creative in himself. He was no longer *Jay*.

And he missed himself.

WALLACE ENDED up at the coffee chat by pure chance—though he would later think fate might have played a small part. Gaynemede's Crossing had eventually drifted apart, and after moving to New Hampshire, he was feeling isolated. Fortunately Adrastia kept tabs on what was going on in the pagan community, and she'd told him about a group meeting in Portsmouth, less than an hour from his new house.

He'd been going for about six months. This group wasn't really into rituals—they just liked to hang out and socialize over coffee and cookies. They also weren't specifically oriented toward the LGBTQ community, but they were very open and accepting. It was a pleasant way to spend an afternoon. Wallace had begun supplying the coffee, since he had a large stainless steel coffee urn that could brew a hundred cups of coffee and keep it hot for the entire meeting. He'd picked it up from a restaurant supply house that was going out of business, along with enough white ceramic plates and coffee cups to start his own diner—not that he wanted to. He just liked to be prepared. He'd offered Julie the use of the coffee urn when he first started coming to the group, and she'd jumped at it. The coffee brewer the church had was so old it was impossible to get the stains and deposits off it.

The group tended to be mostly the same people every month, but on this particular Sunday, a new guy walked in. He was thin and blond, a bit conservative looking but definitely sexy. Wallace had the distinct feeling he'd seen the man before, but he couldn't put a finger on it.

"Jay!" Julie exclaimed the moment she saw him. "I haven't seen you in ages!" Then she ran across the room to give him a hug. Again, the name sounded vaguely familiar to Wallace, but he couldn't recall knowing a "Jay."

The newcomer was clearly friends with a lot of people in the group, and they all greeted him enthusiastically. Those who didn't know him were introduced, including Wallace.

Jay shook his hand and gazed at him with soft emerald eyes that seemed familiar. "Have we met?" Wallace asked.

Jay seemed to look at him more closely for a moment. "I… don't know. Did you go to UNH?"

"No."

Jay shook his head. "I'm not sure." Then he gave him a shy smile. "I think I'd remember you."

Wallace felt himself flush. Was Jay flirting with him? Wallace was a computer geek who'd learned his social skills by carefully observing those around him rather than picking them up by osmosis, as most people seemed to. There were times when he still misinterpreted signals— especially *those* kinds of signals. So he fell back on "Would you like a cup of coffee?"

Over the next couple of hours, as people drifted around the room, inserting themselves into whatever topics of conversation sounded interesting, Wallace noticed Jay kept finding his way back to his side. He found out Jay was in computers too, and they shared an interest in Norse mythology.

"I've found an online course in Old Norse," Wallace told him, "the language the Vikings spoke."

Jay laughed. "Seriously? That must be ridiculously hard."

"Not really. The verb inclinations and noun declinations are challenging to memorize, I guess, but the vocabulary is pretty easy. Most words are close to either modern English or modern German—*sverdh* became 'sword,' *brodir* became 'brother,' and so on." Wallace realized he was rambling about a subject most people found boring, so he shut up. *Gods! Why do I always do that?* Jay was probably wondering how to extricate himself from the conversation now.

At that moment someone over by the snack table said loudly, "Can we take up a collection to buy a real coffeemaker? This coffee tastes like shit!"

Jay, of course, didn't know Wallace was responsible for making the coffee, but Wallace still wanted to crawl under a chair now. He'd allowed himself to think the handsome guy standing in front of him might actually be interested in a geeky guy with glasses that made him look like a startled guppy, but any second now Jay was going to laugh and agree about how awful the coffee was. Then he'd wander away to find someone interesting to talk to.

Jay glanced down at the cup in his hand. "It's perfectly fine to me. I think it's really good, actually." He looked up again and grinned conspiratorially. "So how would a Viking say, 'The next person who insults the coffee will die by my sword'?"

JAY COULDN'T remember where he'd seen Wallace before, but there was a feeling of familiarity about him. Perhaps it was just the way they seemed to mesh. It was more than the shared interest in Norse stuff. Wallace was easy to talk to, and Jay felt comfortable with him in a way he hadn't felt with anybody in a long time. Wallace made him feel like *himself*. He didn't have to prove what a stud he was with computers or compare salaries or any of the shit that had made Jay's life tedious in recent years.

Wallace was cute too. An adorable boyish face framed by soft dark brown curls, and surprisingly sensual lips. True, the glasses weren't very flattering, and Jay found himself wanting to remove them so he could see Wallace's eyes better. But that was just one minor detail.

It didn't matter. Jay was definitely attracted to the quiet, understated computer programmer.

But of course, he was in a relationship. And he wasn't going to hit on someone while he and Doug were still together, even if things were a little rocky. Every relationship had a few rough patches. There was no point in making things worse.

Lunch wasn't "cheating," though, so when the meeting wound up, Jay asked Wallace, "Are you hungry? I was gonna hit the Brewery for a late lunch."

"Sure."

They continued their conversation over cheeseburgers, talking about random things—nothing in particular—and enjoying each other's company until Jay realized how late it was getting.

"I really should get home," he said reluctantly. "My boyfriend will be home from work soon."

It was the first time he'd mentioned Doug, and he thought he detected a slight sagging of Wallace's shoulders when he did, a subtle faltering of his smile. It was the first indication that Wallace had been interested in him. Jay felt awful now. He wanted to reach across the table and take Wallace's hand and tell him, *Don't be hurt. I'd ask you out properly if I could.*

But it wouldn't do any good to say that. It would probably just embarrass Wallace. So he kept it to himself.

"Where are you parked?" Wallace asked.

"Over on Vaughn Street."

"I can give you a ride to your car, if you like."

Wallace's car was in the parking garage just around the corner, so they paid the check and walked there. Then Wallace gave Jay a ride in his old, beat-up Honda Civic across town to Vaughn Street.

He pulled up alongside Jay's new Nissan and said, "It was nice to meet you."

Jay hesitated, his hand on the door handle. A sudden feeling came over him—a feeling he would be making a huge mistake if he got out of that car. He looked at Wallace and desperately wanted to kiss him on those full lips, to see if they were as soft and warm as they appeared.

It's impossible. You know that. Don't lead him on, and don't betray Doug.

"Nice to meet you too," he responded, struggling to make his smile appear casual. "I hope I'll see you again sometime."

"Me too."

"Thanks for the ride." He got out of the car and closed the door. Then he watched as Wallace drove away.

Interlude

2000

WALLACE WAS pretty loopy on Valium by the time the doctor pried his eye open with a speculum. Otherwise he would have been screaming—if not from pain, at least from *A Clockwork Orange* flashbacks. Fortunately the nurse had given him some eye drops to numb everything, and they weren't playing Beethoven's "Ode to Joy" over the PA.

"This will be a little uncomfortable," Doctor Manning said, in one of the great understatements of Wallace's life, as he adjusted the contraption that immobilized Wallace's head. "But it will all be over soon."

Was that supposed to be reassuring?

"We're just going to immobilize your eye now." The doctor slid a ring into place, and Wallace was happy to note he couldn't feel anything when it touched his cornea. "I need you to look at that red dot."

A small red dot appeared on the partition in front of him. It was extremely blurry, so it was difficult to focus on, but Wallace tried to keep it in the center of his field of vision.

"Stay very still."

Something slid in front of his eye, then slid away. A moment later he heard something clicking. The clicking persisted as Doctor Manning manipulated the laser.

At one point Wallace smelled something unpleasant and remarked, "I think I can smell my eye burning."

"Don't talk. You need to stay as still as possible."

THE DOCTOR brought Wallace out to the waiting room, his eyes protected by dark glasses. Adrastia had been waiting for him, and she stood to greet him and take his arm.

"Did they give you your eyes in a box so we can put them on the mantel?"

Adrastia was many things, but motherly was not one of them.

"Keep the glasses on for the rest of the day," Doctor Manning admonished. "And don't scratch. You should be able to use your eyes normally by tomorrow."

"Thanks," Wallace said.

He'd follow the doctor's advice to the letter. He'd paid too much for the Lasik to fuck it up at this stage. But it was going to be excruciating to wait until tomorrow to finally see the world through his eyes directly, without the horrible thick glasses he'd worn since he was a boy.

And though he was embarrassed to admit it, he was desperate to see if a long-held, secret fantasy had come true—that removing the glasses had finally made him handsome.

Chapter Two

May 2001

DOUG WASN'T a very good liar, so it wasn't exactly that Jay didn't know he was hooking up with other men. He hadn't wanted to believe it. But when Doug claimed he couldn't meet Jay after work for dinner on Valentine's Day because his boss and his wife had insisted he join *them* for dinner—on *Valentine's Day*!—the lie was too blatant to ignore. Jay went home that evening, logged into the account he'd created for Doug, and did something he'd promised himself he'd never stoop to. He read Doug's e-mail.

There it was, laid out in front of him and going back at least a couple of years—e-mails arranging meetings with old boyfriends and men Jay had thought of as mutual friends, whenever Jay was at work and Doug had a few hours to spare.

One exchange was particularly hurtful: *I'd leave him, but he pays all the bills. Lol.*

JAY STOPPED paying Doug's bills and kicked him out of the apartment. Then he started going to the gay men's group in Portsmouth again. He'd fallen out of the habit, once he'd settled down—or *thought* he'd settled down. But he wasn't the type of person who enjoyed being alone. "Alone time," sure. He'd never minded being at the apartment by himself for a few hours while Doug was at work. He'd play a computer game, watch a movie, go out to the coffee shop. But not all the time. He needed someone to care for, someone to come home to. It was in his nature.

He'd put on a few pounds in the years he'd spent with Doug, but he wasn't in bad shape. And he was surprised to find himself in demand when he returned to the group. Not that they all fell over themselves

trying to ask him out. But once word got out he was single, he had more
than his share of dates over the course of the summer.

Unfortunately he quickly discovered he didn't mesh well with
the guys who asked him out. It might have been due to his appearance.
He dressed conservatively, had short hair…. In short, he looked like a
businessman. But that wasn't what he *was*. Not deep down. He wanted
to talk music, art, favorite books. His dates would smile and say he was
cute, but they'd rarely have much to contribute to the conversation. And
though a couple had stayed the night—which had been nice, since things
hadn't been good sexually between him and Doug for ages—they hadn't
come back for seconds.

He did date one man for a couple of weeks, a nice guy in his forties
who still hadn't come out to his family or coworkers. Jay liked Ronnie,
though it annoyed him that they couldn't go to any restaurants near
Portsmouth because Ronnie was afraid someone from work would see
him kissing or holding hands with a man. And when Ronnie came to his
apartment, he glanced at Jay's shelf of books on Wicca and joked, "Wow!
You're sure into some weird shit." He was echoing Doug's sentiments
about it, but Jay still found it annoying. It was something he believed in.
Sure, it was unorthodox, but that was no reason to make fun of it.

A couple of days later, Ronnie broke up with him, saying, "We're
obviously very different people."

Jay couldn't deny that was true.

During all this, his thoughts kept traveling back to the afternoon
he'd spent with a handsome man with thick glasses. Jay hadn't felt that
comfortable hanging out with anyone in… forever. Unfortunately it had
been two years, and no matter how much he tried, he couldn't recall the
man's name.

He thought about going back to the Portsmouth coffee chat again,
but he had no idea when they met. Still on Sundays perhaps, but which
Sundays? Two years ago they'd been renting space from the Unitarian
Church in Portsmouth, so Jay called the church to ask about it.

"Oh, those guys," the woman on the phone told him. "I remember
them. But they stopped holding their meetings here over a year ago. I
think the girl who ran it moved up north."

And that was where the trail ended. Jay had been friends with Julie—
the woman who'd run the coffee chats—when they were in college, but

that had been seven years ago. He knew she'd married, but he had no idea where she and her husband might have moved to.

AT THE end of the summer, he ran into Steve again at Café on the Corner. He'd been wanting to find him, but they hadn't exchanged contact info the last time they'd met, so it was just chance that Steve walked in one Thursday evening as Jay was relaxing after work.

"Jay!" Steve sat down without an invite. "How you been?"

"Okay, I guess." Jay gave him the *Reader's Digest* version of his breakup with Doug and the past few months of dating.

"That sucks. I broke up with Caroline a while ago, but it was kind of a mutual thing. I'm happy being single for a while."

Jay sighed and took a sip of his café latte. "I wish I could say the same. But I really hate being alone. Does that sound pathetic?"

"Just a little," Steve said with a laugh. Then, perhaps seeing the look of dismay on Jay's face, he added more soberly, "I think some people are just cut out to be alone and others aren't."

"I'm not saying I'm going to shack up with anybody who will take me," Jay said defensively.

"No, of course not."

Still, Jay felt a bit pathetic. He just hated coming home to an empty house.

"There was one guy I felt a connection with," he said. "More than I ever did with Doug. Though we only hung out for an afternoon."

Steve emptied the packets of sugar he'd picked up at the counter into his coffee. "He didn't want to stick around?"

"I think he kind of did." At least he wanted to believe that. "But this was back when I was still with Doug, so we kind of went our separate ways."

Steve stirred the sugar in. "So call him up now."

"We didn't exchange numbers. I can't even remember what his name was—it was a couple years ago."

"That sucks."

"Yeah." Jay hesitated before blurting out, "Do you happen to know where Julie and her husband moved to?"

Steve paused in the act of taking a sip of coffee, then set the cup down. He looked thoughtful. "Not really. Somewhere way up north, I think. Mark got a job offer in the Berlin area he couldn't pass up."

"Oh." Jay tried to hide his disappointment.

"But I have their number, if you'd like it."

Chapter Three

THE LASIK had certainly improved Wallace's love life. Not that he was sleeping around all over the place now, but he'd had his share of guys hitting on him at the pagan gatherings he attended that summer. And he hadn't snubbed them. Well, apart from the guy who'd boasted about barebacking with strangers. If that was his thing, fine, but Wallace didn't need to wake up with a case of syphilis or herpes or worse.

The doctor had warned him it was possible he'd need glasses again someday, as he got older. "We can do this procedure once more," he'd said, "but after that, the lenses will be too thin to shape with the laser. Even then your eyes will likely change with age, so you could end up with glasses anyway."

"Like the ones I had before?" Wallace cringed at the thought.

"No. Just the sort of reading glasses most people end up wearing. Or in your case, perhaps driving glasses."

Wallace could live with that. He might even be able to find a pair that made him look sexy. Well… he didn't want to get his hopes up too high. He'd settle for good.

The only thing he regretted about getting Lasik was he could no longer see extreme detail on objects right in front of his eyes. He'd been nearsighted, to the point where it was almost a superpower—though admittedly a rather lame one. He'd found that useful for knitting, which he'd picked up as a distraction during interminable business meetings. But he was happy with the trade-off.

WALLACE HAD it in his head for a long time to put together a study group for Old Norse and maybe to learn a bit about runes too. But though a lot of people seemed interested when he gave them a few words or phrases the Vikings would have said, the thought of studying it usually evoked their flight-or-fight response. Suddenly there was somebody across the room they'd been trying to track down all day, or they were desperate to get some more of that delicious mulled cider at the snack table, or they were convinced their appendix might have burst.

"Look at it this way," Adrastia told him when they were at a camping event in Vermont. "Even surrounded by pagans, computer gamers, role-players, and people into *Skyrim* cosplay, you've managed to be the geekiest one at the gathering. You've won! You're the Geek King!"

Wallace gave her a sour look. "Geeks are people who bite the heads off chickens in freak shows. I don't know why everyone thinks it's a compliment."

"It is admittedly an acquired taste."

Wallace ignored her. "I met *one guy* who seemed to find Old Norse interesting—*actually* interesting—but I can't even remember his name." The guy had also been in a relationship, but there was no point lamenting that. Wallace had hoped they'd run into each other at more coffee chats and at least become friends, but he'd never shown up again. Then the chats had shut down.

"I would offer to help," Adrastia said, "but Norse isn't really my thing." Wallace knew that. She was a priestess of Aphrodite. "If you decide to take up Ancient Greek someday, let me know."

Chapter Four

THE DRIVE from Dover, New Hampshire, to Groveton was almost three hours, but at least it was a straight shot up Route 16. Jay listened to Seamus Heaney reading his translation of *Beowulf* to make the trip pass more quickly, and the weather was beautiful. The farther north he drove, the higher the mountains loomed over him and the more untouched the landscape became. On either side of the road, ravines fell away to crystal clear brooks, and forests of ancient trees taller than any in the south climbed up into the hills.

He'd called Julie, and she'd been delighted to hear from him. Unfortunately she'd laughed when he asked, "I don't suppose you remember a guy I spent a lot of time talking to when I went to the coffee chat? He had dark hair and kind of a baby face—cute, but he had really thick glasses."

"Gods, Jay. That was years ago now."

His hopes had fallen, though they hadn't been very high to begin with. He knew he was on a wild goose chase.

But then Julie suggested, "Why don't you come up and visit us? There's a good diner down the road. We'd love to see you."

So that's what he was doing—meeting Julie and her husband, Mark, at Lee's Diner in Groveton.

He arrived at the diner just before one o'clock and found Mark waiting outside in his truck, the driver's side door open so he could stretch his long legs while he read a book. He glanced up when Jay pulled up beside him and hopped down from the truck with a grin.

"Hey! Good to see you!" he said boisterously when Jay got out of his car.

"Is Julie here?"

"Sure. She's inside getting us a table. I stayed out here to wait for you."

Jay tried to shake his hand, but Mark pulled him into a bear hug instead. When he released him, Jay saw the book he still held in his hand—*Brisingamen* by Diana Paxson. The book had been a favorite among Jay's friends in college. It was out of print, but Mark's copy was dog-eared and obviously had been read many times.

He followed Mark into the diner, and Julie waved them over to the table she'd nabbed in the back.

"I think I figured out who your mysterious man with the glasses was," she said the moment he sat down.

Jay felt his pulse skip a beat. It was ridiculous that he'd be so excited about tracking down someone he'd only met once, but it didn't matter. He was. "Who is he?"

But Julie wasn't to be rushed. She waved a hand in the air theatrically. "I don't know why it didn't occur to me before, but two years is a long time. And with all of the stuff going on with the move and everything—"

"Sweetheart," Mark interrupted, "Jay's about to wet his pants waiting for you to get to the point."

Julie snorted. "Oh, fine. There was a guy who started showing up for a while—someone from over near Manchester or somewhere. He had really thick glasses, dark hair…. He supplied coffee for a while with this big industrial coffeemaker, until people bitched about it and we started bringing in the coffeemaker we had at home."

"That was him!" Jay said excitedly. "I remember the coffee urn thing." He paused. "I thought the coffee was pretty good."

"It was fine," Mark said, rolling his eyes. "People just have to have something to bitch about."

"But what was his *name*?"

Julie shrugged. "I think it was Walter or… Wally. Something like that."

"Wallace!" Jay exclaimed. "I remember now. He was adorable and interesting and really sweet…."

Mark laughed. "Jeez. You've got it bad."

Jay ignored him. "How can I get in touch with him?"

"Sorry, hon," Julie said, shaking her head sadly. "I don't know for sure. I have a mailing list for the old coffee chats. His e-mail might be there, but I didn't see anything that jumped out at me as his."

Jay's spirits sank. Maybe he could go through the list himself, if Julie was willing to let him look at it, but would he be any more likely to recognize whatever esoteric e-mail address Wallace was using? And would it even still be a valid address?

"I was thinking," Julie went on cautiously, "maybe if you wanted to start the chats up again…."

Jay stared at her in confusion. "Me?"

"Why not? I hated shutting the group down, but of course we can't run it from here. The old gang is still around the seacoast area. You'd just have to send an e-mail to the mailing list to round them up again. You can get some of them to donate coffee and snacks, and the UU Church will rent you a room for cheap."

Mark smirked at him. "She's been trying to rope someone into doing this ever since we moved here."

"There aren't many pagan groups on the seacoast," she said defensively. "Nobody wanted the group to shut down." She looked pointedly at Jay. "You'd be doing everyone a favor."

The waitress arrived to take their order, and that gave Jay a minute to think. He'd been out of the pagan community for seven years now. He seemed like the last person to be running a group like that. On the other hand, it was just a social group. He wouldn't have to do much, would he?

"Do you think this will put me in touch with Wallace?" he asked when the waitress had gone. He felt a bit selfish dragging the conversation back to this topic, but that had been his primary reason for contacting Julie to begin with. He was certainly happy to visit with her and Mark on top of that. But taking on a new monthly responsibility had been the last thing he'd expected when he set out in the car that morning.

Julie shrugged. "For all we know, his e-mail is in the list. If not, someone from the group might know how to locate him."

Why not? Jay had his weekends free, now that he was single. Even if the group didn't lead him to Wallace, it would be something to keep him occupied—something not tied in with computers and business and stocks.

"All right," he said. "I'll do it."

Chapter Five

WALLACE HAD received the e-mail about the coffee chat starting up again at his baikingu.com domain address and felt an inordinate amount of excitement at the prospect. He didn't recognize the name of the new organizer, Jayson Corey, though it sounded familiar. Even if Wallace didn't know him, he looked forward to seeing some old faces. Maybe one of them would have a clue about the handsome tech support guy he'd gone to lunch with. It seemed unlikely, considering the guy had only shown up once. But several people had seemed to know him. Maybe….

Should he bring the coffee urn? Some people had gotten bitchy about it in the past, until Julie had caved and bought a drip coffeemaker. But Wallace tossed the monstrous thing into the trunk of his car anyway. If nobody thought to bring a coffeemaker, he could dig it out. Better safe than sorry.

He got to the church about ten minutes before the meeting was scheduled, as he'd done in the past. Even though it wasn't the type of event people needed to show up "on time" for—they were welcome to wander in and out as they liked—Wallace had a thing about being late. He walked in the door and at first didn't see anyone in the room.

"Hello?"

"Hey!" someone shouted. Then a man walked out of the tiny kitchenette.

They stopped dead when their eyes met. Then the man with dirty-blond hair and soft emerald eyes smiled and said, "I was hoping you'd show up."

Wallace's mouth was suddenly dry. He swallowed and said, "You're Jayson?"

"That's what my e-mail signature says. Normally I go by Jay."

Jay. That sounded familiar. Wallace kicked himself for not recognizing the name in the e-mail. But really, why would he have expected the person starting up the coffee chats again to be someone who'd only attended once? It didn't make sense.

At last Wallace asked, "Why were you hoping I'd show up?"

Jay's smile faltered. "I don't know. I guess… I thought we kind of connected."

"We only met once." *Did I just say that? Am I a complete moron?*

"I know, but…." Jay looked lost for a moment. Then he gestured toward the snack table, which held just a couple of packages of store-bought cookies. "Well, for one thing, I forgot to bring coffee!"

"Oh," Wallace said, relieved. "I can take care of that."

By the time he'd retrieved the coffee urn from his car, more people had wandered in. He was simultaneously annoyed and relieved—annoyed that Jay was now busy playing host and couldn't continue the conversation they'd begun, but relieved he no longer had to fumble his way through it.

While he was setting up the coffee urn, someone remarked loudly, "Oh God! Not that horrible industrial coffeemaker again!"

He was joking around—Wallace knew that—but it was still embarrassing. Wallace could feel his ears burning as he opened the urn up and poured coffee grounds into the top, pretending he hadn't heard.

Then Jay said, "I wanted him to bring it. I think it brews a nice, mellow roast."

The other guy scoffed at that, but he shut up. When Wallace turned around, he found Jay regarding him with a look of… something almost like affection. Then someone called Jay's name, and whatever it was flitted away as he turned to address the newcomer.

WALLACE HAD a good time at the chat, and he drank far more coffee than a man who had an hour's drive home ahead of him should. He kept moving around the room, dodging whenever Jay drew near, pretending he hadn't seen him approach. It was kind of childish, and he wasn't sure why he was doing it. He needed time to sort things out.

I was hoping you'd show up.

That was kind of creepy, wasn't it? Of course, Wallace had been hoping to bump into Jay here too. But he hadn't come right out and *said* it like some kind of… weird fairy-tale character—a tawny-colored cat with green eyes asking, "Where have you been? You're late!"

On the other hand, it was definitely cool that, while Wallace had been hoping he'd run into Jay, Jay had apparently been hoping he'd run into Wallace. What were the odds of that happening? Wouldn't it be pretty dumb to walk away at this point?

Wallace made up his mind, finally, and the next time Jay zigged, he refrained from zagging. They collided in the kitchenette.

"Hey," Jay said breathlessly, as if he'd been running to catch him, "we haven't had a chance to talk yet."

"No, I guess not."

"Are you getting another cup of coffee?"

Wallace looked down at his half-full plastic cup and grimaced. "That's okay. I think I've had enough."

"I really appreciate you bringing the coffee urn. I don't know what I was thinking, showing up without a coffeemaker. Julie told me people would bring things...."

"Well, I guess they did." The table had been full of cookies and... well, mostly cookies—a lot of cookies—until about a half hour ago.

Jay glanced at the table, but clearly he wasn't all that interested in food. He asked, "So... are you still into all that Viking stuff?"

Wallace debated whether he should be offended by the term *Viking*. The correct term was *Norse*, and even though *Viking* was technically correct in some instances, it seemed as if Jay might be mocking him. But maybe it was just because he didn't know much about it.

"You might say that," Wallace replied. "I've been trying to put together a study group for Old Norse, but there haven't been many takers. Or any, really."

"Really?" Jay said, his green eyes lighting up with excitement. "That would be so cool!"

Wallace blinked at him. "Are you... are you saying you'd be interested?"

"I was pretty good with German in college. Didn't you say it was kind of like that?"

"Well, not so much like the language. But a lot of the vocabulary sounds familiar if you know German—or English, for that matter. If you know both, then it's even better."

"Can I join your group?"

Wallace realized his hand was shaking, so he set his cup down on the table. He wasn't sure why he was so unsteady. Maybe it was shock. "Um... sure."

"When do you want to get together?"

He thought about it, embarrassed by the realization he had nothing whatsoever planned for the immediate future. "Next weekend?"

They haggled over it a minute, settling on one o'clock next Saturday afternoon. Wallace had housemates, which wasn't really a big deal, but they decided to meet at Jay's apartment anyway. Jay jotted his address down on a napkin and handed it to Wallace before turning to go back to the main room.

He took a step and then turned back and looked quizzically at Wallace. "Wait a minute! I've been trying to figure out what's different about you, and I just realized... you don't have glasses anymore."

"No. I got Lasik."

Jay beamed at him. "Nice. Very nice."

Then he turned and walked away. Wallace picked up his coffee cup, saw it had cooled to the point where the cream had coagulated on top, and dumped it into the sink. While he rinsed out the cup, he told himself, *Don't get excited. He's just inviting you over to study. It's not exactly a date.*

But somehow it felt as if it was.

Chapter Six

JAY WASN'T exactly a great housekeeper. In fact, he was a terrible one. The one thing he missed about his ex was the way the guy kept the apartment spotless. Since he'd left, everything had more or less fallen apart. The cat litter box wasn't changed as often—to the cats' obvious annoyance—dirty dishes piled up in the sink, hairballs gathered in the corners, and stacks of books and DVDs had mysteriously appeared in every room.

The apartment itself was different. Jay had been forced to vacate the previous apartment when the landlord wanted to convert the old place into an insanely expensive condo. There hadn't been much available, at the time, so he'd moved into a smaller place and gotten rid of most of the old furniture. Not that he really minded. But his furnishings had been reduced to just a few things and piles of boxes he didn't know what to do with.

He wasn't sure why he'd invited Wallace to his apartment rather than go to Wallace's house. Maybe he was hoping, somewhere in the back of his mind, they'd fool around a bit if there were no housemates around. Jay tried not to think about that. It seemed a bit sleazy. Instead he focused on scouring the place.

By the time Wallace showed up, the apartment was reasonably clean. Jay had cleaned the cat box—though Butterscotch had already seen fit to… christen it again—and he'd done the dishes. A quick sweep had taken care of most of the hairballs, but the stacks of books and DVDs would have to fend for themselves.

Wallace didn't comment one way or another on the décor, and Jay figured that was probably for the best. Hopefully it was clean enough that Wallace wouldn't feel he needed a shower by the time he left.

Oh fuck! I hope he doesn't look in the shower. Jay couldn't remember the last time he'd cleaned the tub.

"Would you like a cup of coffee or juice or something?" he asked.

"Sure, that would be great. Coffee, I mean."

Jay already had the coffeemaker set up. He flicked the switch on. While it brewed, he fished for a topic of conversation. "So how exactly does one go about studying Old Norse? There isn't a textbook for it, is there?"

Wallace lifted a hand as if to push his glasses back on the bridge of his nose—except he wasn't wearing glasses. He stopped, glanced at his hand a moment, then lowered it. "Actually, there's an online course."

"Seriously?"

"Yes. I've printed out the first few lessons."

He held up a notebook, and Jay could see a bunch of papers sticking out of it.

"Oh. Cool."

JAY DIDN'T have a table. He had a couch, some counter space, and some chairs, and he had his bed—a futon on the floor in his bedroom.

"Would it bother you if we sat on my bed?" he asked nervously. "I'm not trying to make a pass at you. It's just the only place we'll have room to spread out."

Wallace gave him a curious look he couldn't quite sort out, then said, "Sure. No problem."

They sat on the futon, the papers spread out between them and their coffee cups resting on the hardwood floor, while Wallace led Jay through the first lesson. He'd already been through the entire course, but he showed no impatience with Jay as they went back to the basics of pronunciation and simple declarative sentences.

For Jay's part, he found the lesson fairly easy, as Wallace had predicted. Though one of the simple dialogues puzzled him. "Never… give… a dwarf—"

"Dwarves," Wallace corrected. "It's plural."

"Dwarves…." The last word he had to look up again in the vocabulary list. "Um… cheese? Never give dwarves… cheese?"

"One can only assume," Wallace said gravely, "that dwarves are lactose intolerant."

"I see. Yes, I imagine that would be pretty bad."

Then they both snickered and started riffing on the idea of dwarves having intestinal distress while they worked their forges deep in the… bowels… of the earth. It was very juvenile, but Jay loved the fact that Wallace shared his sense of humor, even when it was silly.

When Jay finished the first lesson, he was stoked enough about it to move on to the second one. He'd always found Vikings—or more properly, the Norse peoples—to be interesting, and now Wallace made them even more so. He kept dropping little tidbits of information, ranging from the way Norse toilets were constructed to the way women were treated in their culture to the war between the Aesir and the Vanir, two rival factions of gods in Norse mythology.

What worried Jay was the possibility that they might have nothing *else* to talk about. He'd had friends like that in college, who could go on at great length about role-playing games and LARPing but never wanted to talk about anything else. Was Wallace only interested in Norse stuff? But when they wrapped up the second lesson, the conversation didn't falter. Wallace seemed more comfortable now, and they stretched out beside each other on the futon and chatted about all kinds of things—their jobs, what they'd studied in college, how Wallace had pooled his resources with some friends to buy a house in Derry, Jay's interest in painting and writing....

"Do you have any of your artwork?" Wallace asked.

"My paintings from college are packed in storage, but I have some of my sketchbooks handy."

It made him nervous to show the sketchbooks to anyone. Doug had never been at all interested in Jay's artwork, and Jay had eventually tucked it away in a drawer. Now he drew out his old sketchpad and flipped it open. The first sketch was of a nude man lying on the grass near a stream.

"Oh my God," Wallace said in a reverent whisper. "You *drew* that?"

"A long time ago."

Encouraged, Jay flipped to the next picture—another sketch of the same young man, standing this time, still nude except for a cloth draped over one shoulder. "This was a model in one of my art classes. I thought he was gorgeous."

"This is amazing! You should have been an illustrator or a comic artist or something." Then, as if he realized what he'd said could be misconstrued as criticism, he flushed and said, "I mean... you're really good."

Jay couldn't stand it anymore. Wallace was sweet on so many levels and adorable to top it off. He set the sketchbook aside and then tentatively leaned forward, bringing their faces close together, testing the waters.

Wallace looked back at him, his mouth slightly parted, as if those sensual lips were inviting him to kiss them. Then he reached up to brush his temple, causing Jay to pull back.

WALLACE LAUGHED and glanced at his hand. "Sorry. I was trying to take my glasses off." He'd been so nervous, he'd forgotten again. All morning he'd tried to force his thoughts away from anything happening between them. An invitation to study at Jay's apartment was far from an invitation into Jay's bed. But now they were on Jay's bed—surrounded by the lessons Wallace had printed out, true, but it looked as if Jay was making a pass at him.

He looked back into Jay's eyes and wet his lips. It was an unconscious gesture, but Jay gave a soft laugh and something like a growl. He leaned forward again. When their lips met, Wallace couldn't help himself—he whimpered. Then he reached up to grip Jay firmly by the shoulders and fell back onto the mattress, pulling Jay down on top of him.

Am I being too… slutty? In the past he'd had men get turned off by him being too eager. He'd been told he should be less willing, make it more of a challenge so guys wouldn't think he was easy.

Jay didn't seem to have a problem with the clear invitation. He stretched the full length of his body out on top of Wallace's and devoured his lips. Wallace grew hard and felt Jay's erection grinding into his through the material of their jeans.

Jay pulled away from the kiss to gather up the papers and stuff on the futon and set them on the floor. Then he pulled off his shirt. He had an average build. His musculature was defined, though it would be a stretch to call him "buff." Wallace reached up to caress his taut abdomen.

"I'm a little thin," Jay said, as if apologizing.

"You're gorgeous."

Wallace pulled him down again, and they stopped talking about stuff that didn't matter.

Part Two

Chapter Seven

JAY WAS the kind of guy who made instant decisions. The first time Wallace stood with him in a checkout line, he was utterly horrified by the way Jay kept grabbing things off the shelves and tossing them into the cart—candy bars, DVDs, magazines, cigarette lighters….

"You do not need a robot keychain!" he finally exclaimed, snatching the item out of Jay's hand. He put it back on the display.

"But it has glowing eyes!"

It didn't matter. Jay had forgotten about it ten seconds later. He was, in Wallace's estimation, the quintessential impulse buyer. Anything within easy reach might catch his eye and end up in the cart. When supermarkets planned their checkout lanes, Wallace was certain they distributed photographs of Jay and told their employees, "Listen up! This is our target! Put everything at his eye level and make it *shiny*. Understood? Now move out!"

Which is why, when Jay suggested moving in together, Wallace wasn't sure just how seriously to take it. They'd been seeing each other for the better part of a year now. And they were seeing each other a *lot*. The general pattern was Wallace would show up at Jay's apartment on Friday night, after they were both off work. He'd stay all weekend and drive to work from there on Monday morning. Three nights together, four nights apart. And lately they'd begun calling each other during their evenings apart.

So it wasn't that the idea of being with Jay full time bothered him, necessarily. But Wallace was cautious. He liked to think things through carefully before making a decision. And he wasn't convinced yet this wasn't just an impulse on Jay's part and he'd change his mind later.

There were also some practical concerns. Wallace was co-owner of a house. He liked his house, and he wasn't sure he wanted to give it up—certainly not for a tiny apartment an hour's drive away from where he worked. At the same time, Jay couldn't just move into the house. He had three cats, and one of Wallace's housemates was allergic to cats.

And then there was the nudity. Apparently Jay really liked being naked. He'd been to some nude beaches in Vermont with guys from one of the gay men's groups he went to and really enjoyed the experience. When he'd met his ex-boyfriend, Doug kind of put a damper on that. He thought it was weird if Jay even walked around the apartment naked. But now that Jay was living on his own, he was prone to shuck his clothes the moment he came home from work. Wallace loved watching him putter around the apartment in the nude, but... would Wallace's housemates? Probably not.

So that's where things stood for a while. Three days on and four days off. Rinse and repeat. But it wasn't a bad way to run their relationship. They never grew tired of each other's company, and they always looked forward to seeing each other on the weekends.

Then, in December 2003, the Supreme Judicial Court in Massachusetts ruled the state's ban on same-sex marriage was unconstitutional.

THE SJC ruling wasn't the final word—not right away. Things got bounced around between the court and the legislature for several months, while people with no stake in the matter whatsoever gnashed their teeth and wailed about how it would *destroy their lives*. The state of Massachusetts finally began issuing marriage licenses to same-sex couples on May 17, 2004.

This was on a Monday, so Jay and Wallace were at work and might have missed it. They didn't watch television and only checked the news on the Internet occasionally. But that evening they found it plastered all over Facebook. Several of their friends lived in Massachusetts—that, and of course the entirety of western civilization was now collapsing into dust.

But what Jay thought of as cause for celebration appeared to put Wallace in a pensive mood. "What's the matter?" Jay asked.

Wallace shrugged. "I always thought it was impossible. Gay men—and women, of course—would never be allowed to marry."

"So? Isn't it good that things are changing?"

"I guess so."

That wasn't all of it, and Jay now knew his boyfriend well enough to know that. "And...?"

Wallace looked decidedly uncomfortable. "Well…. I just…. It wasn't anything I ever had to worry about."

"Worry about?"

Wallace sighed. "I don't mean I wouldn't want to marry you, but… it's a big decision. Big decisions stress me out."

Jay tended not to stress about things like this. He could imagine being married to Wallace, and the thought made him feel kind of warm and fuzzy inside. But he wouldn't object to just living together for a while, if that would make Wallace more comfortable. He was also good with the arrangement they had for a bit longer.

"I know," he told Wallace diplomatically. "And that's fine. Just because it's becoming *possible* for us to marry doesn't mean you and I specifically *have* to do it."

"It's not that I don't want to…."

Jay kissed him to shut him up. Wallace could work himself up over things like this, and it really wasn't necessary. They'd only been together a few years. It wasn't as if one of them was pregnant and their parents were gnashing their teeth about a grandchild being born out of wedlock. Their religion didn't forbid having sex outside of marriage. There was no reason to rush things.

Chapter Eight

THINGS GOT ugly on the same-sex marriage front during the next few years. Jay and Wallace followed the news and attended the wedding of two friends down in Massachusetts. When the New Hampshire legislature began to fight over the issue, they became more actively involved in the Freedom to Marry campaign. Even though they still lived apart, they reliably spent their weekends together and attended gatherings as a couple—including company picnics.

Everyone in their lives knew they were a couple. Wallace's conservative father had been a challenge. When they visited on the holidays, he was... civil... and he could paste on a smile, though he rarely looked Jay directly in the eye.

Fortunately Wallace's brother was cool. "Take good care of him" was all he said to Jay.

Jay's mother practically cooed over Wallace. "I've resigned myself to never having grandchildren," she said wistfully, "but I'm so glad Jay's found someone who makes him happy." Then she added, "You aren't thinking of adopting, are you?"

Wallace blanched a little. They hadn't even discussed marriage or moving in together since he'd mentioned it years ago. Jay saw his expression and deftly distracted his mother with a question about her baby doll collection.

From his stuffed chair in the living room, Jay's stepfather gave Wallace a commiserating smile.

IN 2008 the New Hampshire legislature voted to create civil unions for same-sex couples. This was the result of three years of squabbling and a general election in 2006, which allowed Democratic legislators to gain the upper hand. But the "separate but equal" status conferred by a civil union was still unpalatable to much of the LGBTQ community in the state, so the fight continued until, in May of 2009, a same-sex marriage bill passed in the legislature by a thin majority.

The governor had five days to decide if he would veto the bill, and he expressed publicly his desire to do so.

To come this close, only to be defeated by the governor—a governor Jay and Wallace had *voted* for, no less—was maddening. They joined a letter-writing campaign to convince the governor this legislation was important to a large number of residents, both gay and straight. Jay wrote passionately of his love for Wallace and his desire to spend the rest of his life with him, even though they still hadn't discussed taking that step. Wallace wrote less passionately but perhaps more logically, about equality benefiting all members of society.

On June 3 the governor signed the bill, announcing his position had been swayed by the many letters he'd received that convinced him this was an issue the people of the state felt strongly about.

Jay called Wallace from his desk at work and told him about the breaking news. It was Wednesday, so they wouldn't be seeing each other for a couple more days.

"Yes," Wallace said, sounding reserved—more reserved than usual, that was. "I saw it go by online."

"We won!"

"Yeah… we did." There was a long pause. Then Wallace said, "I'll see you on Friday."

Jay was puzzled at his behavior, but he knew Wallace could be moody, so he let it go. He stood up to stretch, and George, the coworker in the cubicle beside him, said, "Yeah, GLAAD really came through for you guys."

"GLAAD?" Jay asked, confused. "GLAAD wasn't really involved in this."

George scoffed. "Every time an issue like this comes up, GLAAD swoops in and pumps millions into the state to sway things in you guys' favor. Not that I'm against gays getting married…." His tone didn't indicate he was particularly in favor of it either.

From what Jay had heard, there were some particularly hateful nationwide organizations who were currently under investigation for doing just that, in order to make sure same-sex marriage did *not* pass. But he didn't have direct proof of that, so he decided to avoid the whole argument.

"There was a poll recently. It indicated about seventy percent of the people in the state were in favor of marriage equality."

"Yeah... a poll conducted by college students." He was clearly contemptuous of that. "Look, the governor was dead set against it. Then suddenly he's in favor of it. How else do you explain that?"

"He said it was because people all over the state e-mailed him. I was *one* of them. So was my boyfriend."

"Sure. A couple hundred people wrote letters. Then somebody handed him a nice fat check for his reelection campaign."

Jay knew HR probably had some silly rule against punching a coworker, so he opted to go to the break room and get a fresh cup of coffee instead. The conspiracy theory didn't make much sense. George seemed to be implying the majority of people in the state were against same-sex marriage and the governor had just defied them. If that were true, was GLAAD also promising to buy off all these so-called disenfranchised voters, come the next gubernatorial election?

Jay brewed a cup of Breakfast Blend and inhaled the mellow aroma. It soothed him and allowed him to come back to reality from his brief, unpleasant visit to the Land of Conspiracy Theories. They'd won. And people in New Hampshire might be slightly on the conservative side, but they were also long-term believers in staying out of other people's business. "I don't care what they do, as long as they don't scare the chickens," as his grandmother used to put it. Apart from the occasional debate with guys like George, he and Wallace had never been bothered by anyone.

The law wouldn't go into effect until next January, but as he spooned sugar and creamer into his cup, Jay felt good.

Really good.

Chapter Nine

WALLACE HAD never been so nervous in his life. He'd dressed in his best clothes—not that anybody but him could tell. His best clothes were just slightly less shabby than his regular clothes. He wasn't someone who spent a lot of time worrying about things like that. As long as they didn't have gaping holes in inappropriate places, he figured they were fine.

But when Jay opened the door, his smile was immediately replaced by a slightly puzzled expression. "Hey, sweetie. How was your day?"

He always said that, whenever Wallace arrived at his apartment on Friday evening, as if they'd just been apart since that morning instead of Monday morning. Where the term "sweetie" had come from, Wallace had no idea. He'd hated it at first—he was so not a "sweetie"—but by now he looked forward to hearing the endearment every Friday.

"Good." He came inside, closed the door behind him, and kissed Jay. "How about you?"

Jay went to sit on the couch, still watching him warily. "Fine. Is something going on? You look unusually well dressed tonight."

Dammit.

Only Jay would have noticed. But then that was what all this was about, wasn't it? Only Jay.

There was no point in putting it off. If he did, he might chicken out. Wallace walked over to the couch, but instead of sitting down beside Jay, he kneeled in front of him.

Jay's eyes went wide. "Oh my God! You're not!"

"This is the way it's supposed to be done, isn't it?" Wallace asked stiffly. "I'm sorry if I'm a little old-fashioned."

"Sorry. You're right. Go ahead."

Wallace cleared his throat, suddenly panicking about not bringing a ring. But Jay hated rings. Didn't he? He'd always said he did. Well, it was too late now.

Wallace took Jay's hand in his and said in a shaky voice, "The last ten years with you have been the happiest of my life. I… I want us to be together for the rest of our lives." He realized he was staring at their hands, and that probably wasn't right. So he took a deep breath and forced himself to look up into Jay's soft emerald eyes, which seemed slightly misty now, as if Jay were on the edge of tears. "Jayson Corey... will you marry me?"

Jay grabbed him by both shoulders and yanked him up so he could latch onto Wallace's mouth in a passionate kiss. Then he leaned back, pulling Wallace down on top of him. By the time the kiss was finished, pants had been undone and they'd both rubbed each other to a quick and somewhat messy climax in their underwear.

Wallace groaned and fell down between Jay and the back of the couch, breathing heavily. "You... didn't say... anything...."

Jay chuckled and kissed him tenderly on the forehead. "Yes. Of course, yes!" He paused for a breath. "Did you seriously think it wouldn't be?"

"You always... had the option."

"Don't be ridiculous." Jay smiled and pulled him closer, if such a thing was possible, considering how they were wedged into the couch. "I adore you. And I am more comfortable with you than I have ever been with anyone else. I can't imagine spending my life with anyone but you. So, yes. It's always been yes, since the moment I met you. It just took a while to realize that."

Wallace thought for a long time, then sighed. "You say it better than I could."

"You inspire me."

Chapter Ten

BOTH JAY and Wallace agreed that marrying would present a logistical problem, if they couldn't first straighten out their living arrangement. They had six months before marriage would be legal, anyway. They might as well work on sorting out how they could live together.

Jay's apartment was definitely out. It was too small for Jay, never mind two people. They both liked Wallace's house, though it was a bit close to the road for Jay's tastes. He'd always fantasized about living out in the country, far enough off the beaten path he could walk out of his front door naked without any neighbors taking notice. Even if they wanted to live in that house, there was the slight problem of Wallace's housemates. One was allergic to Jay's cats—that hadn't changed—and Jay had no intention of surrendering his pets. Wallace would have to buy both his housemates out if he wanted to take ownership of the house.

The question was, did he want that? After numerous discussions with Jay and his housemates, he ultimately decided the answer was no. He and Jay needed to find their own place, someplace that was perfect for the two of them.

Fortunately Adrastia had a friend in New Hampshire who worked in real estate.

"DAMMIT!" ROWAN muttered, trying the lock on the side door. The key didn't fit that one any better than it had the locks on the front and back doors. "This is the only key they gave me!"

Jay looked up at the old Victorian, loving the sheer size of it and the old-fashioned design, but the yard was less appealing. It was two acres, so that part was good. It was also on a small dirt road in the country, so there weren't likely to be many cars. But the front door of the house was *right* on the road—no more than twenty feet away from it—and there was a house directly across the road and another just a short distance away on the other side of the property. If he looked out one of the upstairs windows, he'd be looking into the neighbor's windows.

"I'm not sure it's worth bothering with," he said.

Wallace frowned but said nothing. They'd looked at a number of houses over the past few months. This one and an old farmhouse in Barrington had been the best they'd come across. Unfortunately, though the Barrington house had a fantastic three-story barn, big enough to drive a combine harvester into—if they ever felt the need to own such a thing—it had been so out of the way it would have added a half hour to each of their work commutes.

"I'm not giving up," Rowan said. She stepped back and glared at the house, her hands on her hips as if she were about to scold it. "You two stay here. I'm going to crack this baby if it's the last thing I do!"

With that she stormed off around to the back.

Wallace watched her go, then said, "I'm picturing her whipping out a glass cutter and a suction cup."

"Maybe. Or belaying down through a skylight."

How she did it, they would never know, but a moment later she was waving at them through the window on the door. She opened it to admit them. "Nobody stops *this* real estate agent from showing a house!"

"Have you considered becoming an international jewel thief?"

"I thought about it, but I didn't like the hours."

Unfortunately for Jay, the house was gorgeous inside. The living room was cavernous, with a stone fireplace at one end and sliding glass doors at the other, opening onto a deck. The upstairs bedrooms were quirky. The main bedroom was above the living room and pretty large, but the others were at odd angles and not completely rectangular. While this might have been off-putting, Wallace thought it was quaint, and Jay didn't mind them. The upstairs bathroom was a typical bathroom... except the owners had renovated one end of it into a Romanesque bath big enough to fit about ten people, if they all wanted to shower together. One entire side of it was a glass-block window that was impossible to see through, though it admitted light from the main bedroom on the other side. It was impossible to look at the bath and not think "orgy."

But the most awesome feature was the kitchen. It was enormous, and it had an oversized industrial refrigerator and stainless steel sinks, plus a huge gas stove in the center. Had the house been used as a restaurant? Or was the current owner a chef? Rowan had no idea. But it was a beautiful kitchen, and now Jay was torn. He liked the inside of the house but not the yard. He might just have to accept the fact that, without going someplace way off the beaten path—and therefore far away from hospitals, stores, gas stations, and everything else they might need in an emergency—it wasn't going to be possible to get away from neighbors.

ROWAN KEPT sending them listings to consider. They hadn't definitely said no to the Victorian, and she was trying to arrange for them to get another look at it soon so they could make up their minds. But Wallace and Jay were checking out the listings themselves. Not actually going inside—for that they needed to arrange a visit through Rowan—but driving by and looking at houses from the outside.

That was how they stumbled across the property in Rockford.

It was a beautiful house, two stories with a wraparound porch and back deck, a finished basement, fireplace, and a hot tub. It was also situated smack in the middle of eight acres of land, mostly forest. They could see the house from the road if they parked at the end of the 150-foot driveway, but there were no neighbors to be seen without driving farther down the road. It was late October, so the house was overlooked by two tall trees in the front yard blazing in oranges and yellows.

Jay sighed. "I think I just came in my pants."

"Down, boy."

But they called Rowan that evening to arrange for a showing.

Chapter Eleven

ROWAN MET them on the front porch of the house a week later. It was November now, and the leaves had mostly fallen, but Jay loved this time of year. The air was crisp and had an earthy smell, tinged with the scent of woodsmoke. They walked around the porch for a minute, taking in the view from all angles. Not a single house to be seen—just forest on three sides and a country road in front, mostly obscured by trees.

"I love it!" Jay said.

Rowan held the key up. "Why don't we take a look inside?"

The first thing that greeted them when they entered the house was... God. Not the actual deity of course, but there were two cabinets full of angel figurines—hundreds of them—on either side of the door, and one round window had a stained-glass angel in it. Jay stepped forward and glanced up the stairs to discover a large cross mounted on the second-floor wall.

"Wow," Rowan said quietly, standing beside him and following his gaze.

"I'm all for freedom of religious expression," Wallace muttered, "but this is a bit much."

Rowan stepped into the next room, where a pellet stove was burning. "It's okay. There's a fire extinguisher in here, if anyone starts to catch on fire."

Jay laughed. He wouldn't have thought much about a few angel knickknacks here and there. His sister-in-law collected figurines of pigs. There was no reason someone couldn't collect angels. It was just that... there were so *many* of them. As they wandered through the rooms, they discovered more on a shelf in the living room and peering down from shelves in the kitchen. What did it say about the current owners? Jay's stepfather was a religious man. He was a Baptist minister. And certainly the house he shared with Jay's mother had Bibles and crosses and paintings of Jesus. But they were casual touches, here and there. The house they were looking at was either owned by people with bad decorating tastes or people who were really intense about their religion, and the latter possibility worried him. Would they be cool with a gay couple buying their home?

He told himself there was no point in jumping to conclusions. The owners might be very cool people who just happened to love angels. There was nothing wrong with that.

The house was beautiful, with hardwood floors and soft amber-colored pine paneling on the walls. None of the rooms were as large as the rooms they'd seen in the Victorian, but there was a fireplace and a large kitchen and a hot tub on a small side deck. Jay felt very much at home there, but he kept watching Wallace to gauge his reaction, and it was frankly hard to tell.

Later, as the three of them grabbed a late lunch at Pizza by George's downtown, Jay came out and asked him, "Well?"

"Well, what?"

"Did you like the house?"

Wallace took a bite of his pizza and chewed it thoughtfully. He swallowed before replying, "I could see us living there. Maybe converting one of the upstairs bedrooms into a library—"

"Absolutely!" There were three small bedrooms upstairs, in addition to the master bedroom. One would be good for a guest room, but they really didn't need three.

Jay had recently rediscovered the love he'd had of writing when he was young. As a teenager he'd locked himself in his bedroom after school and typed until dinner on the electric typewriter he'd demanded for one of his birthdays. He had piles of bad short stories from that time period. But he'd lost that creative impulse. At least, he'd thought he had. Now, under Wallace's encouragement, he'd begun writing again, and his first novella had already been accepted by an independent press! He pictured a shelf in the library full of his published novels....

Wallace interrupted his thoughts. "I don't know, though. I still like the Victorian."

"I like the Victorian too," Jay said. "It's just... the yard is so... well, not small, exactly. Just... open. What if the neighbors are jerks and we have to keep making sure the curtains are closed in case we walk past one naked?"

"In case *you* walk past one naked," Wallace pointed out. "Some of us like clothing."

"In the house? What are you? A communist?"

"What are *you*? A nudist?"

"Freak!"

"Barbarian!"

Rowan watched this mock battle for a bit, her expression amused as Jay and Wallace attempted to come up with more and more ridiculous insults. At about the time Jay called Wallace a "reincarnated Victorian with attachment issues," she stepped in.

"I don't know how much longer that Victorian will be on the market. The owner is desperate. He's agreed to undersell."

Jay knew the owner of the house they'd just looked at wanted too much. He'd originally listed it for a hundred thousand more than it was valued at, and even when he'd finally been talked down by his Realtor, he still wanted a bit more than market value. But Jay wasn't good at money matters, as Wallace well knew. He acted on instinct. And his instinct told him this was the house he'd be happy in.

The question was, would it be the house they would *both* be happy in? He didn't want to force Wallace to live somewhere he'd be unhappy. Jay would compromise if it came to that. He looked into Wallace's eyes, trying to discern whether his lover really *wanted* the Victorian or just preferred it.

Wallace smiled back at him, but all he said was, "I don't want to be rushed. Let's set up another look at this place in a week or two, if we can."

WALLACE DID like the house in Rockford. But he'd done some research. The town tended to vote conservative. Its state representatives were all Republican, and so were the local elected officials. Granted, conservatives—and liberals, for that matter—in a town the size of Rockford were still friendly to everyone at the supermarket. Politics didn't dominate people's lives there. Liberals and conservatives didn't break out in screaming fights on Main Street. If one person mentioned same-sex marriage to someone else who didn't support it, the other might say, "I'm not really a supporter." That was generally it. He wasn't likely to flip out.

But Wallace hadn't forgotten how ugly the fight had been to get his relationship with Jay acknowledged as legitimate by his state. Even now a small group in the legislature was proposing amendments to get the law changed before it took effect.

Jay and Rowan also hadn't seemed aware of the sounds of gunfire coming from the forest behind the house. Why should they have been? It was hunting season. And probably the majority of people in New Hampshire owned guns. Even Wallace had been given a rifle by his father when he was a teenager. He'd learned to shoot, and he still had it—though it was in storage now. But what if one of the neighbors had an issue with a gay couple moving into the neighborhood? Just how safe would he and Jay be?

They were able to get into the house again a week later.

Rowan let them in with the key, and Wallace was immediately struck by two things. The first was an overpowering scent of pine and... maybe cinnamon apple? The second was Nat King Cole singing "Away in a Manger." Apparently Christmas had exploded all over the house since their last visit.

"Oh my God!" Jay exclaimed, laughing. "It isn't even Thanksgiving yet."

There were no less than three fake Christmas trees in the living room, two in the corners and one tiny one on the coffee table, and the widescreen TV over the fireplace mantel was playing videos of snowy landscapes on a loop. Apparently that was where the Christmas carols were coming from. Rowan found the remote for the television and turned down the volume.

Thank the gods.

Wallace hated Christmas. It wasn't because he was pagan, and it wasn't due to some past trauma caused by writing a hundred letters to Santa Claus when he was a boy and still not getting the toy he wanted. He simply found the holiday excessive, and he didn't enjoy having it shoved down his throat wherever he went from October to January.

However, he also knew Jay *loved* Christmas. He was darting about the rooms, taking in all the gaudy excessiveness—the strings of colored lights, the cartoon pictures of Santa's sleigh and eight reindeer on one wall, the silver and gold garlands hung around the edge of the ceiling.

"Aren't these going to catch on fire?" he asked when they went into the room with the pellet stove.

Wallace and Rowan followed and saw he was talking about stuffed covers on the chairs around the dining table. They resembled elves, and the two nearest the pellet stove were a bit closer to the glass than they should have been.

Rowan opened her mouth to say something, but what Wallace heard instead was a tiny *Yip!* Rowan closed her mouth, startled. They all turned to see a poodle watching them through the glass panes of the kitchen door. She was frantically wagging her tail and panting—perhaps because she was friendly, but it might also have been because the poor girl was wearing a sweater with a tiny Christmas tree and flashing red and green LEDs on the back.

Rowan found the note taped to the door. "The dog is friendly, but please keep her in the kitchen."

"Oh," Jay cooed, opening the door so he could slip inside and pet the little dog. "Did Mommy make you wear embarrassing clothes for the guests?"

The dog didn't appear to be too traumatized by her outfit. She danced excitedly when Wallace and Rowan joined Jay in the kitchen. Each took turns petting her, but they obeyed the note and didn't let her out of the room.

"Don't get too attached to her," Rowan warned. "She doesn't come with the house."

"That's okay."

"Oh, that's right! I forgot. You're more of a cat person."

Jay laughed. "Not really. The cats were my ex's, but he refused to take them when he moved out."

"So… you *don't* like cats?"

"I like my cats," Jay replied, scratching the poodle under her chin. She seemed to have taken to him. "I love the cats I have, and I'll keep caring for them for the rest of their lives. But I'd really like a big Labrador or German shepherd." Then he added to the poodle, "No offense, sweetie."

They'd discussed this a few times. Wallace had grown up with big dogs, and Jay's family had owned a German shepherd when he was a boy. They both liked dogs with *presence*.

Despite the excessive Christmas kitsch, which Wallace knew was simply the owner trying to make the place seem "homey," even if it was somewhat miscalculated, he was developing a fondness for the house. Maybe the overblown décor had influenced him after all, because the place felt… cozy to him. The Victorian was more spacious, but it was completely empty of furnishings, since the owner now lived in another state. It was hard to imagine feeling at home there. But here he could picture Jay in front of the living room fireplace.

Naked.

THEY MUST have stayed a bit longer than the owner had expected, because she pulled in just as they were about to lock up. She had platinum hair, which Jay assumed was treated. He'd seen that color in old movies from the fifties but never in real life.

She smiled broadly at them. "I'm sorry! I can leave for a bit longer, if you'd like more time."

"That's fine," Rowan told her. "We were just on our way out."

The woman extended her hand to Jay. "I'm Theresa Grant. Nice to meet you!"

"Nice to meet you. I'm Jay."

"Are you the one house-hunting?"

"We both are," Jay said. He gestured to Wallace. "This is my partner, Wallace."

He wasn't sure, but he thought the smile faltered for just a moment before she extended her hand to Wallace. "Good to meet you, Wallace."

To be fair, openly gay couples were still a rarity in New Hampshire. Even if she were fine with their relationship, she might be taken by surprise for just a moment. Jay assured himself there was nothing to worry about. This was the twenty-first century. Nobody was going to refuse to sell their house to a gay couple. After all, Mrs. Grant and her husband were moving out. Why would it matter who moved in after they left?

But a week later, after Wallace made an offer on the house through Rowan, based upon the loan amount the bank had preapproved—plus a bit more out of their own savings—Mr. Grant turned the offer down.

Chapter Twelve

"WE DON'T know it was because his wife found out you were gay," Rowan said, though she didn't sound particularly convinced. "I suppose it's possible. We try to keep the buyer and the seller separated until the day of closing so that sort of thing won't happen...."

"Bastard," Jay muttered.

Rowan shrugged. "Maybe he's just being a dick about the price. It might not have anything to do with you being gay."

They'd offered twenty thousand less than Grant's asking price, which was still ten thousand more than market value. He was simply asking too much for a house in that area.

The three of them were seated in a booth at the Chinese restaurant at the end of First Street, a couple of blocks away from Jay's apartment. Wallace had been quiet since Rowan dropped the bomb about Grant refusing their offer. His face seemed calm, but Jay knew him well enough by now to know he was quietly seething.

Wallace set his chopsticks down on the edge of his plate and said, "Offer him another ten thousand."

"That's still 10K less than what he wants," Rowan said, her expression dubious.

"I know. He's not getting that last ten thousand. Not from us."

"The Victorian is still available."

Jay and Wallace exchanged a silent look. Something had changed since the last time they'd looked at the house in Rockford. It was hard to put a finger on why, but they'd both lost interest in the Victorian. The yard wasn't what Jay wanted, and... it just didn't *feel* right—not to either of them.

But they could only go so high on the offer for this house. The bank wasn't willing to approve more than two hundred fifty thousand. Anything more than that had to come out of the money Wallace had received from his housemates when they bought him out. He wasn't willing to bankrupt himself over it, and Jay didn't want him to.

"I think we're going to pass on the Victorian," Wallace said.

"All right," Rowan said. "I'll make the offer."

THE SECOND offer was turned down—rudely.

Rowan called Wallace on the phone to give him the news. "According to his agent," she added, "what he said was, 'If they want it, they can pay full price.'"

"What the hell is *that* supposed to mean?"

"I have no idea. Maybe he's just stubborn about the price he wants. Or maybe…. I don't know. Maybe he does have an issue with you."

It frustrated Wallace that he couldn't tell if this was a case of discrimination or just general douchebaggery. Not knowing made it difficult to determine the correct response. But one thing was clear. He didn't feel comfortable throwing more money at the house. They'd need a financial buffer to handle moving expenses and unexpected repairs, not to mention closing costs.

"Fine," he told her. "We'll start looking at other listings."

CHRISTMAS CAME and went. Thanks to Wallace's dislike of the holiday, it was somewhat subdued, though he made no attempt to prevent Jay from putting up a tree and decorating in his own apartment. He also took his turn slicing vegetables for the Christmas dinner Jay put on for the two of them and a few friends who didn't have family nearby. Jay respected his dislike of Christmas presents, so he didn't buy Wallace anything. But Wallace had long ago learned that not getting Jay a present was a poor life choice. The first Christmas they'd spent together, Jay didn't say anything when there was nothing under the tree for him on Christmas morning, but Wallace caught him a couple of times glancing wistfully at the base of the tree. Those looks made him want to curl up and die.

So the next Christmas, Wallace had bought Jay a home cappuccino maker. Jay was ecstatic. And from that time on, there was always one big present for Jay under the tree on Christmas morning—something to show him Wallace loved *him*, if not the holiday. This year it was an iPad.

There had been some new listings over the holidays, and they'd trudged out through the snow with Rowan to look them over. But nothing had excited them. One house looked quaint, but both Jay and Rowan had been forced to step outside because the smell of mold was so overpowering. Another house was perfect—for a horror movie. Perhaps when it had been new, a hundred years ago, it had been a great sprawling farmhouse for a big family. Now the rooms felt dark and ominous. And the basement was a rat maze of brick passageways and low ceilings.

"I keep expecting to find a sealed door with ancient, evil symbols painted on it," Jay whispered. The three of them were alone, so there was no reason to whisper, but part of him was afraid the house might overhear him and get angry.

"Has anyone heard voices saying 'Get out!' yet?" Wallace asked.

"Not yet," Rowan said, "but if you guys have seen enough, I'm all for leaving before that happens."

There had also been a beautiful colonial home for sale, with enormous rooms big enough to host a ball and an attached carriage house and stable. Jay swooned over it, and the price wasn't bad, but unfortunately it was in bad shape and would have required much more than they could afford to make it livable. It would also never have passed the bank inspection needed to get a housing loan.

Same-sex marriage became legal in New Hampshire on January 1. That didn't mean Wallace and Jay immediately ran out and got married, however. They both wanted it to be special—something with a bit of spectacle that everyone who attended would remember for the rest of their lives. They didn't want to rush it, though the attempt by a group of Republican legislators to repeal the law made them nervous. The attempt was voted down by the New Hampshire House in mid-February, but it reminded them they couldn't put it off for long. If a repeal did succeed at some point, they might still be considered married if it was a done deal. If not, they'd at least have standing if they took it to court.

Then, in late February, Rowan called Wallace again, brimming over with excitement. "He wants to sell!"

"Who?"

"Grant. The… nice man with the house you wanted."

Wallace and Jay were in the Barnes & Noble café. They hadn't been talking—just reading together and drinking coffee in a companionable silence.

He caught Jay's eye as he said, "The owner of the house in Rockford wants to sell us the house."

Jay's eyes went wide.

"Yes," Rowan said. "For the amount you last offered. Are you still interested?"

The way Jay was grinning now pretty much answered that question for Wallace, but he asked suspiciously, "Why? What changed his mind?"

"Christmas."

"He was visited by three ghosts who told him to stop being a dick?"

"I wish. No. They already bought another house down in Georgia. The cost of maintaining two houses, plus all the added expense of the holiday, convinced him he needed to unload the place. You two were his best option."

"I'm tempted to bargain him down to the original offer," Wallace said uncharitably.

"I wouldn't recommend that," Rowan said. "His real estate agent told me she had to agree to a lower commission to make up the amount he feels he's losing."

"Nice."

But he and Jay still wanted the house, so there was no point in dragging it out. He gave her permission to make the deal. Then he took Jay out to dinner to celebrate.

THE DEAL didn't go through smoothly. The banks gave them trouble in the final phases, delaying the transfer of funds for no reason at all, until they missed their closing date. Then there was a mad scramble to get both banks to agree to accept closing on the next business day and get the funds transferred in time. Judging by Wallace's experience buying the house in Derry with his friends and the horror stories he'd heard from coworkers, this wasn't all that unusual. For some reason banks seemed determined to sabotage house sales.

But by the beginning of May, the house was theirs.

Wallace moved in the day after closing. He had no furniture, but he brought a sleeping bag, a mat to lay it on, his pillow, a lamp, and some books. The house was *his*, damn it! His and Jay's. And he was claiming it before anyone could try to take it away from them.

He regretted not having a flag to plant in the front yard, but he did have a plaster wall hanging of the Green Man. He hung it in the entryway.

Jay's lease wouldn't end until June, but they packed up his apartment and arranged for a professional moving company to transport all the boxes the forty miles from Dover to Rockford, as well as hauling them into the house. The movers were young guys in their early twenties who seemed to enjoy working shirtless and showing off their muscles, so Jay and Wallace couldn't complain about the cost. They even bought the guys pizza.

After the movers left, Wallace looked around the rooms full of boxes in dismay. He hadn't been interested in keeping any of his old furniture, and the boxes of books and other things he owned had been brought over in a few carloads. Jay, on the other hand, owned *tons* of shit. He hadn't bothered with much furniture, except his futon, but he owned books and DVDs—literally thousands of them—and box upon box of dishes, models, puzzles, paintings, art supplies... you name it. And of course he'd brought three cats with him, along with their litter boxes and everything else they needed.

Wallace had no idea where to even begin unpacking and sorting through everything, but Jay calmly retrieved a blanket from one of the boxes and ordered him, "Strip."

"Huh?"

"Take your clothes off. All of them."

Jay set the blanket down a moment so he could remove his own clothing. Wallace obeyed, stripping while it gradually dawned on him that they were about to have sex. He didn't object, of course. But the timing seemed odd.

When they were both completely naked, Jay pulled him close for a lingering kiss and a bit of naughty fondling. Wallace quickly grew hard in his hand and reached down to explore Jay's body. But Jay pushed him away, giving him a coquettish smile.

"Not here."

"Where?"

Jay picked up the blanket again and said, "Come on."

He led Wallace downstairs through the cellar and out the side door. A low wall on one side of the hot tub blocked the view for anyone who happened to pass by the end of the driveway, and they were able to walk unseen into the backyard. Here there was nothing but a small patch of lawn with forest all around it. Jay spread the blanket on the grass and stretched out on it.

"This is all ours now," he said, stroking himself while he looked up at his lover. "Let's claim it."

Wallace looked down at him, enjoying the view, and smirked. "Not the house first?"

"We'll claim that tonight. I want to do this in broad daylight, right here—because we fucking *can*."

That somehow seemed appropriate to Wallace. So he knelt between Jay's spread legs and took his hard cock into his mouth.

Chapter Thirteen

How Adrastia talked them into visiting the local SPCA, Jay had no idea. It wasn't that he and Wallace didn't want a dog. They'd talked about it several times, and they were both in agreement—a big dog, something they could wrassle with and snuggle up to on the couch. Maybe a Labrador or a German shepherd, but they weren't particular about the breed. Except Malamutes and other breeds with a ton of fur that had been bred for northern climes. They didn't care about dog hair on the furniture, but they'd feel too guilty in August, when the temperatures were in the nineties.

At any rate, they'd only just bought most of their furniture and gotten most of the boxes unpacked or put in storage. One of their friends was a carpenter, so they'd contracted him to build peninsula bookshelves in the room they were converting into a library. When he was done with that, he'd be starting on a small building near the hot tub—a replica of a Viking longhouse that would hold some replicas of the Norse goddess, Freyja. They belonged to Wallace, and he'd always wanted to put up a proper altar for them. Jay had persuaded him to go "whole hog" and build a small temple of sorts. That way they could host rituals now and then.

With all of this going on, it seemed a bit early to think about adopting a dog. But they'd taken Adrastia with them on a trip to a furniture store in Stratham, searching for sturdier kitchen chairs. They'd already managed to break two of the spindly things they'd picked up a month earlier from IKEA.

On the way back from ordering four chairs—they'd have to wait ten days for the stain and finish they wanted to be applied—she pointed from the backseat and said, "Pull in there!"

Jay took the turn automatically before he realized where they were. It was the local SPCA shelter. "Um… what are we doing here?"

"You said you wanted to get a dog."

"Well, yes," Wallace said from the front passenger seat. "At some point. Not immediately."

Adrastia waved her hand dismissively. "It won't hurt to check the place out."

With a growing feeling of trepidation, Jay parked the car. He glanced at Wallace, but his lover merely shrugged at him. The three of them got out of the car and went inside.

The first thing that greeted them was a room full of cats. Near the entryway was a glassed-in kitty playroom with carpeted platforms of varying heights. The kittens were adorable, but Wallace grabbed Jay firmly by the elbow and steered him away.

"We have three cats as it is, and one of them already tried to kill me."

"I'm sure he didn't know you were sleeping when he knocked the book off the bookcase."

"He dropped a book of hermetic philosophy on my *head*. A facing-page translation!"

Jay merely rolled his eyes. They were there to look at dogs. And he had enough trouble keeping up with the litter boxes as it was.

They spoke to someone at the front desk, who took them back into the kennel. "If you see a dog you'd like," she told them, "just ask, and we'll put a leash on it so you can take it outside in the yard a bit."

Jay saw Wallace glance at a large, brightly lit area near the door. It was glassed in and had a bench for someone to sit on and a dog bed, with several toys strewn around. It was empty, but a cardboard sign read "Raja."

Their guide noticed Wallace's line of sight and stopped a moment. "That area is used to showcase a dog for the day—one who hasn't been getting much attention. People can go in and sit with the dog, play with him a bit. It looks like someone has Raja out in the yard right now, though." She turned to gesture toward the rest of the room, where rows of dog crates were lined up against all four walls. "Feel free to walk around and look at the dogs. Again, if you see one you like, come get me, and I'll put him or her on a leash for you."

As soon as she'd gone, they ventured out into the room. Seeing all the eager, hopeful faces staring out at them—some frantic with excitement and yearning, others more timid but still pleading with their eyes—Jay realized this was going to be emotionally draining. How could he pass by a single one of these poor puppies? How could he leave them to a fate that might ultimately end in them being put to sleep, never having found the person meant to love and care for them? Every dog that whimpered at him made him want to burst into tears.

There were several dogs he liked—and were supposedly okay with cats. Most of them were a bit smaller than he and Wallace had been discussing, such as the female border collie named Sacha who looked up at them with sad eyes.

It broke his heart when Wallace said, "She's nice," but didn't really seem taken with her.

By the time they'd gone around the room, with Adrastia offering her opinions of each dog but Wallace seeming withdrawn, as if he didn't even want to be there, Jay just wanted to get out. He wanted to rescue them all, but that was impossible. And any dog they took would be conditional upon his or her behavior with the cats. Jay didn't want them bullied in their own home. They were stressed enough just trying to adjust to a new house.

As they walked out, Wallace came to a sudden stop. His eyes were fixed on the showcase area, where a large black Labrador retriever stood near the glass, wagging his tail and looking directly into Wallace's eyes. Unlike many of the other dogs, Raja didn't look sad. He was brimming over with joy at the possibility of another human to play with.

Wallace placed a hand on the glass, and Raja tried to lick it. "Let's see if we can take him outside."

Adrastia went to find the woman who'd brought them in, but Jay knew this was just a formality. Some things were destined to be, and from the light that had suddenly flickered to life in Wallace's eyes, Jay knew Raja was going to be their dog.

"DO YOU own your house," the woman at the front desk asked them, "or do you rent it?"

"We own it," Wallace replied. *Technically*, he thought, *the bank owns it.* It wouldn't really be their property until it was paid off. But he knew what she'd meant.

"Oh good! Too many people adopt pets without thinking about whether they can really keep them. Often their landlords have 'no pet' clauses in the lease."

"You wouldn't have let us adopt Raja if we were renting?"

She shrugged. "Not necessarily. We would have required a signed note from the landlord saying it was fine for you to own a large dog."

He supposed he was glad to learn they were being diligent. She'd already given them Raja's history. The poor pup—he was only a year and a half—had been in an SPCA shelter in Indiana for a year, and nobody had wanted to adopt him. The shelter had finally shipped him to the shelter in New Hampshire when a space opened up. If that hadn't happened, he might have been put down.

Wallace shuddered to think how close it had come to him never seeing this wonderful dog. Raja had proven to be affectionate and friendly when they took him out on the leash. He hadn't shown any aggression toward other dogs, and supposedly he was good with cats too. The latter they'd simply have to find out when they took him home.

It had been agony to surrender him back into the care of the shelter employee. But Wallace and Jay were filling out the paperwork now. It would probably just be a matter of days before they'd be allowed to take him home.

When they'd finished with the paperwork, however, the woman who looked it over surprised them. "Are you ready to take him now?"

"Now?" Wallace asked, tapping the nonexistent glasses on the bridge of his nose.

"If you want."

"Um… maybe we should wait…."

"We'll take him now," Jay told her firmly. He turned to Wallace and pleaded, "We can't take him out and play with him, get him all excited that someone might want him, and then just *leave* him here!"

"If you need some time…," the woman began, but Jay rushed on.

"What do we have to have for him? Food and water dishes? A dog bed?" These were all things they could stop and grab at the Pet Life store just down the road.

"Don't forget toys!" Adrastia interjected. "Lots of them."

THOUGH THE cats had their affectionate moments and had more or less warmed up to Wallace by now, slipping into his lap when he least expected to find a cat there, they were still somewhat aloof. They were, after all, cats.

But Raja was another matter entirely. The family dynamic shifted radically when a seventy-five-pound black Lab with attachment issues became part of the household. He needed affection—a lot of it. He was always there, cuddling between Jay and Wallace on the couch, curled up on the foot of the bed, watching them intently as they ate. Having sex was a challenge. It wasn't so much that they were bothered by Raja watching them—or at least they got used to it—but that he wanted to participate. He seemed to think it was playtime. Wrestling, perhaps. And he kept trying to climb up on the bed. They tried closing him out of the bedroom, but he then proceeded to whimper in the hallway, just outside the door, and totally kill the mood. Eventually they managed to train him to stay in his dog bed on the floor. But they had to be careful not to look at him, or he'd assume his banishment was over and try to jump back up on the bed.

The worst, though, was when Jay and Wallace had to go to work. Their shifts were at different times, so they didn't have to leave him alone for eight to ten hours, but with Wallace gone from eight to six and Jay gone from noon to nine, that was still six hours he had to be alone in the house. Since the kitchen had a door that could be closed, they cleaned everything off the table and counters he might be able to reach, gave him food and water, and closed him in there while they were gone. But he broke Jay's heart every morning when Jay closed the kitchen door, by sitting on the other side of it and looking through the glass. He didn't whimper, but his sad puppy eyes seemed to say, "I tried to be a good dog. Why couldn't you love me?"

Fortunately he went into paroxysms of ecstasy when either man came home. All was forgiven. Until the next time.

"What do you want us to do about it?" Wallace asked when Jay told him how hard he was finding it to leave each day. "There isn't a doggie daycare in town."

Jay shrugged. "I don't know. I suppose I could look into one near where I work…."

But Wallace wasn't fooled. They were lying in bed together, Raja sleeping peacefully on the foot of the bed, now that they'd allowed him back up.

Wallace ran a finger languidly along Jay's naked hip. "I know what you're thinking."

"I need a little recovery time," Jay said with a smirk. "I'm not as young as I used to be."

"Nobody's as young as they used to be. Who thought up that silly expression? Anyway, that's not what I meant." Wallace kissed him gently on the shoulder. "You want to work from home. Writing, that is."

It was true. Jay hated being in tech support. He'd loved it when he was in his twenties, but it had grown old. Now it felt as if most of the job was soothing customers who were rightfully frustrated by buggy software—being forced to lie by telling them development was working on it, when he knew their backlog made it unlikely they'd get to the issue for months, if at all. And since the bubble had burst in 2000, he'd been forced to take a twenty thousand a year pay cut. It wasn't worth it anymore.

"My novel didn't do that well," he hedged.

"It sold four thousand copies. That sounds pretty good to me."

"That's not enough to live on."

Wallace kissed him tenderly on the mouth. "I've already run the numbers. As long as I stay employed—there is always that risk—we can afford for you to take a couple years off from corporate work and see if this is likely to be a career for you."

Jay felt excitement welling up in him, but he tried to stamp down on it. "You're just in a good mood because you got laid."

"True." Wallace laughed. "But I'm serious. You'll have to wait until after the wedding, though. That'll set us back a bit."

Jay gasped. "The wedding!"

Chapter Fourteen

WENTWORTH BY the Sea was a Victorian grand hotel built in 1874 in New Castle, New Hampshire. In its heyday it had been splendid, resembling the Grand Hotel in the film *Somewhere in Time*—one of Jay's favorite romantic movies—though somewhat smaller, and had hosted the negotiation of the treaty that ended the Russo-Japanese War in 1905. It had been closed in the early eighties, and by the late nineties, it had fallen into such disrepair it was used as the scene of a murder in the 1999 film *In Dreams*. But then it was mostly demolished and rebuilt from scratch, with only the original grand ballroom, the hotel restaurant, and the hotel lobby remaining of the original structure.

But it looked as it had in the early nineteen hundreds, and it was where Jay had always fantasized about getting married.

"This is going to be insanely expensive," Adrastia commented as they walked from the parking lot to the entrance.

They were walking because Wallace had been uncomfortable with the idea of handing off his car to a hotel valet. It felt too… aristocratic. The entire hotel—along with the marina and golf course that surrounded it—felt a bit rich for his blood. He'd grown up poor and was proud of it.

Jay, on the other hand, was delighted to rub elbows with the well-to-do. As they entered the elegant Victorian lobby, he looked around at the well-dressed men and women lounging by the large fireplace—with a gas flame that produced little heat—or waiting near the doors with their golf clubs and thought, *I could get used to this*. Not that he had any interest in golf. But in being rich? Yeah, that might be nice.

A smartly dressed young woman met them by the front desk. "Miss Denning?" she asked Adrastia, extending her hand, "I'm Tessa Constantine."

Adrastia took her hand and then gestured to Jay and Wallace. "Pleased to meet you. These are the two gentlemen who are getting married—Jay Corey and Wallace Leopold."

If Ms. Constantine was at all bothered by them being gay, she showed no sign of it. In fact, as she shook their hands she said confidentially, as if the thought delighted her, "I believe you'll be our first gay wedding!"

"Cool," Jay said.

Wallace didn't say anything, though he appeared less enthusiastic. They hadn't actually agreed to have the wedding there, since they had yet to discuss pricing.

But as Ms. Constantine gave them a tour, including the gardens, where weddings were often held, and the spectacular ballroom, Jay kept picturing himself and Wallace walking arm and arm through the hotel like Christopher Reeve and... well, not Jane Seymour—perhaps Dan Stevens... back in 1912, when *Somewhere in Time* took place. It was the perfect wedding he'd always pictured.

After the tour, they went to a small room where Ms. Constantine served them glasses of champagne—one of the champagnes they might opt to include for toasts—and laid out brochures on a table outlining the various wedding packages offered by the hotel.

"We have a garden wedding package, if that's what you prefer," she said. "You seemed to like that idea."

"Yes," Jay admitted, "but we're talking about... when?"

"The earliest dates we have available are in mid-November."

"Exactly. How warm is it going to be in November?"

Ms. Constantine laughed. "Well, it could be warm, but you're right. You might not be able to rely on that. In the event it was too cold to hold the wedding in the garden, or say it was raining, we would have a backup plan to move the ceremony inside—in the Garden Ballroom."

"And what about the reception?"

That could be held in the Wentworth Ballroom or the Grand Ballroom. How many guests are you planning on?"

"We estimated about a hundred," Jay said. "At least we're planning on sending out a hundred invites. Not all of them will come, of course." Considering they were talking about a wedding in less than three months, close to a major holiday, he expected a number of their friends would already have other plans.

"In that case, either of the ballrooms would work."

"The Grand Ballroom is the one I want," Jay said firmly. "The one from the original hotel."

"All right. Have you given any thought to the catering? We can supply a meal based upon these menus—" She slid the booklet of menus across the table to him. "—or perhaps you'd just like us to serve an afternoon tea...."

Jay felt his heart flutter a bit. "Afternoon tea? With scones and cucumber sandwiches?"

"There are several options," Ms. Constantine said, sliding yet another menu toward him.

It listed scones and Devonshire cream, along with poached pears, lobster profiterole, smoked duck breast, salmon, cucumber cups, and other things that made him want to swoon. He was seeing himself and Wallace dressed in Victorian tuxes at high tea in a Victorian ballroom, and... yes! A string quartet playing in the background!

Ms. Constantine had been jotting notes and figures down on a notepad during the conversation, and now she tallied some of them up. "If we have the wedding in the garden—with the Garden Ballroom as a backup, in case of the weather—and put the reception in the Grand Ballroom, that gives us a base figure of just under ten thousand."

She seemed to think this figure was reasonable, but Jay felt the bottom drop out of the perfect Victorian wedding he'd been formulating in his head. He was suddenly acutely aware of the difference between *playing* at being wealthy and actually *being* wealthy. Ten thousand dollars? That was insane! They had discussed other details, including local businesses the hotel had arrangements with for things such as wedding cakes, catering, and flower arrangements. These would all be additional expenses, not included in the hotel price.

Jay and Adrastia exchanged looks, and he could tell she knew this was going to be impossible. Wallace's expression was unreadable, as it often was when he was thinking about unpleasant things.

Their host seemed to sense Jay needed a minute to digest the figure she'd just dropped like an atom bomb on his dream. "I'll leave you to discuss it for a few minutes."

"Oh my God," Adrastia said under her breath, the moment the door closed.

"I... didn't expect it to be that much, I guess."

"And that's just the beginning! You don't know how much the tuxes and the wedding cake and all the rest will add up to!"

Wallace contemplated the figures Ms. Constantine had left behind, his mouth set in a grim line. "I would say we're looking at something around... fifteen or sixteen thousand."

"Yeah," Jay said wistfully. He finished his champagne in one gulp.

They had acres of land. It would be infinitely cheaper to put up a pavilion on the front lawn, hire a caterer, and maybe buy a bunch of flowers. With the right decorations, it could be beautiful. Adrastia had already agreed to preside over it. They didn't need to break the bank to prove to themselves and the rest of the world that they loved each other.

When Ms. Constantine returned, she found them sitting in somber silence. That was probably a big hint about what their answer would be. But she smiled cheerfully and took her seat.

"Have you decided? Or would you like more details about anything?"

Jay couldn't bring himself to say it. He looked at Wallace, who gazed back at him, the corner of his mouth quirked up in an affectionate smile.

Then Wallace took a deep breath and turned to Ms. Constantine. "We'll do it."

Chapter Fifteen

WALLACE HAD already anticipated how expensive a wedding might be and had worked out their budget for it. Fifteen to twenty thousand dollars had, admittedly, been on the high side of his estimations, but it simply meant their savings account would be pretty lean for the next several months. They wouldn't starve or miss their mortgage payments. And the look of surprise and delight that lit up Jay's face when Wallace gave the go-ahead made it all worth it.

Wallace himself didn't need anything as elaborately gaudy as the Wentworth for his marriage, but he did need something more than a simple handfasting ceremony in the front yard. That had been discussed, but unfortunately he'd known too many gay couples who were handfasted before marriage was legal for them—and so did a lot of people. Getting handfasted was one of those things gay couples did because they *couldn't* get married. It wasn't that he didn't believe a handfasting was legitimate. Now that marriage was legal, a pagan high priest or priestess could certainly perform a handfasting, and it would be recognized as a legal marriage by the state. But he didn't want to deal with the skepticism of the people he knew—his father, coworkers, and even other gay men and women.

Oh, you got... handfasted? Then you aren't actually married yet?

No. He wanted a *wedding*, dammit. His high priestess would perform the ceremony, and there would certainly be pagan elements, but there would also be the traditional exchange of rings and *I now pronounce you husbands.*

Wallace wanted no doubt about the fact that he and Jay were married. None.

WITH ADRASTIA'S help, Jay didn't find making the wedding arrangements too difficult. The list Ms. Constantine had supplied him with would do, since he otherwise had no idea where to find wedding cakes and floral arrangements in time. He was pretty open to suggestions, except that he insisted everything look plausibly Victorian.

He picked out a design for the wedding invitations that felt sophisticated and old-fashioned, though still striking. Wallace glanced at it briefly and gave his approval. Then Jay roped Adrastia into helping him address and mail them all out.

He tried to get Wallace to do it, since he was one of the two people getting married and all, but Wallace just said, "I don't know why you're wasting time on mailing anything. Who does that, these days? I'll just make up an e-mail list. It's far more efficient."

"Uh… no," Jay said.

So Jay and Adrastia handled the invites.

Wallace did accompany Jay to Jacques Fine European Pastries in Suncook, where they were confronted by a mind-numbing array of flavors for the wedding cake and the fillings between the layers—spice cake, espresso, gingerbread, chocolate truffle, Bailey's, black Russian, apple preserves, lemon, raspberry…. They were given samples of whatever they thought might suit them, and all were heavenly. Jay had always thought wedding cakes were dry, but not these. They were amazing! When he was told he could have different flavor combinations for each of the three layers of the cake, he nearly had an orgasm right there in the bakery. Ultimately he and Wallace agreed on alternating spice cake and gingerbread with black Russian and Bailey's buttercream fillings, all wrapped up in a cake design called "Wheat in the Wind," which had a fondant covering of off-white trimmed with golden shafts of wheat, highlighted with bouquets in fall colors.

Wallace wasn't overly enthusiastic about the flowery theme, but he looked at it and smirked. "Well, it certainly looks gaudy enough for the Victorians."

"Do you object?"

"Me?" Wallace laughed. "I have no taste. If it were up to me, we'd be eating off paper plates and drinking out of Styrofoam cups."

"Ew."

"Exactly. That's why I'm leaving it up to you to make this wedding spectacular."

That was certainly what Jay intended to do. He didn't want to wipe out their savings, but once he was on his Victorian wedding kick, he kept finding more ways to improve upon it. He ran all his ideas and purchases past Wallace and would have put them aside if Wallace had ever said "No, that's too expensive." But he never did.

Jay ordered Victorian tuxes for the two of them online, then dragged Wallace to a local tailor when they arrived to make sure they fitted perfectly. They were nearly identical, except that he'd ordered a dark green paisley waistcoat for Wallace, while his was burgundy. He was used to seeing Wallace in T-shirts and jeans. The man didn't own much else. But the moment Wallace stepped out of the dressing room, even with the tux fitting a bit awkwardly in the shoulders, he looked so strikingly handsome Jay found himself wiping tears out of the corners of his eyes.

When the tuxes were properly tailored, Adrastia took a photo of them in their new library, Wallace sitting in the Victorian chair they'd found at an antique store that summer—not for the wedding, but simply because the library demanded an old stuffed chair—with Jay standing behind him. Then she tweaked it in Photoshop to make it look like an old sepia-toned photo. The result was stunning and nearly indistinguishable from a photograph of the time period.

That gave Jay the idea of small, ornate picture frames with their picture as wedding favors. It was a bit vain, perhaps, but… *cool*. And if a guest didn't want to stare at their picture for all eternity, he or she could always take it out and put something else in the frame. He also got some delicate little teacups with candles in them to balance it out.

He even arranged for a string quartet through a musician friend who happened to know one of the members. They promised to play "Canon in D" for the walk down the aisle, and—best of all—the theme to *Somewhere in Time* when he and Wallace entered the room! They were a bit pricier than a DJ, but Wallace gave him the okay.

When the RSVPs began rolling in, Jay and Wallace were surprised. Most of their invites had been accepted, despite the short notice. Jay had also mentioned the Victorian theme and said, "Feel free to dress accordingly, though it certainly isn't expected or required." An overwhelming majority of those who'd RSVP'd had notes to the effect that they'd see what they could come up with for Victorian dress, often with comments about how much fun they thought it would be.

Wallace looked up at Jay after reading one of these and said with amusement, "We appear to be enabling the steampunk fetishists in our circles."

Chapter Sixteen

WALLACE HAD made certain everyone in his family was on the invitation list. In particular, he wanted his youngest brother to be there—he'd always been closer to Rick than his other two brothers—and he wanted his father to be there. More importantly, he wanted his father to stand up at the altar with him, just as Jay's parents were going to be standing beside their son.

He knew his father was conservative. They often disagreed about politics, and there were some topics they simply couldn't get into without tempers flaring. But they were still family, dammit!

They'd endured the loss of Wallace's mother to heart disease five years before Wallace had met Jay, and they'd lost Wallace's older brother to pancreatic cancer very suddenly just before Wallace and Jay had moved in together. About the same time, Wallace's father had had a minor stroke. He'd recovered, thankfully, but perhaps all these things had made him realize just how fleeting his time with his sons might be. He'd made some gestures toward recognizing Wallace's relationship with Jay. Nothing huge, but Jay had been invited to some family gatherings, and Wallace's father had been pleasant to him, if not exactly friendly.

It seemed like progress.

To people who didn't know him well, it might seem as if Wallace wasn't overly concerned about the wedding. He certainly wasn't enthusing about it all the time, the way Jay was, or obsessing on the details. But it was tremendously important—one of the most important things in his life. He loved Jay, and he wanted that love acknowledged by the world. He didn't want to pretend they were just two good friends buying a house together. He didn't want a small ceremony with just a few close friends so the rest of the world could pretend it had never happened. He wanted to exchange rings on the lawn of the goddamned White House with the president conducting the ceremony on national television and every single lawmaker in the entire country who'd ever voted against his right to marry the man he loved forced to attend, dressed in matching gowns of hot pink.

Jay's family was delighted by the whole affair. His younger brother, Alan, was going to be Jay's best man—Jay had even bought a Victorian tux for him—and his mother jabbered excitedly about it whenever her son talked to her on the phone.

They'd booked rooms in the hotel for Jay's parents, his brother and his sister-in-law, as well as for themselves, but Wallace's family had said not to waste the money on them. They'd be there the morning of the wedding. It made Wallace a bit anxious, because he didn't like leaving things until the last minute, but as long as they made it there before noon, there would be plenty of time.

However, the Friday morning before the wedding, as Wallace and Jay prepared to go to the hotel and meet up with Jay's family for the wedding rehearsal and the rehearsal dinner, Jay logged in to check his e-mail, and his face went pale.

"What is it?" Wallace asked.

Jay took a long time to respond. He opened his mouth as if to say something but seemed to change his mind. He simply rotated his laptop so Wallace could look at the screen.

There was an e-mail from Wallace's father, and as he read it, Wallace felt his chest contract, as if a shard of ice had pierced him through and frozen his insides.

I tried to e-mail Wallace, the message read, *but I must have his address wrong. Please tell him I won't be attending your event. It's a matter of principle.*

Wallace left the room, and Jay didn't chase after him. By now he knew when Wallace needed to be given some space.

Principle.

A matter of principle.

Not a matter of love for his son. Not a matter of respect for how much Wallace had wanted his family to share this "event" with him.

No.

His fucking "principles" were more important than his own *son*.

JAY COULD tell by the look on Wallace's face, when he walked back through the room on his way to his office, he was going to be out of commission for a while. Whenever something really upset him, he shut down. He sort of turned into a zombie and barely responded to anything said to him. And generally he closed himself in his office, so Jay wouldn't try to talk to him. It was his way of processing things.

Shit.

This was *not* the time for it. Not the day before the wedding.

He logged on to Facebook and sent a message to Wallace's brother, Rick. *Are you still planning on coming to the wedding?*

Jay waited anxiously for a half hour while he puttered about the house, making sure their tuxes were loaded into the car, along with everything else they'd need for the weekend. Wallace was still brooding in his office, but nearly everything had been done the night before, so that wasn't immediately a hardship.

Finally a message came back: *Dude! Of course! I wouldn't miss it.*

Thank God.

We've got a problem, Jay replied. He copied and pasted the e-mail into the message.

Fortunately Rick didn't try to take his father's side. Jay would have lost it if he had. *That's pretty shitty. I'm sorry, man.*

Wallace's friend, Clark, is best man. They lived together in the house in Derry. But it was really important for Wallace to have your father standing beside him at the altar. Can you take his place? He didn't suggest Rick argue with Mr. Leopold and change his mind. Even in the short time he'd known the man, Jay had learned that was nearly impossible. If he ever came around, it would be on his own terms, in his own time.

And it might already be too late. Jay wasn't sure the man would ever understand how much harm he'd just done to his son and to their relationship.

To his immense relief, Rick replied, *Anything you need, soon-to-be-bro-in-law. Just tell me where to stand.*

Chapter Seventeen

WALLACE WAS a nervous wreck, and his legs wanted to give out from under him when the theme from *Somewhere in Time* began and his friend Clark opened the door into the ballroom. They were entering from the garden balcony, and across the room, the door to the hallway opened and he saw Jay enter.

He looked amazing. Wallace felt awkward in a tux, as he felt in just about any clothing—or out of clothing, for that matter. But Jay seemed suited to it. He could have been a gentleman from the nineteenth century, popping by the year 2010 for tea before the parking meter expired on his time machine. His eyes immediately found Wallace, and he smiled.

They met in the middle of the room and turned to face the altar at the far end. Adrastia stood directly in front of it, elegant in a custom-made green Victorian gown that set off her red hair. On either side of the aisle were over seventy people. Wallace couldn't believe that many had accepted the invite on short notice, and nearly all of them were dressed in Victorian regalia. Some was more steampunk than authentic, but that hardly mattered. One friend had dressed Indian—as in, from the country of India—but he'd argued it was correct for the time period. Which was true. Similarly, a friend from Nigeria had dressed in a brightly colored Nigerian robe. He claimed to be a visiting diplomat.

Jay's parents were dressed in contemporary but respectable formal attire, but his brother was standing behind Jay in a Victorian tux. His wife was standing with Jay's parents in a Victorian dress she'd somehow wrangled from the theater department in the school where she taught. Rick, to Wallace's delight, had also managed to dress appropriately. The gods only knew where he'd found the suit, but though it wasn't a tux, it was Victorian—complete with a bowler hat—and it looked wonderful on him.

Wallace had never loved his brother more than he did at that moment.

Since neither of them was the "bride," and it would have seemed odd to have both grooms just standing at the altar without the pomp and circumstance of the bridal procession, they'd opted to walk up the aisle arm in arm, with the best men trailing behind. As the string quartet began to play "Canon in D," Wallace cocked an elbow, and Jay slipped his hand through it. Wallace felt as if he might lose it at any moment. Jay seemed a bit more together, but his eyes were glistening.

Jay smiled at him and nodded slightly, and they walked together up the aisle.

IT WAS a pagan ceremony in part, with invocations to the Norse gods Frey and Freyja. They were brother and sister but strongly associated with sexuality—in Frey's case, homosexuality—fertility, and prosperity. Jay and Wallace weren't really interested in being fertile, but sexual and prosperous sounded appealing. Wallace had always had a close affinity to Freyja, and the temple he'd contracted their friend to build in the yard was nearly finished. The moment it was complete, they intended to consecrate it… naked.

They weren't doing the ceremony skyclad or anything the guests might find disturbing, but still Jay glanced at his parents, concerned they might be squirming as Adrastia called the quarters and invited the guardians of the elements to watch over him and Wallace. His mother was crying and dabbing at her eyes discreetly, but she was smiling. And his stepfather, the Baptist minister, was beaming proudly.

"Repeat after me," Adrastia told him. "I, Jayson Corey, take you, Wallace Leopold…."

"I, Jayson Corey, take you, Wallace Leopold…."

They continued through the vow, Jayson echoing her and placing the ring of white gold on Wallace's finger.

"To be my lawfully wedded husband,

"To have and to hold, from this day forward,

"For better or for worse,

"For richer or for poorer,

"In sickness and in health,

"Until death do us part."

When it was Wallace's turn, his voice broke after the word "husband," and he had to take a moment, but Jay held his hands and tried to convey through his smile how much he adored him. The thought that this normally taciturn man could almost fall apart at this moment seemed… adorable. And beautiful.

Wallace cleared his throat and managed to get through the vow, ending with, "Until death do us part."

"You may kiss."

They did, while everyone applauded.

"May I present to you all," Adrastia announced loudly, "Jayson Corey and Wallace Leopold—husband and husband!"

Chapter Eighteen

THEY HAD told everyone not to bring wedding gifts. They'd combined two kitchens' worth of dishes and just bought all the furnishings they wanted. They had little need for more. But of course some people brought gifts anyway. They were stacked neatly on a small table, alongside a beautiful hardcover book that detailed the history of the hotel. This is what they used as a guest book, encouraging people to sign and write notes on any of the pages inside.

Wallace and Jay stood outside the Grand Ballroom, shaking hands with the guests as they entered for the reception and exchanging hugs and kisses. Then, once all of the guests were inside, Jay took Wallace's arm again and escorted him into the ballroom.

It was amazing. The Garden Ballroom had been nice but somewhat modern. Now, as the hotel event coordinator introduced them, they stepped back in time to 1912—a magnificent Victorian ballroom with high chandeliers and a burgundy oriental carpet, filled nearly to capacity with men and women in suits and gowns from the period. Though this was an alternate history—one in which two men could walk arm and arm as husbands.

And rather than inspiring disgust and causing heads to turn away in embarrassment, they were greeted with applause.

"WE SHOULD have rehearsed more," Wallace muttered.

"Keep smiling," Jay said cheerfully, "and follow my lead. One, two, three. One, two, three."

They danced in time to the waltz while their guests looked on in amusement. Wallace was right. They should have rehearsed more. Wallace was stiff and awkward, nearly stumbling over Jay's feet. Jay had waltzed before—a long time ago—but he wasn't very good. Certainly not good enough to lead a partner with no experience at all.

But it didn't matter. It was their first dance as a married couple, in front of a ballroom full of friends and family, and it was perfect.

"Just a few more steps," Jay assured his husband, "and then we can sit down again."

But that wasn't to be. The moment the music stopped, Wallace breathed a sigh of relief, and a room full of clinking champagne glasses induced them to kiss. But as they turned to walk back to their table, Jay's stepfather suddenly swooped in and grabbed Wallace by the hand.

"Oh no, you don't! I still have to have my dance!"

Wallace gave Jay one helpless glance before he was spirited away to the strains of "Voices of Spring." Jay turned to find his mother waiting patiently beside him, so he took her hand and escorted her into the middle of the dance floor.

At the end of that waltz, he was startled when Rick swept him up for the next dance. Jay glanced around and was delighted to see many of his guests dancing in same-sex couples, whether they were gay or straight. It was very sweet.

"Thank you so much," he told his new brother-in-law, "for stepping in at the last moment. It meant a lot to Wallace."

Rick smiled but answered seriously, "Not a problem, man. Just… you know… take good care of him."

"Is this the if-you-ever-hurt-him speech?"

Rick laughed. "Maybe. Though I'm not likely to break your legs or anything. Just… you know. Don't."

"I won't." Hadn't he just promised to care for Wallace for the rest of their lives in front of the gods and a roomful of people? Jay couldn't conceive of ever wanting to hurt him. But he had no problem reiterating it. "I swear."

WALLACE WAS finally able to escape their guests—seventy wonderful wedding guests had become a ravening horde in his mind the moment they'd begun passing him from one person to the next for dances—and staggered back to the table. Jay was sitting there already, and Wallace glared at him as he plopped down onto his seat.

"You lied to me. You said there would just be one dance."

"Can I help it if you're adorable and everyone wants to waltz with you?"

"Gods! It was like that story where someone puts on a pair of cursed ballerina slippers and can't stop dancing!"

Jay poured him some more champagne. "You need another drink, my love. I think the worst of it is over." Despite his words, he was beaming as if this was the best time he'd ever had.

And Wallace had to admit it was, despite how challenging it was to his introverted nature. He took a sip of the champagne. They hadn't opted for the most expensive brand, but it was significantly better than others he'd tasted.

"What's left on the agenda?"

"Not much. I think we just have to cut the cake."

Wallace looked at him suspiciously. "You promised not to smear it in my face. You remember that, right?"

"Are you mad?" Jay exclaimed in horror. "These tuxes cost a fortune!"

"Just checking."

Jay smiled and leaned in for a kiss, and suddenly the air was filled with the sound of silverware tinkling against champagne glasses. He sighed. "I hope nobody breaks their glasses. The hotel will probably charge us a thousand dollars apiece for them."

"Then you'd better make the kiss worth it," Wallace said, and he pulled his husband in close.

Epilogue

TWO YEARS later—after the Rockford town clerk's office had mysteriously "never received" the signed documentation for Jay and Wallace's marriage and made them fill it out again, and after they'd spent a day in Concord protesting yet another attempt to overturn same-sex marriage in New Hampshire—Jay finally persuaded Wallace to accept one of the invitations to his father's house. The man had invited them to go there for holidays several times, but Wallace had steadfastly ignored him.

It wasn't that Jay had any great love for his father-in-law. And he certainly didn't blame Wallace for shunning him. But he also knew Wallace was still fuming about it, and it was still tearing him up inside. Jay wanted them to at least start talking again for Wallace's sake, if nothing else.

It was an awkward Thanksgiving dinner. Mr. Leopold put on a forced cheerfulness and acted as if nothing had changed since the last time they'd gotten together. He was friendly to Jay, as always, though he couldn't quite look him in the eye.

When one of the other guests—an old family friend, apparently—shook Jay's hand and introduced himself as Frank, Wallace's father said, "Jay is… Wallace's partner."

Jay would have let it slide, but Wallace's nostrils flared, and he said curtly, "Husband."

"They were married a couple Novembers ago," Mr. Leopold added, as if he'd meant to say that all along.

Frank seemed oblivious to the tension between father and son. "Really? That's interesting. One of my coworkers just married his partner last summer."

ON THE car ride home, Wallace muttered, "Well, that was fun."

"He'll come around eventually. He just needs more time to process it."

Wallace sighed. "I suppose. But he should have sucked it up and been there. He could have processed it all he wanted—*after* the wedding."

"I know."

They rode in silence for a few minutes. Then Wallace reached across the CD holder and took his hand. "I'm glad you twisted my arm and made me go."

"I didn't twist your arm. I just suggested going."

Wallace quirked up a corner of his mouth. "Well, anyway… I don't want to spend the rest of my life not talking to him. Even though he deserves it."

"He could have been worse," Jay pointed out. There were definitely gay couples dealing with more hostility from their parents than a refusal to go to the wedding.

"True," Wallace said.

He continued to hold his husband's hand as they rode through the night, thinking it might be chilly enough to warrant starting the pellet stove when they got home. Or maybe even start a fire in the fireplace. Then he and Jay could curl up in front of it with some cocoa, their dog snoozing at their feet. No doubt the cats would wedge themselves in somewhere.

It was a simple life, despite the gaudy ostentatiousness of their wedding. They weren't the kind of guys who wanted expensive cars or Italian suits or wall-to-wall entertainment systems. They just wanted… cozy. And they wanted to be with each other. Wallace was perpetually baffled that he had to keep fighting so hard for that—against his father, against narrow-minded assholes in the state legislature, against people who didn't want to do business with him and town clerks who'd made it difficult to register their dog two years in a row, because someone kept "accidentally" forgetting to list them as a household in the computer, as opposed to two friends living together.

But as he glanced over at Jay's handsome face and received a reassuring smile and a gentle squeeze of his hand, he knew it was worth the fight.

JAMIE FESSENDEN set out to be a writer in junior high school. He published a couple of short pieces in his high school's literary magazine, but it wasn't until he met his partner, Erich, almost twenty years later, that he began writing again in earnest. With Erich alternately inspiring and goading him, Jamie published his first novella in 2010, and has since published over twenty other novels and novellas.

After legally marrying in 2010, buying a house together, and getting a dog, Jamie and Erich have settled down to life in the country, surrounded by wild turkeys, deer, and the occasional coyote. A few years ago, Jamie was able to quit the tech support job that gave him insanely high blood pressure. He now writes full-time… and feels much better.

Visit Jamie: jamiefessenden.wordpress.com
Facebook: www.facebook.com/pages/Jamie-Fessenden-Author/102004836534286
Twitter: @JamieFessenden1

By JAMIE FESSENDEN

Billy's Bones
The Christmas Wager
Dogs of Cyberwar
The Healing Power of Eggnog
A More Perfect Union (Multiple Author Anthology)
Murder on the Mountain
Murderous Requiem
Saturn in Retrograde
Screwups
Violated
We're Both Straight, Right?

GOTHIKA
Claw (Multiple Author Anthology)
Stitch (Multiple Author Anthology)
Bones (Multiple Author Anthology)
Spirit (Multiple Author Anthology)

Published by DREAMSPINNER PRESS
www.dreamspinnerpress.com

SOMEDAY

BY B.G. THOMAS

This one is, of course, for my *legally* wedded *husband*, Raymond.
My knight in shining armor.
Who says I saved him too.
He's the one who supports me and puts me first no matter what, even though he doesn't always understand me.
I love you with all my heart!

Acknowledgments

THANKS ARE due to a number of people. My daughter, Jayli. My dear friend Dani Elle Maas for all things Dutch. This couldn't have been done right without lots of help from Renae Kaye—thank you. Thanks to Noah Willoughby and Jan Valdez and so many others for their research help. And of course to Andi, Nicole, Jason, Brian and Stacia for all you did to make this story the best it could be.

And I want to give a very special thanks to Jamie, Scott, and Michael for joining me in this anthological endeavor. It wouldn't have happened without you.

And I must not forget the Freedom to Marry website. Simply wow!!

1991

THE FIRST time Lucas Arrowood saw Dalton was on his way to his first day of kindergarten. His mother was walking him to school, he was very excited, and his right shoelace was flopping, untied.

"Baby," said his mom. "Let's sit down and try to tie your shoe."

He looked up at her, excitement temporarily quashed. He couldn't do it. Couldn't tie his shoe. And he was supposed to be able to. His mother had tried to show him how—over and over again—but he couldn't get the laces to go where they were supposed to go, and it just fell apart. He *couldn't* do it. If his teacher found out, would they make him go home? Would he have to wait until next year? That would be horrible!

"Hey, you can do it. It's easy!"

Lucas gave a little jump, turned around, and sighed as he looked into the narrow dark eyes of the most beautiful human being he had ever seen.

"Want me to help?" the boy asked, flipping his mop of dark brown hair out of his eyes with a toss of his head. "I taught a bunch of kids last year when I was in kindergarten."

A bunch of kids hadn't known how to tie their shoes? That perked up his ears. Lucas looked up at his mother.

She smiled. "Do you want him to help?"

Then he realized something. He *did* want the boy to help him. He thought he would do *anything* the boy wanted him to do, even ask his mom to take the training wheels off his bike (which was a big scary because he was afraid of falling and getting hurt!).

"Sit down," said the boy, pointing to the landscaping wall along the sidewalk.

Lucas sat.

"What's your name?" asked Lucas's mother.

"Dalton Churchill. Like *Winston* Churchill. Only it's Dalton."

He smiled, and Lucas *knew* Dalton was the most beautiful boy on the planet.

"Who's Winston Churchill?" Lucas asked.

Dalton shrugged and got down on one knee before Lucas. "I don't know. I think he's a minister. Okay, now, first you pull your laces up and then cross them over, like this." Dalton demonstrated.

"I can tie a knot," Lucas said, wanting very much not to look like a complete dope in front of Dalton. Then he frowned. "It's the other part I get mixed up on."

"That's cool," Dalton said, tying the knot. "Okay.... So here's the tricky part. First you make a loop and stick it up so it looks like a tree—see?"

Lucas nodded. He wasn't sure the upward turned loop looked much like a tree, but he wasn't going to tell Dalton that.

"Then you take the other lace and wrap it around the bottom like this—like a dog running around the tree."

Lucas smiled. "My neighbor has a dog. His name is Super Mario."

"That's a great name," Dalton said, laughing.

Then he finished showing Lucas how to tie his shoe.

"Wow," Lucas said.

But then Dalton untied the shoe.

"Hey!" cried Lucas.

"Now you do it," Dalton said. He nodded. "You can. I *know* you can. *Easy*."

Lucas wanted to yell, "No, I can't!" but he quite suddenly knew he could not disappoint the pretty boy with the beautiful eyes. He sighed. What had Dalton said about a tree? He made a loop with one of the laces.

"Just like that, but the other one. Unless you're a southpaw."

Lucas looked up through his own dark bangs. "Huh?"

"Southpaw means left-handed."

"Oh!" Lucas giggled. "I'm not."

"Tree!" Dalton ordered, brows knitted together.

So Lucas made a loop with his shoelace.

"Yes!" Dalton said with such enthusiasm Lucas would have thought he'd ridden down to the corner and back on his bike without training wheels. He laughed and then thought about dogs running around the base of trees. A moment later, Lucas had tied his shoe. His mother clapped.

"Yes," shouted Dalton. "I *knew* you could do it, Lucas."

Dalton walked the rest of the way to school with them. But even better, he also promised to walk Lucas to school the next day.

2

"I STILL think he's a little young to be walking to school by himself," Lucas's mother said that night over dinner. "His mother should be walking with him."

"But he's a Big Kid," Lucas said. "He's in the *first grade*. Besides, he won't be walking alone anymore. He'll have me with him."

His mother raised her eyebrows.

"I'm going to marry him someday," Lucas said and dipped his fish stick in the puddle of ketchup on his plate, then took a big bite.

His mother laughed. "You can't marry Dalton," she told him.

"Why not?" Lucas asked. Why couldn't he?

"Because *boys* can't marry *boys*," she explained.

Lucas gave her a curious look. Took another bite of his fish stick. "Why not?" he asked. That didn't make any sense.

"Boys marry *girls*," she said, and she wasn't smiling now, and that made Lucas feel funny. "Two boys can't have babies. You get married so you can have children."

"We could adopt," he said, wondering why that wasn't obvious. "Like your friend Angie. Didn't you say Angie got a baby because it didn't have a mommy to love it?"

Lucas's mother sighed in that way that told him he should stop. But it was frustrating. He *wanted* to talk about it. Today he had met the boy he was going to marry one day. He knew it.

"It's not legal. A marriage is between one man and one woman."

"But what if two boys fall in love?"

She bit her lower lip. "Lucas…."

"Can we take the training wheels off my bike?" he asked, changing the subject.

It worked. She laughed again. "What brought that on, honey? There's no reason to rush."

He nodded and stuffed the half fish stick that was left into his mouth.

"Lucas! You're going to choke!"

"Sowwy, Mhum," he mumbled through a mouthful of fish.

Why did he want to take the training wheels off his bike? Because he didn't want to look like a little kid in front of Dalton. That's why. It turned out that Dalton was a Big Kid. He was in first grade.

Lucas smiled.

Because he knew what he knew.

Today he had met the boy he was going to marry.

1998

1

IT WAS the summer between sixth grade and junior high, and Lucas was in the basement of Diego Hernandez's house—Diego was a friend of Dalton's. Diego and Dalton were going into the eighth grade, and it was a big deal that he'd let Lucas even come.

Diego'd had a pool party with like fifteen kids swimming all afternoon. Diego's father had cooked hamburgers and hotdogs on the grill, and there had been a ton of food. Lucas thought Diego's family must be rich.

And now, somehow, Lucas was left with the handful of hangers-on—Dalton and two giggly girls and Diego of course—after the party wound down.

He'd been feeling wonderful.

But that came to an end the minute Diego announced it was time to play spin the bottle.

Spin the bottle? Wasn't that the game where you had to kiss girls? Girls in *bathing suits*?

He looked at Dalton (who looked so nice in *his* trunks and his sexy bare chest).

And what did Dalton do? Shrug. *Shrug?* Was Dalton wanting to do this? Did he want to kiss girls?

Lucas looked at the two giggling girls, who were eyeing Dalton and Diego. Of course they were. Who *wouldn't* look at Dalton?

He glanced at Diego, who was okay, but *God*—he was no Dalton.

"I'll be right back," Diego said and scrambled up the stairs.

Now the girls were looking at Lucas. They were giggling again. It didn't seem like the same nervous laughter inspired by their glances at the other boys.

This was not good. His stomach was clenching. He felt like puking.

Diego came back down the stairs, and to Lucas's total surprise, he had a bottle of alcohol.

Please God, thought Lucas. *Please make that the bottle we're supposed to spin and not anything else.*

"Okay!" said Diego. "Here's the rules. First you take a drink—"

Oh no.

"—and then you spin, and you have to kiss *who*ever it lands on. *No* exceptions."

Oh no!

Lucas looked pointedly at Dalton. *Really?* he tried to beam. *Alcohol?* They were twelve. Well, Dalton was thirteen but.... *Booze?* He bobbed his head to the side, trying to tell Dalton that he wanted to *talk* to him alone about this!

Dalton shook his head. He dragged his fingers through his hair, pulling his mop of bangs out of his face. They immediately fell back where they were before. Where they always were.

"Okay, everybody." Diego pointed at the floor. "Sit!"

The girls were there in two seconds, Diego was already sitting, and Dalton was making his way over. He nodded at Lucas. Nodded again. *Come on*, he mouthed.

Lucas felt like crying. He felt like running. He looked at the stairs. Considered bolting.

"Come on, Lucas," Diego said. "Dalton said you're cool."

He felt like he'd been slapped.

Lucas watched as Dalton sat down. Dalton was looking at him with those pretty brown eyes of his, but right then it didn't seem to matter how pretty those eyes were. He felt like he was being betrayed.

Please, Dalton said soundlessly.

Lucas sighed, walked to the circle, and took his place.

Diego waggled his eyebrows. "It's my house, so I'll go first." He opened the bottle and took a swig, squinted his eyes as he swallowed, screwed the lid back on, put it on the floor, and spun.

It made this weird glassy sound, almost musical and almost creepy at the same time, against the wooden floor. It seemed to go on forever.

Finally it stopped, pointing at the ginger girl with tons of curls. Julie, he thought her name was.

Once more the girls giggled—what was it about girls and giggling?—and Julie leaned over the bottle, holding her long curls out of her face, and kissed Diego. Then she sat back, blushing and covering her mouth.

"Okay, Julie. Your turn."

"Okay. But do I have to drink?"

Diego nodded enthusiastically. "You bet."

So Julie drank, and she winced like she'd sucked on a lemon—"That's not *too* bad," she said—and spun the bottle. *Woop woop woop* it went on the floor, and who should it land on?

Dalton.

Of course.

Lucas bit his lower lip. No. Please, no.

They kissed.

God.

Lucas wanted to cry.

Somebody was kissing Dalton. And it wasn't him.

Dalton drank. He didn't flinch at all. He twirled the bottle.

It landed on the girl with the hair bleached so white she could have been an albino.

And once more, Dalton was kissing a girl.

This was twice Dalton was kissing girls!

Bleached Hair took a swallow of the alcohol—her expression changed less than Dalton's!—and then sent the bottle spinning.

The bottle stopped. It was pointing… Directly. At. Him.

Lucas shivered.

He looked at the girl.

She didn't look very happy about it either. B.H. shrugged, started to lean over, and….

"What's your name?" he blurted. "I'm sorry. I-I don't know…."

She cocked her head. "Samantha."

Lucas looked over at Dalton—who was nodding. And now it really was all he could do not to cry. He looked back at Samantha. Saw the expression on her face. What was it? Was it hurt? Did he do that to her? Had he hurt her feelings?

So Lucas smiled—or hoped he was smiling—and closed his eyes and bent in… and…. They kissed. It was light. It was fast. And it was his first ever in the world kiss.

He took a deep breath and hoped-hoped-*hoped* that no one noticed how much he was trembling.

It wasn't too bad.

Why are you doing this?

But then why did *anyone* do this? What was the big deal? It wasn't gross, exactly, but why on Earth did two people stick their mouths against each other's? Who was the first person to even think of such a thing?

Why was *he* doing it?

Lucas turned and saw Dalton's eyes on him. They were weird. Shiny.

"Your turn to spin," Diego cried.

God. I have to do this again.

He reached down and prepared to spin that bottle.

"Hey," Samantha said. "You gotta drink first!"

Lucas sat back, looked around at all the faces watching him. "Do I *have* to?" His mother would be very upset if he drank alcohol. She hadn't wanted him to come to the party in the first place. Thought Diego was too old, and Lucas had insisted that was silly. Diego was only one year older. And she liked Dalton. Finally she had said okay, but only if he was very good and didn't get into trouble.

Wasn't drinking trouble?

They all nodded or said, "Hell yeah," or "If *I* had to, *you* have to," or worse, "You chicken?" The last was from Diego.

But worst of all was Dalton. Dalton knew Lucas's mom would be mad. That this could get him into all kinds of trouble. But he still said....

"Drink, Lucas."

I should go. I should run. I should get the heck out of here!

But what would Dalton think? What would Dalton's friends think? He so wanted to look cool in front of them. If he didn't take a drink, they would think he was a scared little kid.

He *felt* like a scared little kid.

Then, before anyone could say anything more (or call him chicken again), Lucas grabbed the bottle, looked at it—vanilla-flavored vodka; at least it was flavored—screwed open the lid, and taking a deep breath first, drank. It went down sweet and hot and—*ka-pow!*—it hit his stomach hard. *Whoa.* He actually felt dizzy for a minute. People drank this crap?

Julie laughed. Samantha said, "Yes!" Diego said, "Good!" Dalton said, "You okay there, tiger?"

Tiger?

"Yeah," he said. "I'm great." Then before he could change his mind, he spun the bottle. It landed on Samantha again. Thank God. At least it was the same girl.

The kiss was almost as fast, and he was so thankful she didn't try and make it last. Somehow he didn't wipe his mouth, although he found he wanted to.

Samantha drank and twirled the bottle.

It landed on Julie.

The two of them looked at each other in surprise. Samantha looked at Diego, her face a question.

"Go on!" growled Diego. "*No* exceptions. None."

Samantha looked at Julie, who shrugged, and then they did it. They kissed.

Wow. Girls kissing. Who'd have thought such a thing?

He bit his lips—thought about it.

Well, why not?

And then Julie was kissing Diego again. And then Diego and Samantha. And then Samantha and Dalton. (*Aaaarrrgh!*) And then….

Dalton sent the bottle spinning—

(*woop woop woop*)

—and it landed on Lucas.

Lucas's eyes flew wide. His mouth fell open. He looked up into Dalton's equally surprised face. Lucas closed his mouth with an audible click.

Dalton sat back on his heels. "I'm *not* kissing my best friend!" he objected.

"Oh *yes* you are!" shouted Samantha. "Julie and I kissed, and I am not missing *two* boys kissing!"

Lucas's heart was trip-hammering.

He locked eyes with Dalton.

Dalton locked eyes with *him*.

"God damn *do* it, Dalton," snapped Diego.

"*Fuck*," muttered Dalton. Lucas had never heard him say "fuck."

"Do it!" said Julie.

"*Fucking do it*!" said Samantha.

Would he?

And then Dalton's eyes closed and he leaned toward him and—

This is it.

—they kissed.

It lasted only a second. A brief moment. Dalton's lips against his. Lucas thought his heart would explode.

And he quite suddenly understood why people kissed.

2

THEY DIDN'T stay much longer. Diego's parents caught them.

And they made it clear they were calling *everyone's* parents. "Drinking, Diego! I can't believe you all are drinking!" Apparently Diego's dad hadn't cared about the kissing.

"Do you think they'll really call?" Lucas asked. "Mom will kill me if they call. She didn't want me to go in the first place. She'll say, 'This is just what I knew would happen!'"

He glanced down at Dalton's hand. He shivered. He wanted to take that hand in his. After all, they'd kissed. Shouldn't they hold hands? He wouldn't be so afraid of what might happen if Dalton held his hand.

Why didn't Dalton say anything? Didn't Dalton care that he could get into a whole *lot* of trouble?

"I don't want you to tell anyone," Dalton said.

Lucas stopped. "Huh?"

Dalton turned. "Nobody can know."

"*Huh?*"

"Nobody can know we kissed." Dalton made a slashing motion through the air. "*Nobody.*"

"B-but why?" Lucas asked. He felt like Dalton had just reached into his chest and squeezed his heart.

"*Oh, come on,*" Dalton cried. "How can you ask that? You want everybody calling us *fags*?"

Lucas opened his mouth to answer and found he didn't know what to say. *Fags.*

It hit him.

I'm a fag.

I'm gay!

Wow....

He smiled. The squeezing in his chest stopped. He quite suddenly felt like he could fly.

"What the hell are you smiling about?" Dalton snapped.

Lucas shook his head. "Dalton, does it matter what people think?"

"*Lucas*! If people think we're *fags*, our whole high-school lives are *over*!"

"But Dalton.... What if it's true?"

"*What?*"

Lucas shrugged and tried not to laugh. "If they call me a fag, then they'll be right. I *am* a fag."

Dalton's mouth fell open.

Then Lucas saw the sudden dawning knowledge on Dalton's face: "*Oh God,*" Dalton said. "That *marriage* thing! When you proposed to me when you were in *kindergarten*! I thought you were just being a silly kid."

Lucas shrugged. "Maybe I was. Maybe I wasn't. I don't know."

"Lucas."

Interesting. Now Dalton looked like *he* was going to cry.

Dalton took a step closer. "Lucas. You can't *know* you're gay."

"Why not?" He spread his hands. "I asked you to marry me when I was... what... five? Today I kissed a girl for the first time. I didn't like it, Dalton. Not one bit. But—*wow!*—I sure liked kissing you."

Dalton looked at him in complete shock. "*Lucas*...."

"What?" He grinned even wider. "You know *you* liked it. You felt it too. I *felt* you feel it." Because they'd kissed two times. The bottle demanded it twice. The second time Dalton's mouth had lingered on his just a little bit. He was sure Dalton had shivered.

Dalton shook his head. "No."

Lucas nodded hard. "Yes. Yes, you *did*."

Dalton shook his head again. "No."

Dalton's denial was pissing him off. "Oh yes, you did," he said defiantly. "You're going to kiss me again too. Not only that, but one of these days you *are* going to marry me, Dalton Churchill."

"No!" shouted Dalton.

And then he turned and ran down the sidewalk.

Lucas sighed.

There was a part of him that hurt.

But there was a part of him that knew he was right.

Dalton *had* liked kissing him. He *had* felt it.

And one of these days—legal or not—he was going to marry Dalton. If it was the last thing he ever did.

Lucas went home. He'd forgotten all about his worries about getting in trouble.

3

NOBODY AT school said anything about the kissing. At least the boy-boy kissing. Junior high started without a hitch for Lucas and continued without Dalton's macho reputation being damaged in any way.

Everything was status quo.

Dalton was still skittish around Lucas for a while, and that hurt. But at least once Dalton's fears were alleviated, he started hanging around Lucas again. For a while Lucas thought Dalton might end their lifelong friendship, worried that perhaps Dalton thought hanging with the "gay kid" would be bad for his reputation.

After all, Diego snickered with friends when they passed Lucas in the hall. Or ignored him altogether. Or sometimes they would roll their eyes with great exaggeration and say, "Seventh graders!" with great disdain. Lucas thought it was hilarious (although he didn't voice that thought). As if a *one*-year difference in age gave them great maturity and wisdom.

As it turned out, worry about a gay rumor was needless. Lucas wasn't ashamed and had been prepared for it, but nothing happened. It surprised him. He thought *gay* was tattooed on his forehead.

Lucas would study himself in the mirror—with his near-perfect skin (he never drank soda or ate so much as a fun-size Snickers bar), the huge amount of gel he used to give himself the perfect JC/Joey Fatone from *NSYNC hairstyle, his surprising long lashes and how it made him look like he was wearing both eyeliner and mascara (he wasn't), his ludicrously Disney-animation-character-sized brown eyes—and he'd think, *"God, I look* so *gay!"*

But not one whisper.

If he'd wanted a girlfriend, he could have had his pick of at least a dozen girls. Girls told him he was pretty all the time. *Pretty!*

He longed for a rugged face and body like Dalton's. Dalton was getting pubic hair. (He'd seen him in the shower room at school—it was his first time seeing Dalton naked since they'd taken a bath together in second grade and... *wow-wow-wow!*)

How Lucas had gotten to be twelve without *any*one calling him a faggot, he couldn't guess. But he began to suspect a big part of that was due to Samantha—or Sam, as she liked to be called.

Interestingly enough they struck up a friendship after the great spin-the-bottle debacle. She'd walked up to him during lunch one day at school—he was sitting all alone—and asked if she could sit next to him, and when he nodded, she sat down.

"You *liked* kissing Dalton, didn't you?" she asked without preamble.

Then before his filters could kick in, the words came out of his mouth as if they'd been fired from a cannon. "Oh *God*, yes!"

She nodded. "I know, because when we kissed, I might as well have been kissing a mannequin. I felt the same way. But oh my *God*! When I kissed *Julie*? Explosions! Waves crashing on the beach like that old stupid movie my mom loves. *From Here to Infinity* or some such thing." She shivered. "Kissing the boys was... sorta gross. Sorry." She did something with her mouth that was a strange combination of a smirk and a sneer. "Nothing against you, Lucas."

He grinned. "No. I get it."

"But kissing Julie? Oh. My. *God*. My insides turned to *jelly*."

Lucas grinned even more. "I get that too. But about Dalton—*not* Julie."

Sam nodded vigorously. But then she frowned. Let out a long drawn-out sigh. "It's too bad neither one of our wet dreams is dreaming about us," Sam stated flatly.

"Oh no, Sam," Lucas said, shaking his head emphatically. "You don't understand. Dalton *is* going to realize he loves me one day."

She raised her eyebrows.

He narrowed his.

"Don't say it, Sam. I know what I know. He's the one. And I won't hear you say anything to squash my dream. Got it?"

Sam burst into laughter. "I got it! And if there is anything I can do to help, let me know, okay?"

From such a beginning, a friendship was forged.

After that they hung out more and more. It seemed Dalton felt funny about hanging out with a seventh grader at school, but Sam had no such compunctions. She was happy to hang out when Dalton was busy—or grounded—and she often tagged along when they went to see a movie. And of course Dalton had no interest in going to the mall with her and shopping for the things she wanted to shop for, so that was Lucas and Sam alone, and soon everyone assumed they were dating—if what junior high school kids did was called dating. The only trouble had been the fact that she was a year older than he was, and some kids didn't think that was cool.

Sam couldn't care less. She had quite suddenly dropped the bleached-blonde look and dyed her hair so black it looked wet. She wore tons of black eyeliner and took to using a foundation that made her so pale she looked dead. In time she was a full-fledged goth. What did she care about the no-no's of dating a boy a year younger?

Even Dalton thought they were boyfriend and girlfriend, no matter how much Lucas guaranteed him otherwise.

"You're the only one for me," he would say, and Dalton would get cross and remind him again and again that they weren't "fags," no matter how many times Lucas told him that he was.

"You can't know you're gay when you're twelve!"

"Who told you that?" Lucas asked with a laugh.

"My mother."

Lucas looked at his hero, dumbfounded. His mother? "Why were you talking to her about something like that?" Lucas wanted to know.

"After Diego's party. I told her you said you were gay." Dalton glared at him and put a hand on his hip.

Lucas didn't tell Dalton how gay he looked doing that.

"And she said that at our age we're this raging cauldron of emotions and feelings and hormones and stuff. That we don't know what we want, and it's normal for boys to get crushes on other boys."

Lucas laughed. "We're a cauldron? Did she really say cauldron?"

"Yes!" Dalton's other hand joined his other hip (and Lucas didn't mention how gay *that* looked either). "She said we're all mixed up, and we don't know anything, and we get horny and do stuff because we can't do it with girls. And she said that was a good thing so we're not getting some girl pregnant!"

Lucas felt his face flush. He had missed for just a second what "stuff" meant, but when Dalton added the part about not getting a girl pregnant, he realized what his mother was talking about. The very thought of doing stuff with Dalton turned him into a cauldron of emotions and hormones.

"She said you'd get interested in girls soon enough, and then all this silliness would stop."

But Lucas knew otherwise. He didn't know how he knew, he just did—as sure as a compass pointed north.

"They don't understand," said Sam later. "Straight people like what they like so much, they can't imagine anyone liking anything else."

That was the night Sam told Lucas she had been crying her eyes out because she had finally told Julie how she felt. Julie had not only let Sam know she didn't feel the same way, but that she thought the whole idea was disgusting.

"She said I was *gross*," Sam said and cried on Lucas's shoulder—literally.

Lucas could only hug her and tell her that he didn't think she was gross and that he could understand how she felt. Dalton thought boy-boy stuff was pretty gross too.

Which made what happened soon after all the more surprising.

1999

1

THE NEXT spring, Diego—he who had been ignoring or snickering at Lucas for months—invited him and Dalton to a slumber party.

"He wants *me* to come?" Lucas asked, incredulous.

"Yup," Dalton assured him.

"Wow," he said.

"But he doesn't want you to broadcast it, okay?"

Lucas looked at Dalton, hurt.

"You have to understand," Dalton explained, fidgeting, which Lucas thought was odd. "Diego is one of the most popular kids in school. He has a reputation. You're…. Well…. You're just too…."

"What?" Lucas asked. *Too gay?*

"Girly," Dalton said, and then at least he had the class to flinch.

"Girly?" Lucas asked, surprised. He slumped. Girly? He'd never thought of himself that way. Geeky, maybe. He did think he *looked* gay. But a girl? "You don't think that, do you, Dalton?"

Dalton quite suddenly looked miserable, and Lucas's heart sank. *He does.* Lucas was prepared to be called gay or faggot or fairy. But he'd never considered himself girly.

"Well, you're certainly not a stud," Dalton said.

"And *you* are?" cried Lucas and gritted his teeth so he wouldn't. How would that look?

He knew the answer, of course. Yes. Dalton *was* a stud. He was as manly a man as a thirteen-year-old could be. Not only was Dalton getting pubic hair, his legs were starting to get hairy, and so were his armpits. Lucas would find himself staring at Dalton's legs when he was wearing shorts, gazing at his pits when Dalton's arms were raised. The hair fascinated Lucas, and he found he longed to touch it. To see if it was as soft as it looked. But it was more than that. Dalton was starting to get more muscular, his chest was getting broader, his biceps bigger. Yes. A stud. Dalton really was turning into a man. It was very exciting and made Lucas's tummy all fluttery and filled with apprehension.

"Oh, Lucas," Dalton said, and the look on his face hurt Lucas all the more. It was pity. And the last thing Lucas wanted Dalton to do was pity him.

"Well, if I'm girly, then why does he want me sleeping over?"

Dalton looked away. Cleared his throat. "He likes you, Lucas. He just doesn't want other people to *know* he likes you."

The words hurt. They physically *hurt*. "Do you feel like that, Dalton?" *Like me but don't want people to* know *you like me?*

Dalton looked back at him, and then to Lucas's relief, a steely expression came to his face. "No," he stated firmly. "You're my best friend."

His best friend! Lucas's heart leapt.

"I don't give a shit what people think about it either."

Lucas laughed. Joy filled him. At last! What had changed? "Thanks, Dalton."

"You got it, tiger!"

Tiger?

Lucas's heart leapt again.

2

THEY WENT skinny-dipping as soon as Diego's parents left for the evening, making them promise to be good and not to get into the liquor cabinet—

"I've taken stock," Diego's father had said, "and I'll *know* if anything's missing!"

—and not to have any girls over.

Fat chance of that.

Lucas hadn't expected the pool to be open. Sure, it was spring, and the temperatures had been in the seventies for some weeks, but he hadn't been prepared, hadn't brought his trunks. But then Diego announced that no bathing suits were allowed in the pool *tonight*—this was guys only after all—solving that problem, but Lucas became so anxious he thought his heart would explode.

He hadn't seen Dalton naked except for that mere glimpse in the shower room at school, and now that he could really look (although surreptitiously at first), what Lucas saw that evening was amazing. Dalton had gotten so… *big*. And he was so hairy down there. Sure, it was dark out, but the lights coming up from the pool were enough for Lucas to see.

Lucas could not ever remember being so stimulated.

He'd been very shy to take off his clothes in front of the two older boys. But then Dalton smiled at him so warmly when he finally stood naked before them, and Diego looked at him in a way that made him begin to get hard. That made him seriously blush until he saw the same thing was happening to them.

He wasn't as big as them down there, but then Diego wasn't as big as Dalton either—a fact that made Lucas immensely proud of Dalton. That was the way it *should* be. Diego also had foreskin, which Lucas had never seen in real life, and he thought it made Diego's penis look kind of funny, like an elephant trunk or something.

But then the time for checking each other out was over—and Lucas somehow knew they were all doing the same thing, it wasn't just him— Diego let out a holler and dove into the water.

It was wonderful. The pool was heated, so even though there was a chilly bite to the air, it didn't bother them. They swam, and Lucas found it exhilarating to be swimming without a stitch of clothing on— vulnerable and yet powerful at the same time. So freeing. He wasn't sure why. Shouldn't it be like taking a bath? But it wasn't.

Soon they were laughing and splashing each other and playing grab ass, and Diego even grabbed him somewhere else, and Lucas's heart had nearly leapt from his throat.

A boy! Had touched his penis! *God.* If only Dalton would touch him there! He wished he had the nerve to touch *Dalton* there. But of course he didn't.

Then when it was time to get out—they were all turning into big human prunes—because it had gotten even chillier, they scrambled across the deck and through the sliding doors into the family room—the very same room where a game of spin the bottle had once been played. After drying off with huge, obviously expensive, and luxurious towels, Diego and Dalton made no move to get dressed. They simply sprawled casually on the love seat and the couch as if they lay around naked together all the time.

God! Maybe they did!

Lucas found he didn't like the idea.

Diego jumped up, turned on his parents' big stereo system, and said he would get them all something to drink, and Lucas worried it would be vanilla vodka again, but luckily it was just some Pepsis.

After a bit Lucas got over his worry about sitting around without any clothes on—stopped worrying that Diego and Dalton were comparing him to themselves (and that he didn't measure up) and in no time found it began to feel quite natural to be naked.

They started talking about the normal things boys talked about.

Sports—which Lucas cared little for but pretended he did.

Cars—Diego liked Camaros, but Dalton loved Mustangs—he was a Ford man all the way.

Music—Aerosmith's "I Don't Want to Miss a Thing" (which as far as Lucas was concerned was the only good thing about the movie *Armageddon*) was playing on the stereo, and all thought it was a hot song, even if it wasn't as cool as the Run DMC version of "Walk This Way." Lucas was disappointed that Diego gave the thumbs-down on Savage Garden's "Truly, Madly, Deeply." But then Lucas had a personal reason for liking that one—it made him think of Dalton. Diego did like "You're Still the One" even if it was country because Shania Twain was a fox. And then they all sang along with Will Smith's "Gettin' Jiggy Wit It," which was fun and somehow... well... *sexy*. Because Lucas had a deep suspicion that getting jiggy wasn't only about dancing.

Movies—Diego loved *Armageddon*, but Lucas preferred *Deep Impact* and was happy as could be when Dalton agreed.

Television—they all agreed that Bart on *The Simpsons* was too funny—

"Eat my shorts!" cried Diego.

"Ay caramba!" exclaimed Dalton.

"Don't have a cow, man!" Lucas added in his best imitation of Bart (and he was thrilled when everyone roared with laughter).

—and *The Sopranos* was really cool (and Lucas got a clue and didn't mention how much he liked *Touched by an Angel* or *Buffy the Vampire Slayer*).

Then somehow the subject changed to girls.

Because by then Diego had brought up Buffy himself and couldn't stop talking about how much Sarah Michelle Gellar turned him on and how he would like to stick her with *his* stake, and he thrust his crotch out and wiggled his penis.

"You're not going to stick anybody with it floppin' around like that," Dalton observed.

"Don't worry," Diego informed him. "I can make it plenty hard."

Lucas flushed at that. Flopping penises and talk about getting it hard struck something deep, deep inside, and anxiousness swept over him again.

Dalton said that it was Jennifer Anniston that got him hard, and then they looked at Lucas and he blurted, "Gillian Anderson," because he couldn't say David Duchovny, of course, even though Lucas got all excited whenever the actor for *X-Files* smiled.

"Oh, yeah!" Diego said. "That red hair! And those boobs!" He held his hands cupped out in front of him as if the actress had breasts bigger than Dolly Parton's. "I wonder if her hair down there"—he pointed at his own pubic hair—"is as red as up here?" And then he was fluffing a nonexistent bouffant.

And how gay did that look?

That's when they started talking about "real" chicks. Diego asked Dalton about someone named Rebecca, and Dalton said, "Ah, she's okay." And Diego said, "Didn't you take her to Dairy Queen last week?" and Lucas couldn't say anything—his mouth simply fell open when Dalton replied that yes he had, but it had been no big deal.

Rebecca? Lucas closed his mouth quickly. Who was Rebecca, and why hadn't he heard about her before?

Dalton gave him a guilty look.

"Did you kiss her?" Diego wanted to know.

"No," Dalton said, and Lucas couldn't get over how relieved he was.

"You gonna take her out again?"

"Maybe," Dalton answered, looking down, decidedly not at Lucas.

"You think you could nail her?" Diego looked very eager as he asked the question.

Dalton simply shrugged.

"What about Sam?" Diego asked, and it took Lucas a moment to realize that Diego was talking to him—about Samantha.

"What about her?"

"Have you tapped some of that?"

Lucas gave him a questioning look.

Diego rolled his eyes. "You know. Fooled around with her."

"*Sam?*" Lucas almost laughed but through some miracle didn't. And he knew when he told her about this later, she certainly would. "No."

"*Nothing?*" Diego said, incredulity in his voice.

Lucas looked at him, feeling like some animal caught in the headlights of an onrushing car. "We kissed," he blurted. Which was true. They had. Not ten feet from where he was sitting right now. It wasn't a lie.

"Cool!" Diego said eagerly, then reached down and started fondling his penis. "Get any boobage?"

Now Lucas really had to fight to keep his expression neutral. Diego was getting hard.

"Boobage?" Lucas asked.

"You get to play with them yet?"

Lucas glanced to his right and…. *Oh God, oh God, oh God…!* Dalton was touching himself down there too.

He forced himself to look away, even though it was the last thing he wanted to do. He tried to think of another way to answer Diego without lying. He'd accidentally sort of grabbed one of Sam's breasts once when he spun around to ask her a question and hadn't realized she was standing closer to him than he'd thought. He'd been horrified, and she'd thought it hilarious.

But he tried something else instead.

"I feel funny about answering that," he replied. "I think it would really hurt her feelings if she knew I was talking about her that way. I really like her, Diego." And that was the truth.

Diego sighed. "What the hell *ever*. She sure seems to be into you."

"What about you and Julie," Dalton asked Diego (thank God!).

"We make out all the time," Diego said. "And I've played with her boobs. *God*, I *love* her boobs. She's rubbed my dick through my jeans."

"Wow," Dalton said.

"But she won't let me take it out! It's so fucking frustrating. Jorge, my cousin, gets blowjobs all the time. *God*, I want a blowjob *so* bad!"

"Me too," agreed Dalton, then so did Lucas, because it seemed to be what he was supposed to say.

Both Diego and Dalton were totally hard by now. Their erections stood up like pillars, and it was all Lucas could do not to stare. Lucas covered his own hardening penis casually—letting a hand fall in place as if he didn't even know he was doing it—embarrassed and incredibly excited at the same time.

"Do you jerk off yet, Lucas?"

Lucas froze, stunned at Diego's question. Did he jerk off? Oh, yes. He'd discovered masturbation about a year before, and it was quite simply *brilliant*. He almost always pictured Dalton when he did it, although he was never quite sure just what to picture them doing. He would focus on that all-too-short a look he'd gotten of Dalton naked that day in the shower and then pretend that Dalton was encouraging him to masturbate—watching and urging him on.

And now—oh God, *now*—he had a perfect picture for future nights alone in his bed.

"Let's see," Diego said. "Show us what you got, Lucas!"

It was more a command than a request, and Lucas could feel his face blazing with embarrassment.

Diego was openly stroking himself now, and watching the foreskin slide back—you would never know he was circumcised or not when that happened—and then up over the head was fascinating, and Lucas found he couldn't look away.

He gulped hard and turned to Dalton, who nodded his encouragement. And God, his penis. It was so big. Lucas couldn't believe it. Dalton was slowly stroking it, and his balls were hanging over the edge of the couch. Lucas's balls weren't nearly as big. Neither was his erection. Would they laugh?

Horribly, he felt the sudden urge to cry.

But then Dalton nodded again, and Lucas was stunned to see— yes—*hunger* in Dalton's eyes.

So taking his soul in hand, Lucas leaned back and slowly, cautiously, spread his legs.

"*That's* it…," Diego hissed, and Lucas blinked in surprise.

Almost in terror Lucas glanced over at Dalton, and he was smiling, nodding again. "Yeah, Lucas. You've got nothing to be ashamed of."

Really? Really? He had to be at least an inch or more shorter than Diego, two for sure less in length than Dalton, and had not half as much pubic hair. No hair on his legs either, only a wisp under his arms.

And they didn't think that what he had wasn't good enough. He was almost dizzy with gratitude.

"You guys too," he somehow managed. Because God—they were so sexy. Especially Dalton, of course. He wanted to go to his friend right then. Beg him to let him touch him… down there.

Now Diego was explicitly masturbating; it was no longer casual. That is what they all were doing—he watched Dalton again and thought his hero's erection was just as beautiful as the rest of him—masturbating.

"Do it," Diego said. "Do it!"

So Lucas did. It was all he could do to keep himself from finishing in seconds. He watched them both, but he was watching Dalton far more. He had dreamed of this—literally. Dalton had been his first wet dream and the star of several since then. His mouth slowly opened, his throat began working, and he didn't know why.

"Look at him," Diego hissed. "*So* fucking hot." Suddenly Diego was on his feet and, a second later, standing directly in front of Lucas, his erection less than a foot from his face. "Lucas." He was whispering huskily. "You like it. I know you do. You want to suck it. I can tell. Suck me, Lucas, *please*!"

Lucas drew back, horrified.

What? Suck it? Diego wanted him to suck his *penis*?

Diego reached out, put his hand behind Lucas's neck, and gently at first, and then not so gently, pulled him forward.

Lucas shook his head. Diego's erection drew closer. No. *No!*

"No!" he cried and somehow resisted Diego's strength.

And then Dalton was standing there. His erection was big and hard and God, no! Was he going to do the same thing? Force him to—

"Diego. He said no. *Fucking* lay *off*."

Diego fell back a step. "Damn it, Dalton! Look at him. He wants it. All he needs is a little encouragement. You can see he's a cocksucker! He's just afraid 'cause he's a virgin."

"He said *no*," Dalton reiterated, his voice rumbling.

"He wants it!" Diego practically shouted.

"No!" Lucas was fighting to keep himself from crying now. His erection was almost gone. "I don't want to!" But then he saw Dalton's erection and quite suddenly knew that if it had been Dalton who asked, he would have done it.

And maybe liked it.

If he'd ever had *any* doubt that he was gay, it was gone in that instant.

Dalton gave Diego a little push. "Sit down," Dalton commanded, and with a loud groan, Diego did what he was told.

Dalton sat down next to Lucas and put his arm around Lucas's shoulders, sat close enough that their thighs were touching. Dalton's penis was still hard, but not like before. "Do you want to go home?" his best friend asked. "We can leave right now. You know…. If you *want* to."

But feeling Dalton's thigh against his own, their skin touching, looking down at Dalton's penis, Lucas knew. As much as Diego had scared him—almost ruined everything—Lucas did not want to go home.

"N-no," he said. "I want to stay."

Then Dalton laid his cheek against Lucas's head, and oh, the weight of it and the heat of his leg against Lucas's. The arm around him. It was all the most exciting moment Lucas had ever experienced. His penis surged back up to its full length. And when Dalton asked him if he was sure, he told him yes, he definitely wanted to stay.

So Dalton pulled his arm from around his shoulder, scooted over, and leaned back in the corner of the couch—looking at him. So Lucas did the same, sat back in the other corner, and when Dalton began to stroke his beautiful penis—cock, Diego called it a cock, and of course he had heard that before—then Lucas did the same.

"Oh fuck," Diego said. "That's so fucking *hot!*"

Lucas didn't even look, for he'd forgotten Diego was even in the room. He didn't care. He truly only had eyes for Dalton. He was watching Dalton's face now, his beautiful face.

Dalton was speeding up, and his breath was catching, and he was grunting, moaning, and Lucas was as well and feeling his orgasm rushing up on him fast. Then before he knew it, Dalton was shouting and it was happening. Great jets of sperm were shooting high into the air, and with a cry, Lucas was ejaculating as well, and it was so *exquisite* it hurt, as well as nearly made him black out from the unbelievable power of it. It felt like someone was roughly squeezing his testicles, and that hurt, but as his sperm—his cum—launched out of him, he knew only pleasure undreamed of.

Then he thought maybe he did pass out there because he was swimming in a thick warm blackness and slowly became aware that Dalton was shaking him awake.

He was smiling shyly at Lucas and asking him, "Are you okay there, buddy?"

Lucas was. Oh, he was!

He looked around him, and Diego wasn't there, and he could look back into Dalton's beautiful eyes and fall in love.

Diego came back into the room carrying towels and handed them out, and they cleaned themselves off—*boy, what a mess*!—and then Diego said maybe they should get some shut-eye.

So they put on some underwear; Lucas put his shorts on as well for good measure. They pulled the couch apart—it turned out to be a sofa bed—opened it, and Diego said he would take the love seat, which sent Lucas's heart racing again. He would be sleeping with Dalton!

Diego turned out the lights, and Lucas and Dalton got in the big bed. Lucas wondered if Dalton would cuddle with him.

He didn't. He kept firmly to his side of the bed.

It wasn't a comfortable bed.

But both were okay: the uncomfortable bed and Dalton a foot away. It was only a foot after all.

Lucas didn't care.

Something new had begun, and he couldn't wait to see what it would be.

3

DALTON'S PARENTS drove them home the next morning, and then Dalton walked him to his door. He had been strangely silent all morning, and Lucas couldn't help but be worried. He couldn't even finish the breakfast that Diego's mother had made them.

Then as they stood on the front stoop, before Lucas could say anything, Dalton said, "I am so sorry, Lucas."

Lucas saw pure agony on his friend's face.

"Dalton?"

"I—I don't know what made me let you go to Diego's."

"*Let* me?" Lucas said. "I wanted to go!"

"But you didn't know what you were getting yourself into. You didn't know what was going on. What Diego had planned. Fuck. What *I* was going along with!"

And, God! There were tears in Dalton's almond-shaped eyes! One rolling down his cheek!

"But you did?" Lucas asked quietly.

"I did." Dalton's eyes were glistening. "I set you up." He shut them. "Oh God, Lucas. I'm *so* sorry. I want to fucking punch myself! I deserve it. I deserve to have the shit *beat* out of me!"

Lucas shook his head. Right then all he could think of was how wonderful it had been to sleep the whole night so close to the love of his life—and he knew, just as he had somehow known on the day they both met all those years ago, that Dalton *was* the love of his life. When he realized Dalton couldn't see him shaking his head, he reached out and laid a hand on his best friend in the world's arm.

"Stop," he said. "You didn't *make* me do anything."

Dalton opened his eyes, and tears flowed down his face. "Lucas…. We never touch each other." Dalton looked away. "He wasn't *supposed* to touch you."

Lucas blinked. Wait. Dalton sounded angry there at the last. Angry that Diego had touched him?

"And I *swear*," Dalton said so loudly that Lucas jumped. "I *swear* I had no idea he would try and force you to…." He covered his face with his hands and let out a long moan.

It wasn't the same kind of moan he'd made when he had his orgasm last night.

It was awful.

"He kept asking me about you…. He kept saying you were prettier than any girl at school and kept asking me if you and I had ever… fooled around. And I said no…. But I thought you wanted to."

Lucas's stomach leapt. *You know.*

"So he begged me to ask you to join us."

Lucas felt his stomach *drop*. "J-join you?"

Dalton opened his eyes but didn't meet Lucas's. "We get together sometimes and… you know… jerk off."

Pain shot through Lucas's heart. "L-last night…." Lucas trembled. "Last night wasn't… the first time you two…." He couldn't finish saying it. *Couldn't.* He didn't want to hear what Dalton would say.

But he had already said too much.

"No. We've done it several times. For a year now. Before the pool party."

Now it was Lucas who wanted to cry.

"Did…." *Don't ask!* But now he *had* to know. "Do you guys ever… suck each… other's—"

"No!" Dalton was shaking his head in denial. "Never."

The relief was immense.

"But you kept telling me you were gay, and I thought you might want…." Dalton looked away, not finishing his sentence.

Then Lucas was speaking before he even knew he was going to.

"I would have for you. I realize now I *did* want to. But *you.* I would have done it to you. Not Diego."

Dalton shook his head. "No. It's over. I told Diego it was all over. I'm not doing anything else with guys again."

The relief was replaced with sorrow. *No! You can't take this away!*

"My mom was right. We're just confused. Horny. All those hormones rushing through us. It's just because we can't have sex with girls. And that's good so we're not getting some girl pregnant."

A cauldron of emotions and hormones. He remembered the conversation well.

A car horn honked. Dalton's parents.

"So from now on," Dalton said, "I'm just going to jerk off alone. It's better that way." He turned and stepped off the stoop. "I am so sorry, Lucas."

"Dalton!" Lucas called after him.

His friend turned around.

"I meant it," he said quietly. "I would have done it for you. I would have sucked *you.* I *will.* I will right now if you want."

Dalton's eyes went wide. "No! I'm done. I'm not doing any of that anymore. No guys ever again. I'll wait until I'm older. Until I'm ready to be with a girl. And I won't make her do anything. It'll be when she's ready."

"But Dalton. You wouldn't be making me. I *want* to." Lucas knew it more and more and more. It was true. He *did* want to. He was getting hard again just thinking about it.

Sucking Dalton's beautiful cock.

"No, Lucas. I can't. I won't." He took another step back. "I love you, Lucas. Just not that way. If you're gay… then, okay. But I'm not."

But if that was true, why didn't he sound like he meant it, Lucas wondered. He didn't sound like he meant it at all.

Then as Dalton was turning, Lucas stopped him again. "Dalton?"

Dalton looked back.

"If you change your mind, please don't do it with Diego."

Dalton gave a half laugh. "Believe me, I won't."

"Or any other guy. Let me be the first. Please."

"I'm not gay, Lucas."

"Then just promise me this. If you ever decide that maybe you are… please? Let me be the first?"

Dalton looked at him long and hard, opened his mouth, shut it, looked away, looked back.

"Okay," he said so quietly Lucas could barely hear him.

"Promise?" Lucas asked.

"I promise."

The car horn blasted again.

"I have to go," Dalton said, and with that he was running down Lucas's driveway.

And Lucas was happy.

It wasn't what he really wanted. But he'd take it.

The promise of a possibility.

It was enough.

2003

1

DALTON'S SENIOR prom was a week away.

And Lucas wasn't going *with* him.

Dalton was taking a girl.

It wasn't like Lucas didn't know ahead of time, but it still hurt.

Rebecca. Rebecca D'Angelo.

Aarrgh.

What kind of name was that anyway?

But it wasn't like Dalton and Rebecca hadn't been on again, off again since… well, freshman year. And before.

So when the foreign exchange student from the Netherlands, Etienne De Vries—whom everyone called Steve because they couldn't pronounce his name—came out when he was a junior, Lucas went for him.

Etienne was more than happy to take him. He told Lucas it had taken a lot of guts for him to come out. He'd been afraid, which surprised Lucas because scared was the last thing he would have ever suspected Etienne of being. He was on the football team. He was in the glee club and even the speech club.

"It helps me with both my English and my accent," Etienne explained.

Etienne was the epitome of brave.

They began dating—movies, going out to eat, walking in the park. Lucas even attended Etienne's games, though sports had always bored him to tears. Actually knowing someone on the team helped, though.

What was really incredible was how cool most of the kids at school were. Lucas wouldn't walk down the hall holding Etienne's hand (and he certainly wouldn't put his hand in Etienne's back pocket or let Etienne do the same), but it was nice. It certainly threw Dalton's theory that letting people know he was gay would mean his high-school life was out the window.

The problem was… sex.

Etienne wanted it, and Lucas didn't.

The kissing was fine. Some touching. He'd been fine with the groping and rubbing through their jeans. Making out hadn't been bad, rolling around in the backseat of Etienne's car. They'd even progressed to taking their cocks out and masturbating—first together and then eventually each other. Lucas finally held another cock besides his own, and it was exciting. He couldn't deny it.

But it wasn't Dalton's.

He couldn't help but wish that the first penis he ever held was Dalton's.

Etienne had been pushing for more. He wanted them to suck each other. Etienne had half attempted doing it to Lucas already. And he couldn't stop talking about fucking. He had even found a book at Not Just Another Book Store on Main—*The Joy of Gay Sex*—so they would know how. The assistant manager had let him buy it.

"I was so scared he wouldn't let me. He gave me this long hard stare, and my heart was pounding, and then suddenly, he just rang it up, and I gave him the money, and then I was *out* of there!"

The problem was, Lucas didn't want to do that. He wasn't ready.

(Not with Etienne.)

He did, however, want to go to prom. And when Etienne asked him, he hugged him hard and told him he'd be honored.

Which meant Lucas decided it was time to tell his mother he was gay.

They were sitting on the couch when he did it. He had made tea and baklava because he loved how it all looked on the coffee table. And because he wanted to show off his newly discovered passion for baking—a fortunate by-product of his new job at a recently opened local bakery. He wore a new peach polo shirt he'd bought himself with the money he made at The Sweet Spot. Lucas had wanted everything to be perfect. This was an important conversation.

After he told her, she looked at him, blinked, gave an ever so slight sigh, and visibly relaxed.

"Well, of course I knew," she said quietly.

"You did?" Lucas asked. He wasn't sure if he was surprised or not. He hadn't hidden it—years after he first started scrutinizing his reflection mornings and evenings, he still wondered how even statues couldn't know he was gay. He just wasn't all that masculine. But neither had he insisted his room be painted pink, nor had he flapped his wrists and called everyone "Miss Thang."

"Well, honey, you've been in love with Dalton your whole life, and you didn't go out of your way to hide that stack of *Playgirl* magazines in your closet. Didn't you expect me to put your clothes away? You didn't even put them in a box or anything like your father did with his *Playboy*s."

Lucas blushed. Both for himself and the father that he'd never really known. There were only shadows of memory that might not have even been real—might have been the stuff of dreams. His father had died in Panama when Lucas was three. He had a vague recollection of *tallness*, but then anyone would have been tall to a three-year-old, right?

He could believe she knew he was gay, but the magazines! He blushed all the harder. Did she know what he did when he looked at them? He always tried to use his dirty sweat socks to clean up with. Sweaty socks *got* stiff after all.

"I just wondered how you got ahold of them," she said, eyes filled with curiosity but still maintaining a quiet cool that almost embarrassed him more. Disappointment he could have planned for. Anger. But this level of calm? "Some man at the newsstand didn't sell them to you, I hope. Didn't ask for something in return?"

"*No!*" Lucas assured her with a gasp. He'd found them at a garage sale. He'd been far too afraid to buy them, so he bought some *Sports Illustrated* instead, asked for a bag, and then switched them when the lady was busy with another customer. It wasn't stealing after all.

His mother nodded, but again it was only ever so slightly.

"That I would *not* have liked."

"So you're not mad?" Lucas asked. "You're not disappointed?"

She shrugged and patted at her blonde (beginning to go gray) hair, which was formed around her head like a loose football helmet. "Not really." She took a bite of baklava. "I mean, goodness, Lucas. It wasn't like you haven't given other hints. I mean, really—baklava? That's not easy to make. None of my friends have sons who would dream of making something so fancy. Or daughters either. They're very tasty, by the way." She popped the remainder of the little snack into her mouth and smiled while she chewed. Then, "And I haven't had to worry about you getting some girl in the family way," she said in a weird echo of what Dalton's mother had once said. "I guess you'll be marrying him after all?"

Lucas frowned. "No, Mom." He let out a long, dramatic sigh. *God, of course she knew I was gay!* "Dalton is straight."

Finally the look of surprise he was expecting. "Dalton? Straight?" She laughed.

"What's so funny?"

"He just seems so gay to me," she replied and then reached for another delicious triangular dessert.

"*Dalton?*" Lucas was stunned. Dalton? Dalton was a stud. If she thought Dalton acted gay, then, "What do you think of me?"

She waved the comment away. "You're Lucas."

He didn't know what to say about that.

She drank some tea. "This is really quite tasty," she replied. "No wonder the British like it so much. A lot of trouble with the boiling and the teapot and the steeping bags. My Mr. Coffee beats that hands down. But then I guess I'm spoiled. It wasn't that long ago I used a percolator. So Dalton isn't your boyfriend?"

The way she said it, Lucas almost missed it.

He came close to laughing, but then he thought about Rebecca. Seeing Dalton walking down the hall holding her hand. Or worse. When he would have his hand in *her* back pocket. And worse yet. When she had her hand in his. He frowned.

"What's wrong, honey?" his mother asked.

"No," he said sadly. "He's got a girlfriend."

She gave him a consoling look. "I'm sorry, Lucas. The boy I had a crush on in high school didn't like me either." She sighed.

I don't have a crush, he thought, irritated.

"He was so cute." She smiled at what he could only assume was some memory. Then she sat up and her brows rose high and a little color spread out across her cheeks. "But his best friend liked me! And we got married a few months after I graduated."

His father? "Dad?"

"Your father!" She nodded happily and leaned back into the couch. A faraway look came to her eyes.

It was then that it occurred to him that he should tell her the other thing. It wasn't like she would be mad. "I do have a boyfriend, though."

There was only one flicker in her eyes. A tightening of her lips. Had she just stiffened? Maybe she wasn't quite as cool as she was letting on. "Oh?"

"His name is *Etienne*," he said, careful to pronounce it correctly— *A-tie-enn.*

"At-ee…. That's a mouthful, isn't it?" she asked and made a very strange little sound. Lucas didn't even know what it was. Was it a laugh? What was it?

"He's from the Netherlands," Lucas said. "He's a foreign exchange student. Most people just call him Steve."

She folded her hands over her knees and nodded. "I think for now I better stick to Steve."

"Okay…." *God.* He tried to guess what she was thinking. Was she…? "You okay, Mom?"

She froze for a second… and then relaxed again. "Yes."

He didn't believe her. "What is it, Mom?"

She gave him a half smile, paused for a very long time, then said, "Oh, Lucas. I told you. I've known forever about you. And… well… it *became* okay."

"Okay?" he asked. There was a tug at his heart.

"It was you," she said with a wave. "You were always that way. And I was a young mother and very naïve, and I kept… I don't know… resisting. Your father was gone, and you were my only child, and your grandmother is gone…."

He'd never known her either.

"And I would read in the women's magazines in doctor's offices that…." She paused. "That boys raised without a strong male role model could become homosexual." She sighed. Made a noise that might have been a laugh. "There! I said it out loud! Ho-mo-sexual!"

She reached for another baklava, then seemed to change her mind. She rocked for a second.

Lucas bit his lip. His stomach was doing weird things. He couldn't tell where this was going.

"I kept wondering if I did something wrong. That's why I tried to get you to get involved with sports, Little League, that kind of thing."

That had been a disaster. He'd hated it, and the kids had hated him hating it—he couldn't even hold a bat right and he didn't want to. So he always struck out. He lasted for three games, and she finally let him drop out. It had felt like a thousand!

"I watched you grow, and it soon became obvious that it was foolish to want you to be any other thing than what you are. It became... *okay*. I mean, it wasn't like carrying on the family name meant anything to me—although with it just you and me, I was sad for a bit that this would be the end of our family."

Then she did laugh, and she snatched up her tea and took a drink, and Lucas could see the laugh was real (which was a relief), and whatever had been settling over her was gone. The tightening in his stomach relaxed.

"I realized that there have been thousands of families that have ended since the caveman times, and the Earth has continued to spin along just fine." She put her cup down and reached out and placed a hand on his. "What matters is love, right?"

He smiled, his heart swelled, and he gave her one single nod.

Then she rolled her eyes and sat back again. "And then there was Dalton. I've known him nearly his whole life. He has always seemed like a son to me. And it was like... well, it's *always* been you two. I didn't have to really *think* about it. I think I've imagined you two being married since you were at least fourth grade or so."

Lucas's mouth fell open. "But you were the one who told me two boys can't get married."

She shrugged. "Well.... I did some reading there too..."

Which wasn't surprising. For as far back as he could remember, she always had a book or a magazine in her lap. She'd never been a soap-opera-watching mom.

"...and I saw how so-called legal marriages are in many ways a relatively new thing. Many cultures just got together and said, 'Okay! You two are married! Let's dance around the fire!'"

They both laughed at that.

"This marriage license thing and legal documents and all that stuff? Hell! That doesn't make a marriage! It's love that makes a marriage. Love and commitment, right?"

"Yeah," he said. But that didn't mean he didn't want to be legally married. It had always confused him that he couldn't. Why not? Why shouldn't he be able to marry whomever he wanted to? But recently he'd finally accepted that he'd never have that piece of paper. What other choice did he have *but* to accept it?

"*Right*?" she insisted.

"Right!" he answered and rolled his eyes *just* as she had.

"Anyway…. Yes, I always knew. It was fact. One we never talk about, but yes. I left a couple of magazines around the house open to articles that talked about celebrities coming out, hoping you would talk to me about it."

Lucas blushed. He'd seen the magazines and had been excited to read those articles, hoping that one day his mother wouldn't be too shocked if he finally got the nerve to tell her *he* was gay. He thought she might be okay since she'd already read about famous people doing the same—Rupert Everett and Ellen DeGeneres years ago (as if she hadn't been obvious), Will Young the year before.

But he hadn't been ready.

"And there was Dalton, who has always watched out for you, taken care of you, and I just naturally figured you two would move in together one day and he would *keep* taking care of you. And all would be… well, normal."

The tightening in his stomach came back.

"But now you say that it isn't going to be Dalton? Now it's this… Steve? Someone I've never met? And you say he's your boyfriend?"

"Ah…," he said.

"So do I get to meet this boy?" She bit her lower lip.

You aren't quite ready, are you? But you're damned close. And that was pretty fine.

"Well… he's going to be picking me up the night of the prom…."

And finally a warm smile spread out over her face. "Oh, baby. Wow. The prom!"

"You're okay with that?" he asked, nerves jangling.

"Yes, honey. I am. In fact, I'm proud of you."

"Oh, Mom!"

He would never be clear on just who hugged who first. All that mattered were those last four words.

I'm proud of you.

He could not have dreamed of anything better.

2

ETIENNE SHOWED up exactly on time. He knocked on the door while Lucas was upstairs because his mother insisted. Lucas was ready. He'd been ready. For forty minutes! He'd almost gotten dressed hours early, and his mother reminded him that he might be sweaty before they had their first dance.

"You don't want to be all stinky when he gets here, do you?"

He'd burst into laughter at that, then fallen from his chair and realized that people really do fall on the floor laughing.

"Honey!" she yelled up the stairs. "A-tie-enn is here!" Not at all the way the French pronounced it—*Eh-tea-in.* No. *A-tie-enn* was how his name was pronounced in the Netherlands.

And Lucas loved her more than ever—trying *and* pronouncing it right.

What a mother!

Three days ago she had gotten a call from the principal of the school saying that there had been some controversy over the fact that two boys were coming to the prom as dates, and after evaluating everything, the school board had decided it might be best if that didn't happen.

Then without batting an eye—and Lucas had been there to witness it (he didn't need to hear the other side of the conversation to figure out what was going on)—she said very quietly and very forcefully that Lucas most certainly *would* be attending the prom with Etienne De Vries. She pointed out that Aaron Fricke had sued and won a court battle in 19-*fucking*-80 (Lucas had never heard her swear in his entire life) and that she would hold a press conference and do a little—well, not so *little*—suing herself. She also *promised* the principal would wish that his mother had never met his father when she was done.

She never yelled. Had barely raised her voice.

But *wow*, the power.

The next day the principal had called back to apologize and let it be known that the board wasn't going to stand in the way of two human beings enjoying their prom.

So Lucas couldn't help but stand up and look at himself in the mirror one more time, adjust his tie for the four-thousandth time, touch his hair to make sure it was perfect, and go to meet his date.

He left his bedroom, watching his feet as he walked (the shoes were very shiny), feeling almost stoned (he wasn't), and stopped at the top of the stairs. He took a deep breath.

God. I am a fag. I am truly a fag. The girl is the one who is supposed to be doing this. Waiting for the boy to come pick her up. I'm not a girl.

Why am I the one? Letting him come to get me? I should have gone to get him*! Now* that *would have been a statement. If I had done something manly for once in my entire life! Maybe if I had been more of a man instead of such a fruit, then maybe, just maybe, Dalton would have wanted* me.

It was right then that it hit him.

Being more of a man wouldn't have helped at all.

The only thing that *had* appealed to Dalton about him was that he was girly. If he'd been more of a man, he didn't think that Dalton would have given him the time of day.

Dalton. Wasn't. Gay.

But I am.

And it's time to be grateful for what I have, instead of looking for what I don't.

He came down the stairs, and it wasn't Dalton standing there—Dalton was standing at the foot of someone else's stairs, making someone *else* very happy—it was Etienne who—

Be honest! He's gorgeous.

He is.

Lucas's heart sped up.

—was standing there in a near-matching tuxedo (Lucas's cummerbund was purple paisley, the concession Etienne had given him for being different), and he *was* gorgeous—*fucking* gorgeous—and how could Lucas not be happy?

The look on Etienne's face!

I need to love him.

Etienne deserves it.

He deserves better than a guy who is in love with someone else.

After all, I am the one who went to him.

Etienne truly was beautiful. There was no way, looking at him, that anyone would have guessed he wasn't American. He wasn't darker or paler or taller or hairier or anything-er. That was until he talked. The accent came through strong then!

But yes, he was gorgeous. Sam had assured him of that.

Taller than Lucas, he had long dark blond hair and a lovely palish complexion that was just as clear as Lucas's. Etienne had taken his advice on what to do about acne. He was one of the only kids at Terra's Gate High School without pimples or with only a hint of them.

Standing there, looking up the stairs at him, wearing his black tuxedo with the shining lapels, he really was extraordinarily beautiful.

Why can't I see how lucky I am? How half-full my glass is?

His hair was like a small lion's mane around his face, his lips full, his brows thick, and his eyes were a shining blue. And Etienne was looking at him. Looking at Lucas the way he'd always wanted Dalton to look at him. Lucas's heart swelled, and tears stung his eyes.

God, Etienne even had a rose.

"Wow," Etienne said in that musical accent of his. "*Wow.*"

Lucas giggled—it was out before he could help it, even though it was girly. He went to Etienne, who started to kiss him then froze and looked at Lucas's mother.

"Don't let me stop you," she said.

So he did. It was a sweet kiss. And then Etienne was pinning the red rose on his lapel. A matching lapel. They'd decided on classic black tuxedoes.

"Okay, I'm taking pictures!" cried Lucas's mother.

So then she posed them—several times, trying to get everything just right—and took picture after picture, and Lucas had to finally get her to stop so they wouldn't be late.

Etienne held the car door open for him, closed it after Lucas got in, ran around the other side, and got in himself. Then he looked at Lucas in a way that made Lucas's stomach clench. Before he even saw it coming, Etienne leaned over and kissed him.

Lucas gave a mental shrug. *Relax.*

It was nice. Wasn't it?

"Tonight's the night," Etienne whispered. "I've got it all planned out."

Hmmm? What? Lucas looked at him, puzzled.

He leaned in very close, placed a hand on Lucas's crotch, and whispered in his ear. "Fucking. I'm so ready. And if you don't want me to do it to you—" He leaned back and looked at him with eyes so blue they almost looked topaz. "—then you can do it to me. I followed the instructions. I'm ready. You know… clean."

Lucas's face blazed. "Oh." It was all he could say.

Oh God, oh God, oh God was what he was thinking. *What am I going to do?*

"My… brother—you know, the family I'm living with—he got us a room at the motel out on the edge of town."

Oh God, oh God, oh God….

"Do you have any idea how I feel about you, Lucas?"

That look! That look on his face! He means it!

"But…." *But I don't love you.* "But we can't stay the night in a hotel! What will my mother say?"

Etienne smiled at him shyly. "I guess we won't spend the night. Your mom will forgive us for being out late, though. Right? It's prom after all. She probably went to the prom."

Lucas gulped.

"And aren't we supposed to lose our virginity at prom?"

He kissed Lucas again, and then they were on their way.

3

THEY GOT their pictures taken first thing, and no one even blinked. In fact the girls taking the pictures cooed over them.

Lucas was embarrassed, but it was fun. It would have been more fun if his head wasn't whirling.

Etienne wanted them to lose their virginity tonight? Tonight? They hadn't even tried blowjobs—although he had to admit that was his fault. He had wanted to… but then he couldn't. He'd dreamed about it. He had imagined himself doing it to Dalton for years. At one time the idea had seemed kind of gross—but that had been a very short time.

That had changed when he'd seen Dalton's erection that night at Diego's. After that it was surprising how he'd changed his mind. And how many times he'd kicked himself for not going for it when there had been opportunity. Now? Now he would have done it to Diego if that had only meant he could have done it to Dalton as well.

"Lucas. Etienne. Wow!"

He spun around, and there was Dalton. And Rebecca. Talk about "wow."

"You two look incredible," Dalton said.

No. It was Dalton that looked incredible. Amazing. Marvelous. Astonishing. *Beautiful.*

He had gone with classic designer. Black with a dark charcoal trim and matching gray vest and tie. His shirt was so white it was dazzling.

But nothing compared to Dalton himself.

He hadn't shaved. Not today at least. There was a heavy shadow of beard, and it made him look even more masculine than Lucas already knew he was. Dalton hadn't gotten a haircut either, had turned his back on that cookie-cutter style so many of the boys had tonight, that cut every boy's mother insisted on—

"You'll look back at these pictures your whole life—you'll want to look wonderful! You can grow your hair back…."

—and instead gone with his usual shag.

Lucas couldn't stop looking at him. Looking at his face, his narrow, stunning brown eyes, his mouth, his lips….

He remembered what it was like to kiss those lips. He'd never forgotten. He dreamed of those kisses.

He'd thought of those kisses when he kissed Etienne.

"*Hello!*"

Lucas jerked and looked away from Dalton to see Rebecca—a funny look on her face—staring at him, hand raised. She waved it.

"Hello?"

"Hello," Lucas said and then saw that she was beautiful, and of course Dalton was here with her tonight. Her gown was red, and it was gorgeous. Her long dark blonde hair was swept back and over her shoulders, and she was even wearing long gloves. Dalton was straight, and he was with the perfect woman.

And Lucas bit down hard on the insides of his cheeks so he wouldn't start crying. Instead, after taking a deep breath, he said, "You both look gorgeous—you especially, Rebecca."

Her smile was dazzling, and it was like a knife to the heart.

"Shall we go in?" asked Dalton, and when Lucas looked at him and the way Dalton was looking back, for just one second he thought he saw….

No. Stop. Stop looking for something that isn't there. Dalton is with her.

"Baby?" said Etienne, and Lucas turned to him and saw the troubled look on his face—

I did that.

—and he leaned in and kissed him lightly on the lips, right in front of everyone.

Including Dalton.

"Everything is fine," Lucas lied. Then he nodded. "Yes. Let's go in."

4

THEY EVEN sat at the same table.

It might have been better if they hadn't. He wouldn't have had to look at them having fun.

Rebecca laughed, and she looked like she should be some kind of movie star or beauty queen. Dalton waited on her—the perfect gentleman—getting her faux champagne and little treats and of course asking her to dance.

It was a relief when Sam showed up and joined them. They'd turned into the finishing-each-other's-sentences kind of friends, and now he could talk and distract himself from thoughts of losing his virginity or watching Dalton with Rebecca. And she'd come stag because she refused to come with a guy, and the girl she sometimes saw was totally on the down low. Even Lucas didn't know her name.

His first dance was with her. It was easier dancing with a girl, especially when there was nothing sexual there. It made him think that he could dance with a boy—could dance with Etienne—before the night was over.

Etienne had to ask Lucas to dance three times before he could. Funny that he'd fantasized about this for years, and yet it took three times to get him out on the floor.

And it was… nice. Nice that the body fit against his the way it should. Nice that there was a hard chest against his instead of soft breasts.

And a certain sexiness in knowing his crotch was pressed against a male crotch. That he knew what was there instead of the sort of scary mystery of what lay there with a girl.

Then to his surprise, soon other people asked him to dance. Julie, Sam's old crush. Rebecca—that was a shock. Even Diego—which made him uncomfortable at first since he clearly remembered the night the guy had tried to force him into sucking his cock. But it had been four or five years, and Diego seemed to be a different man. He even slipped Lucas his phone number.

Dalton didn't ask Lucas for a dance, though....

And after a while, Etienne didn't give him a chance. He made sure he got all the rest of the dances.

Their dancing wasn't universally accepted. There were some sneers, a few frowns, at least one not-so-whispered *"Fags!"* But for the most part, it really was magic. Dancing under aluminum-foil-covered stars and silver streamers to the music of the band. With a guy. No pretending at all. He was dancing with a guy, in front of his whole school.

Etienne was looking at him with pride and love and *God-I'm-giving-you-my-virginity-tonight.*

And I'm going to take it, Lucas thought, even though somehow he'd always assumed he was going to be the one to be taken. But he hadn't followed any instructions, hadn't gotten himself clean—not in that way.

It had never occurred to him.

They danced to "Wannabe" by the Spice Girls (which Lucas couldn't help but dance to despite the lyrics that made him nervous) and "Show Me Love" by Robyn (Lucas loved Robyn) and "Semi-Charmed Life" by Third Eye Blind (who could resist the beat?) and "Hot in Here" by Nelly (which also made Lucas quite nervous but obviously pleased Etienne, to go by the flashing in his eyes) with its lines about shooting my steam and taking off your clothes (the chaperones were letting them play this song?).

The ballads were the worst.

How could Lucas tell Etienne that he couldn't slow dance? But did it have to be Jewel's "You Were Meant for Me," even though it was sort of a breakup song?

"You *were* meant for me," Etienne told him, holding him close and swaying to the song and—*God, God, God*—Etienne was hard. Lucas could feel it pressed against him and damned his body for responding. What message was that giving?

That song led to "A Thousand Miles" by Vanessa Carlton, and when Lucas saw Dalton dancing with Rebecca over Etienne's shoulder, he had to pull away and go back to the table.

"You okay?" Etienne asked, and Lucas made some excuse about needing some air, and it was only logical that Etienne asked him if he wanted to step outside.

Why not?

It got him away from having to watch Dalton dance so close with Rebecca.

Would they be having sex too? Lucas wondered, which of course reminded him that, apparently, he was losing his virginity tonight.

There were other people who'd had the same idea, and most of them were hanging in the shadows so they could smoke and make out. Etienne took him by the hand and led him to one of those shadows and soon was kissing him.

He was a good kisser, there was no denying that, and Etienne was male, and the feeling of that muscular chest against Lucas's and his strong arms wrapped around him made his body respond once again.

Etienne shifted his hardness against Lucas's and said, "God, that is so damned sexy. I can't wait for us to get our clothes off. You?"

"I…. I…." What to say? "You just don't know…."

Etienne flashed him a smile, and his perfect teeth shone in the dark from the reflection of the streetlights that lined the sidewalk.

"I bet when we rub them together we can get a fire going, *denk je niet*?"

Lucas gulped. Etienne was slipping into Dutch again. He did that when he got particularly excited or romantic. It was cute. Maybe even a little sexy. But hell, he had no idea what Etienne was saying. He could be asking for a recipe for chicken parmesan for all Lucas knew.

"Oh, Lucas," Etienne said with a sigh. "You have no idea what you do to me." He trembled and pressed his hardness against Lucas's.

Definitely *not* the recipe for chicken parmesan.

"You're so *mooi*. Beautiful. Like a *meisje*—like a girl."

And there it was, that dreaded word. Girl. He *wasn't* a girl!

"Oh, Lucas!" Etienne said and kissed Lucas again and then held him, pushing him up against one of the pillars, getting ready to kiss him once more, and…

…that was when Lucas saw Dalton and Rebecca.

They were kissing too.

Hell, not just kissing. Making out! They looked like they were going to start having sex right there. It hurt and made him angry and made him want to puke.

And then Etienne was kissing him again, and it felt good to be wanted when someone else couldn't be bothered, and Lucas finally surrendered and knew that later tonight, he was going to truly be with another guy for the first time.

Somebody who cared about him.

5

THEY GOT to the Haven's 24 Inn about eleven. Etienne already had the key, so there was no embarrassing moment with the front desk clerk at the little no-tell motel. No disapproving looks or comments when two young men wearing tuxedos tried to get a room on the night of the town's high school senior prom.

It was with fear and excitement that Lucas got out of Etienne's car—or at least Etienne's sponsor's car.

I can't believe I am doing this. I am finally losing my virginity!

But that was when he saw Dalton's car. He wasn't prepared to see the little Honda parked outside the hotel room three or four doors down from the one Etienne was leading him to. For a moment Lucas thought he would die.

But then Etienne unlocked the door and, to Lucas's total surprise, scooped him up and carried him over the threshold and to the bed. He kissed him and then left him long enough to light some candles that had obviously been put there earlier. Then Etienne locked the door, went to the bathroom, and when he returned, he had a bucket with a champagne bottle sticking out of it, which he placed on the table on Lucas's side of the big bed. He popped it and poured it into two lovely fluted glasses.

"To us," Etienne said, and Lucas sat up and took the offered glass. They clinked, sipped, and then kissed.

It was sweet. It really was.

Etienne had gone to a lot of trouble to make this evening perfect, that was clear.

I'd be stupid to let this pass me by. It wasn't what he had dreamed of, but that fantasy wasn't going to happen, was it? Dalton didn't love him. Or wouldn't. Couldn't? But this young man loved him. He wanted to make love. God. He wanted Lucas to… fuck him.

Quite suddenly he flashed on Dalton. He couldn't help it.

Were he and Rebecca naked yet? Were *they* fucking?

"Baby?"

Lucas looked at the man who was so very busy looking at him—*really* looking at him and no one else.

Let it go, he told himself. *Take what's right there wanting you.*

"Oh, Lucas. *Ik hou van jou,*" Etienne said with a soft gasp. "You know I love you, right?"

Lucas gulped. Love? Had Etienne ever said anything about love? "I know now." The thing was, Lucas didn't know whether to be excited or scared, thrilled or horrified. Love? Etienne loved him?

"You didn't know already?" Etienne asked.

And oh, the look of surprise on Etienne's face. Had he really thought Lucas knew? That Etienne loved him?

I didn't know!

Liar. You knew.

"We never said it before…," he reasoned. Carefully.

"Well, I do. I *love* you, Lucas. Please tell me you love me too."

But as he looked into those pleading eyes, Lucas knew he didn't. He didn't love Etienne, and he couldn't say that he did.

Just like Dalton can't tell me he loves me when he doesn't.

No. He couldn't say it. So he kissed him instead.

That's what Etienne needed. Or near enough.

Etienne put the champagne glasses aside, pushed Lucas back onto the bed, and kissed Lucas in a way he'd never dreamed possible. And he kissed back.

He thinks this means you love him too.

I never said it.

Doesn't matter.

That night he was going to do what Etienne wanted. It wasn't the way he'd imagined losing his virginity, but there were far worse ways. And who knew? Maybe he could learn to love him.

Lucas took a deep breath. In his head he heard his mother say, "Let me give you this one piece of advice. I'm not stupid enough to think you'll wait until you get married to have sex. Damn it, you can't *get* married! But do this, Lucas. Make sure the first time is special. Don't just throw it away like a piece of garbage. Make it something you'll remember forever. Make it something that when you're fifty or sixty or eighty—"

Eighty? Would he ever get to be eighty? That was older than she was!

"—that you can look back on and smile. Will you do that for me?"

This is a good first time. And God, Etienne certainly knew how to kiss.

Suddenly Etienne pulled away and sat up on the edge of the bed. He was panting. He was wiping at his face.

What the hell? "Etienne? Are you okay?"

There was a long pause.

"This is wrong…," Etienne whispered.

Lucas propped himself up on his elbows. "*What's* wrong?" he asked, confused. Dazed from the passionate kissing.

"I…. I need to tell you something."

"What?" *What did he want to say? Screw talking!* The time for talking was past.

"I'm… I'm not telling you everything. *That's* what's wrong."

You're not telling me everything? Well, Etienne, that makes two of us. He closed his eyes, took a deep breath, then slowly let it out. He reached out and touched Etienne's arm. "Etienne?"

"I'm leaving, Lucas. This summer. I'm going home. And I don't know if I'll be back."

At first the words didn't make any sense. They had taken Lucas completely by surprise. Leaving? Not coming back? What was he talking about? *Going home?* "Going home?"

Etienne turned and looked at him, and there were tears in his eyes. "Lucas. I'm a foreign exchange student, for Christ's sake. I was here for a year. It's time for me to go home."

Lucas froze. Then it hit him. Of course. Why hadn't he realized that?

Because you weren't thinking about it.

"Before we go on, you need to know. If we do this…. We might not see each other again. I can't promise you anything but tonight. And a few more weeks."

And for some reason, that was a relief. Lucas relaxed.

Etienne looked away. "Something else."

"What?" Lucas asked. He touched Etienne again.

"You won't tell me?"

Tell him? Tell him what? "Tell you what?"

"That you're in love with *him*?" he asked in a tone that was almost a snarl.

Lucas shivered. God. Did he even do Etienne the injustice of asking who? Lucas swallowed. Tried to decide what to say.

Etienne sighed. "I knew it," he whispered. "You love Dalton."

"Yes," Lucas said before he even knew he was going to say it.

"You know he's straight, right?" Etienne wiped his face. "That he can't love you back?"

Crying? Was he crying?

Etienne turned, and yes, he was crying.

"Yes," Lucas said.

There was a long pause. "So now what?"

Lucas took a deep breath.

"But do this, Lucas. Make sure the first time is special…. Will you do that for me?"

He'd told her that he thought he could.

He thought that if he made love with Etienne right now, it was something he could look back on and smile.

He reached out and touched Etienne's face. "Make love to me, Etienne," he said in a voice barely above a whisper.

And Etienne was kissing him again. He pushed him back onto the bed once more, climbed onto him, and *kissed* him. Then he rolled Lucas over onto his side. Soon the clothes began to come off, shirts first, and their bare chests touched. Etienne's was so big for such a slim (skinny) guy, but smooth. Smooth as Lucas's. Not a single hair.

Then belts were undone and zippers came down. Lucas looked down and marveled at the sight of Etienne's underwear-clad erection, the wet spot, knowing that meant Etienne wanted him.

I can do this.

He scooted down and pulled at Etienne's underwear, securing them under his hairless testicles, freeing Etienne's cock.

It was a lovely cock. He had a foreskin since he'd been born and raised in the Netherlands, but this one was tighter and shorter than the last one Lucas had seen. It didn't look anything like an elephant's trunk.

Do it.

Suck him.

He was opening his mouth, bending forward, when there was a pounding on the door...

6

AND HE heard Dalton's voice.

"*Lucas!* Are you in there?"

The pounding got louder.

"Lucas!" Dalton was shouting.

"Fuck!" cried Etienne.

There was a moment of silence and then pounding again. But it wasn't their door. It was the door next door.

Shit.

Now, shouting. Some man shouting. Lucas could hear it even through the walls, through the door. This wasn't a luxury hotel, after all.

"Who the fuck are you?" came a strange voice.

Dalton's voice wasn't quite as easy to make out. He'd stopped shouting. Sorry? Was that it? Something about a wrong door?

Then Lucas was off the bed and running to the door. What if the screamer hurt Dalton?

"Lucas!" That was Etienne. "Where are you going?"

It couldn't be helped. How could he do anything else?

Lucas yanked the door open, only half zipping up first, and stepped out to see a big man, even bigger than Dalton—wide and heavy as well as tall and muscular—raising his fists.

"I'm sorry, man," Dalton said, holding his hands out before him. "I was just looking for...." Then Dalton saw him. He locked eyes with Lucas—and God, the emotions reflected in those eyes!—and...

Dalton didn't see it coming. Didn't see the big man swing, didn't dodge. The fist hit him square on the jaw, and he went down like a felled tree.

"Dalton!" Lucas screamed and launched himself at Dalton's attacker. He ran, jumped, landed on the man's back and, without realizing what he'd done, put him in a chokehold.

It was a valiant try, but it was like trying to ride a bull at a rodeo. The man had to be double Lucas's weight, at least—Lucas weighed no more than a hundred and twenty pounds. A swift elbow to his stomach and the air *whooshed* out of Lucas's lungs with an "*Ooof!*" He went stumbling back, and before he could fall, the man's locomotive fist hit him. He whirled around and went down hard. And then he was swallowed by darkness.

The last echoing thing he heard was, "Lucas!"

7

LUCAS WOKE to a circle of faces peering down at him. He had no idea how long he'd been out—in fact didn't really understand fully that he'd been unconscious at all. Only that one minute he'd witnessed a big fist hurtling meteorically toward this face, and the next there was a simply unbelievable amount of pain, and he was spinning, and then the ground was coming up at him. More pain, the wind being knocked from him again, and there, inches from his face, the butt of a crushed out cigarette, and…

…then he was here.

Wherever here was, although here was softer than the concrete where he'd been before.

A cigarette butt. There had been a cigarette butt. And had there been a trundling roly-poly bug as well—looking as if it were the size of a tank?

"Lucas! Thank God!" That was Dalton, and oh… oh… the look on his face. Before he knew what was happening, Dalton swept him up in his arms. "Lucas, baby, you scared the shit out of me."

Baby? Had Dalton just called him baby?

"Wha-what hap-happened," he asked, and God, suddenly he was hurting. His head was buzzing, and his jaw was killing him, and there was the taste of copper. Blood? Was that blo—

But suddenly he didn't care.

He was in Dalton's arms.

Bliss!

He opened his eyes to see Etienne and Rebecca—fucking Rebecca—looking on. The sneer on her face! And…. Oh…. Lucas swallowed hard. The anguish on Etienne's.

"Wha…. Who?"

"Your boyfriend rescued you," Rebecca snarled.

"Etienne?"

"Not the wimp," she snapped. "Your *other* boyfriend."

Other boyfriend? What other boyfriend?

"He was like fucking Superman or something," Etienne said, distress coming through his voice as well. "He just beat that big guy up."

"The guy who punched me?" Lucas asked. Because that was what happened, right? That big bruiser who had tried to hurt Dalton?

"Dalton?" Lucas pulled back, and Dalton gave a shrug and ran his fingers through his shaggy mop of hair and….

God! Dalton's hand! It was bloody. All scuffed up.

"Dalton!" He grabbed Dalton's hand—Dalton hissed—and then more gently brought it to his mouth and kissed the abused knuckles, not caring about blood, only that Dalton was hurt. Helping him. "Oh, Dalton…."

"Oh. Fuck. This. *Shit!*" Rebecca said. "Et, can you give me a ride home?"

"What?" asked Etienne. "No, I can't give you a ride home. Lucas and I are…."

"Lucas and you aren't doing shit! Can't you see that?" She tossed her gorgeous blonde hair.

"What? Lucas?"

Lucas looked at Etienne, saw the confusion. And something more. Hurt?

"Dalton!" Etienne said. "Do you think you can let go of my boyfriend?"

Rebecca let out a puff of air. "God, this is *pathetic*."

Dalton started to pull away, but Lucas held on. He wasn't letting go. Not yet.

"Et!" snapped Rebecca. "Can't you see we lost?"

"Lost?" Etienne said, his voice filled with confusion and, yes, hurt.

"*Christ*, I know you're not *that* stupid. Can't you see the way they're looking at each other? They've only got eyes for each other. They've chosen each other. We. Lost."

Etienne shook his head. "Lucas? Is that true?"

The pain in Etienne's eyes made Lucas's heart hurt, but… he turned back to Dalton. Did he dare hope? Was Rebecca right? Surely not. But then he saw it. Saw what she had seen. God! The look in Dalton's beautiful eyes. Could it be?

Dalton gave a single nod.

"No," cried Etienne. "He's straight." He stepped up to Dalton and shoved him. "He's straight, Lucas. You can't choose him. Choose *me*! Please!"

"Et!" Rebecca shook her head. "You're groveling. Show some pride, man. Let's get out of here."

"No! Lucas!"

Lucas looked at him.

"Choose me! How can you have anything with a straight guy? You think he can make you happy? I can make you happy! I—I'll find a way to stay here in America. And I will make you happy."

"Lucas?" It was Dalton.

Now he was looking at the one he'd loved since the day a boy taught another how to tie his shoes. And he was seeing love in his eyes. He was sure of it.

"Pick me," Dalton whispered.

"But…." *You're straight.* He started to push away—Etienne was right, wasn't he? How could he choose Dalton, as much as he wanted to?—but this time Dalton wouldn't let go.

"Pick me, Lucas. I'm so sorry I've pushed you away. Tell me it's not too late. Pick me?"

"Oh, Dalton."

And then they were kissing.

No bottle to spin tonight. Only fate. Only their whole lives.

He heard a sob, but he couldn't break the kiss. He just couldn't. It was Dalton who did first, and when—with guilt and a little shame—Lucas glanced at Etienne, he saw that his boyfriend had turned and was leaving the room. Rebecca was already gone. Etienne dared one last look back, but Lucas could only shrug helplessly.

He didn't know if this was truly real.

But he had to find out.

Etienne turned and left.

And now there were only the two of them.

8

LUCAS OPENED his mouth to ask how, but before he could ask anything, Dalton was kissing him again. Soft at first, and then harder. It hurt Lucas's jaw, but he wasn't about to stop him. He had waited far too many years for this.

But then... then he had to stop. He had to know. He had to know what this was. Was it for real?

With a little cry, he pulled his mouth from Dalton's and asked in one breath. "How?"

"How?" Dalton repeated.

"How can this be happening?" Lucas asked, surprised to find he felt almost angry. "You said you weren't gay."

Dalton shrugged. "I don't know if I am."

Now Lucas did push away. "Then how can you ask me to choose you? At least Etienne is *gay*! He *loves* me."

"I love you," Dalton whispered. "I've always loved you." And his eyes! They were filled with a maelstrom of emotions.

"But you're not gay.... How can we have *anything* if you don't want me the way I want you?"

"Like this?" Dalton asked, his voice still barely above a murmur, and he took Lucas's hand and placed it on his...

God. He was hard! Dalton was hard. But how?

"I don't understand...."

"I went to get ice...." Dalton's voice hitched. "For...."

"Ice?" Lucas asked, confused. What did ice have to do with anything?

Dalton nodded. His Adam's apple bobbed. "And I saw Etienne's car. I just froze. I realized that you must be here with him. Why else would his car be here? I started... fuck. I started shaking. I just suddenly saw the two of you naked together."

Just like me.

"I got the goddamned ice and went back to the room and Rebecca. She was already naked. And all I could think of was you. Here I had her, naked and ready for me at last—"

At last?

"—and all I could think of was you. I looked at her smiling, trying to look sexy for me—and I saw your face. I looked at her breasts... and they... they weren't right. They weren't doing anything for me. All I could think of was your pretty bare chest...."

Lucas's eyes widened. What? "My pretty chest?"

Dalton's eyes filled with desire. "So flat, with just the smallest amount of definition. So smooth. Not one hair...."

Dalton had looked at his chest?

"Your sexy little nipples. And right then I knew... knew I didn't want her. I wanted you."

"Me?"

"But there she was. What was I supposed to do? She was motioning me over to the bed, and I saw all she had to offer. A normal life. Marriage. Kids. Everything I wanted."

"And we can't get married," Lucas said, his eyes filling with tears. "Can't have kids."

"But then she did it, Lucas. Made it impossible. She actually said that she wanted to suck my cock, and then... all I could think of was you. That night."

"That night?" Lucas asked. What night?

But then he knew. Or thought he did. "When I asked if I could be the first to do that to you?"

Dalton nodded.

"But all you could promise was that you wouldn't let another guy do it first."

Dalton shook his head. "No. I realized I couldn't have my first time be with anyone but you. It had to be you. It has always had to be you. I don't know how I couldn't have known. But I love you, Lucas, and I want you. Please say yes."

Lucas let out a laugh. Dalton had to ask? "Yes," he said.

And then they were kissing again.

They didn't stop this time.

Dalton lay down on the bed next to him, and they kissed and touched and held each other. Lucas's face still hurt, but he didn't care. He wanted this. Needed it. It would have taken a lot more pain for him to consider stopping.

He could touch Dalton's chest now, and God, had he ever imagined anything like this? Dalton's chest was so different from his own. Different than Etienne's. Bigger. Harder. And hairy. Not overly so, but oh so soft and spread out everywhere. He wanted to feel it against his face, and when he had the chance, he lowered his head and lightly rubbed his cheek against it. So sexy. So, *so* sexy.

But then Dalton was rolling him over on his back and kissing, kissing, kissing downward. He kept traveling down, down Lucas's body, and was there any way Dalton couldn't see his straining erection?

"Oh, Lucas," Dalton said with a heady growl. "My tiger. At last."

At last?

Dalton unsnapped Lucas's trousers and had them unzipped before he realized what was happening. A few quick yanks later and his pants were open and his erection springing out, and then… oh God, then he was in Dalton's mouth!

Dalton took him deep, and Lucas arched up off the bed and almost came in that instant. He wasn't sure how he didn't. Dalton was humming, causing the most amazing vibration through his cock, and he had to bite down on the insides of his cheek to stop himself from finishing too soon. It worked. The bite set off the pain in his jaw, and his ass dropped back to the bed. Now Dalton was bobbing up and down on his cock, and he reached down and clutched at Dalton's shaggy hair and let out a sob. He couldn't believe how it felt. Nothing could have prepared him for this. Certainly not his hand. Not the hundreds of ways he'd masturbated in his life. Nothing came close.

And just as he thought he could stop it no longer, even dropping his jaw to his shoulder more than once, Dalton released him and began to gently suck his balls. Oh, oh, oh! Exquisite! Torture! Exquisite wonderful torture!

"P-please, Dalton. P-please stop. I'm going to cum!"

But instead of stopping, Dalton let out a cry and took Lucas's cock back into his hot, wet mouth, and it was over. Lucas thought he would die from the pleasure of it. A shock traveled through his entire body, and he unleashed a lifetime of need into Dalton's mouth, his semen jetting out of him and into the love of his life. Dalton swallowed greedily, moaning almost as loudly as Lucas cried.

He thought he would black out. Maybe he did? For then Dalton was on top of him and lightly kissing him and using tongue to ask for permission for more. Lucas opened his mouth, accepted Dalton in, tasted himself, and felt his cock hardening again (if it had ever really gone soft). They kissed for a long moment, but that taste reminded him of what he really wanted. He pushed at Dalton's chest and somehow managed to get him to roll off, and then he just kept rolling until he was on top. Dalton had no shirt to unbutton—and did Rebecca still have it? he wondered for less than a second—and at last he could worship that chest. Touch it and kiss it, make love to it, find Dalton's nipples and suck on them and delight in feeling them harden in his mouth and how soft that hair was on his tongue.

Now it was his turn to travel down, down, down that lightly furry belly to the place the skin disappeared into Dalton's pants. The bulge in those trousers looked huge. Much bigger than he remembered. Could the fabric make it look that big?

Time to find out.

He had Dalton's pants undone just as fast as Dalton had had his, and suddenly there it was (at last!): Dalton's erection.

It was bigger. Lucas was sure of it.

But Dalton had been thirteen then. He was eighteen now.

It was beautiful.

Thick, so thick Lucas could barely get his hand around it. And long. Longer than Lucas's own modest six inches. It was surrounded by a soft forest of hair that looked almost sculpted—a soft pillow for Dalton's cock to rest upon. It throbbed in Lucas's hand, and a big crystalline drop formed at the head.

Lucas had to have it.

He licked it off, and his tongue tingled and delighted at the taste while Dalton cried out. Then he was taking it in his mouth, and God, if being sucked was pleasure, this was even more.

It was so alive!

The feel of the skin and the taste and the musky scent. It filled his mouth, and his sore jaw objected, and his sore jaw be damned. He took as much into his mouth as he could before gagging and retreating a bit and experimenting until, yes, he could take it deep, and he began to suck in earnest. He let his tongue move and massage the underside and was rewarded with more fluid, and he sucked more. Now Dalton's fingers tangled in *his* hair, and Dalton was crying, telling Lucas how much he loved him, and it was music.

Lucas found he couldn't stop. He thrust his own erection against Dalton's leg. Couldn't stop bobbing and sucking and seeing how deep he could go. He played with Dalton's big balls, wanted to taste them too—like Dalton had done—but he just couldn't stop. He wanted Dalton. He wanted all of Dalton.

"Oh! Oh, baby. I… I'm going to…!"

Yes, yes, yes!

Please!

And Dalton poured into Lucas's mouth, thick jet after jet after jet, and any fear that he'd ever had that he wouldn't like it was cast away in less than an instant. It was thick and sweet, so sweet, with only the slightest tang. He swallowed and swallowed and swallowed again, and then before he could stop himself, he was riding another orgasm, shooting all over Dalton's pants leg.

Couldn't be helped now.

He collapsed onto Dalton, his cock slipping from his mouth, and rested his sore face against Dalton's hitching belly, felt the still-hard erection against his neck and throat.

He'd done it.

He had sucked Dalton's cock.

It was wonderful.

He told Dalton he loved him and slipped off to sleep.

9

BEFORE THE night was over, Dalton fucked him. He offered himself, but they both knew the way it would be between them. Who knew what might happen one day? But that night and through the months to come, it was Dalton inside him.

That first morning, waking in each other's arms in that no-tell motel, Lucas asked it again for the first time since they were kids.

"Marry me, Dalton."

Dalton sighed, rolled over, and threw a leg on top of Lucas. "Not that again! Lucas, we can't get married. We're never going to be able to get married."

"I heard about this church," Lucas said. "They've got one in Kansas City. It's called MCC. It's a gay church. And they do these things called Holy Unions. They're not legal of course, but—"

"Then why bother?" Dalton interrupted. "It won't mean anything, Lucas!"

"But what does that matter? It's the ceremony, isn't it? The commitment?"

Dalton looked at him. Kissed him on the nose. "Baby. I don't need any ceremony except to be in your arms. And I'm sorry, I'm not doing any 'Holy Union.' Unless it's legal, I'm not doing it. And that's never going to happen. Not in our lifetime."

It hurt, made Lucas's heart hurt. But then Dalton was kissing him and making love to him, and he forgot all about marriage and Holy Unions.

For a while.

They learned a lot about each other's bodies in those months of summer before Dalton had to go away to college.

And way too soon, those days of summer were ending.

10

"ARE YOU sure about this?" Lucas asked for what felt like the millionth time. It all seemed too impossible. Dalton's parents? Well, they were nothing like his mother. That was for sure. Lucas knew they were why it had taken Dalton so long to come out. Or was about to.

"I'm sure," Dalton said and kissed him, right there on the doorstep in front of Dalton's home.

Heart in his throat, Lucas followed Dalton into his house. His very big house. Dalton came from money, and the house was in the nicest neighborhood of Terra's Gate.

It wasn't the first time Lucas had been in Dalton's house, of course. He'd known him his whole life—or at least most of it. The house wasn't the same one he'd lived in back in those shoestring days. Dalton's father had climbed the corporate ladder pretty quickly and had considered moving to Kansas City. Thankfully Dalton's mother prevailed, saying that the quiet of a small town—even a college town—was a better place for Dalton to be raised. Lucas wasn't sure what he would have done if Dalton had moved away.

The smell of food filled the house. They were having dinner with Dalton's parents, and Lucas was so nervous he wasn't sure how he would eat.

Dalton was coming out to his family tonight.

More—he was telling them that they were lovers.

Lucas couldn't get rid of the feeling that this was a very bad idea.

They already were pretty unhappy with their son for changing his college plans at the last minute. He was all set to go to the University of Missouri in Rolla—a science and technology school. Perfect for Dalton, who had always been one for taking apart and putting things back together (starting with the tying of shoes). But then he had elected to stay in Terra's Gate instead and go to Wagner University. His parents had acknowledged it was a good school, so they hadn't fought it too much. They just couldn't understand why he'd chosen to stay.

The reason, of course, was Lucas.

"I can't bear to do it," Dalton had said, and no matter what Lucas did to try and convince him otherwise, his mind was made up. Of course Lucas hadn't had his heart in it. Which made him feel guilty. But *he* couldn't bear the idea of Dalton leaving either.

"Mom?" Dalton called out. "We're here."

The one source of relief was that Dalton's father wasn't home yet. His Lexus wasn't in the driveway.

"Hello, boys."

They turned as one, and there she was. Mrs. Denise Churchill. Looking like she was dressed for a business dinner in a white blouse buttoned high and a black skirt and sensible heels. She was a handsome woman—no, beautiful—with brown hair cupped around her head and face like a bonnet. She was smiling, but it didn't quite reach her green eyes. She was studying them both, and Lucas couldn't help feeling that she was actually looking inside his head.

"Hello, Mrs. Churchill," Lucas said.

"Lucas." She nodded, then turned to her son. "Do I get a kiss, Dalton?"

"Sure, Mom." Dalton went to her, and she put her arms around his neck, and he gave her a peck on the cheek.

"I hope you boys are hungry. I've made a big beef roast with all the fixings: salad, mashed potatoes, rolls—they're not as good as what my mother made, but they're good. Do you like carrots, Lucas? I cooked them with the roast."

"Yes, ma'am," he replied.

She raised a brow high enough that it disappeared under her bangs. "Ma'am? Mrs. Churchill? Why so formal tonight? What happened to Mrs. C? You're making me nervous." She gave her son a steady gaze. Then turned. "I've made iced tea. Would you boys like some?"

They followed her out of the living room and into the kitchen. It was a big kitchen. Easily twice the size of Lucas's, with a big island in the middle with both electric and gas burners and a grill. The cabinets were all glass faced, and Lucas knew from experience that all you had to do was touch them and gentle lights came on inside for late-night visits. The floors were heated as well.

"Will you pour, son?" asked Mrs. C.

The pitcher was on the island, along with glasses and lemon slices. Dalton poured and gave the first glass to Lucas—even though he shook his head no—and the second to his mother before taking the third for himself. He pulled Lucas to the counter that separated the kitchen from the dining room and sat them down together.

Again Dalton's mother studied Lucas. "I made German chocolate cake for dessert. I wish it could have been pie, but they're not my strong point. Not from scratch, that is."

"I *love* German chocolate cake," Lucas said.

She smiled. "I know. Dalton told me. He said you make one to die for, yourself. I wanted to make sure we had something you enjoyed. I hope it is as good as yours."

Lucas's gut clenched. For some reason he wasn't feeling good about this. He hadn't before. He wasn't now.

Mrs. C took a sip of her tea, then placed it on the counter. "Your father should be here soon. I think I'll fix the potatoes. Would you get the pot, Dalton? Drain it there in the strainer in the sink. That's a good boy."

Dalton got up, rolled his eyes at Lucas, and went to the stove. He snagged some oven mitts that matched the kitchen colors beautifully and grabbed the big steaming pot. Then he poured it into the sink.

"Does your mother make mashed potatoes from scratch, Lucas?" she asked, back to him and plugging in a hand mixer. "Or does she use the instant boxed stuff?"

Geez. What the hell was wrong? She had never seemed to love him, but she'd never been like this.

"It depends," he answered. "If we're in a rush, she uses the boxed stuff. But when it counts, she makes them from scratch. Sometimes she adds cheese and chives."

She paused. "Well, I guess with her having to work, she doesn't have as much free time. It's good she tries."

Then she began to make her mashed potatoes, with short orders to Dalton for cream and real butter. She used the mixer with her right hand and took a sip of her iced tea with her left. Then she held it high. "Dalton, dear, slip some vodka in this for your mother. Not too much!"

Vodka?

Dalton got a pained expression on his face, took the proffered glass, and left the room.

Vodka in her tea?

Lucas knew she was no teetotaler, but vodka *in* your tea? What happened to martinis? The ones she trained Dalton to make when he was a kid and pretty much why Lucas had guessed his boyfriend—

(Boyfriend! He still couldn't believe it.)

—had all but stopped drinking himself.

When Dalton came back, she was adding the butter to her potatoes and hardly looked as he handed her the glass.

"You didn't put too much in?" she asked, loud enough to be heard above the noise of the mixer. "You know when I have too much I lose my tongue, and I must keep that tonight!"

The comment did nothing but make Lucas all the more nervous.

When she was finished with her mixing, she was also half-done with her cocktail. She wasn't playing around tonight. At least with her martinis, she sipped. She put a lid on the pot with the potatoes, checked the roast in the big oven set in the stone wall, and then asked them if they "would like to retire to the living room?" She lagged behind, and it was only when she sat down on the chair next to the love seat that Dalton had insisted he and Lucas use that Lucas saw why. Her tea was near full again and suspiciously lighter in color.

"So how was your day, boys? The summer is almost over. What did you two get up to?" She crossed her legs, and Lucas noticed she was wearing hose. Lucas couldn't believe it. His mother hated them with a passion. She didn't like wearing hose at work as an administrative assistant—

"Glorified secretary is what I am," she would state with a sigh.

—and she certainly wouldn't wear them at home. Not even for company, and definitely not for Dalton, a boy she had known for pretty much his entire life. So why was this woman wearing them. For Lucas? He hadn't ever noticed them before. In fact, she'd always worn pantsuits or obviously expensive and even ironed jeans (and who ironed jeans?).

"We went swimming," Dalton said.

"At Wagner Public?" she asked.

Dalton shook his head. "No. Smithville," he answered. Which was a lie. They'd gone to a pond that a nearby farmer had dug up in the middle of one of his cornfields and let the rain fill. Apparently he'd made it for local gay naturists, which meant skinny-dipping. Dalton had heard about it from Diego Hernandez and actually gone with a group of guys almost a year ago—

(which made Lucas very jealous until Dalton promised that he hadn't done anything with Diego or any of the guys)

—after he turned eighteen. Lucas wasn't quite eighteen yet, but Dalton reasoned that it would only be the two of them. What could happen?

"You didn't drink, now, did you?" she asked and took a healthy swig herself.

Dalton assured her that it had been nothing but colas. Which was true. What they'd done was make love. Twice. Dalton had even insisted Lucas top him, which wasn't Lucas's favorite thing (it almost seemed wrong—it was only the second time he'd done it), but still, it had been bliss. Dalton had loved it, cried out in joy, and being inside Dalton had felt amazing.

Mrs. C turned to him and quite without warning was looking directly into his eyes, seemed to be watching the movie in his mind. He blushed hotly, as if she really had seen what he had been seeing.

She pursed her lips, nodded once, and looked away. For a second Lucas thought he would puke.

Then she started talking about what she'd done that day: breakfast with Sharon Solomon and then a meeting for the annual Kingston Charity Dinner—of which she was secretary—and how she was concerned with the lack of donations with any real worth for the auction.

"I mean, *please*," she was saying as Dalton's father came into the room. "A necklace of only six carats? Last year we had one that was 18.6—and I thought that one was rather cheap. How chintzy are people getting?"

"Next year they'll be donating cubic zirconium, right, dear?" Mr. Churchill added, standing in the doorway like some ancient god.

They all turned in unison.

Lucas actually trembled.

"I know, *right*?" Mrs. C said.

Dalton's father was a tall man, taller even than Dalton's own six feet, and his face looked as if it had been chiseled from stone. His features were hard, and his hair barely looked real, was cut military short on the sides with the top in short frozen waves. He wasn't as blatantly muscular as Dalton, but he was wide shouldered and very fit. Dalton said he ran five miles every morning before work. He also said the ladies loved him, but Lucas couldn't see it. The man was as cold as marble. Always had been.

Mrs. C had been the warmth of the family.

It amazed Lucas that Dalton was as passionate as he was. And in retrospect—the sudden understanding hit him in a way that almost made Lucas gasp aloud—what had surely been yet another reason Dalton had taken so long to proclaim his love.

"Good evening, Lucas," Mr. C said as Mrs. C got up and headed for the bar.

"Good evening, Mr. C," Lucas replied, trying the honorific he had used growing up and Mrs. C had insisted on earlier.

"Dinner is pretty much ready," Mrs. C said over the clinking of ice against glass. "All I have to do is put the rolls in. Ten minutes. You want me to do that now or give you a chance to sh—"

"Now will be perfect, dear," he said, interrupting her as she slipped him a short glass filled halfway with a tea-colored liquid. Scotch?

Whiskey? Lucas had no idea. His mother wasn't a drinker—not even wine. There had been no alcohol in the Arrowood household while Lucas was growing up. No martinis to learn to make. "Dalton, would you take my briefcase up to my study? It's in the hall."

"Yeah, sure," Dalton said, and once again Lucas was alone with one of these unknowable people.

"'Yeah, sure,'" Mr. C said in a gently mocking tone. "Can you believe that, Lucas?"

"Sir?" Lucas all but squeaked.

"There. See? 'Sir.' I don't know what's happened to Dalton this past year. He's lost all sense of respect. I suppose it comes with his age. Thinking he's a man—"

He is a man.

"—thinking he's old enough to make the decisions that will affect his entire life."

Mr. C laughed, and Lucas felt a chill. He opened his mouth to say "Don't you think he's old enough to make his own decisions?" because he felt Dalton *was* old enough, *was* a man. There were countries where a boy became a man at thirteen. But then he closed his mouth and left it unsaid. He could *see* that Dalton's father didn't agree. Not at all.

"Can I get you a drink, Lucas?" Mr. C asked.

Lucas. Not son. Mr. C had called him son for as far back as Lucas could remember.

He was getting a very bad feeling.

You're letting your imagination get away from you. You're just making mountains out of molehills.

Nervous about Dalton coming out. Coming out as gay. Coming out about their being lovers.

"No, thank you, Mr. Churchill," he answered, all thoughts of calling the man Mr. C abandoned. "I'm not old enough. I'm only seventeen."

"Seventeen?" the cold giant said quietly. "Really?"

"Not old enough for what?" asked Dalton, returning to the room.

"Of course, he's *only* seventeen," said Dalton's mother, one step behind. "He's a year behind Dalton. He's *always* been a year behind Dalton, darling."

"Not old enough for *what*?" Dalton asked again.

"For a cocktail," Mr. Churchill stated, almost vaguely, almost as if Dalton weren't even in the room.

"*Dad*!"

God! I've stumbled into The Addams Family *or something.*

"I won't tell if you don't," said Mr. Churchill.

Lucas gulped. "Thank you, sir. That's okay." And truth to tell, he wasn't interested. The thought of alcohol always made him think of a certain forever-ago day with spin the bottle and vanilla-flavored vodka, which had burned and tasted nasty and not anything like the bottle had suggested.

"Suit yourself," Mr. Churchill said.

Thankfully dinner came as quickly as promised. There was no grace, not even the simple "God is great, God is good, let us thank him for our food. Amen." that Lucas's mother insisted they say before every meal. And the meal was amazing. Mrs. C had always been a good cook.

They were soon at the dining room table—it was a strangely cold room, with wallpaper that looked like burlap to Lucas—and Dalton's parents sat at either end of the table, Dalton and Lucas across from each other. Lucas would have been more comfortable at a table like the much smaller one at home, sitting next to Dalton. Equally thankfully, the odd and disquieting conversation turned much more like the ones Lucas was used to at the Churchills'. Was Lucas sending out college applications yet? What movies were good right now? Which ones a waste of time? Mr. and Mrs. Churchill mentioned the books they were reading—Lucas hadn't heard of either of them—and was shy when he mentioned that he was reading *The Da Vinci Code*. Was the book too common for them? Then there was talk about if anyone thought the Chiefs would do well this year, which meant Lucas was completely lost.

It was after dinner that everything went wrong.

11

THE CONVERSATION started with a question.

"So, Lucas, you didn't tell me what college you're looking at attending," Mr. Churchill said over coffee on the patio. It was late summer, and even though it was after eight, the sky was still bright. "Or are you planning on college?"

He'd already asked that, hadn't he? And why hadn't Lucas answered? No. He'd started to answer, and then Mrs. C had cut in, asking Dalton if he'd ever finished reading *Trainspotting*….

"I just figured I'd go to Wagner University," Lucas said. "It's a top-rated school, and town residents don't have to do the whole dorm thing. And I'll probably qualify for some scholarships too. I've got a pretty good grade point average."

"It's 3.8," Dalton supplied proudly.

Mr. Churchill barely glanced his way before seeming to dismiss his son.

"And your major?"

"Not sure yet. I'll start with the general required classes that any major calls for. Get them out of the way."

Mr. Churchill nodded. "Dalton here"—and he pointed—"is going to the University of Missouri at Rolla."

Lucas did a double take. What? He turned to Dalton, who seemed equally surprised.

"No, I'm not, Dad. We talked about this and—"

"*Sir*," Mr. Churchill said, steel in his voice, clearly correcting his son. "Or Father. What's happening to you? Is frolicking with this boy softening your brain while it hardens your cock?"

Lucas gasped, Dalton's mouth fell open, and Mrs. C let out a "Richard. *Must* you be so crude? I thought we agreed to subtlety. *Ease into this.*"

They know! My God, they know. Lucas's heart leapt, and his stomach turned to lead. *I knew it.* He'd known something was up from the moment he and Dalton walked in the door.

"Subtlety is for *pussies*," Mr. Churchill snapped. "And I didn't realize until a week ago that was what my son *was*."

"Dad!" Dalton protested.

"What did I *just* say?" Mr. Churchill shouted. "*Father* or *sir!*"

Shit, thought Lucas, and his stomach began to roll, dinner the worse for wear for it.

"*Sir*," Dalton replied quietly.

"Now, as I was saying. Dalton will be attending University of Missouri in a few weeks. As a matter of fact, we will be going up a week early. As a family. Exploring the town. Touring campus."

"Da.... Father," Dalton said as Lucas watched helplessly. "I've already told them I won't be attending. We can't just show up and expect—"

"I've spoken to the dean," Mr. Churchill interrupted. He seemed to do a lot of that—interrupting. "I've arranged everything. *Explained* everything. Told him how you've been influenced"—he shot Lucas a look that made him so unsettled that for a second he thought he would lose his dinner—"and how you need to be away from it."

It? Had Mr. Churchill just called him an "it"?

"Like some kind of drug." The last dripping with disgust. "I told him that a man needs to get away from his childhood home, *learn* to be a man. The dean—the pussy—was not sympathetic with my feeling about your perversion—"

Again gasps, both from Dalton and Lucas.

What happened? wondered Lucas as he sat there—stunned. He felt like he was underwater. One minute they were having dinner. Contemplating the Kansas City Chiefs' prospects for the coming season—to which Lucas was not able to add anything—and the next Mr. Churchill was talking perversion?

"—but he *did* agree about the importance of leaving the nest. And in this, your mother and I both agree, it is very important."

"*Dad*," cried Dalton, ignoring his father's demanded title.

"It is time for you to be a man. Part of that means you can't be around *him* anymore." Mr. Churchill made a dismissive gesture at Lucas. "It's one thing for you two to play around at thirteen, fourteen. It's normal. Boys do that. I jerked off with my buddies...."

Mrs. C's eyes popped wide. "*Richard*. Please."

Mr. Churchill turned to her slowly, eyes flashing. "Denise. Why don't you go off and do something womanly? Make plans for your charity. Moan about the carats of that damned necklace. Count the coffers. I don't know. I don't really care. But if you don't have the stomach for this, then leave."

Lucas's eyes went even wider. That sense of being underwater intensified. He was stunned into incomprehension.

Mrs. C stood, eyes downcast, and went inside. She didn't even spare them a backward glance. No apologies. Nothing. Just left the room like a scolded puppy.

Mrs. C. The most formidable woman Lucas had ever known.

We were talking about the Chiefs.

Mr. Churchill, wife now discharged, snapped his attention back to Dalton. "It's not that I don't understand. He's pretty as a girl." He pointed at Lucas with his chin. "He's got an ass like a pair of grapefruit. *I'd* fuck him if he weren't underage—"

"*Dad*!" Dalton stood up fast.

"'*Dad*' what?" Mr. Churchill all but roared.

"That is my *lover* you're talking about."

And Lucas thought he might cry. But not from Mr. Churchill's ugly words.

Lover. Dalton had said it. Love surged up and through him, banished the stunned fear that had filled him. Said it in front of this roaring lion.

Mr. Churchill, though, growled. He actually growled. "*Lover!*" He flicked his hand at Lucas. "This isn't your 'lover.' This is your cum dump!"

"That's *it*!" Dalton declared. "Come on, Lucas. We're leaving."

"You step out that door and you won't *ever* walk back through it. Not even for your clothes."

Deathly silence followed. Lucas thought his heart would simply stop. Had Mr. Churchill just—

"Did you think I didn't know? Of course I knew. I was shocked when Rebecca told me that you begged that little pansy to choose you over the Dutch faggot. *Begged*, she said. I didn't want to believe it. *My* son begging *anyone*, let alone a boy. But Jesus bald-headed Christ, Dalton! He *is* a boy. He's underage, and if his mother pressed charges, you'd go to prison. Have you thought about that when you're screwing his tight little ass?"

Dalton's eyes went wide. Dalton clearly *hadn't* thought about that. Not really.

She wouldn't, though. She said Dalton was safe. She wants me to be with Dalton.... "She wouldn't do that," Lucas blurted without thinking.

"Am I speaking to you, Lucas? Did you somehow get that idea?"

"N-no," Lucas managed.

"Then shut the fuck up." Mr. Churchill turned back to Dalton and stabbed a finger at his son. "No. I didn't want to believe it. But then I checked your e-mail. Saw those ridiculous messages back and forth. You acting like some love-struck simpleton. The 'I love yous' and the 'No, I love you mores,' and dear *God*, the 'I want to suck your cocks!' *You* said it!" He shuddered. Then, in a mocking tone: "*Oh*, Lucas. I want to suck your beautiful *cock*." He grimaced. "But the worst was the pictures. Cocks and asses and goddamned *assholes*! I thought I would puke. *That* was the last straw."

"Oh my God," Lucas whispered. And watched as Dalton's face crumpled.

"Now you listen and you listen well. Lucas will now leave this house, *never* to return. And *you*, Dalton. *You* will go to University of Missouri at Rolla, and if you don't, then you are never to return to this house either. And I'll fuck your trust fund. See if I don't."

"That's from Nana," Dalton objected angrily.

"*See* if that stops me."

Mr. Churchill spun back to Lucas, and he flinched at the expression on the man's face. "*Now* I'm talking to you, you little cocksucker."

The evening started with a question. It ended the same way. With several.

"If you actually do profess to love my son, don't you want what is best for him? Do you really want to ruin his life? Do you really want to doom him to a life of *faggotry*? What kind of life can you give him? A life living in some gay ghetto? Always in danger of losing his job if anyone found out about him? About you both? When he could have a position in the community? A wife, kids? If you really do love him"—and once again his face twisted in distaste—"then ask yourself if you want the best for him. And if you do, then get out. And if I ever see you within a block of this house again, I'll run over you with my car. See what that does to you."

"Dad!" Dalton cried. "Fuck!"

Lucas leapt to his feet and fled from the patio.

"Lucas, wait!" Dalton shouted and raced after him to the front foyer.

"Dalton! Get back in here now!"

Now the tears were coming. "Get back out there," Lucas hissed. He began to shiver, unable to believe everything that had just happened. He looked up into Dalton's beautiful almond-shaped eyes, feeling as if the world had come to an end.

"I'm not," Dalton said firmly.

"Yes," Lucas replied. "Because, my God. He's right! What kind of life can I give you? You have everything here. With me? You have my tight little grapefruit ass." Tears rolled down his cheeks, hot and wet.

"I have love with you, Lucas."

"You'll find someone else. Easy. One week at Rolla and you'll have the women lining up." With that he ran out the front door and down the walkway that led to the house and then turned right and followed the sidewalk into the night.

He never got any German chocolate cake.

12

LUCAS WEPT on his mother's shoulder, in her arms, as he hadn't since he was a child. Over. He couldn't believe it was over. He'd waited all his life for Dalton, and now, God, how much the world had changed in one evening.

The noises she made as she held him were comforting. Not shushing, not telling him to stop, just a mother's lies to let him know all would be right in the world.

This was the third time he'd burst into tears since he'd gotten home, sweaty, out of breath, his side an agony of pain—he'd run nearly all the way. She'd made him chamomile tea between the second and third bouts, with lots of honey. During assurances that he didn't know that it was all over. That anything could happen.

And then, somehow, she was right.

The doorbell rang.

Lucas jerked, pulled back, looked out the kitchen door and down the hall. "Huh?" Who?

Then before even his mother could get up, the door opened. "Lucas?"

"Dalton?" he cried, heart leaping.

He jumped up, kitchen chair flying back, and then Dalton was in the room and sweeping him into his arms, covering his face with kisses.

Lucas tried to object, tried to say what he should say—*What are you doing here? You need to get back!*—but the relief was so immense, and he was in Dalton's arms, and Dalton was kissing him, and Lucas could only kiss him back.

But even in the midst of passion, his cooler head finally prevailed—that and his mother clearing her throat loudly—and he pulled back and said, "Dalton! What are you doing here? Did you hear what your father said? He means it. He'll disinherit you."

"I snuck out, baby," he said.

"God, Dalton! Don't think he hasn't noticed. You've got to go back."

Dalton shook his head. "He's out like a light, my little tiger. He hit the scotch and hit it hard after you left and staggered off to bed drunker than I've ever seen him. I had to get over here. I ran all the way." Which explained the sweat.

Lucas knew all about running all the way. Thankfully Terra's Gate wasn't that big a town and nothing was that far a drive from anything else—but with *drive* being the operable word. Running all the way had exhausted Lucas. That and crying his heart out.

"I just couldn't let things lie the way they were. I had to see you. Lucas… I love you so much. I'm willing to lose everything. Tell me. Give me the word and I'll tell him to fuck off."

God…. It sounded wonderful. But then…. "No. You've got to go back." Because he had to. This was Dalton's whole life. And that did matter to Lucas. "And you go to Rolla," he said and felt his heart break.

Dalton shook his head. "No."

"Yes," Lucas insisted.

"At least for the first year," Lucas's mother said, surprising them both. Lucas had almost forgotten she was there. They turned to her just as she said, "In a year Lucas will be eighteen. And to tell the truth that will make me feel better. For all the mother reasons." She nodded. "And if that bastard of a father of yours has a fit, then let him. But don't give him any legal ammunition. We can also check with the bank when your father isn't aware of what's going on. See if he really can touch your Nana's trust fund."

There was a long pause as they digested her words. And tried to sort their swirling emotions.

And then they began to talk. They kept it short to make sure Dalton's father didn't find out that Dalton had left the house. They came up with a plan.

It wouldn't be easy.

But it was better than the alternative.

Then Lucas's mother drove Dalton home—both insisting Lucas stay at home.

When she got back, she held him again.

"That young man loves you so much," she said. Then she was crying with her son. "And it's going to work, baby. It's going to work. I know a year seems a long time, but years and years from now when you look back, you will know it was worth it."

"Are you s-sure?" Lucas asked through tear-filled eyes.

"Of course, baby. In the end, love always wins."

2004

1

LUCAS'S FINAL year of high school—the supposed best year of a person's life—wasn't easy, nor would he *ever* consider it his best. Or at least he hoped not. First and foremost, he ached for Dalton, who was a couple of hundred miles away. Sometimes it felt as if an ice pick were being twisted around deep in his chest. It made it hard to concentrate on his schoolwork, hard to sleep, hard even to pay attention to an episode of *Will & Grace*.

They were able to get away with all the e-mails they wanted. There was no way Mr. Churchill could check Dalton's computer or chaperone Dalton's online activity 200 miles away.

Lucas often thought those e-mails were the only thing keeping him from going crazy.

That and his mother once again saved the day. Several times over 2003 and into the next year she drove them down to Rolla, and while he and Dalton weren't able to make love, they did spend wondrous time together—gazing at each other over shared sodas at an ice cream parlor near Dalton's school (Lucas's mother sat reading *Beachcomber* across the room), holding hands during a movie, or going for walks. Lucas found it particularly exciting how little anyone cared that the two of them were together. In fact, Lucas delighted in meeting Dalton's friends, gay and straight alike. He also didn't mind that Dalton's gay friends were either coupled or not at all Dalton's type. He couldn't help a little jealousy. Those gay men got to see Dalton anytime they wanted.

Lucas's mother also kept another promise, which turned out to be a bright and shining element in the darkness of their exile from each other. They went to a lawyer. And because Dalton was legally an adult, there wasn't anything his father could do about it.

Turns out the man, a Jerry Drake, didn't like Richard Churchill one bit. And he let it be known that Dalton's Nana had been clever.

"He can prevent you from getting your trust until you're thirty, but after that he—can*not*. And if he so much as tries, then *his* trust will go to the Kansas City Home for Wayward Felines. Here's the thing you'll be glad to know. It's a lot of money. Both funds. Mr. Churchill is a vengeful man, and while he's very financially comfortable, he's not going to want that much money getting away from him—especially to a bunch of cats."

It wasn't until after the relief of finding out that Dalton's father couldn't—or in all likelihood *wouldn't*—ultimately prevent Dalton from getting his trust fund that the words "that much money" sunk in.

"Just how much is it?" Lucas's mother asked.

They were all quite surprised at the figure. "Goodness, Dalton. That would pay for all of your schooling and pay a substantial down payment on a house."

"And more," said Drake.

Dalton had been thrilled, even though he was at least temporarily blocked from getting the money that would solve almost everything for a possible twelve years. Because Nana had known her son well—and not cared for the man he'd turned into.

Dalton's father *hated* cats with a blue-blooded passion.

And so Lucas got through that year. At first his grades suffered. The pain of not having Dalton a touch away was hard. But two things turned that around.

First he took the pain and sexual frustration and anger at Mr. Churchill and redirected that energy into studying. Then the Supreme Court of Massachusetts ruled the state's ban on same-sex marriage was unconstitutional, just as 2003 ended, which only fired him up all the more. If Massachusetts allowed gays to get married, then he and Dalton could move! It would mean they could really get married and not have to worry about rites like Holy Unions. He graduated with a 4.98 average and was class salutatorian.

During that time Dalton had come down for Lucas's birthday with a group of friends, and after a small party and cake—and afterward, dinner with just the two of them and Lucas's mother—Dalton asked her if he could please, now and finally, take her son away with him for the night. Blushing, she gave her blessings.

They went to a nice hotel this time.

And they made love well into the night.

This time Lucas didn't object to Dalton's desire that they top each other. It was a symbol that they were at last together.

The only thing that prevented their night from being perfect was that when Lucas brought up their ability to go to Massachusetts to get married, Dalton balked at the idea.

"I want us to be legal everywhere, Lucas. Not just in one state. It's just not real to me otherwise. Please. Why is marriage so important to you?"

Lucas pulled a sheet up to cover himself. He didn't know why, but Dalton's apparent decree against them getting married made him feel funny. Exposed. Wrong somehow. As if what he wanted was wrong. He'd never worried about concepts like sin, but now he was feeling something akin to it.

He couldn't even look Dalton in the eyes.

"I love you, Dalton. And I want what I've always wanted. I want what everyone should be able to have. I want you to be my *husband*."

Dalton snuggled close, reached out with a gentle hand, and turned Lucas's cheek so they were *seeing* each other. "Oh, tiger. We are married. I feel that. Don't you? I have for a while. But tonight? I couldn't feel it more."

That nickname! Dalton rarely used it, but it got him every time when he did.

"You're inside me right now, Lucas. I am inside you. There's no one for me except you."

"There's no one for me except *you*, Dalton." And Lucas's heart surged and ached at the same time.

"I don't need a piece of paper, Lucas," Dalton said. "I am yours forever."

"You promise?" Lucas asked, felt the ache even deeper—even as his heart soared even higher.

"I do. See? I'm saying it. *I do.* Do you take me, Lucas?"

Lucas's eyes filled with tears, and he nodded, allowing himself to push away the hurt and embrace the joy.

2

BUT HIS real soaring point came when Dalton took him to Lucas's senior prom. When they arrived, Lucas had been quite nervous, especially with what Dalton had done earlier that day. Lucas had been a wreck, sure that something ugly would happen. Thankfully that wasn't the case, and Dalton had arrived looking dazzling in his tux.

"You got it!" Lucas exclaimed.

"I knew I would. I know the runnings and the schedule of that house as clearly as I know anything"—he leaned in close—"like the shape of your beautiful little ass."

Lucas had blushed at that. But he'd had another physical reaction. It had delighted Dalton.

"After prom," he said.

The class for the most part embraced them. There were even clapping when the two of them took to the floor and danced to Shania Twain's "Forever And For Always." It was corny, but with its lyrics all about keeping each other and waking up together for all their days, it was enough to make Lucas feel as if he were dancing a foot off the ground.

It was what he had wanted for always.

A perfect evening—until they met Mr. Churchill in the parking lot.

He was leaning against Dalton's car, arms crossed, the look on his face—well, indescribable. There was just so much there. Anger for sure. Lucas thought he could see hatred, determination. More. So much more.

Assurance. That was what it was, Lucas thought.

Triumph.

"Did you think I wouldn't find out?" Mr. Churchill asked, his voice like stones.

Lucas tried to pull his hand from Dalton's, but his lover held firmly to his.

"I'm not surprised," Dalton said, his voice matching his father's, stone by stone. "Who was your spy?"

Mr. Churchill raised an eyebrow. "Spy?"

"Was it the principal? One of the chaperones?"

"Does it make any difference?" Mr. Churchill's eyes flashed. "Maybe I just drove down to see if your car was here."

"Whatever," Dalton said. "Now, what do you want?"

Mr. Churchill stood up straight. Dropped his arms to his sides, his hands now fists.

Dalton let go of Lucas and stepped half in front of him, his own hands curled into fists.

"I am here to tell you that you are no longer my son. I am no longer paying for your college, and it will be twelve years before you get one cent of your trust fund."

Which meant that the lawyer Jerry Drake was right. Mr. Churchill didn't want to fuck with his own money.

Dalton let out a huff of a laugh. "That's okay, Mr. Churchill," he said.

He didn't say "Father," Lucas heard immediately. Nor Dad. And Lucas didn't know whether to be sad or not. He'd longed all his life to know his own father. Now Dalton was rejecting his right before Lucas's eyes.

"It's okay, is it?" Mr. Churchill asked, eyes now blazing. He raised his fists, not quite before him, and took a step.

"Who's this old fuck?" came a voice, and to Lucas's surprise, it was Gabe, one of the stars of the football team. Gabe was a big guy, muscular and tall and broad shouldered. He stepped up so that he too stood in front of Lucas.

"It's Dalton's old man," said John Sanchez, another member of the football team. He joined Dalton at his other side.

Within minutes several more of Lucas's fellow students, including a few girls, had joined them. Lucas was tingling in surprise. What the hell was going on?

"Yes," Dalton said. "It's okay."

Mr. Churchill seemed suddenly unsure.

"You know you're not coming back to the house," he said, his voice not as strong as before.

"I don't need to," Dalton stated. "I cleaned out my closet and most of my stuff while you were at work today and Mom was at one of her meetings. I guessed maybe that's how you knew something was up."

Mr. Churchill stood taller and puffed out his chest. From the chuckles, Lucas didn't think he was fooling anyone. "So what's up, Dalton?"

"I'm not coming home," he said, then stepped back and took Lucas's hand again.

Gabe stepped to the side, but it was also clear he wasn't going anywhere.

"I've made a choice. I've chosen Lucas."

Mr. Churchill gave one single tremble before regaining his composure. He clenched his jaw, and his brows turned into one single slash. "You've chosen this little faggot over me?"

Dalton put his arm around Lucas's shoulders, pulled him close. Lucas didn't know what to do. Part of him wanted to turn and run, part to ask Dalton *one more time* if this was really what he wanted to do, and part wanted to melt against his man. He chose the last, and his heart surged with love.

"Yes. I've chosen the little faggot."

Another little tremble. Barely suppressed rage. His fists clenched and unclenched at his side. Lucas was sure that if it weren't for their companions, also known as witnesses, Dalton's father wouldn't be holding back.

"How… can… you?" Mr. Churchill said through gritted teeth.

"Because I'm a faggot too," Dalton said, stunning Lucas out of any ability to do more than lean against his lover.

The look of shock on Mr. Churchill's face would have been comical had the situation not been so sad. Dalton having to pick….

"And you?" growled Mr. Churchill, waving at the crowd around Dalton and Lucas. More people were joining. "What do you all think about this? These two?"

"I'm a faggot too," Gabe said.

Lucas had to fight to keep his mouth from falling open. Gabe? Gay?

"Yeah," said Jack. "Me too!"

Two girls stepped up, abandoning their dates. They grabbed each other's hands and raised them high. "And we're dykes," said one of them, and the second agreed.

Lucas smiled. He saw it now, saw it as one student after another joined him, mocking Mr. Churchill, each saying they were a homo or a cocksucker or a muff diver. It was like something right out of that movie *To Wong Foo*. Lucas's smile spread even wider. Bliss.

"What are you smiling at, you little fairy?" Mr. Churchill snarled.

"Something faggy," Lucas said. And laughed. God, suddenly this man who had seemed so scary now just seemed pathetic.

He looked up at Dalton, who was looking back at him. And then bending to kiss him.

Lucas kissed back. It wasn't a long kiss. Nor deep. But when he turned back to Mr. Churchill, he saw abject horror on the man's face. Dalton's father ripped his gaze from Lucas's and scanned each of the people around him.

"You're all freaks," he rumbled. Then back to Dalton. "One last chance."

"No, Mr. Churchill—"

Dalton's father flinched at that.

"—*you* have one last chance. Take me the way I am, or go away."

Mr. Churchill shook his head. "Fuck," he whispered. Once more he looked at Dalton and Lucas and his classmates. "Freaks."

"Yeah," said Gabe. "We're all freaks. Now get out of here. *Now.*"

Mr. Churchill's eyes went back to Dalton.

Dalton nodded.

And Mr. Churchill left.

Later, back in the room Dalton had gotten them for the night, after they made love (it was very quiet and sweet and almost sad), Dalton began to cry. It started with one heavy tear that dropped from Dalton's face to Lucas's. Then he began to sob, and Lucas held him tight and told him that he loved him and everything would be all right.

Because just like his mother had done for Lucas countless times, that's what you did for those you loved.

2004—2008

1

DALTON TRANSFERRED from the U of M to Wagner University for his second year. With the residential discounts, he saved quite a bit of money. Of course he had to get a part-time job to pay for his schooling, but with his savings and the scholarships he qualified for, it was all doable.

Lucas could have gone to nearly any college he wanted in the country—even outside the country. He chose to stay in Terra's Gate.

Lucas's mother didn't try to convince him to leave. She told him only once that she thought it might be a good idea, and—in a haunting way that almost echoed the words of Dalton's father—that a young man needed to leave the nest. To get away from his mother and discover life on his own.

But she softened that with, "Although I'm not sure what I would do without you."

She made it clear that she just wanted him to stay or go for the right reasons. And as much as she loved Dalton, she really did think they were too young to move in with each other.

But she didn't stop them.

"I'm not stupid," she said.

Interestingly enough when it came to a gay son (and one with a lover), her life and her decision on her path were completely different from what Dalton's parents took—and the parents of some of Lucas's other friends.

She didn't use religion to condemn.

She didn't even use it to find some biblical reason why Lucas wasn't going to hell.

She turned her back on her Baptist upbringing and instead began to take a two-year nondenominational course to become a minister.

"A minister, Mom?" Lucas asked the morning she told him over a cup of coffee. It was their Saturday morning ritual. Coffee and whatever new recipe for scones or biscuits or muffins he'd found that week on the Internet. He'd had no idea he liked baking until he'd gotten that job at The Sweet Spot, and it turned out he liked cooking as well, which was a good thing since it was easier for him to take on that duty in his and Dalton's household. Not that he was the only one, but with Dalton fixing things around their apartment (which gave them a break on their rent), it seemed only fair.

She shrugged and gave him one of her funny little smiles. "Why not? There have to be those who make a difference. Those who start building the bridge to a world where people see that God loves my son—almost as much as I do."

He hugged her tight, and they toasted each other with touched coffee mugs and ate their pecan scones.

2

LUCAS AND Dalton had a small apartment on the edge of town over a garage. Not much. But it didn't need to be. They were together. It was all that mattered to either of them.

Lucas's mother made them curtains and a quilt for their bed.

Dalton's mother didn't do anything.

It didn't matter. It was an incredible time. So exciting. Everything Lucas had ever dreamed. Dalton said the same thing, and why shouldn't Lucas believe him? Dalton had given up everything in the world to be with him. So despite the loss of Dalton's family's love, there was still love.

Playing house—but for real.

They didn't see quite as much of each other as they might have hoped. Conflicting class hours and job shifts cut into that time. But it was better than Dalton living two hundred miles away.

And sometimes Dalton brought him flowers.

When they had the time and schedules permitted, it was all the little things that made Lucas so happy. Shopping for groceries, cooking, and doing the dishes—one of them washing, the other drying (their little apartment didn't have a dishwasher)—even going to the Laundromat was like living a dream.

Lucas's mother kept asking why they didn't use her washer and dryer. "You could have dinner here, and we could watch a movie." Comments that flew in the face of her advice about leaving the nest. It was sweetly amusing. And sometimes they took her up on her offer. But Lucas felt that even the ritual of the Laundromat was romantic. Was there anyone there that didn't know they were a couple? Washing their underwear together. Smiling at each other as they folded sheets (and underwear).

"Wish *my* husband helped with the sheets," said one older lady, hair up in curlers, one night.

Sometimes they shared their rare alone time with friends. Friends made their life together even more real, and they had a surprising number of friends. DVDs, potlucks, games—but most assuredly not spin the bottle, and most especially when Diego came over.

But one of Lucas's favorite times was when they would simply sit at their kitchen table, a small round wooden thing that had needed a few screws for one of the end hang-down leaves. (It was twenty dollars at a garage sale, including three chairs.) That was magic. Lucas would look across at his lover and be happier than anything.

And of course there was making love. In any room, over their fragile little table, up on the kitchen counter—thank goodness Dalton was tall—the shower (and one hurried time in the alley, Dalton fucking him up against the rear wall of the garage, and the excitement of getting caught was *fire*).

But especially in their bed—not childhood twin beds but a queen they'd found on Craigslist. Making love. Falling asleep in each other's arms. Waking up and making love again. Lazy weekends when neither had to get up and rush out to go to class.

"You realize how lucky you are?" Sam asked him one evening. They spoke on the phone because she had moved to New York and somehow been one of those rare people who was in the right place at the right time and was now some kind of big-time DJ at a big-deal club. "Because I'm telling you, finding this dyke a real girlfriend and not some crazy freak has been insane. I think I used up my luck getting my gig at the Phaze."

Lucas smiled. "Yeah. I know."

"Good."

"Is it really that hard to find a girlfriend?" he asked.

"Not finding them. The joke is true. When lesbians meet, they're trying to move in the next day. At least they want to move in with *me*. I've learned to wait after letting one chick move in and discovering she was bringing about a hundred cats—"

Lucas had to fight a laugh. Sam *hated* cats.

"—and another wanted us to get matching clit piercings to prove our love, and I was like, *fuck* that shit. Can you imagine how much that would hurt?"

Lucas didn't have any idea. He wasn't even sure what a clitoris looked like. "Bad?" he ventured. He certainly wasn't interested in either him or Dalton getting their dicks pierced.

"You're fucking-A right! I don't even like a little nibble down there. Ms. Pierce-My-Clit liked hers bit. Christ!"

Lucas laughed and tried not to picture the images Sam was conjuring.

"God, Sam. I miss you *so* much. It gets lonely around here."

"I know, baby," she replied. "But it's not forever. I know it seems like it. But it's not. Remember we thought high school would never end? Can you believe it's been almost two years?"

Sometimes he could. Sometimes it seemed longer. Especially on long lonely nights. But he told her he didn't anyway.

They talked a little longer, then had to sign off because she had to get ready to head over to the Phaze, and they made promises that someday he and Dalton would visit her.

3

BUT THE power came when Lucas and Dalton had evenings when time and events allowed them to sit on their couch and watch their little TV and cuddle and eat microwave popcorn.

They watched New Jersey pass its Civil Union law—Dalton scoffed at that, said it might as well be a Holy Union, but Lucas saw hope. He never gave up hope.

They watched Kurt Hummel come out on *Glee*, and Lucas was both dizzyingly happy… and a little bitter. If only there had been a Kurt

Hummel on television for him when he was in high school. What a difference it would have made.

But then he remembered all those kids standing up for him the night of prom. He really, in the great scheme of things, had little to be bitter about. Especially after what they had already survived.

The year Lucas graduated from college, California passed same-sex marriage.

And Lucas's hope rose ever higher.

I'm going to marry him someday came the echo of a memory that went back as far as he could remember.

It sounded good. And he knew it was true.

One day, somehow, he just knew he would marry Dalton.

But then in November of that same year, the citizens of California voted to constitutionally ban same-sex marriage by 52.2 percent of voters; same-sex marriage was overturned.

It was the second most crushing event of Lucas's young life.

Lucas asked if he could leave work early, and his boss let him go without hesitation. And as he left the bakery, he stopped him, looked at him with tears in his eyes. "Never give up," the middle-aged man told him. "Love will win."

"You believe that?" Lucas asked him, a man who had turned out to be gay and someone Lucas could talk to through the years.

"I do," he'd said. Despite the fact that he was single himself.

If he can believe, can't I?

When Lucas got home, he found Dalton sitting in the dark, watching some moronic black-and-white movie. There were five empty beer bottles on the table in front of him. He'd been crying.

Lucas went into their small kitchen. There were seven bottles of Budweiser left. He suddenly felt the overwhelming need to have one. Did Dalton need another?

What the hell.

He opened them both, took them into the living room, sat next to Dalton, and handed him one of the beers. Dalton looked at it for a moment as if he didn't know what it was and then chugged down what must have been half of it. Lucas simply sipped at his. He'd never grown a fondness for beer.

They sat for a long time while Lucas tried to make sense of the old show. A man kept referring to an elegant woman as Nora. They drank a lot. There was a dog. Apparently they were trying to solve a crime?

"This is why I didn't want us to get married," Dalton said, almost startling Lucas despite how quietly the words had come. "Can you imagine? Being one of those couples that got married and had fucking voters take their marriages away? What must they be going through?"

"They can't take their marriages away," Lucas replied, just as quietly. "Their marriages are here." He touched his chest. He touched Dalton's. "In their hearts."

Dalton looked away from both his beer and the TV, studied Lucas. Another tear rolled down his face, shimmering blue in the light of the television.

Neither said anything for a long time.

Finally: "Then I guess we're already married, right, Lucas Arrowood?"

Lucas nodded. "Yes, Dalton Churchill." Even if he did want that piece of paper.

Dalton kissed him then, and they abandoned their beers and Nick and Nora and the dog, Asta, and they made desperate love, and Dalton—who took a long time to cum (although Lucas didn't really mind; he needed to be taken long and hard that night. It made him feel alive)—fell asleep almost immediately afterward.

Lucas lay in the dark for a long time, though.

I'm going to marry him someday came the echo once more.

It was going to happen.

It was going to happen if Lucas had to will it into being.

2009

1

LUCAS'S MOTHER found the lump early that year. When she broke it to Lucas, all she could say was that she didn't want to believe it. She'd simply been taking a shower. She felt the BB-like knob, and she gasped and came fully awake.

"Have you gone to the doctor?" Lucas asked. It was the only thing he could say. Part of his brain had completely switched off. He felt drunk—and not in a pleasant way. In that way when he'd realized he'd drunk too much and couldn't figure out how to put his socks on, let alone answer an important e-mail. Like he was trying to swim up out of a deep dark place and tying his shoes took major concentration.

Cancer? Isn't that what a lump means?

"I have an appointment in two weeks," she said and took a drink of her coffee. It was Saturday morning, their ritual get-together, and Lucas had made eggs Benedict. A product of learning cooking as well as baking.

"*Two weeks?* Mom! Two *fucking* weeks?"

"Lucas! *Language.*"

Lucas stood up, nearly knocking over his cup of coffee. "Fuck watching my language! You can't mess around with this stuff."

She sighed. "I know, baby. But it's going to be okay. God's got a plan for me, and I don't think it's for me to die." She reached out and touched his hand. "Sit, baby. Sit. I'm going to be okay."

He sat, heart pounding in his chest, stomach clenched, throat working. He didn't believe her.

You can't. You can't die, Mom. You. Can. Not.

Lucas looked at his mother. Studied her face. Suddenly noticed lines around her eyes he hadn't seen before, a shimmer of silver in her blonde hair.

When had she gotten older?

Same time you did.

But he had been doing nothing but playing for the last couple of years.

Well, and working his ass off to get good grades. There was that. And the part-time job. And keeping the apartment up.

Which was why he hadn't noticed the lines on his mother's face, the silver in her hair.

"Mom," he sighed. "I'm so sorry."

Her eyebrows rose. "For what? You didn't do anything. It's not your fault."

He sat there for a long time, trying to absorb what was happening. It was not how he'd expected that morning to go. Why, he'd made eggs Benedict to celebrate.

Now how did he tell his mother?

She reached out and patted his hand. "It really is going to be okay, honey. 'I can do all things through Christ who strengthens me,'" she quoted.

You could put the New Age in his mother, but you couldn't take the Jesus out of her, Lucas thought.

He swallowed. Hard.

"It's not that, Mom. It's Dalton. He's gotten a job offer. A really good one."

She sat up straight, beaming. She clapped. "Oh, Lucas! That's wonderful! What will he be doing? Certainly not creating the zombie apocalypse virus you're always teasing him about?" She laughed.

Lucas shook his head. How could she laugh at a time like this? It's why he loved her so much.

Lucas shrugged. "Something about microbocal or -bobal or -crobial diseases? Shit. Surveillance? Pathogens?" He shook his head. "I don't get it. I never really have. That's why I bake cakes."

"You two can finally get out of the crappy little apartment."

"I like that crappy little apartment." He managed to keep from snapping.

She laughed. "Of course you do. It's got your wedding bed in it. You'll always love that apartment."

Lucas's face blazed, which only seemed to tickle her all the more.

"Mom! You don't understand. We'd be living in Oakland. Oakland, *California*."

Her smile faltered for less than a second. If he hadn't known his mother better than he knew even Dalton, he might have missed it. "Well, I've always said you needed to fly from the nest. And halfway across town, especially a town like Terra's Gate, is hardly flying the nest."

"Well, I can't go," he stated.

"Why not?" she asked.

"I can't let you go through what you're about to go through alone."

A sweet but sad smile lifted the corners of her mouth, and she reached out and touched his cheek. "Oh, baby. Don't you see? We don't even *know* what I'm about to go through. It could be simple. It might not even be cancer. There's no telling. We don't know if it'll be surgery or a mastectomy or what the treatment will be. We don't even know for sure that it's cancer."

From the look on her face, Lucas could almost believe it.

"Mom?" he said. "Mama?"

And then they held each other tight.

2

IN THE end, she went with them.

3

AND SHE lived.

She decided against the mastectomy, which was directly against the advice of her doctors and Lucas's appeals.

"I've made up my mind, and that's it. Now you decided to move in with Dalton—which was against my advice—but what did I do? I shut—my—*mouth*. And you know what happened. I was wrong. Well, this is my decision. I want to keep my breast. If the lump was as big as my cousin Shelly's, which was as big as a plum, then I'd do it. But this really is BB-sized, and I'm taking a chance. No, I'm not going to be luring too many men these days with my boobs, but—"

"Mom!" he cried, shocked.

"—I've got a nice rack, and—"

"*Mom!*"

"—I'm not winning any beauty contest with my face, never could, and especially not at my age, and—"

Lucas's face had blazed at the conversation, and he found he could no longer respond.

"—what chance do I have of finding me a man otherwise?"

Lucas wanted to point out that if all a man wanted was a nice rack, he didn't want her marrying him.

But then he really didn't have any say, did he?

So he shut up, and she stuck to her guns, and yes, there were days where he held her head while she puked in the toilet and bought her pot to give her an appetite and even shaved her head for her because she couldn't stand to find it in clumps on her pillow in the mornings.

And she survived.

More than survived.

She thrived.

She got that minister's license too.

2010—2014

1

NOT ONLY that, but she fell in love with the RN who administered her chemo—a man five years her junior named Marcus DeWolf—and got engaged. She fell in love with him because even he told her she should have gotten the mastectomy, and any man who married a woman because of her breasts was a scumball who deserved to get cock cancer.

She accepted his proposal without a second thought.

She accepted it as he kneeled on the floor in a restaurant with Lucas and Dalton in attendance. He wouldn't think of doing it any other way.

But she didn't marry him.

She told everyone that she was not getting married until her son did.

"Mom," Lucas cried in exasperation. "*Marry* him! Just because I can't get married doesn't mean *you* shouldn't! I can't live with it!"

"You can and you will!" she shot back.

"But people don't care that you aren't marrying because I can't," he countered. "It's not going to change anything. It's not going to change the laws. Please, Mom. *Marry* him! A good man doesn't come along every day—believe me, I know."

"I've made up my mind, and if there's anything you should know, when we Arrowoods make up our minds, they're made up for good. If he's the good man you say he is, he'll wait."

Luckily he was a good man.

Marcus waited.

2

DALTON'S JOB was the answer to unspoken and even undreamed fantasies. Exactly what he had always been suited for, and it paid beyond anything they had ever imagined combined. And the icing on the cake was that he loved it.

They bought a little Eichler house in a neighborhood of Oakland called Sequoyah Hills (although Lucas wasn't sure why since the plant life was mostly yuccas and palm trees and the like). But they loved it— the candles on the cake. The front door opened onto an enclosed small courtyard with a hot tub (they had to get it fixed, and that took a few months) and yuccas and an awning that could be pulled out during the rainy season (Oakland's answer to winter). Most of the rooms had glass doors that gave access to the courtyard, and it was all quite lovely. It was, like Dalton's job, unlike anything either of them had imagined, but they almost immediately couldn't envision living anywhere else.

If there was anything better than the cake and the icing and the candles, it was that Dalton was making enough that the house would have been paid for in less than ten years on his salary alone.

Lucas's job assured it.

It started as a fluke. He saw a Help Wanted sign at their favorite bakery. He got the job. His old manager gave him a glowing recommendation. And before he knew it, they were allowing him to try his recipes.

That was when his business degree turned into something he'd never expected.

Within a year he was looking at his own store.

He didn't even have to worry about his first employee.

His mother was there for that.

2015

1

ON THE morning of June 26, Lucas took the old TV—the one from that first apartment over a garage in Terra's Gate, back before they could afford a fifty-inch flat-screen television—to work with him. He set it up on the counter near the register, heart in his throat, hoping for the best. His customers certainly didn't mind. More of them were GLBT friendly than not. Customers of On the Rise, Lucas's thriving bakery, pretty much needed to be. Lucas was very out—not that he was capable of being anything else—and often featured baked goods that made it clear that his shop was GLBT friendly as well, especially this time of year when Gay Pride was being celebrated across the country. The cases were filled with rainbow cookies and muffins, and because of the possible SCOTUS decision, lately cupcakes with two artificial rings stuck into the icing and wedding cakes with two grooms or brides atop them (not that he hadn't made plenty of them over the last year—Prop 8 had been overturned three years before, after all).

So anyone offended by things gay rarely stepped through the front door unless it was because they just couldn't resist Lucas's specialties— cheesecakes, key lime pie, and his coconut cream—all made from the scratchiest of scratch. Not to mention his crème brûlée, which was to live (and not) for.

And of course his mother's favorite—baklava. They would always associate it with his coming out.

In fact, many of his most loyal customers were hanging around that morning—which was saying something considering it wasn't yet even seven o'clock—and it was a surprisingly large crowd. The front of On the Rise was only big enough for four small tables and the front counter. It made Lucas incredibly grateful, despite his nervousness. These people could have been anywhere, but they were here.

His mother was there too, even though he'd insisted she didn't need to be there on her day off (which with the size of the standing-room-only crowd turned out to be untrue).

"Nonsense," she told him when she'd arrived shortly after him at five that morning. Tying on her apron, she began setting bread out to rise. "Did you think I wasn't going to be here with you when the good news comes down?"

"*If* it's good news," Lucas said, unable to shake his worry.

His mother tsked him. "Lucas, what other decision can be made? Especially with Justice Kennedy on our side? Look at everything he's done for the gay movement. He voted against DOMA. He helped strike down the antisodom—"

"It takes a *majority*, Mom," he replied, cutting her off. He was blushing. Hearing his own mother talk about sodomy was too much, at least right now. "It's not just *one* judge's decision."

Yes, the almost certain (but not totally certain) outcome was that this was the day that everyone in the United States—at least matrimonially—would at last be equal. But again, no one could really be sure: witness the lesson that liberals learned when they didn't get up and go vote against Prop 8.

Lucas would never forget that day. Who would have ever thought it would pass, and by such a small percentage, or that it would take so long to be overturned?

Yes, the right decision should come down, but would it even be today? There were those who thought it could be days before it happened. But how wonderful would it be to enter Gay Pride weekend with the right to marry!

It didn't help that Dalton wasn't with him. Lucas had tried to be understanding. They didn't know if the decision would come down today. And Dalton had made it clear that "a piece of paper" meant little to him. And as world-shatteringly important as Dalton's job as a brilliant microbiologist might be, Lucas still thought Dalton should be able to take one *frigging* day off to be with him on this possibly momentous day.

At least now Lucas had some idea of what Dalton actually did for a living. He helped figure out the basic workings of infectious microbial cells so that drugmakers could develop new medicines. Hopefully that had nothing to do with creating zombies.

And dammit, everyone was here! Why not his man? Husband in heart if not in legal deed.

"Wait," someone shouted and pointed to the little television. "Look!"

The screen showed the huge crowd in front of the Supreme Court Building, but now—now there were people running down the vast white steps! What? What?

The crowd began to shout. To roar!

The cheer that rose up was deafening. Lucas thought his heart had actually stopped. He couldn't believe it. Was it? Was it?

And then the CBS News special report came on, and the room, which had been filled with cheers, went silent as Charlie Rose and then Jan Crawford told them that all their dreams had come true.

Same-sex marriage was now the law of the land.

Then, like a firework streaking up into the sky then bursting into gorgeous fire, Lucas's heart soared as well, and it felt as if it too had exploded.

Gloriously—*just* like that firework.

He was shouting, screaming, dancing for joy, crying, laughing.

His mother threw herself into his arms, and he hugged her back fiercely. Then there was somebody else hugging him and someone else and someone else. Wait! Was that her boyfriend, Marcus, hugging him? When had he gotten here? Then there were more hugs. Lucas found he couldn't stop crying. Every fear and every hope he'd had for... how many years? Twenty? Twenty-five? No. Twenty-four. Since kindergarten. That was it. A day he could still clearly remember—being told that boys couldn't marry boys, even if they were in love.

God. If only Dalton were here. If only. A different kind of tears threatened, and he shook his head and told himself, *No, no, I won't go there. Dalton, if you need to be looking in a microscope right now instead of—*

"Lucas?"

He almost didn't hear his name at first because he'd heard it shouted a dozen times in the last few minutes. But when his name was said again—

"*Lucas?*"

—he jumped. Because wasn't that...?

He pulled away from the young lady he was currently hugging—her head full of rainbow dreads—and turned to see…

Dalton.

His eyes went wide.

"Dalton," he cried, and his heart jumped. Dalton was here, and it was too good to be true! Like something out of a movie, and he started to hug him but…

Dalton dropped to one knee.

"Dalton?" Lucas said again, and although it was barely a whisper, his voice seemed almost to echo since—except for a few gasps—a hush had fallen over the room. Even the TV had gone mysteriously silent.

Dalton reached into his pants pocket, and although there was certainly some part of Lucas that realized what might be about to happen, that part of him felt as if it were very far away—on the other side of a canyon, the Grand Canyon perhaps, or ever farther. Miles. The Moon. The planet Altair IV, even.

Because could this really be happening? After all these years, was the impossible happening?

Dalton pulled his hand out of his pocket to reveal a small black box. The kind that could really hold only one thing.

And that part of Lucas that felt like he might be on Altair IV was quite suddenly a whole lot closer. Maybe even in the room.

"Lucas Arrowood," Dalton said, his voice clear and strong (but still cracking slightly on "row") and his beautiful brown eyes shimmering with tears (Dalton? Tears?), "you are the love of my life. For years I said I would not marry you unless it was legal across this entire country. And now it is. Therefore, Lucas, it is long past time for me to ask. I shouldn't have waited for the Supreme Court to give me permission."

And now he was coming out of whatever strangeness—fog, high—had fallen over him for that endless moment because—Oh God—years from now he would want to remember every single second of this.

"That young man loves you so much" came the echo of his mother's voice from years before. "And it's going to work, baby. It's going to work. I know a year seems a long time, but years and years from now when you look back, you will know it was worth it."

Dalton opened the box, and yes, it was a ring. A man's ring. A gold band. And Dalton knew him; there was some bling too, wasn't there? He looked up from the row of small diamonds and into Dalton's handsome face.

"Lucas, will you marry me?"

And thank God he could speak, and the words came out of his mouth even as his vision blurred as tears filled his eyes.

"Oh, yes. Yes, Dalton. Yes!"

A cheer filled the room.

It joined the one echoing across the world.

2

"WE ARE gathered here today," said the Reverend Alice Arrowood, "to bring these two men together in legally wedded—"

(and there was much emphasis on the word "legally")

"—and what *I* know to be *holy* matrimony."

Lucas's heart began to pound. Began? Hell, it had been pounding all day and all last night as well. He hadn't slept but an hour or so. Partially it was Mother's and Marcus's very uncomfortable sofa bed— she'd insisted he and Dalton not sleep together the night before they were to be wed—

"I don't care if you've slept together for ten years. It's bad luck. And unseemly!"

—and in part because he'd been way too nervous to sleep.

He was so nervous right then he didn't know how he was standing. No. He knew.

He glanced next to him. Sam was right there. His "Best Person." Who else should stand next to him?

Then he shot a quick look to the man standing next to Dalton.

Diego Hernandez. At one time that was the last man Lucas would have wanted to see there on this very important day. But life changes people; Diego's husband was sitting in the front row.

Lucas looked up at Dalton now, and a rush swept over and through him, and his heart skipped a beat. Dalton was so incredibly handsome in his tux. And the way Dalton was looking at him! Lucas thought he might faint.

He forced himself to turn to his mother, who looked radiant in her robes and stole. She'd made them both and designed a stole with symbols, religious and otherwise, sewn down either side. Christ believer she still was, but she'd accepted New Age teachings with open arms, and she wanted all people to feel comfortable when she performed their weddings. It was the reason she'd nixed using rainbow fabric. All people meant *all* people—straight as well as another orientation, sexual or otherwise. So instead the long scarf-like piece of deep blue fabric had a pink triangle—point upward—among the other emblems.

"But you know," Lucas's mother continued, "these two men became bound a long time ago with one little boy teaching another little boy how to tie his shoes. More than Keds were tied that morning. I think that maybe their hearts were as well."

Lucas turned back to Dalton, his focus shimmering in and out, and he thought he could almost see that boy right now.

"'Mamma,' Lucas said to me. 'I'm going to marry that boy someday.' It caught me by surprise. This was 1990…'91?" She nodded. "Yes, 1991. And not 2015, and I was *all* discombobulated."

Laughter rippled gently across the room.

"'But boys can't marry each other,' I foolishly said, and Lucas looked me in the eye and asked why not, if they love each other.

"And now, today, a far wiser woman, I am blessed to preside over the celebration that recognizes that love. Today they promise before us all to dedicate themselves to each other completely. In body. In words. In mind. And in heart."

Lucas wiped at his eyes, saw Dalton do the same and—*God!*—the love shining in his eyes! Unbidden, Lucas's filled again and tears spilled down his cheeks. *My love!*

"These two men already have love and a wonderful relationship. So now I only remind them of what they already know. Lucas? Dalton?"

They both turned to look into her shining face.

"Your marriage today is one that you created. *I* do not do this. You create. I tell you to create something wonderful. Something good. A good marriage is in the small and in the big and knowing that in God's eyes, in Love's heart, there is no small or big. It is all the same. It is listening to everything your partner says… and *hearing* it. It is never being afraid or too old to take each other's hand in your own, no matter where you are. It is saying 'I love you.' Every. *Single*. Day."

For one second her eyes flashed to the front row. He knew who she was looking at. Marcus DeWolf, the man who insisted she had no more than a week to marry him after today.

And right next to Marcus was Diego Hernandez's husband. And next to him a surprisingly adorable young lady named Jill. She had an orange streak in her hair, and from what she had told Lucas, she loved Sam very much.

Boy! You never knew what could happen in life.

In the end, it made Lucas all the happier.

"Loving someone is never going to sleep while you are angry," Lucas's mother continued. "Kissing every time you part. Every time you see each other again. Standing together against a world that at times will not understand you. It is forgiving… and *forgetting*. It's allowing each other to be separate as well as together. Letting them grow into what they will be and not be encased—frozen in time. It is not only taking the right person unto you, but by being the right person for him.

"Now repeat after me…."

Lucas did. And he heard Dalton chorus the words with him and was filled with utter joy.

"I, Lucas, take you, Dalton, to be my *lawfully* wedded husband—"

(and there was much emphasis on the word "lawfully")

"—my partner, my *one* true love. I will honor and trust you. Laugh and cry with you. I will be at your side at the best and worst of times, whatever may come. Today, tomorrow, and forever."

Forever! Yes, forever. And a feeling swept over him that felt like the end and the beginning of the world at once—and in a way, it was. It was the end of one world…

…and the beginning of another.

"Do either of you have anything to add?"

Lucas froze. Add? Hadn't they decided to go with classic vows? He hadn't written anything—come up with anything. His mother had promised to take care of everything.

But then he looked up into Dalton's beautiful eyes, and he knew he had to say something, and before he even realized it, the words came, easy as could be.

"Dalton, I have loved you nearly my entire life, and all I've ever wanted to do is marry you. But the world? The world said I couldn't. That my love—the only love I've had or wanted—wasn't *good* enough. I had faith, though, even if there were times when it was almost impossible. I held on. I knew. I *knew* that one day I would be your husband. And that you would be mine. Because you know what husband means? It means *caretaker*. And isn't that what we do? Take care of each other?

"I knew one day we would be married. I would will it into being if I had to. And I have heard that 'where attention goes, energy flows.' That's what Mama has been saying these last few years. And that 'thoughts become things.' And finally, it has happened. We *can* get married. We can take that piece of paper that I believe is so much more than just a piece of paper. It is a symbol of our love. And I love you, Dalton. Today, at long last, despite all the couldn'ts and shouldn'ts and can'ts, today I make you mine and give myself to you—forever...."

Was it good enough, he wondered. Had it sounded stupid?

There was a sigh through the room.

Dalton's eyes were glassy with tears, and oh, oh, oh, the love shining there.

I said the right thing.

How have I been so lucky to have this man?

Lucas's mother cleared her throat. "Dalton? Is there anything you want to say?"

"Yes," Dalton replied in a voice that was so quiet Lucas could barely hear him. His eyes were full now. He too cleared his throat, and then he spoke...

"Lucas, I stand here today in front of all our friends and family of choice..."

His voice hitched, and Lucas could only guess it was because his parents were absent, even though they'd been invited. The two of them hadn't even bothered to refuse to come. They had simply not replied at all.

"...and.... And I want to tell you I'm sorry."

Lucas started. Sorry? What? Why was he sorry?

"I'm sorry this day took so long in coming. So long. You wanted a Holy Union, and I wouldn't give it to you. You wanted to fly off to Massachusetts and get married, and I wouldn't do it. I told you I wouldn't marry you unless it was legal everywhere and not just in one state. I told you we didn't need to get married anyway because a marriage license was just a piece of paper. And I was wrong and I was wrong and I was *wrong*. I should have given you that Holy Union. Because what we have truly *is* holy. The only holy thing I've ever really believed in. I should have married you in Massachusetts. And California. And Connecticut too. *Any* damned state you wanted. To show the world and our government and everyone we knew that I was very serious about our love.

"We moved to Oakland, California. I should have married you that day! We could have moved anywhere, and so what if our marriage was only legal in a few states? Because we would have already been spiritually married when we had our Holy Union! And now I know that our marriage is legal? Now that we *have* a license? You are so right, my love. It *is* more than a piece of paper. You're right. It *is* a symbol. Like the American flag is more than pieces of red and white and blue fabric stitched together. And our license is more than a piece of paper. More than words on paper. It is a symbol that now—at last, after a thousand years and more of our love *not* being recognized as real—*now* it is real.

"As our president said, now we've made our union a little more perfect. And now that it is, why, I would marry you in any state you wanted. I'd marry you in all fifty of them if you wanted. So I could show the whole country that you're mine.

"And baby? There is nothing that I can think of that is more perfect than being in a union with you."

Another sigh went through the room. Someone sobbed.

Lucas could only stand there, stunned. It was taking everything out of him not to burst into tears. He couldn't believe what he'd heard. Dalton—*Dalton*—who was rarely the most demonstrative person, and certainly not in front of people, saying such words?

Lucas's eyes blurred again as they filled once more with tears. His throat seized up, and his tongue lay useless in his mouth. He found it was all he could do not to throw himself into his man's arms.

"Can you forgive me?"

Forgive? Forgive what?

"Can you forgive me, my love?" Dalton asked again.

Lucas stood for what seemed like forever, trying to speak, knowing he had to respond.

"Forgive me for making you wait so long for this day?" A tear rolled down Dalton's cheek.

Lucas's heart swelled until he thought it might burst. "Oh, Dalton...." He swallowed hard. Oh God. He took a deep breath. "Forgiven...," he managed. "And forgotten."

Now someone really was crying, and he wanted to tell them to please stop because it was all he could do to hold himself together. There was still more to go!

Lucas's mother took control then, saying those very important words.

"Now do you both have the rings?"

Lucas grinned and reached into his pocket—remembering Dalton reaching into his such a short time ago and watching him do it even now—and he pulled out Dalton's ring. Just the way Dalton wanted it. A solid gold band. Simple. No bling. But it told the world that the only thing it *could* be was a wedding band.

"Wedding rings represent an unbroken circle of love," Lucas's mother continued. "Love has no beginning and no ending. It is forever. May these rings forever remind you of the vows that you now give.

"Now, Lucas, place your ring upon Dalton's finger. Lucas, do you take Dalton to be your lawfully wedded husband?"

"I...." This was it! He took Dalton's big beautiful hand in his own and slipped the gold band upon his finger. "God, yes. I do."

"Do you promise to love, honor, cherish, and protect him, forsaking all others and holding on to only him?"

Yes. Oh, yes! "I do." Now he couldn't help but cry.

"And Dalton. Place your ring upon Lucas's finger."

Once more Lucas's heart began to pound as Dalton took his hand and slipped that lovely ring on his finger. This was it. This was it!

"Dalton, do you take Lucas to be your *lawfully* wedded husband?" She smiled.

"I do," Dalton said, his voice so strong and sure and deep.

Lucas trembled.

"Do you promise to love, honor, cherish, and protect him, forsaking all others and holding on to only him?"

Lucas and Dalton locked eyes.

"I do," Dalton said.

God! Oh God!

Heart pounding!

Heart pounding so hard!

"And now—"

And now? And now? Lucas glanced at his mother. What was that twinkle in her eyes?

"—before my pronouncement—"

Wait. What? Before…? He narrowed his eyes.

"—there is one more thing."

One more thing? Mom!

"Dalton, take Lucas's left hand in your right."

Lucas looked at Dalton, who gave a slight shrug, then did as he'd been asked.

"Now hold them up."

They did as bid.

And then *she* pulled something from a pocket in her robe Lucas hadn't noticed. What was it? String? Was it a piece of—

Then he knew.

God, he knew.

It was old and tattered and gray….

Quick as a wink she tied it around their wrists. If it had been an inch shorter, it wouldn't have fit.

"And now… with this Holy Shoelace… I pronounce you husbands."

Husbands? This was it? This was it!

"Well, boys, you may now kiss."

And they did.

God, they did.

3

THEY CHOSE Provincetown for their honeymoon. Dalton had insisted, even though it could have been Boston. It surprised Lucas. Provincetown was so… gay. And Dalton wasn't much for waving rainbow flags or holding hands in public.

P-town turned out to be gorgeous.

And they did walk down the streets hand in hand.

"I promised your mom, after all," he said. "No. I promised you."
Then they kissed. Right there on the street.

They stayed at Romeo's Holiday—which was purported to be the
gayest B&B in the country. They had breakfast at Joe Coffee & Espresso
Bar and dinners at the Lobster Pot at Crowne Pointe, and of course they
didn't forget to eat at the Crown & Anchor's patio café at the Central
House Bar & Grille—all *very* gay. They shopped and went to art galleries.
And they swam at Herring Cove Beach—it was Dalton who talked
Lucas into getting naked, and Lucas was surprised at how freeing it was.
Swimming naked in a pool years before was one thing. Swimming naked
where people could see you was something else. Of course he was with
the sexiest man on earth, so that had helped.

But the biggest surprise of all was when Dalton asked Lucas to go
to the courthouse with him.

"But…. But why?" Lucas asked.

"I want to marry you," Dalton replied, staring into his face, eyes
once more ashimmer.

What? "But we're already married, Dalton." At last. At long last.

"Did you think I was just blowing hot air when I said I'd marry
you in all fifty states? That I wanted to show the whole country that
you're mine?"

Lucas's eyes went wide, and as it was wont to do where Dalton was
concerned, his heart started to race. "Y-you mean it?"

"I do." Then he grinned and chuckled and said, "I *do*."

"Oh my God, Dalton…." Lucas was all but speechless.

Dalton pulled something out from under the bed and had Lucas
sit down. He placed it in his lap. It was a photo album. The picture on
the cover was from their wedding (and how he'd gotten it already Lucas
didn't know). A picture of their hands with their wedding rings.

"Open it, baby," Dalton said.

So Lucas did. The first page had their names in a lovely script
and the words, "Lucas Arrowood and Dalton Churchill's Big Album of
Wedding States."

What? Lucas wondered.

He turned the page, and across the top was written, *Alabama*. The
second and third pages said *Alaska* and *Arizona* respectively. It was on
page five that he found their portrait from their wedding. Above it was

the word California, of course. Lucas's heart began to race all the more. Did this really mean…?

"We're already married in California. Now let's get married in Massachusetts, like we should have a long time ago. What say you, tiger? Marry me?"

Lucas looked up from the album into Dalton—his husband's—face.

Had he ever seen anything more beautiful in his entire life?

Then, before he could think—

(as *he* was wont to do)

—Lucas said, "Yes."

And they did.

B.G. THOMAS lives in Kansas City with his husband of more than a decade. They've been married twice. First in 2005—although it wasn't legal. They jumped the broom (as well as the sword) and were married in heart in front of their friends and loved ones. Then in 2014, they flew to Baltimore and made it legal (and couldn't have without the help of B.G.'s fans who practically funded the entire weekend!). He can't get enough of seeing that gold wedding band on his hand, even two years later.

B.G. loves romance, comedies, fantasy, science fiction, and even horror—as far as he is concerned, as long as the stories are character driven and entertaining, it doesn't matter the genre. He has gone to conventions his entire adult life where he's been lucky enough to meet many of his favorite writers. He has made up stories since he was a child; it is where he finds his joy.

Excited about the growing male/male romance market, he submitted a story and was thrilled when it was accepted in four days. Since then the stories have poured out of him. "It's like I'm somehow making up for a lifetime's worth of stories!"

"Leap, and the net will appear" is his personal philosophy and his message to all. "It is never too late," he states. "Pursue your dreams. They will come true!"

Website/blog: bthomaswriter.wordpress.com

By B.G. Thomas

All Alone in a Sea of Romance
All Snug
Anything Could Happen
The Beary Best Holiday Party Ever
Bianca's Plan
The Boy Who Came In From the Cold
Christmas Cole
Christmas Wish
Derek
Desert Crossing
Grumble Monkey and the Department Store Elf
Hound Dog and Bean
How Could Love Be Wrong?
It Had to Be You
Just Guys
Men of Steel (Dreamspinner Anthology)
A More Perfect Union (Multiple Author Anthology)
Red
Riding Double (Dreamspinner Anthology)
A Secret Valentine
Soul of the Mummy
Editor: A Taste of Honey (Dreamspinner Anthology)
Two Tickets to Paradise (Dreamspinner Anthology)
Until I Found You

Published by DREAMSPINNER PRESS
www.dreamspinnerpress.com

By B.G. Thomas (CONT.)

GOTHIKA
Bones (Multiple Author Anthology)
Spirit (Multiple Author Anthology)

SEASONS OF LOVE
Spring Affair
Summer Lover
Autumn Changes

Published by DREAMSPINNER PRESS
www.dreamspinnerpress.com

From left to right: Michael Murphy, J. Scott Coatsworth, B.G. Thomas, and Jamie Fessenden, at the Dreamspinner Press Author Workshop in March 2016.

Also from Dreamspinner Press

PIECE US
BACK
TOGETHER

Cate Ashwood
L.J. LaBarthe
Raine O'Tierney

www.dreamspinnerpress.com

Also from Dreamspinner Press

RANDOM
ACTS OF
KINDNESS

A DREAMSPINNER PRESS ANTHOLOGY

www.dreamspinnerpress.com

Also from Dreamspinner Press

www.dreamspinnerpress.com

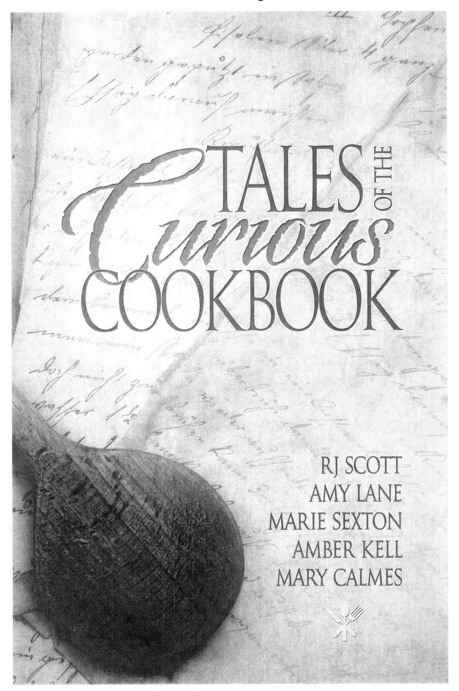

CPSIA information can be obtained
at www.ICGtesting.com
Printed in the USA
LVOW10s1115071117
555290LV00009B/120/P